THOUGHT MECHANIX

THOUGHT MECHANIX

A NOVEL BY

DEREK SCHREURS

Out of the ground the LORD God made to grow every tree that is pleasant to the sight and good for food, the tree of life also in the midst of the garden, and the tree of the knowledge of good and evil....Genesis 2:9

Order this book online at www.trafford.com
or email orders@trafford.com

Most Trafford titles are also available at major online book retailers.

Printed in the United States of America.

ISBN: 978-1-4669-0551-1 (sc)
ISBN: 978-1-4669-0552-8 (hc)
ISBN: 978-1-4669-0553-5 (e)

Library of Congress Control Number: 2011961398

Trafford rev. 12/07/2011

 www.trafford.com
North America & international
toll-free: 1 888 232 4444 (USA & Canada)
phone: 250 383 6864 ♦ fax: 812 355 4082

ALSO BY DEREK SCHREURS

DEBIT FUND

"A forensic accountant's life, job, and girlfriend are suddenly threatened when he unwittingly stumbles upon questionable financial practices during a routine assignment. A modern-day financial thriller."

AUGUSTINE PURSUIT

"A sunken Spanish treasure ship, a failed real-estate development and a centuries-old pursuit provide for a thrilling adventure full of unexpected twists and exciting possibilities."

For my friends (you know who you are)

PROLOGUE

Yasin sat in the van, looking out of the window and thinking about the toppling of the statue. Saddam Hussein, the Supreme Ruler of Iraq was on the run, driven from his palaces by the infidel Americans on the eve of Yasin's thirtieth birthday. He could not believe how quickly the world had changed. The day before, watching the tearing down of the statue, he had been unable to go to his job at the National Museum of Iraq in Baghdad, because Republican Guards had commandeered the museum to provide unsanctioned positions to return sniper fire to the advancing Americans. Yasin was directed to leave, to go home, and to speak to no one about the military presence in the museum. He learned later that the Republican Guards were in violation of the Geneva Convention for engaging in warfare from a protected site.

Well, it was no longer protected.

The museum contained all of the treasures of the Mesopotamian era dating back over five thousand years. Artifacts and relics that Yasin had helped maintain and restore for the past twelve years since he entered his first year of Archaeology at the University of Baghdad. He spent his summers cataloguing, and hoping to work full-time afterwards. That was until the first Gulf War shut down the museum for nine years. When it opened, Yasin was there, working tirelessly to restore the displays. He was there when Saddam Hussein praised the reopening for the Iraqi people. And until now he spent every day restoring artifacts from the great civilizations of the past. That was until he was forcibly evicted by Saddam's guards, idiots who had no respect for the history around which they stockpiled their mortars and rocket-propelled grenades.

Now, three days after the statue of Saddam was toppled, he was again at the museum, thankful he could do something to preserve the history within its walls. As an added bonus, he was about to enjoy a very profitable night. He watched from the passenger seat of his Mercedes extended box van as Saleh, the driver, pulled up to the delivery entrance of the museum. He could not believe what he was about to do.

Saleh, his cousin's friend from the southern province of Basra, had approached him several months earlier, saying that there would be an opportunity for him to make a lot of money. When the time was right, he was to ensure that Saleh and his people would be able to gain access to the museum. For one night's work they would pay him one hundred thousand American dollars. He laughed at first as he sat with his cousin, Saleh, and another darker, unfriendly man, drinking tea and discussing arrangements. He was only half listening as they planned; his attention focused on the groups of young men sitting in the café, talking in animated voices about American's expected attack.

"The security is too tight," he had told them. Guards with submachine guns occupy the hallways of the museum now.

They laughed. "Don't worry. On the night we need you to identify the rarest pieces there won't be any guards to worry about."

Now he sat in the passenger seat of a van at the rear entrance of the Baghdad museum, waiting for a second van to arrive. Yasin realized that these people knew far in advance about the American invasion. They picked him because they knew who he was and what he did at the museum. He would make their lives easy. Yasin thought about the displays and the treasures that lay inside the museum. They would be worth an untold fortune. But to him it was ridiculous to steal the artifacts and relics that lay within the museum. Who would buy them? he wondered. Surely no other museum in the world would pay for the stolen items. And they were all catalogued, so anyone in the antiquities market would know where they came from and steer clear away.

Saleh explained that private galleries and collections of the wealthy would pay handsomely for the contents of the museum. More importantly, these were people who appreciated the significance of the treasures within the museum and would treat them with the respect they deserve. That made Yasin happy, and it would make him very rich.

No one had to explain to Yasin the true potential of what they were about to undertake—ransacking a museum devoid of security. The Republican Guards had all fled in disarray. When they left, the electronic grid that protected the most precious artifacts and relics was blown to bits by the advance strikes of the coalition forces. Nothing was protecting the national treasures. It was the perfect time to strike. The looting would take two days. The plan had been carefully laid out in a café. Yasin's job was to help identify the valuable pieces. Once he was done, two teams would crate up the chosen pieces for removal from the museum. The items would then be secreted out of the country before the Americans could set up proper checkpoints. Sufficient money would grease the palms of those who would help clear the path to get the items out of the country.

The other van pulled up. Six men exited the back. Two of them held small Russian made sub-machine guns close to their torso. The other four each brandished metal batons, ready to do damage. *Nothing was left to chance,* Yasin thought, as he followed Saleh to the loading ramp. Jumping ahead, Yasin removed the set of keys from his pocket to unlock the overhead doors of the loading bay. He made his way upstairs to the displays, placing small stickers on the items he felt were the most valuable. The sound of smashing glass and wood followed him, as the thieves found the easiest was to access the treasures that lay within each case he marked. He wondered why he was doing this, but he soon let the thought leave his mind. Better his cousin's friend than the Americans taking the loot.

On the third floor were the Sumerian relics. The main exhibit in the room was a collection of clay tablets. In the middle of the display there were two clay tablets beautifully displayed in sealed, gilded-wood cabinets. Yasin ignored it on his way to the weapons room.

"What's in here?" Saleh stopped at the case, peering inside.

"They are early examples of Sumerian writing. Just notes written by a scribe."

"Why do you not mark it? It must be important." Saleh stared down through the glass, his eyes scanning the odd-shaped wedges cut into the clay tablet.

"It is the earliest example of writing, probably six thousand years old," Yasin commented. "I do not think it would be valuable to a collector. The writing is meaningless. The linguists who have studied it could not even transcribe any meaning."

Saleh smiled to reveal a mouth missing several teeth, his eyes crisp and alert. "Ahh. That is where you are wrong. It is not what is says that makes it important. It is the fact that it is possibly the first of its kind. The first clay tablets depicting cuneiform writing. Being first is what will bring top dollar. We will take them."

Saleh smashed the side of the case and proceeded to remove the clay tablets. Each weighed slightly more than a paving stone. He handed them to one of the men, who placed them into the crates one by one.

Saleh followed Yasin through the labyrinth of rooms and corridors for another two hours until the entire museum was categorized. One of the vans had already left with its first load by the time they returned to the loading dock.

Saleh thanked the curator for his efforts as they climbed down from the loading dock. Yasin again asked about the money. Saleh laughed lightly, promising, as he reached inside his tunic, that the cash would arrive once the artifacts were sold. Yasin did not see the knife Saleh had taken from its sheath under his rib cage. The blade entered Yasin's body under the arm, hitting his heart. He was dead before he hit the ground. A moment later, two of the men added Yasin's body to the crate they were about to nail shut.

1

Gyrating across the stage with a bottle of vitamin water as his only prop, the rotund ball of a man waved his arms in the air in an exaggerated fashion. Moving quickly across the platform, he pivoted his legs to change direction. Diminutive on the massive stage, he moved across it with wide swings of his legs, spinning his hips horizontally with penguin-like movements. He was a short, stout, round man with little body hair and creases in his face from an affinity to expensive vodka. At the far end of the stage he stopped to look directly out at the audience, his voice rushing out of him like a freight train.

"Energy," his voice boomed through the loudspeakers. "Everything you see, say, and hear, comes from energy. Every action, every reaction, is an output of energy. Movement and stillness, sound and silence, voice and…" he paused for effect, "thoughts…they are all energy. Outside of these walls the people that you will interact with tomorrow will help you to create energy. Or take it away. It's entirely up to YOU."

Hans Pedersen was in his element. Born in Denmark, raised in America, and founder of Thought Mechanix, he was the creator of the immensely popular motivational series known as the Rules of Possibility. Pausing after emphasizing the last word, he pointed to the camera and at the studio audience, capturing everyone's attention with his intense gaze.

"During the next twenty-one days I will take you on a journey that will both entertain and amaze. What I say will scare you. Excite you. Energize you. Everything that you want is out there for the taking. You, and only you, control your destiny by how you accumulate and dispense the energy that you generate.

"Each day a new concept will be introduced. I will ask you to complete a series of lessons to improve your skills. Each day you will enhance your ability to control your thoughts. To control your life."

A large wall lit up behind Hans. The name of his company, Thought Mechanix, filled the screen, followed by the trademark name of his motivational series. He wiped his brow with a cloth as he rotated his body sideways. The twenty-one sessions were predominately displayed on the screen.

Hans waved his hand majestically down the screen. "The Rules of Possibility will change your world forever..."

Jason Wakefield concentrated hard on the television, trying to replace his day of destructive encounters using the rules of thought energy. It was past midnight but the refresher course was necessary, a constant reminder of the source of his success as the founder and still managing partner of Wakefield and Associates, his accounting and advisory firm in the heart of New York. His late-night review of the motivational seminars presented by Hans Pedersen helped him regain focus. It had been a few years since he'd first discovered the man and his genius, and he needed a recap.

Sinking into his expensive Italian leather couch, sipping a Corona, his favorite Mexican liquid meal, Jason momentarily shifted his gaze from the plasma screen to the panoramic view of the brightly lit Manhattan skyline stretching beyond the window of his penthouse. It was his favorite perch from which to watch the round man deliver the ideas that garnered Jason his success. Tapping the Grid became his daily regimen of mind development—straight from the pages of a Rules of Possibility session—he would ignite the experiences of the past, propel his decisions further in order to succeed to the level he desired. He simply had to rely on the untapped energy of thought. It was his mantra. Even if he wanted to he could not ignore the success that stared him in the face each day.

His interest in the Rules of Possibility ran contrary to his impoverished upbringing. Raised on a farm in the heartland of America, Jason, an average student, enrolled in the local college to avoid following in the footsteps of his father, a struggling dustbowl farmer. A keen interest in math and much help from his professor earned him a scholarship to Stanford, where he excelled beyond both his own expectations and those of his sponsor. His latent math talent was not something that Jason knew he possessed growing up in the small rural enclave. The only serious number crunching he had witnessed was his father's, when he counted the proceeds of each year's dismal crop. So survival was a calculation he took seriously. Halfway through his degree in math, when business schools came trolling, he was bitten by the bug of commerce. After grinding through an MBA, he wound up in Manhattan, where he worked his way to becoming a CPA. His natural math talent gained him early success, as he was able to assimilate and analyze the details on a company faster than anyone else in the firm. He was soon called on to complete the most difficult assignments.

But the work became a relentless grind. The fourteen-hour days, the lost weekends, and a shallow social life were depleting his ambition. His farm boy leanness was lost in the years of sweat equity in the firm. His physique quickly evolved into that of a deskbound drone.

That was until he discovered the Rules of Possibility.

He had been channel surfing after a particularly grueling audit client that had kept him at the office sixteen hours a day for a month. When he made it home to his apartment at two that morning after the audit wrap-up party ended, he was too wired to sleep. Hans Pedersen's gyrations on the tube caught his attention. The fleshy man was racing from one end of the stage to the other, sweating profusely into a towel as he engaged an enthusiastic studio crowd. Jason did not know it at the time, but he was watching a rerun of the first infomercial released by the fledgling self-improvement company. Staring at the screen, seemingly too mentally zapped to comprehend, the message being delivered by the little man stuck nonetheless.

A month after zoning out on the late-night motivational speaker, he saw an advertisement about Hans Pedersen in an in-flight magazine while on his way to Philadelphia for an audit. After reading it, he slipped the magazine into his briefcase. Not one to believe in coincidences or mass-marketing, he was however intrigued enough by the claims of the publication to enroll in Pedersen's seminar series taking place a few weeks later in midtown Manhattan. It cost a thousand dollars, *but what the heck*, he thought. *Maybe there would be some good ideas to get him out of the bull pen of his stagnant career.*

The week was a blur. The wild-eyed Hans yelled his theories at the two hundred or so participants. Jason tried hard to concentrate, but the esoteric process was not crystal clear to his analytical mind. He did not know how he would accomplish his goals by following the Rules. Even so, after that week-long journey into the strange world of Thought Mechanix, he bought the Twenty-one Rules of Possibility DVD series.

In fact everyone did, which Jason thought was unusual. *How was it that after the week-long session everyone wanted to continue the program?* And yet, despite his internal argument that the seminar was a waste of time, some psychobabble to take money from desperate young professionals, he paid for it with a credit card that had very little room left on its limit.

In the first assignment, the first Rule—thinking consciously— Jason was instructed to establish goals. The initial task was to listen to one's thoughts for an entire week to ascertain where the mind was headed. He conducted the first exercise with religious fervor; then he listened to the entire series of DVDs he was expected to follow after the initial week-long retreat—twenty-one segments, twenty-one days—each day providing a single Rule to the TMI recruits, as they were called.

But the meditative music and strange exercises seemed to have no lasting effect. Despite his commitment, he ended the process feeling less focused than when he started. The only thought that remained was that he had just blown a grand on some hocus-pocus.

His mind routinely came back to the third segment—Energizing Memories. Throughout the sessions dealing with listening, propelling thought energy into the universe, and even the most bizarre Rule of all— directing his thought receptors—he kept trying to convince his mind to shed the past. To no avail, his life *was* his past. *Wasn't it like that with everyone?* Yet despite his skepticism, he continued to work on the lessons and develop the skills promised by the short, round man.

After the first month, he faithfully attended the weekend updates with hundreds of other TMI Recruits. Soothing music, mental exercises, and an hour-long webcast activated an energy level that propelled Jason forward, as if driven by a force guided by someone else.

Soon the changes began to take shape. Literally. Jason began to gain back the fireman-physique he enjoyed in his youth on the farm.

The soft-center of his professional accountant body firmed up with his intense daily exercise regimen. Jason's blond hair, chiseled jawline and deep-set eyes were his own, but the comfortably toned body was the result of Thought Mechanix. The less-than-athletic, unassuming grinder in the bull pen of a Big Four firm was one more success of Thought Mechanix.

Once he completed the program, he attacked his career with an unseen force of confidence. Jobs that he wanted to work on came his way. Assignments he dreaded were unexpectedly taken on by another group. Miserable clients left the firm but still commending their relationship. His star was rising. Within three years he took control of his future, rising to the ranks of partner. All at once he was directing the work and capturing large clients at the drop of a hat. Success came easy. But it wasn't enough. Like a drug, the success pushed him further. He requested a shift to the corporate advisory group. The Firm's management board turned him down. He insisted but was rejected a second time. So he left to start out on his own.

Now, at thirty five, he was the managing partner of Wakefield and Associates, a Manhattan based, eleven-partner boutique firm, living happily single in a Manhattan penthouse, working more hours than the lowliest grunt. He still had no social life and dated only occasionally. He was a sought-after bachelor, but the firm became his passion, a driving force that was infectious to all those who joined. The clients rolled in. Hans Pedersen and Thought Mechanix Inc. became a client, a crowning achievement to the man's own Rules of Possibility seminar.

2

Wakefield and Associates worked only with the best companies, and only the best business school grads became Wakefield employees, each of whom were expected to complete the Thought Mechanix Rules of Possibility program as part of their initiation. Jason generally insisted that his clients also attend the seminar, if they hadn't already, which was usually the case. Just like the internationally accepted ISO 9000 industrial certification ensured that a company adhered to rigorous operational standards, TMI RoP began to be a required symbol on the letterhead of any company of significance. Hans Pedersen insisted that his program offered an even greater chance of success than any other management program, including ISO and even Sigma 7. Wakefield and Associates was one of the first to display the TMI RoP symbol on the firm's literature. The claim that Thought Mechanix made was that the symbol changes how the world perceives your company. Hans went further to state that the symbol attached to a company "changes how others *think* about what you can do for them."

Since attending Hans Pedersen's workshop, every one of the provocative ideas espoused in the month-long DVD series had improved Jason's life and career. Jason never thought of himself as an evangelist, despite his unending support for the benefits of the Thought Mechanix methodology.

"We have to let up." Jason listened as his fellow partner, and best friend, Timothy Greer spoke. "This has been an incredible ride. I can't thank you enough for the opportunity you offered, taking me away from the drudgery I had grown accustomed to."

"Don't forget the money," Jason chimed in with a grin. "How many other accountants do you know who are making seven figures, working the hours you do?"

"Yeah, the money's great too. But people, and by people I mean our illustrious governing body, are beginning to circle the wagons.

They don't like our delivery system. They feel it lacks the necessary professional distance from our clients."

"We don't audit many of them."

"True, you are behaving more like a management consultant than a public accountant. Still, we are CPAs and being a Certified Public Accountant requires a certain duty of care."

Timothy started to sound preachy, which is why Jason brought him on board in the first place. He needed someone to mind the store. He appreciated the advice, though he was not always inclined to take it.

"Our clients hire us to deliver a comprehensive approach to help them run their empires. We interpert data, guide them into understanding what decisions are best, and make sure it gets properly recorded and reported. What more could anyone ask for?"

"Cute. What is expected is that we 'cease and desist' from acting like an in-house financial and business counsel while at the same time releasing financial statements that represent results that we had an obvious hand in creating."

Timothy was not telling the managing partner anything he did not already know.

"What's the solution?" Jason knew where this was heading.

"The Thought Mechanix endorsement needs to be curtailed, maybe for a little while anyway, as Blair and our other partners have suggested. The threat from Gunter Tang makes it hard for us to win this battle with Blair."

"It's a frivolous lawsuit at best. Blair Stanford knows that." Jason had dismissed the threat almost as soon as he handed the file over to his lawyer.

"It's not the lawsuit..." Timothy knew that his managing partner knew what he was talking about. An internal power struggle was under way, and the lawsuit was just fuel for the other side.

"My success—your success—and the growth of most of our clients comes down to the implementation of the Rules of Possibility created by Hans Pedersen and his organization. Thought Mechanix has been the key to our success. How can we deny access to that formula to those who come looking to implement its strategies?"

It was true. Once Jason established a reputation as a doer within the TMI fraternity, he was the first person many graduates of the TMI RoP program turned to for help when implementing the strategies for their businesses. He built the firm around the referrals. Within a year, the TMI founder even sought him out to help evolve the organization. It became a closed club, one that he was not willing to give up easily.

"You and I need to stay aligned with this." Jason spoke with conviction. His best friend had broached the subject before.

But Timothy played the voice of reason. "With the Tang situation, now may not be the time to be so adamant."

3

The incident prompting the delivery of the lawsuit happened a month earlier, in the same office that Jason occupied at Wakefield and Associates since its first day in Manhattan. It was a long month made longer by the expectation of bad news. But the day of reckoning had come, as he knew it would.

After Timothy left his office, Jason sat in his leather swivel chair and stared out of the window, recalling his encounter with the dangerous Gunter Tang. The meeting was not one he would forget, as it was the first time since he completed the motivational series, the Rules of Possibility, that he felt the control over his stellar career was suddenly out of his hands.

The meeting with Gunter Tang took place on a sunnier day than today. The Asian tycoon sat stoic across from him, a man not to be taken lightly. Jason had heard stories that made Al Capone look like a Goody Two-shoes. The man was belligerent to his staff, sanctimonious when handling problems that affected his business dealings, and to make matters worse, right about his current disagreement with Wakefield and Associates. The sneering, self-indulgent gaze caught Jason squarely in his ego. Tang interrupted before Jason could begin, his thin accent, a cross between Mandarin and German, filling the room.

"Do not take me for a simpleton, Mr. Wakefield. My company does not have any significant dealings with your firm, and I suspect we will not be having any more, given the circumstances. You had an opportunity to help me, yet you chose to remove yourself from the deal."

"Gunter," Jason began, "our firm strives to ensure the privacy of all of our clients. When Talon Enterprises entered a rival bid to acquire FinnStart , I could do nothing else but step aside from the negotiations. Talon Enterprises is a client. Once they entered the deal I was compelled to back away. I could no longer think for either party. Thoughts… "

Remember to choose your thoughts with care. Jason let the rule slide across his consciousness.

Tang cut him short.

"Cut the Thought Mechanix crap. Since my second-in-command brought the TMI RoP into the organization, I had nothing but dissention from my employees, who now all think they should be empowered to build fabulous lives and great careers. My factory workers don't have careers. They get handouts. Do you really think that some uneducated, minimum wage single mom with two bastard children will ever reach high enough to climb out of despair just by listening to a dozen theories on how to think better? They don't need to think, and judging from their lot in life, probably don't want to know that something better is just beyond their grasp. For each one of them who challenges their station in life, there are a dozen waiting to take their place. Not everyone in this world needs, or should be given, the tools for success. It would destroy them."

Tang had delivered the tirade with care. He was very interested in TMI, but he did not want Jason to get the impression he cared. Or what he knew that made him so interested.

Jason was getting hot, his anger coursing just below the surface, raising his blood pressure to a dangerous level. He tried to keep his ego in check. Taking a deep breath before responding, anxious not to get into an argument about TMI, he paused a moment. He learned early on that not everyone was ready to accept the positive thought energy that provided success. In fact, even he could feel the negative energy coming to the surface more often of late. The feeling was not pleasant.

"Mr. Tang. Let's keep this civil. Clearly we have different philosophies—"

Again Tang cut him off. "This has nothing to do with points of view about management. This has to do with the fact that you backed out of negotiations with my company at a crucial juncture in our bid to acquire FinnStart Communications, and that move resulted in your client being in a position to offer a better, more competitive bid to wrestle the company out from under me. I have come to learn that you have been actively involved in another deal involving Talon

Enterprises...and I can't help but think that you led FinnStart away from me in order to make that happen."

It was Jason's turn to interrupt. "Let me make one thing perfectly clear to you, Mr. Tang. The FinnStart deal was shopped around for two years before Tang approached Wakefield and Associates to help orchestrate a deal. No one was interested in the company, certainly none of Wakefield's existing clients."

The small electronics company made specialized radio equipment, transmitters and long-range radar devices primarily for commercial use. FinnStart made it known that they wanted to align themselves with a company with complementary products and were willing to wait for the right company to come along. They threw out the Tang deal at first glance.

Gunter Tang was known as a predator whose primary intent was to gain control of a select piece of technology that a company possessed, then strip and abandon the rest of the business as scrap. No matter how convincing Jason was as to the merits of the deal, they wouldn't budge. When Talon swooped in to acquire FinnStart, the deal surprised Jason as much as anyone.

Jason focused before speaking, ensuring that his mind was very direct in its message. The sudden change of tone cast a pall over the room. But if Gunter Tang noticed, he did not let on. Jason had heard of the man's reputation, but that did not matter to him. His need to win trumped his concerns.

"Wakefield and Associates does not engage in information piracy. Your deal was strictly confidential. I shared nothing with the acquisition realm over at Talon Enterprises. As I told you repeatedly, once they presented an offer I backed away. You can be assured that I have personally reviewed the files, e-mails, correspondence and telephone records of all staff members involved on both files, and there is not one shred of evidence that implies impropriety on our part. It was an unfortunate coincidence that sadly did not work out in your favor. We are clearly not at fault, legally, professionally or morally, so please do not try and grind out something that wasn't ever going to happen."

"It wasn't? That's not the way I saw it taking place." Gunter Tang never said anything accidentally. He operated his business empire like a warlord, leaving no enemy behind to come back and mount a challenge. Originally from Hong Kong, he fled the British Protectorate on the heels of the Chinese takeover at the end of the millennium. Keeping a few trusted lieutenants behind, he set up his operations on the waterfront in Vancouver, on the west coast of Canada. To ensure he was not overly taxed on his worldwide operations, he only brought essential personnel to the city, sending the profits to Gibraltar and other tax havens around the world. Tang Enterprises spanned the globe, entering into every facet of commerce, eagerly gobbling up companies that could not compete.

Tang was not a typical rags-to-riches billionaire. He grew up in the shadow of his father's potent criminal organization, which sent him to private schools and allowed him to enjoy luxury early in life. Criminal jealousies eliminated his family before he had a chance to assume the reins. That didn't stop Gunter. Taking the emergency millions that his father put in reserve with a Swiss trustee, Tang built his own empire after his father was killed. He avoided the underworld, deciding instead to compete in the legitimate world of commerce. It proved to be a perfect plan. Recently his plans had turned to something more ambitious than just the accumulation of a massive balance sheet.

He had seen Wakefield utilize his distinct brand of advisory services with several of his key company heads, applying the Thought Mechanix Rules of Possibility framework in several divisions. It was providing stellar results in the two divisions—one an animation company and the other an electronics manufacturer. Although it caused utter disruption in his company as the managers began to incorporate the ideas, Tang saw the bigger benefit. He had seen men manipulated by brainwashing before and that was how he perceived this motivational mumbo-jumbo. He had bigger plans.

Tang grinned through his thin moustache. He flexed his lean muscles of his forearm, honed from years of martial arts training. A black belt in several disciplines, he rarely needed to use the lethal force but was thankful he possessed the tools. Although he was now a "legitimate" businessman, he did not forget the other effective methods of compliance he learned from his father. If Tang thought about it, he couldn't have cared less about Talon buying his target acquisition. He would deal with that little problem in his own way, when the time was right. He wanted to rile the accountant. The message had been sent; it was time to change his approach. Clearly he hit the nerve he needed.

"And how did you see it taking place?" Jason held his ground, but in a flash his mind formed the thought that this problem would not go away as easily as he expected.

"Exactly as it was supposed to; you will approach the management of Talon Enterprises and present the original offer of mine to take over FinnStart. I suggest you do not take no for an answer." Tang leaned forward slightly so that Jason's field of vision included only him.

"In addition, I insist you deliver a message to my managers. This motivational mumbo-jumbo is creating havoc in my organization and it has to stop. You will renounce the effectiveness of the Thought Mechanix program in a formal release to my company. With such a statement, I will be able to regain control of my wayward management. Finally, Wakefield's continued involvement with Hans Pedersen will stop immediately."

Tang sucked in a breath as he stared down the accountant. He didn't really care about seeing his demands through. He just needed the young accountant to be off-balance enough to give him what he really wanted. He had his own designs for the powerful brain tool.

"I can't do that—" Jason started.

"You can and you will. Stick to accounting. Motivational redirection is not what the world needs of its bean counters. But, since your firm instilled the ideas in my management team, you need to be held responsible. My lawyers will be filing a breach of trust lawsuit against your firm and you personally regarding your involvement in the FinnStart deal. You, your firm and the 'amazing' Thought Mechanix guru are in for a battle for your meddling in my company affairs without my permission. There was no authorization given for you to manipulate my employees and turn them against my organization."

Before Jason could mount a protest against the threats, Gunter Tang had already stood up and was headed out of the office.

4

A grey mist shrouded the Horseman who stood guard over the entrance to Central Park. Jason stared out of his office window towards the Thought Mechanix building. It was kitty-corner from where he stood in his office at Wakefield and Associates. His view was as clouded as his mind, as the words and warning from Timothy rattled his brain. He was thinking about that meeting with Tang a little over a month ago. He hadn't heard any more of the matter since the volatile mogul's abrupt exit from his office, until his discussion with Timothy. He had thought it was over.

To make matters worse, he had chosen not to mention the outcome of the Tang meeting with his partners at the last two weekly meetings. Had he chosen to share the Tang confrontation with the other partners of Wakefield and Associates, things may have been different. This was not the first such incident. He remembered their somber faces the last time Thought Mechanix caused a concern. It was etched in his mind like scratches on a blackboard. Yet he knew that despite the unwanted exposure, these were the same people who as early as six months ago lauded Jason for his ingenuity, laughed as they puffed on Montecristos at the annual retreat, and patted each other on the back and congratulated themselves for having created such an innovative firm.

They have no backbone, Jason thought as he turned back to his desk. His partners were no longer the lean and hungry accountants eager to change the face of the profession they sometimes mocked. Their conventional indoctrination as CPAs won in the end. The gauntlet forced upon them by their professional body, the AICPA, had the entire group, save one, turn tail. It was his enterprise, and although he was responsible for creating and nurturing it into the successful advisory machine it had become, he had become a liability, so the managing committee seemed to intimate. Jason knew that it was more than the pressure from the governing body to whom they answered. It was Gunter Tang that had them spooked. To challenge the partners on this fact was to admit that the man scared them, which was reason enough for him to be sacked. Tang was someone whom most people were afraid to challenge. It wasn't the threat of a lawsuit from Tang's organization that fueled the fear. Tang had a reputation for ruthlessly eliminating obstacles to his success, like the horrific burning death of Steven Joel, the CEO of Action Life, only weeks after he opposed Tang's attempt at a takeover. Jason could see the charred body of the flamboyant entrepreneur in the eyes of his partners as he passed them in the hallway.

Jason looked out of his office window one last time at the Horseman as it emerged from a rising fog, standing guard in the center of the Grand Army Plaza roundabout. The corner office had an unobstructed view across Central Park. From his vantage point, he could look southeastward to the museum of Natural History halfway down the park, south along Park Avenue to the Zoo, or straight across to the entrance to the Park. He had a bird's eye view of the same people that Hans saw. But to Jason they were just ants, representing the multitude of moving parts that made up the New York machine.

Was he their servant or their master?

Wakefield and Associates had its roots as a professional accounting office. The majority of the three hundred people who worked for the firm were professional accountants, although not all of them. The consultants who helped deliver the TMI RoP implementation strategies came from all walks of life: engineers, MBAs, even psychologists. The division was independent, yet an integral part of the success at Wakefield. The twelve partners making up the firm enjoyed a success none had ever dreamed possible. The firm had grown at an astounding thirty-seven percent a year rate for the past decade. Despite the growth, none of the partners, except one, was prepared to compromise on the fundamentals of the core accounting business that grounded the firm. They were entrenched in what had become *their* firm, with no intention of leaving. Wakefield and Associates brought them the financial rewards they had missed out on with their former careers. But they were also focused on the accounting profession. Advisory services were left to the two advisory partners in the firm, Jason and his best friend Timothy Greer. The partnership was starting to see audit work slip though their fingers because of the advisory division, and they were anxious to get back into the traditional stream. It was comfort food.

Jason paused for one last look out over Central Park before leaving his office. He knew that the consultancy practice caused his fellow partners unease. *But, damn it, they knew what drove the numbers and were happy to sign on when times were good and the money was rolling in. One lawsuit and the shit hit the fan.*

He grabbed his coffee mug and headed out of his office to the boardroom. He was greeted with a few odd stares from the administrative staff as he passed through the central bullpen. Rumors of the latest lawsuit to hit the firm were running rampant. It was time to put an end to the speculation. Jason was determined not to lose control of the momentum he had built within *his* firm.

The boardroom was tucked away on the opposite side of the floor from his office. Unlike most prestigious accounting firms, Wakefield did not waste prime real estate on space that was used only occasionally for large client meetings and staff gatherings. The boardroom was at the back of the building and had only interior windows, whose function to catch light from the external offices was eliminated by a series of electronically controlled blinds.

Jason took one last deep breath, yanked open the thick, frosted-glass door and entered the room. *All but two of the partners are present for the hanging,* Jason thought, as he caught the eyes of the man that would conduct the inquisition.

"Have a seat, Jason."

Blair Stanford's chiseled face rarely expressed emotion, but he stared up at the founder of the Partnership with smugness. "The Stanford," as he was known around the office, had joined Wakefield and Associates five years earlier, bringing with him a mid-seven figure practice dredged up from the dying embers of a scandal-ridden Wall Street firm brought down by sloppy audit work of a now defunct hedge fund.

"Blair, nice to see you so upbeat. I'm surprised to see you so relaxed. But then again, you've been down this sort of road before."

Jason nodded, cocking his head as if he were bowing to a fellow combatant inside the UFC cage.

Clearly there was no love lost between the two men. Jason Wakefield regretted his decision to woo Stanford into his practice almost from the moment the man set foot in the office. By the time he had come to realize the folly of his growth-at-all-costs decision, The Stanford had already embedded himself into Wakefield's business arena, quickly recruiting three of his prior partners that now made up the core of the executive committee.

Blair Stanford ignored the sarcasm. Instead, he stood up, his six-foot-four frame commanding attention from the partner group as he began the meeting.

"The Gunter Tang incident is far more volatile than a crooked hedge fund. The man is more than a mere menace; he's dangerous, and he has taken a true dislike to your newfound passion. This man will stop at nothing to get what he wants. Rumors of dead associates who have tried to challenge his authority are not exaggerated—"

"Now you just sound scared, Blair." Jason smiled wryly, knowing what was about to come.

"Don't taunt me, young man. Nothing scares me." Stanford's voice boomed against the back wall of the boardroom like a tsunami. He let the echo linger like thick fog as the others in the room looked around uneasily.

"Then why are you letting a punk like Gunter Tang tell you, the great Stanford, what to do within his own firm?"

"This is bigger than Tang. He is just one of several clients unhappy with the increased emphasis on the Thought Mechanix bullshit. For all intents and purposes, we're almost seen as a part of that insidious organization that poisons minds. It might have been the great fuel for your rising star, and make no mistake, we appreciate the success you have had…" Stanford lingered on the word, "…but it is clear that your focus has had a significant divergence of late. Enough to worry the executive committee of the firm."

Stanford continued to rant, never failing to emphasize that the advisory side of the practice comprised only twenty-percent of the firm's business. "It has become abundantly clear that our illustrious governing body wants nothing to do with Hans Pederson's psycho-babble."

"Like you give a shit what they think," Jason shot back.

"It's not about me, Jason. It's about the rest of the people in this room. They joined you to build a practice that would rival the best of Wall Street, not traipse off and offer some crackerjack, late-night infomercial advice on how to live your life better."

"That 'crackerjack' advice, as you so eloquently put it, has made all of you very wealthy. And saved you from ruin," Jason chimed in. It was well known that Wakefield and Associates was the only place willing to take Stanford after the scandal.

"Don't start with me." Stanford raised his voice again. He could hold his own in any room and was not about to accept the insolence of this young buck. The comment warranted a challenge, but Stanford checked himself before speaking. He had a job to do, and the reward it offered was too good to pass up. It was time to put an end to the charade. Regaining his composure, he lowered his voice, set his calm steely-eyed glare upon the firm's young founder and issued his decree.

"The Partners have taken a vote. By unanimous decision they have chosen to expel you from the partnership, effective immediately."

5

Jason stared at the men sitting around the large table, an expansive slab of raw, unfinished lumber cut from a single Douglas fir. They averted their gaze back to Blair.

"You can't expel me. You need just cause. There is no litigation against me or the firm, as far as I am aware. I'm not inclined to go anywhere just yet. Besides, it takes a unanimous vote to extract a partner. Tim would never agree to this."

Jason surveyed the faces of the men around the table and realized that his best friend was not present.

"Mr. Greer will also be moving on."

"I assume you have already delivered the ultimatum to Tim."

"No need. Tim resigned on his own volition this morning."

"I don't believe you," Jason responded with an edge.

"Trust me. He knew a good deal when he saw one. His resignation will not go unrewarded."

"But no such luck for me." Jason sat back in his chair. It was done. He may as well let them conclude with their fiasco.

"While there is no currently pending lawsuit, Gunter Tang has filed a complaint with the AICPA. They have asked us to act and avoid a scandal.

"Cute, Blair. Somehow I don't see you as the white knight of our profession."

"We do what we have to do." Stanford feigned a slight grin and stood up, dismissing Wakefield with the command that he clean out his desk and leave the office by the end of the day.

Blair Stanford was no slouch when it came to successful transitions. He rose to the ranks of managing director of his old firm, ducked under the indictments strewn about during that firm's demise at the hands of hungry district attorneys, and surfaced as the de facto leader at Wakefield despite Jason's attempt to remain at the helm of his sleek, wave-riding practice. Jason's ever-consuming obsession with the field of "energy management" would be his downfall as it turned out. Stanford could taste the victory, and Jason could see it in his eyes.

Blair Stanford stared back at the young nonconformist, who was finally going to be set back a peg or two if he had anything to say about it. Jason Wakefield was a disgrace to the profession as far as he was concerned. To assist in his total destruction was like Sparta pushing the barbarian hordes through the gates of Hades. One of his clients in particular, the Diocese of the Roman Catholic Church of New York, was particularly forthright about the direction of Jason's practice. Stanford had consolidated power amongst the traditionalists of the firm over the past year when they watched Jason start to integrate his processes into his client's businesses. The idea of entering into some sort of joint venture with their clients went counter to everything they believed. With the urging of powerful influences, including the AICPA and others, he decided to act.

After dealing the death blow to the firm's founder, he sat back in his chair, content in the knowledge that it was over for the young Jason Wakefield. By week's end, his epoch of power would be completely and irrevocably over, for once and for all.

The palace coup was successful.

The man sure knew how to move in tight circles, Jason thought as he returned to his office to clean out his desk. Wakefield and Associates, the firm that he founded a decade earlier was no longer his to morph into his own design. A little shocked at how swift was his extraction was, he knew the days of Wakefield and Associates were long gone. By week's end the signs would be replaced with some reference to Blair Stanford.

Jason was not entirely disheartened. Accounting was no longer something he was interested in pursuing; instead, he was driven to give his clients what they truly needed—and wanted. Long before Tang initiated his expulsion, Jason could see that the rest of the partners, except one, wanted to devolve into the traditional role of external number cruncher. It was a worthy profession, one that provided the backbone of corporate governance.

But Jason had created Wakefield and Associates to be unlike traditional accounting offices. He succeeded for a time, until its size forced it to gravitate back to its traditional role. Too many accountants in one place stifled the creativity, he figured. What he could not understand was how it happened despite the lucrative dividends paid out each year through the TMI practice. Had it change slowly, over time, or was it an instant conversion, reaching a tipping point that forced the partners to swing back to their comfort zone?

Gunter Tang had provided the catalyst with his unsubstantiated and impossible-to-prosecute lawsuit. Being the author of his own downfall was difficult to accept, but he knew that spending more time on TM client advisory engagements allowed others to take over the reins. The plough moved swiftly in a different direction.

Time to move on, Jason muttered to himself. Timothy knocked as he pushed open the door to Jason's office. He was holding two lattes. Before sitting down, he handed one of them to Jason.

"Thanks," Jason replied.

"Thought you could use a double after that meeting." Timothy returned a wry smile. "I'm coming with you, you realize."

"So I heard. Took the easy way out: slit your wrists instead of sticking your head in their noose."

"Ha. Very funny. But you're right. I'm just a coward to the core." Timothy mocked up a stance of self-pity, his fiery-red hair drooping over his eyes as he lowered his head in shame.

"At least you did not give them the satisfaction." Jason took a sip of the latte, quickly spitting the coffee back through the tiny exit on the lid. "Ouch, that's effing hot."

"Just the way you like it." Timothy laughed at the pain his friend was suffering, as good friends are inclined to do—don't offer a hand if it's not needed when a stifling guffaw will suffice. "It's not a done deal for you."

"Are you kidding? You should have seen the wolves salivating? They were more than eager to eat their young. Despite their tacit commitment to the direction with the firm, they are all still accountants at heart. Look at Russell. Can you imagine him delivering a TMI Rules of Possibility speech to his timber brokerage client? They all like the ideas, the energy, and the results, but none of them are prepared to spend the time delivering the message."

"It is exhaustive work," Timothy admitted. Even he found it easier to crank out financial statements at fifteen large a pop instead of delivering advisory services. The TMI stuff, as with all advisory work, was partner intensive. It demanded time and commitment with very little staff leverage—the grease that made the machine work.

"I don't think any of them are afraid of hard work. Russell clocked twenty-seven hundred hours last year, and took the summer off. It's the subjective themes, the delving into Hans Pedersen's direction that scares them. They can't have anything against Thought Mechanix. It made this firm. It made them all very wealthy." Jason sounded more intense than he intended.

"Hey, you're preaching to the converted." Timothy held up his hands in mock protest.

"I'm not preaching."

"Well...lately you have been a bit too enthusiastic about the new stuff coming out of TMI. Baines called you an evangelist."

"I thought he was kidding. Obviously not," Jason commented as he unfolded a file box to collect his desk contents.

Timothy raised an eyebrow in classic Belushi style. The two shared a moment of realization. Jason had dipped over the edge. He cautioned his clients about this exact dilemma: being too immersed in the passion that drove the success in the first place. What he taught was the necessity to remain semi-detached, to hover over the enterprise at a discrete mental distance and watch it function. By getting caught up in the creative energy that built the organization without stepping back to ensure the pieces were all fitting together was a formula for disaster. *Train your mind to accept the thoughts of those around you* were his instructions to his clients. Again, he relied on the steps defined in the Rules of Possibility as a backdrop—*listen in order to learn.*

Jason realized he was no longer listening to the noise around his universe. He had blocked everyone out, expecting them to be as committed to the direction of the firm as he was. Wakefield and Associates attracted the clients they did because they delivered an exceptional product. Jason pounded the TMI concept into every one of his prospective clients. Those who joined did so because they liked the message.

But not everyone liked the message. Those that did not care for the TMI message just never even came to the party. As the firm grew—as partners were added—they brought in their own clients. Those clients heard a different message. Jason had created an organization that no longer bore his signature.

"Before committing to the spin-off, it might be a good idea to meet with Hans. I'd like to make sure he is okay with the concept. We'll center our product line on implementing the Rules of Possibility." Jason was getting excited.

"Hold on, cowboy." Timothy was becoming a clear mind to the wayward preacher. "Wakefield Consulting needs to become its own brand. What we need to do is spin the TMI process with our own style."

"You mean steal his ideas." Jason paused for a moment as his mind toyed with the idea of his own packaged philosophies being gobbled up by the hungry masses.

"His ideas are just regurgitated philosophies from a cast of self-help gurus. In 1937 Napoleon Hill wrote *Think and Grow Rich,* in which he described the brain as a broadcasting and receiving station for thought. His theories quoted numerous other great leaders who knew the secret of thought transmutation. However Hans came upon his ancient formula, it's been done before."

Timothy could tell that Jason was hearing something he already knew by the way he contorted his mouth, pushing the cheekbone into his eye socket. It was a poor imitation of a constipated pirate.

Jason fired back, "Yeah, I know all that, but then why is Hans such a phenomenon? Look at his numbers. Over twenty million people have attended his seminars or completed the RoP DVD program. In just the last three years. That number jumps to over fifty million if you count the earliest programs."

Not trying to compete with the metrics, Timothy provided a comparison. "In the seventy years since it was first published, Hill's book has sold fifteen million copies. That's two hundred thousand a year on average. So there are a lot of people who already know how to achieve success like the great ones."

"And yet it doesn't happen!" Jason sobered up his enthusiasm. "It doesn't happen because people want to be spoon-fed. Pedersen's program—delivered by the TMI RoP method—has been more successful because he goes one step further than Hill: he provides a paint-by-number approach to the theory of thought."

"We can improve on them. Make them less esoteric. Can you imagine if the average person truly understood what Hans Pedersen was getting at? The reason your clients have succeeded with his concepts is because you've figured out how to deliver the goods in a way that people can understand. In a way, that makes all the thought-receptor stuff more about helping people work together and less about getting inside of people's heads."

"Still, it's not my style to steal anything from anyone. I was a boy scout, remember, and a Rotarian. Not to mention a CPA."

Timothy laughed, spilling some of the frothy milk onto his tie as he tried to hold the latte steady.

"Oozing with ethics, are we? Come on, Jason. This is business. Survival of the fittest. Dog-eat-dog. If we do this right, we can be bigger than Thought Mechanix."

Jason was not sure he liked what was coming from his right-hand man. Ethics were the foundation of his career. He never did anything just to succeed. There were certain issues he would not compromise on. If Timothy was so inclined...

A small twitch of Timothy's lower lip followed by a wide grin stopped Jason's thoughts.

"Why are you such a prick? You had me going. Not that I don't agree with you about our chances, but let's do this right. We can still succeed with the endorsement from Hans."

"Yeah, you're right. Let's try it the proper way first." Timothy continued to smile as he looked the wounded puppy. "Go see the man and ask if we can play in his ballpark."

6

Hans Pedersen stood at his window and looked down on the Fifth Avenue entrance to Central Park. The entrance of the tranquil park was in sharp contrast to the hectic fray of the city. A small plaza, anchored by a statue of a horseman, stood between the city and the park—as if trying to prevent outward expansion, while Fifth Avenue and Sixtieth Street formed a asphalt shield, separating the park from the small plaza, allowing it to transition from the chaotic to the serene, from a city of urgently moving traffic to a haven of lush, green tranquility.

The scene changed like rolling waves. Each moment brought different people, movements and noises, filtering up into the remarkable domain where Hans stood. When he watched the tide of pedestrians navigating their way through their little patch of New York, he would inevitably focus in on one person who stood out from the masses. Maybe they were taller, moving faster, or weaving erratically through the crowd. Perhaps they were dressed differently, or looking around with a where-am-I-now-and-how-did-I-get-so-lost look. Regardless of which individual he picked, it was clear to Hans that his or her life had purpose. Good or bad, productive or useless, there was still purpose.

Within a heartbeat their lives—both real and imagined—would rush in his consciousness to be analyzed, contemplated, and then mostly discarded.

But not always.

On occasion, Hans would catch something unusual or trivial, but nonetheless interesting, that would cause him to act. A quick phone call to one of his security guards at the entrance below would bring a swift reaction. If he was lucky, the particular person who had caught his attention would agree to an interview. And when they did, the world was one step closer to perfection, according to the Thought Mechanix founder.

Today Hans was focusing on a blue-suited businessman crossing over to Central Park South, away from the plaza. The man was known to him. Whether he was preparing for a confrontation or just leaving an altercation was unclear, but the gait at which the man walked signified he was desperate to distance himself from the office building he had just exited. Beside him, a less formally attired, stern-looking man scanned the crowd as he kept pace with the man who was obviously his boss.

Deciding against the intrusion into his already distraught morning, he turned away from the window to attend to the papers sitting on his desk. He picked up the phone after settling into his soft brown leather chair to summon his assistant.

Amy Gloss entered a few minutes later, holding a foot-thick sheaf of papers against her body with one hand and balancing a coffee in the trademark white and green cup in the other. Dumping the sheaf of pulp onto the desk, she casually whirled around to close the door before sitting down across the desk from Hans. She waited for instructions, sitting patiently in wait, staring at Hans more as a disciple than an employee, because regardless of how she came to know Hans, the man had saved her life.

From the age of thirteen Amy had lived on the street, forced there by a drunken father who had already destroyed her mom. She did whatever she needed to in order to survive. Amy was one of Hans's first random acts of kindness that resulted from his astute observation of the masses that passed under his office window each day. She never tired of relaying the story of that cold, rain-soaked afternoon. After having taken up residence on the south end of Central Park, in the woods near the Pond, she began hustling passersby for money and food. She felt secure amongst the wealthy of Fifth Avenue. It was certainly safer than uptown—more discarded food from the tourists and the pimps left her alone. The only trick was hiding from the foot patrols and park sanitation crews whose job it was to keep people like her out of sight.

After a third week of seemingly endless rain battering the city, Amy was desperate. She had been tossed out of almost every shelter she could find. Despite attempts at looking "normal," she did not have the wardrobe to even blend into the disorderly chaos of stores. Amy tried not to steal, and only took drugs occasionally offered to dull the pain of loneliness. She had few friends, many of them dead, or sucked into drugs and prostitution to survive. She had done all of that without emotion, without thought.

That rainy, grey day when she met Hans Pedersen was not like any other. Amy had lost hope. Eyeing cars as they sped out of the Grand Army Plaza crescent, she wondered if jumping in front of one of them would be painful, or if she would die instantly. She wondered whether anyone would come to her funeral. Then she realized that there would be no funeral. Two minutes into planning her suicide, a man approached her. He offered her sanctuary from the street. She only had to agree to be interviewed by a motivational expert.

At first she walked away, skeptical of the man's intention. A moment later she turned and followed him. A least it was a way to get out of the rain. That was six years ago. A lifetime! Since then, Amy took all that life presented, not turning down many opportunities, and thankful for her redemption.

The confident emerald eyes glinted with expectation as they scanned the desk of Hans Pedersen. They disclosed none of the misery that they had previously experienced. Amy did not suppress those memories; she used them as fuel. Her life now had purpose. In some ways she had not changed. Her clothes were still plain in a way that took nothing from her smooth beauty. Had her life taken a different turn at thirteen, had her father not been an abusive drunk, had she not been relegated to the streets to survive, she could have been the high school prom queen, the valedictorian, class president, an honor student—anything. But then, she wouldn't be where she was—where she was meant to be—inside the inner chamber of one of the most powerful organizations in the world. With a purpose.

Amy was the success story that kept Hans at the window, the same window that reflected so many more failures than successes. Many of the random acts of kindness that he had extended to the downtrodden of New York made Hans feel like an imposter. Still, he did not believe the failures were a direct result of the application of his Rules, and yet he could not seem to engage everyone who he approached. Some people were perhaps too stubborn. Others—too many to count—were too negative. He ignored the negative energy that seemed to overpower his good intentions. He did this because he was so sure that his successes were more significant. Hans did not want to see what was really happening around him either. Too many good things were being accomplished, so how could what he was doing possibly be bad for the world? He refused to see the perverse ways in which people were applying the Rules. The lucky individuals who connected with what Thought Mechanix was all about—the Amys of this world—spurred him to continue.

At least, that is, until the recent encounter with the source of his success. That encounter scared him into realizing it was time to stop the charade. It brought him back to the beginning, to Siena, Italy, fifteen years earlier.

7

*T*wenty-seven, single, and traveling on a shoestring budget trying to write his dissertation to achieve the lofty title of Doctor Emeritus in history was not how Hans Pedersen pictured his life. After seven years of schooling, paid for out of a now-depleted trust fund, he had hoped for a more solid foundation. After studying for three years at Oxford, he was considered one of the few experts on the Etruscans, the little known early settlers of the Tuscan region of Italy.

He had no politically sensitive bad habits that would alarm the boards of the universities to which he applied for positions. Yet after finishing his studies, no one offered him a job that would allow him to pursue the direction of his studies. They were all looking for star material. Optics seemed to be the order of the day. Brains were no longer enough to fund a Chair at a first-rate university. At first glance they all seemed to enjoy his style, and thus granted him small speaking engagements because of his theatrics. His dry material, seldom published in academic journals, was delivered with such wit and energy that the lecture halls were packed. But he was more of an amusement than a serious consideration. His physique was not appealing. It entertained the students but offered no access to any endowments. There was no prospect of tenure. They all wanted something more...useful.

In the end he accepted a nominal position in a second-tier French institution, kept as low a profile as his cylindrical body would allow, and tackled the challenging assignment of the Etruscans, a seldom explored, craftily ignored advanced civilization that received only a footnote in the history of the world. But their mystery-shrouded story accommodated the religious powers of Rome. Hans had previously written a very minor paper on the marriage customs of the Etruscans, a topic that held his interest enough to consider basing his entire academic future on a doctoral thesis to study every aspect of their little-known move from Asia Minor and the role they played in the rise to prominence of the Romans.

He was now pursuing the next phase of research in his pursuit of his PhD. The trip from Paris to Siena with a second-class Eurail ticket took fourteen hours, depositing him on the footsteps of the hilly Italian town a few minutes after sunrise on a sleepy Sunday morning in the middle of May. It was down to the wire. His professor had demanded that the dissertation be done by the middle of June in order *to give him enough time to grade the effort before the annual July exodus from the scorching heat of Paris.*

Hans received some direction from a former professor about a little-known order of monks in Siena who had collected a varied history on the Etruscans, which they had brought with them during the exodus of the last crusades. Professor David Guy told Hans that he had first heard of the Dominican order when he spent a year as a guest lecturer at the University in Siena. The monks were not very well known, and when he tried to interview them for a paper he was writing, they politely obliged, although it was clear they were holding back much of their knowledge. The professor gave him the name of a monk that he should meet, Brother Franco Agostino.

Siena was a town that time had left behind. It stopped growing after being ravaged by the black plague in the fourteenth century. Once a rival to Florence, it never recovered, content with staying in the minors as Florence joined the big league. It was a quaint town on a hill, made famous by a cathedral that housed a plethora of art unrivalled in Christendom. To be famous during the Renaissance an artist had to contribute to the mosaic of talent filling the space of the Duomo of Siena: Michelangelo, Bernini, Nicola Pernini, Duccio, Donatello. In total, over forty artists spanning two centuries created the masterpiece of Siena.

The address Hans held in his hand was of a nondescript building next to San Martino, a small church on the Via d. Porrione, two blocks opposite Il Campo from the Duomo. As Hans walked across the large open space to his destination, he spied postcards depicting the Palio delle Contrade, an event that overtakes the city each July and August. The Palio is a famous horse race between the best ten of the seventeen Siena neighborhoods—the winner being given the honor of displaying a banner of the Madonna in their district for the remainder of the year. As he walked across the large empty expanse, Hans enjoyed the solitude, which would be nonexistent in those crazy days of summer when the center of town would swell to over fifteen thousand.

The smell of fresh bread from the early morning activities of a local panificio scented the air. He was hungry. After a detour and a quick pastry, he climbed the steep roadway leading out of the square. Standing outside the door of the monastery, his eyes were drawn to the crest on the door. Old and worn, it depicted a winged-horse that carried a sword-wielding knight. Behind the knight, a cloudlike stream appeared to be flowing into a golden urn. The knight's free hand was reaching to the urn, holding onto the tail of one of the wispy clouds. Hans translated the Latin inscription in his head: I am knowledge, I am one.

As he stood gazing at the intriguing crest, he was interrupted by the raucous sound of an approaching motorcycle, which sped around the corner at a pace suggesting that the rider was unaware the early morning street was occupied. Vehicles, unless they were commercial or emergency plated, were forbidden on the sloped streets of the medieval town center. A second later, the machine hit Hans head on, sending him rolling down the sharp-angled street just as the door to the monastery opened. Lying a hundred paces from the entrance, Hans saw four brown-cassocked men rushing his way just before he passed out, and the last sound he heard was that of a motorcycle roaring off in the distance.

Hans woke up in the dark. He was lying in a bed. Feeling groggy, like he'd had too much to drink, he tried to stand but could not easily move. He could see the outline of a window, with faint light streaming in around the edges. There was an odd sensation on his right leg. When he felt down, it was clear his leg was in a cast. He wondered how long he had been there, trying hard to remember where "there" was. The darkness was disorienting. Reaching over to the small bedside table, he fumbled around for a lamp. His hand found a small switch.

With the light on, Hans surveyed the room. It was miniscule, barely enough room for the twin bed. Only a wooden crucifix adorned the entrance above the door. The light that entered came from a window no more than a foot square. Taking another attempt to stand, he was able, with only a little discomfort, to shift his body upright, his leg sticking straight out, almost touching the door. Instead of standing, he simply reached for the doorknob and twisted. Nothing happened. He gripped and turned it more firmly. Locked. Just as his mind wondered why, he could hear a key turn and the door opened.

"No, you are not a prisoner." A man in a long brown robe smiled at him, answering the question that Hans was only thinking. His English was fluent but halting. "We locked the door to make sure you were alright. The passageways can be a bit treacherous, and given your condition we were concerned you would be further injured if you moved about without guidance."

Again, before Hans could ask where he was, the monk spoke.

"You are at the Sumer monastery in Siena. We are an order of Dominican monks. You had just knocked on our door when a motorcycle struck you and broke your leg."

"How long—"

"I am Brother Alphonse. I have cared for you for five days."

Hans was now completely disoriented. Had he been unconscious for five full days with no recollection, even of the accident?

Again the monk spoke, anticipating the question. "We kept you anesthetized to prevent the leg from moving."

"How—?"

Brother Alphonse smiled "It was not some religious mumbo jumbo. I am a trained physician."

Hans looked down at his leg. Sure enough, the cast appeared to be professionally set. "Why did you keep me here, instead of bringing me to a hospital?"

"This is a hospital, of sorts. We look after ourselves. Have always."

Hans felt his antennae rise. What did "always" mean?

As if on cue, Brother Alphonse responded, "Later. Now we should get some solid food into you." He pointed to a disconnected IV hanging from a hook near the bed.

It took another three weeks for the leg to be strong enough for partial pressure. He hobbled around on a set of aluminum crutches. The deadline for his dissertation was now only a fortnight away. Hans had lost all hope that he would be able to finish the dissertation, visions of his doctorate gone. Now it was a matter of deciding what to do with the rest of his life. Stand-up comedy entered his mind. He had a journal full of incidents that would knock them dead at the Montreal Comedy Festival. Actually, he knew that his sponsor would give him one final extension. But maybe he did not want it anymore.

Given free rein over the monastery was comforting after the initial security of his room. He spent many days touring the buildings and grounds. The main building was carved into the Tuscan hillside, a nondescript portico opened into a narrow courtyard surrounded by sheer granite walls. A steep staircase wound its way to the top of the bluff, where the property spread out. There were three sides to the monastery complex. A fourth section of granite that rose to the top of the mountain completed the square; beyond that the azure sky protected the monks from any intruders. The buildings were modest in decoration, although several statues and even a large fresco suggested the property had been occupied by less pious residents in the past.

Fifty monks and other laypersons lived in residence. Alphonse estimated that their numbers were three or four times that, the others being on missions throughout the world. He did not elaborate. Hans had met all fifty within the first week, as he was encouraged to participate in their activities. They were standoffish, as if not *permitted to engage the intruder in conversation. A few times he wondered whether the Order was some sort of a cult.*

Alphonse laughed at the suggestion. "We are a simple order, with a direct purpose handed to us by our founders. There is no coercion here, as you shall see."

Hans asked about the contact he had been given only a few days after he awoke from the induced coma. Brother Alphonse promised to introduce him to his superior, Brother Franco Agostino, when he was ready. So instead he kept close to the physician, who plied the younger man with questions about his paper.

After the two men spent an afternoon of physiotherapy at a nearby terme, the topic of his pending obligation came up. Hans once again was astounded by the monk's insight.

"You needn't worry about finishing your dissertation. Your probable path will be more fruitful to you."

"Probable?" Hans was more confused than ever. Had his visit to Siena been expected? The more he spoke to Brother Alphonse the more he suspected that the conversation with Professor Compton was not accidental. And he began to wonder about the motorcycle accident.

8

"I don't believe you." Hans spoke into air as his Bluetooth signal delivered his exasperated voice four thousand miles across the ocean.

"Believe what you like but the numbers don't lie. There is something happening. If you proceed with your plans, it will be a disaster. What you have started cannot be stopped. Everything that was planned has been destroyed."

"Why. Why can't it stop?" Hans pushed further, trying to figure out what they knew of his attempts to subvert the Order.

"Because *you* have stopped believing. You have forgotten why you are doing what you are doing."

"No. I know exactly what I am doing. What you don't realize is that I have found the fourth connection. And I now know what I have to do."

"You can't go through with it. The fourth book is a myth, a fabrication. You know that. I know that. Whatever you think, don't be fooled. It can only spell disaster." The smooth voice that had guided Hans for all these years was becoming edgy.

"You believe it doesn't exist because that is what the Order has been convincing itself of for centuries. But it is real. I have seen it. The stories you convinced yourself of are not true. The fourth book will undo everything that has been done. I know it is the right thing to do."

"Please listen to reason. It is a lie. If you do this you *will* destroy everything. You will destroy it all."

Hans had stopped listening, but in the back of his mind he was uncertain as to what he should do. He spent most of the last fifteen years doing their bidding. Until recently, he was convinced that he was the new messiah. But the numbers didn't lie. Violence and anger were more predominant now than ever. Perhaps *he* had unleashed this fury on the world.

Hans recalled his methodical indoctrination into the Order of Sumer, his fate determined without his knowledge. He was handed an opportunity that few were ever given in life. As the years wore on, Hans began to see far beyond the vision that the Order of Sumer had set. The Order never had a destiny to deliver a message to the world. Their task was to protect the secret. At least, that was what he was told.

The beginning of his present journey began at the end of his stay in Siena, when his Mentor told him a different truth. A message needed to be delivered when the time was right and the correct alignment of the celestial bodies was set in the heavens as their forefathers had predicted. The time was right, and he was ordained to bring the message to the masses. It was during those final days of Hans's stay with the Order that the Mentor taught him how to understand and control the power of the Book of Thought. Hans needed to understand it all if he was to become the messenger.

Blinded by his success, the years allowed Hans to forget that he was only a messenger, a messenger created by a sacred bond in a small village in Italy when he was poor and destitute. Instead, *he* became the message. He forgot who created the Rules of Possibility. At least he had conveniently forgotten until recently, when the Mentor delivered his not-so-gentle reminder. It had come from as unlikely a source as his decade and a half of success. Hans, the former historian, knew the true history of creation known only to a handful of living souls. He had thought that the Order of Sumer had forgotten about him. He'd followed their destiny, did exactly what they asked of him, to a point.

Yet now they were checking on his every move, to the extent that they placed a spy in his organization. It was the last straw. He had done nothing that they didn't expect. What they wanted he had delivered, and made countless millions in the bargain. They were not going to take that away from him, at least not without a fight. That was how he saw it. It was clear to him that his new direction was considered unacceptable to the Order. He regretted not telling the truth, but he did so to protect the message.

Now it was too late. He had deceived them, and they had found out.

Now that they knew he was about to embark on a path of enlightenment, the rules were about to change. In the early part of the past decade he delivered a candy-coated message, just as he had promised. They delivered the material in piecemeal, and he performed. As his wealth grew, Hans used the power it provided to learn as much as he could about his benefactors. Through a series of private agents and brokers, he acquired every artifact he could find concerning the Order and their hazy tie to the elusive Etruscans. By doing so, he thought he had guaranteed his continued existence. But the infiltration of his organization by one of their own made it clear he could not trust anyone.

Except Amy.

9

"Thought Energy."

Hans Pedersen spoke with intensity as he stared into the bright lights beaming down from the top of the rafters above the balcony of the Isaac Stern Auditorium. He had electrified his audiences with powerful, life-altering performances. Tonight was not going to be any different. Constant motion, enough sweat to fill a five-gallon drum, and loud outbursts of vocal energy captivated the crowd.

But Hans Pedersen was no different when he wasn't performing. He could not see the eyes of the twenty-eight hundred participants in this seminar, but he could *feel* the energy they emitted. He could feel the thoughts behind the eyes. They were palpable. It was what Hans Pedersen lived to achieve.

He reached the end of his Twenty-One Rules of Possibility. The participants had heard them all before. They were all veterans to his program. But tonight was going to be different. It was time to go further. Beyond expectations. Beyond acceptable limits.

The enthralled crowd—each one of them shelling out three thousand dollars to hear the latest from the Thought Mechanix founder—listened with rapt attention.

Hans stared up at the logo of his company shining on the screen. The name was the result of a rant from a former girlfriend who had accused Hans of brainwashing his clientele. She called his clients "people in need of brain repair" and said that he was a "thought mechanic." She ranted that he was no different than the Jim Joneses and David Koreshes of the world, or scores of others who promised salvation to the masses. A few months after the tirade she was killed in a plane crash on her way to one of his seminars. Afterwards, the name Thought Mechanix stuck.

Hans appreciated the name more than his ex-girlfriend could ever imagine. It fit perfectly with how he achieved his success. At last count over fifty million sets of his DVD series, Rules of Possibility, had sold worldwide. The series had been translated into over ninety languages. Hans was wealthy beyond reason. But his success did not slow his relentless pursuit to deliver his message to as many people as he could until it made a difference.

Tonight's performance was a world premiere. Hans had made numerous public appearances each year for the past decade. Tonight's audience was handpicked, like those who would attend the four others he planned. Each person was of particular importance. It was clear that every one of the people in the room had completed the twenty-one day, self-guided course, delivered by Hans in his vigorous style. In fact, Hans was sure of it because he made it a prerequisite of the guest list.

Hans Pedersen had a message to deliver to the audience invited to attend the evening's presentation, a message that would require the undivided attention of everyone in the auditorium. He was about to change history and he wanted as many willing participants as he could enlist. For too long he watched as people learned the lessons delivered by Thought Mechanix only to squander the potential with ill-guided thoughts. Hans did his best to use his influence to silence, re-educate, or even eliminate those who would disparage the good the program delivered. But he was unable to monitor everything done in the name of RoP.

Not that the results weren't impressive. Although he would never admit it, many of the accomplishments of these nefarious converts were stellar, potentially more important than any single positive testimonial, though it was unlikely those people would ever appear in an infomercial.

"How many people here can feel the energy in the room?" Hans listened for the crowd. It was loud, like a congregation response to an evangelist.

"How many of you feel that energy every day, every moment of every day? How many people here control that energy to get what you want out of life? Most of you probably feel that your individual world was created by you, by your power, by your intellectual strength, or by brute force." Hans glanced sideways at a manicured, grey-haired man sitting at the end of the first row. They exchanged a knowing smile. "Are you really in control of your Universe?" he bellowed. "Or does your Universe control you? I can tell you the answer, but you are not going to like it."

With these questions, the murmuring was not as pronounced. He hoped for the same reaction in the other seminars he had scheduled in London, Moscow, Beijing and Tokyo. There was a low buzz in the audience. After a slight hesitation, Hans readied himself for the revelation. He knew that there were many in the crowd who so much wanted to achieve what the Rules of Possibility promised, but they failed. They failed because they missed the message. They missed the message because they were wrapped up in trying to achieve their own success instead of accepting the lesson as it was intended, a lesson that even for him became blurred in the decade since he created the Rules of Possibility.

Tonight was the culmination of months of planning that was intended to change all of that. In the audience were business men and women, senators, congressmen, clergy and, most importantly, enough of his clientele who truly believed in his word, his exclusive knowledge. It was time to reveal the truth. Time to eradicate all links to his past.

He paused for a moment before speaking, looking out over the crowd, knowing he had exactly the people he needed to succeed.

"Energy. It is around us, it is us. Einstein knew what we all take for granted. We are all connected by energy. But what does that REALLY mean? I am about to share with you the answer. It will prove invaluable to your future. To every person in this room who is connected to every other person in this room..."

Hans kept speaking but his voice was not being carried over the loudspeakers. He looked to his right, at Amy, his protégé, who was responsible for the event and probably the only person who knew what was about to happen next.

A second later the lights went out and the entire auditorium was sheathed in blackness. A few women screamed. As the audience started to shift in their seats, an explosion rocked the stage directly beneath Hans. Within seconds a thick, arid smoke rose up from the source of the explosion. Dark grey swirls of cloudy heat scorched the people in the first three rows.

Moments later panic set in as another explosion rocked the back of the auditorium, setting off a chain reaction. The black tie crowd forgot what they were listening to, abandoned the Rules and ignored the people around them. Each person was focused on his or her own survival. The younger, more athletic patrons clambered over the weaker participants, crushing them into the velvet seats of the historic auditorium. Screams cascaded over the sounds of sirens approaching from outside.

The seats were soon empty, replaced with a thick layer of gray-blue smoke that stung the nostrils. What went unnoticed by the people as they scrambled out of the New York landmark was that the ensuing fire that followed each explosion was a non-event, causing very little damage to the structural integrity of the building.

Hans had been thrown back against the back of the stage by the first explosion. Blinded momentarily by the bright flash of light that accompanied the explosion, he could not see the panicked crowd as they emptied out of the exits.

"What the hell?" The motivational icon bellowed to the empty wings of the stage, where his security detail stood a few minutes earlier. Receiving no answer, he rolled onto his side to stand up just as the second explosion collapsed a part of the entrance arch at the far end of the room. Instead of standing, he crawled towards the exit on his hands and knees. Before leaving the stage, Hans was blinded once more by a singular flash of light near the stage door, its source quickly disappearing amidst the chaotic retreat of the Thought Energy guru.

10

Three hours after the debacle at the Isaac Stern Auditorium, the offices of Thought Mechanix were in a state of quiet pandemonium. No one dared speak directly to the man who had created their world. Employees wandered the rooms of the two converted floors of the Plaza Hotel in Manhattan careful to avoid eye contact with the security details that now patrolled the hallways and offices.

A steady rain fell outside, giving the summer-scorched ground of Central Park a well-needed soaking. The energy released from the electric storm raging outside was more or less insignificant to the energy battle that ensued in Hans Pedersen's office. Looking south to the dark edges of the Park, Hans stopped breathing for a moment as he listened to the explanations and excuses. He knew that powerful factions were beginning to tear at the heart of his organization. Even though Thought Mechanix was a popular target of many self-serving groups, he could sense this was different.

What he didn't know was that the core of his world was about to implode. His seminars and their results were affecting the traditional way of life for tens of millions and the livelihood of scores of thousands. This explosion was not the first incident, but it could not have come at a worse time. The power brokers who sought his demise were fighting back. Until the previous night he was convinced that they could not stop him, even if they wanted to, now that he possessed the ultimate knowledge.

Hans turned his back to the window of his elaborate office on the top floor of the Plaza Hotel. He had acquired a controlling interest in the Plaza during its recent renovation through one of his earliest unsolicited testimonials. A well-known developer who credited RoP for his success approached Hans with a generous offer to occupy the top two floors of the luxury landmark, a 1907 building being restored to its former glory and more.

Hans had added his own touches to the floors he acquired. It was a head office that displayed his unique business to anyone lucky enough to enter the inner-sanctum of his organization. Shelves and walls were adorned with gifts from thankful RoP graduates. The diversity and value of these pieces would rival the collections of many public museums. It was a testament to his success, a crowning achievement over those who thought they controlled his actions.

He could do whatever he wanted.

Of the many pieces in his collection, his most prized artifact was a set of four scrolls, each displaying two columns of angular phonetic symbols—Sumerian writings. Hans glanced at the display then shifted his gaze to the woman standing next to it.

Amy Glass did not speak as she entered the room. She waited for the inevitable grilling. Even though the security at the Stern was not her responsibility, she felt she had let her boss down. What concerned her more, though, was that her late-night investigation clearly revealed that the work had been done by an insider, someone with an in-depth knowledge of the planning behind the seminar.

Amy placed her weight onto her left foot, the soft curves of her hip shifting like a gazelle with the movement. Dressed in covert clothes, the black Lycra jump suit outlined her trim, athletic body. At six feet she towered over the five-foot-six founder of Thought Mechanix. Like all of his employees, Amy considered Hans Pedersen to be of a stature beyond her personal expectations. He was a messiah. Amy knew it was one of the problems that plagued the organization—others of influence were losing ground to his teachings, despite the fact that the message had not changed for a decade. Once considered a cult of the desperate, when subscribers reached ten million worldwide opponents stood up and took notice.

Amy tucked a loose strand of blond hair behind her ear. She pursed her ruby red lips before finally speaking.

"I know who it was. I just don't think you are going to like it."

"Who?"

"Mark Clarkson."

This was a surprise. Mark knew he was only months away from conducting his own seminars, following in the footsteps of this mentor. Hans abandoned his plan to chastise his protégé.

"Why did he do it?"

"He disappeared today. The security scanners have him leaving the building an hour before the explosions shut down your seminar."

Hans stared at his executive assistant. "So what? Mark has a habit of keeping strange hours. Why do you think he was involved?"

Amy trained her dark eyes on her boss, silently reproaching him. She hadn't been trained by the Russians, but her covert tactical skills were rarely questioned. Taking a letter-sized manila envelope from the leather bag on the ground beside her, she handed its contents to Hans.

"Because of these." Amy continued while he looked at the pictures: "Mark came into your office last night a few minutes before eight. The hidden security cameras that I had installed, despite your misgivings, took those pictures at three-second intervals. Mark shut off the security grid into your room and walked directly to this cabinet," she pointed to the glass case she stood beside, "and snapped pictures from every conceivable angle.

"He then went back to his desk, emailed the pictures to an address in Italy, took everything that looked remotely personal from his desk, and left the building at eight-twenty. He was supposed to come to the Stern and help wrap up the question period after the seminar. He conveniently missed the explosions."

"I think you may be jumping to conclusions. Besides, the tablets are purely ornamental."

"Sure boss," Amy laughed.

Hans ignored the quip, pushing instead to get to the root of the accusations. He knew the pictures would be useless to anyone who tried to translate, although no one else knew. Hans was not about to risk the organization he built to a petty or ambitious criminal. The real tablets were not in his possession. They were never his to have. Three of the tablets displayed in the cabinet were excellent forgeries from pictures he had taken personally many years earlier. The fourth was a genuine fake that he had added to his collection recently. The knowledge contained in the fourth tablet was the basis of what he was about to reveal at the Isaac Stern that night. It was what Mark must have hoped to steal.

"The contents of all four were reproductions with suitable modifications; the original text is safely hidden away."

He trusted no one.

Amy laughed, "You trust a lot of people. I probed into Mark's background a little further this morning. It appears he was once affiliated with the Order of Sumer." She said the words carefully to watch Hans's reaction.

Hans stopped smiling for a moment, the mention of the Order sparking a tinge of fear. He checked himself before speaking. Not that it mattered. He had asked Amy to follow up on too many queries about the Order for her not to be aware of how he felt. But he had never fully explained to her how they had provided the training and backing for his start-up, to experiment with the powerful philosophy and try to harness its potential. The Order was integral to the implementation of the initial Rules of Possibility seminar. It was their message to be delivered. A few years after Hans started, after the Order was satisfied with the results, they faded into obscurity. At least they were dormant until the recent contact. Obviously, their involvement had continued unabated since the beginning. It had only become more clandestine.

"How did our background check miss that?" he asked as calmly as he could.

"It seems Mark Clarkson has an alias. His real name is Mark Calvecchio. He came to America three years ago on a student visa, formally changed his name then went to Canada for a few months before joining Thought Mechanix. When our security group ran the routine bio on him, which only starts when he re-entered the U.S. from Canada. After last night, I conducted a more in-depth Internet search."

"What do you think he was looking for?" Hans asked the obvious question.

"I have started new background checks on all other active employees."

"Where were the pictures sent?"

"No idea. Our Internet provider is proving to be a little paranoid about privacy issues. It will take me a few days to convince him that our request is legitimate."

"Don't bother. I'm pretty sure I know," Hans replied as he looked out the window at the downpour soaking Manhattan.

11

Mark Calvecchio sat in the diner across from a man he thought was a phantom. The existence of the great man had been spoken of since he joined the Order, but evidence of his physical being had never been confirmed. The deep-set raven eyes pierced his own, demanding attention as he spoke in hushed tones. Mark listened silently as the man chastised his behavior. For a moment his mind wandered, as he looked out past the dime-a-song jukebox to the empty, rain-soaked street beyond the window. It was late. He had arrived at the all-night diner just before two in the morning. The Master had arrived twenty minutes later.

Mark looked back at his dining companion, but by the time he refocused his energy on the conversation it was too late. The searing pain between his eyes told him all he needed to know. His failure would not be tolerated.

"You screwed up," the echo reverberated.

"Hans was not supposed to be on stage." Mark rubbed his temples, hoping to relieve the incoming pain.

"That is inconsequential. You, however, failed. For two years you have been carefully groomed for this moment. For two years I waited patiently for you to make your move. It was a calculated risk to bring Hans back to me and retrieve the knowledge that is rightfully mine. And you failed."

"It doesn't matter," Mark retorted, now oblivious of the pain.

"What do you mean it does not matter?" The man across the table became insistent. "Does he not understand what is at stake?"

"The fourth tablet in his possession. Trust me. I checked everywhere. The tablet in his office is a fake. Gibberish. I looked at the details of the tablet. Nothing. He has kept his secret hidden very well."

"Impossible. We were very careful, watched his every move."

Mark realized that the older religious man was not convinced of his candor. He sat silently waiting for his punishment.

The man who had flown in from Italy to deal with this issue also sat in silence as his mind reeled from the information he had just received. Now he had no idea whether Hans even possessed the knowledge of the fourth book or whether he had concocted some elaborate hoax. He needed to find out if this peon did any good after two years undercover. His sources told him that the fourth book had been found, that it was not a myth. But he had to have that knowledge if he was going to accomplish his plan. It seemed now that Hans may just be in the way.

12

Amy waited a few moments until she realized that Hans was not about to start the conversation. She noticed that about him. He listened better than anyone she had ever met, even the disenfranchised stoners of her street life who could barely string a dozen words together.

She began: "I've run the reports you asked for. A line bio from our database of every one of the attendees at last week's seminar." She pushed the stack of paper across the smooth cherry wood. "Do you think that anyone in there could have been responsible besides Mark?"

"Do you?" Hans's habit of deflecting a question with another started when he was a smart ass in elementary school. Amy was the most informed person on his staff. After he helped her get off the street, she became his most trusted assistant. Despite a lack of formal education, she had a computer-like mind and a photographic memory that was never challenged. At Thought Mechanix she thrived.

"Of the twenty-eight hundred participants, only sixty had never attended a workshop or purchased the RoP program. You handpicked each one of them. There were only seventeen empty seats. This was a sold-out show. I started by listing those who did not come. Seven were out of the city and six were otherwise indisposed, so that left four others. More detailed biographies of those people are on top of the pile. I thought you decided Mark was the culprit." She spat out the words. Mark and she were close; they could have been bedroom partners if they hadn't felt so much like brother and sister.

"You take on these problems personally." It was more of a statement of surprise than a question. No one but the two of them shared that original theory.

"Why? Do you think I don't like your ideas?"

"Because people use people."

"Do you really believe that—" Amy bit her tongue.

"Even me?" Hans laughed. "Everything I do is about using people, using them to help themselves." He stared at his reformed protégé a moment, fixing on her eyes. "Except you. For some reason, it seems that you are not capable of using people. Even if by doing so benefits both parties concerned."

Amy did not turn away as her intense eyes absorbed the stare. "I used you, didn't I?" Amy tried to sound indignant.

"No. You allowed me to exploit your situation and, in return, alter the course of your life. I used you to prove that my theories worked. It helped sell millions of copies of RoP. Whatever you decided, it was better than walking in front of that car."

"What did you say?" Amy had never told him anything about the day they met.

Hans ignored the question. Instead, he grabbed the first page on the top of the pile and began to read. "Tell me about these people. Do any of them fit the description of a crazed lunatic?"

"So now you think it was a crazed lunatic that set off those explosions. I thought you were convinced it was orchestrated by your rivals. By Mark."

"What I need to find out is whether he had any help."

"It seems to me that he had the motivation, the means and the opportunity. Why would he need help?"

It was time to break the news. Hans reached over and grabbed a file folder perched on the edge of his credenza. He slid it across the desk towards Amy. He watched as her initial curiosity turned to shock. A picture of Mark Clarkson on a morgue table stared back at her, a deep gash evident across his neck.

"Oh, my God," Amy brought her hand up to her mouth as she choked back a salty taste of bile. She could not believe it was Mark on the slab. At least it explained the unanswered calls. All of a sudden her world became a little less certain.

"Mark was killed late last night. I checked the security tapes during the seminar. At the moment of the Isaac Stern Auditorium explosion he was at the office. So someone else must have been involved."

"What is happening?" Speaking half to herself, Amy stared down one more time at the picture, then lifted the photo to read the report it was paper-clipped to inside the folder. A picture from a security camera showed Mark being attacked by a hooded assailant. He was just leaving a local diner that they had frequented together.

As she stared at the photo, the face of a man in the window of the diner made her blood turn cold. *What was happening?* She focused her energy to maintain composure, hoping that Hans had not noticed her reaction.

When she looked up his eyes revealed a telling knowledge.

"They found the body right here in the building. He was stuffed into a garbage bin that was scheduled to be picked up the next day. A sanitation worker spotted the body as it was falling into the garbage truck. Someone took his TMI identification. So we need to double our security efforts."

"Do you think anyone else is in danger? Are you in danger?" Amy was suddenly afraid. Was *she* was on borrowed time? Should she be more afraid for Hans? He had too much left to accomplish. Others, obviously, did not share her conviction.

"I've hired enough security to form a small army. No one will be in harm's way if they follow protocol. What we need to do is find out the connection between the two events."

"There is always a connection," said Amy, quoting one of Hans's more famous lines.

13

Hans was on line One.

Jason stared for a moment at the flashing light before picking up. "Your ears must have been ringing," he started. "I was just talking about you. I'd like to discuss a proposition."

"*We* need to meet," Hans replied without exchanging pleasantries.

"What's going on?" Jason heard the thin agitation in his client's voice. The edge always made him nervous, some uncertainty that he could not control.

As Hans started to reply, a noise in the background made it difficult to hear. It was a grinding, mechanical noise that filled the phone, painful to the eardrum.

Jason moved the phone away from his ear as the sound intensified. A few moments later it died down.

"What the hell was that?"

Hans could be heard in the background yelling. The voice was faint. Jason suspected that his hand was over the mouthpiece. Then a moment later the clear, distinctive voice of Hans Pedersen came back on line. There was no evidence of the loud pitch that interrupted them a moment earlier.

Jason repeated his question, "What the hell was that?"

"It's nothing. The technicians are installing some high-density microphones to track the calls coming in and out of here. It was a bit of feedback. That's what we need to meet about. I need your help with a situation that has developed. Maybe outside of your area, but I can't think of anyone else I can trust."

"I'm flattered," Jason replied, never knowing if he should take the man seriously. Hans was a success, no doubt, but he had a way of alienating people with his crass expectations. It was a false sincerity, yet Hans was also genuinely charitable. Jason never knew what to believe. Whatever the motivation, it was a perfect opening to unveil his idea.

"You should be. After all, you are just an accountant."

"Funny guy. Coincidentally, I need to bounce an idea or two off you as well."

"Great. Hop across the street. I'll make sure the security lets you through."

"Security?"

"I'll explain when you get here." Hans hung up the phone.

Jason took the elevator down to street level and made his way across Park Avenue to the Plaza. He waded through the usual crowd of protestors in front of the Thought Mechanix headquarters. Hans's success brought with it a litany of naysayers and fanatics who believed that the round ball known as Hans Pedersen was evil—the antichrist, a profiteer and a charlatan—or at the very least a fraud.

Jason had heard them all. Talk shows devoted weeks of commentary on the daily workings of the organization, an organization challenged primarily because of its success, from its humble beginnings to global dominance in less than two decades. Whenever Hans was in the news, the anchor would preface the story with the usual warning that the opinions expressed in the story were not those necessarily shared by the station—blah, blah, blah. As far as the media was concerned, Hans Pedersen was not significant enough to warrant serious attention. At least they were not interested in exploring the numerous claims of the conspiracy theorists. Many people resented the notion that the short, unassuming college academic was able to accomplish all that he had on his own. His teachings came out of nowhere. It challenged the norm at a time when the norm was taking it on the chin.

Jason followed the controversy with rapt attention. He was a convert to Thought Mechanix. He'd experienced firsthand the awesome power of the mind, power created by training the mind to have the ability to focus its thoughts. Most of his clients balked at the notion that they could benefit from the hocus-pocus, that is until the applied methodology proved itself time and again.

One of the unauthorized documentaries of the Rules of Possibility claimed that in excess of one-hundred million people—from all walks of life and from virtually every country in the world—had adopted the TMI philosophy. Hans refused to comment on the numbers. Claims were made that many informal groups began meeting on a regular basis to recite the teachings espoused by the decade-old self-help DVD series. It was being referred to as a cult—a cult with dangerous aspirations.

During one of Jason's early meetings as the accountant for the organization, Hans had referred to the concepts as being older than organized religion. When Jason pushed him for an explanation, it was met with the usual press release answer—*We all have to believe in something, it might as well be something useful.* The dig was not lost on the various religious leaders around the world.

As Jason exited the elevator, he could see that the Thought Mechanix headquarters was in virtual shutdown. No one was getting in, or out, without a physical and verbal search. Jason waded his way through a crowded lobby towards an unusual scene—two enormous machines filled the waiting room area. As he approached the reception, Jason was directed to place his leather bag, complete with laptop, on the small conveyor in front of the machine. He felt the urge to reach for a nonexistent boarding pass. After his laptop passed the test, he was directed to enter a second machine.

"What is this, an x-ray?" he asked, as the security guard directed him to stand in front of the machine and to place his feet on the two stenciled footprints on a rubberized mat. A bluish scan traveled from the top of his head to the floor.

"It checks for inorganic implants in the body. A threat that has many airports around the world spooked about the next phase of terrorist ingenuity," the operator commented as he directed Jason to the inner sanctum of Thought Mechanix.

Jason figured Hans was taking personal security to a new level since the Stern explosion. He wondered how the man felt about the intrusion.

Before he could speculate, Hans rounded the corner into the lobby with the answer.

"It sucks. I feel like America the day after 9/11. I keep looking over my shoulder. My mind is full of suspicion. With no clear motives, it's hard to say who hates me."

Jason looked sideways at Hans. "Really? Have you ever paid attention to the protesters out front?"

Hans held out his hand to welcome Jason. A broad smile crossed his pudgy face. "Oh, them. They're harmless. Come on, you've been scanned, so I assume you're safe."

"What's that all about?"

"Protection against the newest suicide bomber rage—surgically implanted explosives. I asked for the best..."

Jason shook his head. "You have got to be kidding. Anyway, I take it from the Fort Knox decor that you don't think that Stern was a random event."

Hans shrugged. "It appears the terrorists are getting smarter. Unfortunately, even my organization is not safe from the disenchanted of the world."

"According to the media, some of those disenchanted claim that Thought Mechanix contributes to their success." Jason mentioned the burning fact that Hans tried to distance from his program. Jason did not mean to dredge up the issue, but always maintained a frank relationship with his clients.

"You cannot imagine how people will look for a wealthy scapegoat to solve their woes." Hans slapped Jason on the back. "You have to be careful what you wish for..."

"And your wish is..."

Hans stopped in the lobby, turned and stared at Jason. He let the thoughts flit through his mind, knowing that Jason was not capable of interpreting his dilemma without further access. Swiveling on his heels, he pointed out the mayhem surrounding the two of them.

"My wish is dangerous to conjure up. All of which is much more than you can imagine. Sometimes the burden is too much."

Hans was not ready to elaborate. He had to make sure that Jason was ready, although he had few options. The accountant embraced TM RoP like it was his own. He implicitly understood the concepts to a tee. He delivered the message to everyone he came into contact with. Many of the businesses that applied the Rules to their organizations did so under the direction of Wakefield and Associates. It was like the two of them were in partnership without the messy ties of ownership.

Despite the fit, Hans was not so sure he liked the way his program translated into a practical business application when Wakefield was involved. TMI was not about trying to create successful commerce. Yet that seemed to be where everyone gravitated—thinking themselves into wealth. But it was about much more than that. The way in which his past had recently resurfaced seemed to confirm this. But it was clear to Hans that Jason was more than just a successful graduate, despite his desire to focus the energy on business success.

As they headed for Hans's office he explained. "I don't believe it was a random event. But not for the reasons you may think. You were right in your earlier assessment that Thought Mechanix has enemies. The Rules of Possibility have changed a lot of lives. But for every thousand personal success stories, there is the periodic suicide, murder or failed marriage blamed on TMI. There is no screening, no oversight. That's what I wanted to talk to you about. But before I get into that, why did you want to see me?"

Jason explained his concept to deliver a polished product, whose foundations would continue to rest on Hans's programs. He summarized his argument, and it was a compelling argument, for someone interested in focusing the profound power of the Rules on achieving commercial gain. It took Jason fifteen minutes to deliver his sales pitch.

Hans's face betrayed no emotion as he stared over his fingers at the enthused Jason. Even his most promising candidate could not see what was unfolding. *Was he truly short-sighted about the power he possessed? Just blinded by the money?*

"Any neophyte could make money—lots of money—peddling thought migration, as if it were a carrot and at the end there's a shiny red convertible. Once the participants focus on using the Rules to create wealth, they lose focus. Napoleon Hill, among others, espoused these ideas three quarters of a century ago."

"You know about him?"

"Do you think I was the first to figure out the power of thought? A rather large and austere fraternity has shared this knowledge down through the ages. A dangerous knowledge."

"What do you mean?" Jason was beginning to think maybe he had underestimated his client.

Before he received his answer, a petite woman in her mid-twenties, thick blond hair cascading over her right shoulder, knocked at the door and entered. Hans's executive assistant glided into the room.

Jason always liked seeing Amy. He thought about her a little too much since the last financial meeting.

"Hey, Jason." Amy made eye contact, locking her gaze on him for a moment, forcing Jason to look away.

"Sorry for the intrusion, Hans. The police are here. They have some information on the Stern explosion."

Hans moved over to his desk and grabbed a file folder, which he handed to Jason.

"Take a few minutes to review this proposal for me. It is one of the items we need to discuss. Talon sent over this agreement. I'd like your opinion on the numbers. It looks too good to be true, but I've said that about everything so far. I'll be back in a few minutes. Grab a drink from the fridge."

As he headed out the door he turned to Amy, "I need to make a move on the next infomercial. There is a chance to do a global webcast and I don't want to miss out on that chance."

Jason stood up and walked to the mini-bar built into one of the walnut-lined walls and grabbed a bottle of vitamin water from the fridge. As he drank, he glanced around the well-appointed office. The walls were adorned with original works of art, one of them a Matisse. Hans didn't collect art, Jason knew that. Hans collected items of distinction—a statue by Auguste Rodin, a Fabergé egg, an original Mark Twain manuscript. The list of assets was endless. Jason studied the growing list each year as he struggled with how to get the best tax breaks from the seemingly never-ending purchases.

Before settling into the leather side chair to study the contents of the folder, he went over to the case next to the window. The stone tablets were as impressive as ever beneath the thick glass. Hans had once explained the significance of the writing, but Jason wasn't buying into the story. At the time, when they first met, he was too immersed in the idea of landing the motivational guru as a client to pay attention, so he listened politely then quickly forgot the gist.

Jason sat down to read the proposal from Google, but he had trouble concentrating. His mind wandered. Hans had told him something he had never volunteered in the past about Thought Mechanix: that the theories were not original, despite guarded claims to the contrary. So Hans was not the first to tap into the power of thought migration. He'd have to find out who was part of the "large and austere fraternity" to whom Hans referred.

A few minutes later Hans and Amy returned.

"No big deal," Hans was saying as they entered the room.

Jason noticed that Amy's nod was not as convincing, her emerald eyes displaying none of the optimism that suggested agreement with her boss.

A flurry of activity followed them into the room. One of the men who entered looked like he was about to help launch the space shuttle, with a phone in one ear and a headset plugged into the other. He was followed by two assistants. They barged into the office en masse.

"Mr. Pedersen. We've gotta go in five. The set is ready. The audience will be in position by the time we get to the studio." One of the assistants was already grabbing whatever she felt was needed from Hans's desk as the other started to eyeball the man, seemingly trying to determine what it would take to make the rotund pint presentable on stage.

"Shit. I thought the session would have been cancelled, all things considered." Hans looked at Amy as he gestured to Jason with his hands, as if it was only too obvious the world would be compelled to reschedule in light of the recent events.

"No time to stop. You set the ambitious schedule yourself."

The Thought Mechanix production guy scoffed as his helpers tittered. "The studio waits for no man. Space is booked, cameras ready. It's a hundred thou an hour. Our production team has been working on this segment all week. We only have another month to get the entire twelve segments filmed. The television time has already been spoken for. Let's not be late."

With that he clapped, turned, and left the room without looking back, expecting to be followed.

Hans spun around, grabbed his gabardine jacket from the hook next to the door. "Come on, Jason. It's the third installment of the new infomercial to promote RoP II—The Next Step. You'll find it particularly interesting. Your new firm will like where I'm headed with this. It is vintage thought migration—with a twist."

Hans winked at his accountant, a tacit gesture that Jason's proposal to use TMI would be approved. Hans needed to keep his accountant close. He needed to tell him the real purpose of the new series before it was too late. It was time to recruit Jason into his plans. Hans only hoped that the accountant would still be interested once he knew the truth. He would reveal everything when the time was right.

Jason bit. "What kind of a twist?" He looked over at Amy, who just shrugged.

Hans left the room without answering.

"I don't think he's answered even one of my questions today," Jason said to Amy as the two of them picked up speed. Hans had already rounded the corner at the lobby and was heading past the security machines to the elevator. They extended their stride to keep up with the revolving legs of the five-foot-two Pedersen.

"He's not been himself since the explosion. He's distracted...more than usual."

"Wouldn't you be distracted?"

"This is different. He seems scared."

"Scared?"

"A few weeks ago when I was in his office he received a phone call. From somewhere in Italy. I recognized the country code. The call was short, less than a minute. Hans was ashen-white after the call. The color had drained from his face as if he had sprung a leak. When I asked what the matter was, he dismissed it as a prank call. But I could see in his eyes that he was troubled."

"What do you think is going on? He mentioned something about a fraternity of people who understood the source of his knowledge," Jason commented.

"Did he tell you who it was that called?" Amy asked him.

"No. Why would he?"

Amy looked around before she answered, "I checked the Internet phone log—"

Before Amy could finish her sentence, they had reached the elevator. Amy looked over at Jason and mouthed her words over her boss's shoulders: *I'll talk to you later.*

At street level, Hans strode towards the waiting limousine. Jason kept pace beside him, expecting to return to the office without receiving an answer to his idea.

"Come and watch the taping. You can spare the afternoon, I suspect. I'll explain a little more on the way."

The driver opened the door as Hans approached. Amy and Jason climbed in behind him. Amy slid next to Jason on the plush leather, her thigh touching him as she sat. She did not move away, distracting Jason from what Hans was saying.

Hans was offering them each a sparkling water from the fridge.

"The new ROP II infomercial will revolutionize how people think. When I designed the first ROP, I wasn't sure if I understood the power that the *thought matrix* gave to people. I was stunned by the impact. Rules II opens the floodgates to a new paradigm for our world."

Hans was giving the standard media line to Jason. He would give him the real explanation of the purpose of RoP II once he knew his accountant was fully committed—*once he discussed London*. Until then it would be better if Jason continued to see only the commercial aspects of Thought Mechanix.

"The third segment is being taped today. The intro segment and the second segment are already in the can. They deal with how thinking influences our perspective of the world around us. I'll give you a copy. But this third segment is the start of "the meat" of the new Rules. It deals with how the process of replacing our memories with thought energy actually works. This is the key to utilizing the brain. If you could even begin to understand the power of focusing your memories to achieve control over those around you by producing energy, you would not find it so difficult to balance your life."

"What do you mean?"

"Let's say, for example, that you were thinking about Amy." Hans looked over at Amy and smiled. She'd been part of such a demonstration before. "You know, wondering about how she feels right now."

Jason blushed, providing a weak protest.

Hans continued.

"Instead of trying to recall all of the previous memories you have of Amy, thus restricting your thought by focusing on the past, think about what it is you want Amy to think. Build forward momentum in your thought process. That is how thought energy will generate real-time results."

"What do you mean by 'real-time'? A thought is just an internal manifestation: my brain communicating with me about things that have already happened. Even the immediate thought is history once it is released. You taught me that."

"Rather than give you the entire story, we'll wait for the taping of this segment of the infomercial. The presentation at the Stern was supposed to be a revelation of this concept. Now it will have to wait. I'm not going to make any more public appearances until the purpose of the attack has been discovered."

For a moment nobody spoke. Jason was feeling somewhat awkward, the soft touch of Amy's thigh against his own leg now felt like a stinging needle. Amy made no attempt to move, and he suspected she was enjoying the pressure she was exerting.

The limousine was heading under the Holland tunnel to New Jersey, where the studios were located. Traffic was light, unusual for this time of day, brought on most likely by the start of summer vacation. The heat rising out of the tunnel formed a haze.

Jason stared through the fume-fuelled mirage as the car headed under the Hudson. He had diligently listened and followed the Rules of Possibility seminar series that Hans had introduced over a decade earlier. It had changed his life. And it would make him and his clients wealthy as he continued to incorporate the methodology into his consulting business.

But he wanted to know more. He was wondering how much bigger or better the concept could get. Already millions of people—tens of millions—were using the tools to live better lives and, according to each one's personal ambitions, to succeed. What could Hans possibly introduce that would improve upon his breakthrough RoP? Jason had spoken many times to Hans over the years about the true power of the seminars he created, but this was the first time he offered a glimpse of what was behind Thought Mechanix.

Sitting across from Jason, Hans too was lost in thought, quietly looking out the window as the vehicle exited the tunnel. Five weeks earlier it became clear that whatever subterfuge he employed to distance himself from his past had not worked. The plain brown envelope that arrived over a month ago was not marked with a return address. But Hans knew exactly who had sent it by the distinctive writing on the brief note attached to the journal. It was the gothic handwriting of a man he thought was long since out of his life. Despite his misgivings, Hans felt duty bound by the instructions carefully laid out in the note. To Hans, it finally all made sense. The clarity of what he was told was so simple that he knew why he was chosen to deliver the message to the world, why he was given the knowledge to create Thought Mechanix. Now that so many believed, it was time to clarify the message he was destined to deliver.

But the explosion at the Isaac Stern made it clear to Hans that not everyone wished for him to succeed.

14

Father Thom stood at the edge of the crowd, having spent two hours winding his way through the labyrinth of corridors lined with priceless works of art to finally arrive at the Chapel made famous by the reluctant artist. He stared silently at the ceiling, contemplating the musings of a whispering tour guide a few feet away. He heard the word *ass* and looked up past the pointed finger of the American guide to what was clearly the naked form of God's buttock, pointing directly to where the Pope would stand to read the Gospel. He wondered whether the urban myth was truth or a convenient anecdote to spice up a rather boring tour of pillaged artwork.

The Sistine Chapel was completed in 1483 as a temporary chapel in anticipation of the tearing down and rebuilding of the original St. Peter's Basilica. Pope Julius II was not interested in being without a house of worship during the construction, so he built the unassuming square, somewhat ugly, adjunct to the Vatican as a last resort. When it was time to adorn the small chapel, the competition of the contemporary artists of the day claimed a victim. Michelangelo was appointed by the Pope, after a suggestion by Raphael, knowing how much the young sculptor despised painting. It is to his enemies that the artist owes a debt of gratitude for his greatest work.

Either way, he thought, as he glanced at his watch to note it was time to go, *it was compelling.*

Delayed by the throngs of people at the exit, Father Thom quickly made his way to the spot in St Peter's Square near the obelisk where he was to meet his ride to the summer home of the Cardinal of Siena. It was surprising to him that the mathematical model he'd sent from his parish near Calgary had created such a flurry of interest. His email outlining his findings had been forwarded only a week earlier. Three days later a reply email included a travel itinerary for a flight to Rome. What he thought were interesting anecdotal details about a struggling religion obviously turned a few heads. Such a quick reply meant that he was being taken seriously.

Now he was standing on the steps of St Peter's, unexpectedly fulfilling a lifelong dream.

Thom Watson's first love was mathematics. He became a priest after serving in a peacekeeping mission in Africa with the Canadian Forces. Bombarded by scenes of hopelessness, poverty and loss of humanity, he made the easy decision to devote his life to the Church. Now the church was experiencing a loss of its own, and he decided he had to do something about it.

His life was simple. For the past fifteen years, he had presided over a parish located on the outskirts of oil-rich Calgary, a distinctly Canadian city sprawled on the fringes of the Rocky Mountains. When he wasn't birthing, baptizing or burying a member of the congregation, he spent a considerable amount of time exploring numbers. He poured over Church statistics just as others might compile sports scores. His early interest in mathematics earned him a role as an outcast growing up and contributed to more than a few of the beatings from the class bully. Most of his childhood was spent in his room or at the church with his mom.

It was his passion for numbers that prompted Thom to send the email. He had been keeping a tally of the world's congregations, as something was going terribly wrong with the level of church participation—the reduction of devoted church attendees was caused by a very clear and very real threat. Compelled to alert the church hierarchy that the dwindling numbers were not an accident, he sent his results.

The steps leading up to the Cathedral were packed with tourists. Father Thom was not sure how the Cardinal would be able to find him, but he had been assured that this would not be a problem. He was instructed to stand by the obelisk in the center of the piazza and he would be spotted.

Waiting by the Egyptian tower, Father Thom stared up at the dome of the great cathedral as he wiped the sweat forming on his brow. Like the thousands of others in the square that day with no place to find shade in the center of Piazza San Pietro, the summer heat was taking its toll. Rome was in its second week of record-setting temperatures as each day soared above 35 degrees Celsius. The morning newspaper he had purchased from the small grocery store next to his hotel splashed a headline that blamed the heat for at least fifty deaths in the city. His hotel on the Via Moncenigo was a bit on the seedy side, so with no air conditioning, he feared he may be next if he had to spend one more night in the damp heat of the room. The only saving grace was that it was close to the Vatican. The Cardinal had made the arrangements. Given the quality of the rooms, Father Thom suspected that despite their urgent interest in meeting with him, perhaps they did not give much consideration to his research after all.

A man dressed in a brown cassock adorned with a white rope around the waist emerged from beneath one of the columns that lined the large walkways on either side of the square. The brown robe stretched across his torso, as if the muscles inside were ready to burst out of the constricting fabric.

Father Thom saw the man approaching, looking from side to side as he made his way across the lengthy Piazza. But he was veering to the left, away from where he stood. He held up a hand to wave. *This could be the person,* he thought.

Unbeknownst to Father Thom, the cassocked man had been observing him for some time, to make sure he had come alone.

The man in the cassock saw the hand movement, changed direction, and caught up to where Father Thom was standing.

"You look just like your picture," the man smiled as he held out his hand. He spoke with a thick accent.

Father Thom figured him to be Bulgarian or Czech, certainly not Italian. He grasped the man's hand warmly, but he could not recall sending a photo with his email.

"Cardinal Agostino is waiting in the car. He suggests that we avoid the Holy See, as it is difficult to gain privacy. The walls have ears, as they say. Your communication is of great concern to Cardinal Agostino."

Father Thom was led by the cassocked man to a black sedan waiting on the edge of the Piazza. A penchant for all things numerical, he noticed that the license plates of the car were not issued by the Vatican.

"Does the Cardinal not live in the Vatican?" Thom questioned, pointing to the license.

"We often hire vehicles. The Vatican fleet is not as modern as it should be."

When they reached the car, the brawny priest opened the back door of the sedan, ushering Father Thom inside with a firm hand. He then took his place behind the wheel and pulled away from the curb without looking, almost sideswiping a three-wheeled Fiat turning onto the street. The sedan left the front of the Piazza San Pietro and headed north along the Via Del Mascherino.

Agostino greeted Thom with a syrupy smile, one reserved for patronization. He was interested only in hearing what this savant with numbers living in the backwater of Catholicism had to say. The numbers were not unexpected, but the extrapolation provided by the young priest had him worried.

"It's a pleasure to meet with you, Father. I trust your accommodations are sufficient."

"I—"

"Yes, I'm sorry. With the summer tourism season it was difficult to make reservations on such short notice." A drippy smile followed.

Father Thom watched as Vatican City disappeared into the distance.

"Are we not meeting at the Vatican?"

The Cardinal of Siena looked over at his guest. "The analysis you sent by email deals with matters that the Vatican—the Pope—would rather not deal with directly. The official policy is that Church attendance is on the rise worldwide and that Catholicism is leading the charge. Unofficially, we all know the truth."

Thom nodded knowingly.

Agostino continued. "So in order to not raise any undo concerns, these matters are dealt with outside of the normal workings of the Holy See. Now, tell me a little about Canada, and your Parish. I'm interested in knowing what goes on outside of this bastion of faith."

"My Parish is nothing special. It's in a small community. A wood-framed church with a small cemetery attached. The main congregation comes from surrounding farms."

Father Thom elaborated on his daily routine as the Cardinal maintained an interest as best as he could muster. He let the young priest drone on as the sedan weaved its way out of Rome towards Siena. Once on the E35 the sedan picked up speed. It would take another four insufferable hours to reach their destination, but it was crucial that Agostino confirm the information compiled by the Canadian priest.

The early evening sun neared the crest of the horizon as the black sedan turned onto the drive leading up to a sixteenth-century country home where Cardinal Agostino lived when he wasn't in Rome or London. It was in his capacity as the Grand Master of the Order of Sumer—as Brother Franco Agostino—that took up most of his time. For now. Being a Cardinal of the Holy Catholic Church allowed him the opportunity to pursue his true goal. A goal for the Church that his position in the Order would help him achieve, a sacred vow that he took very, very seriously. Nothing could get in the way of his duties as the Grand Master of the Order of Sumer. Mere lives lost, lives that were temporary anyway and which were inconsequential to the preservation of what the Order protected.

The Cypress trees on either side of the cobblestoned driveway cast long shadows on the waning day, a long day for Thom, as he had slept for only a few hours after the plane landed at Leonardo da Vinci Airport before making his way to the Piazza. Now at the end of the long drive, Thom was starting to feel the effects of jetlag. His eyelids felt like they were being drawn down by lead weights as he struggled to stay awake.

Cardinal Agostino's voice broke the spell of sleep.

"Here we are, Father. We'll eat first and then work."

"Where are we anyway?"

"Siena. At my country estate. Whenever I have a chance I like to do business here."

"Church business," Thom echoed.

"Always," the Cardinal replied with a wry smile, "always."

Thom was led by inside by Agostino, as the cassock-clad priest took two bags from the trunk and followed them inside the magnificent home. Nothing he had seen of the homes of Calgary's wealthy oil barons prepared him for the opulence before him. This was old money. His eyes scanned the tapestries hanging from the three-story-high walls of the entranceway. Several marble statues stood guard over the door leading into the house. On a wall facing him was a massive painting mounted on a gilded frame. He stopped to absorb the scene of the gigantic painting.

"It was painted by one of the great Renaissance artists. A student of Leonardo Da Vinci, who painted in the master's shadow his entire life. It is not as famous as Da Vinci's works, but in some ways it was better."

Agostino came to stand beside Thom. He enjoyed the picture. It was his favorite. The painting depicted a garden scene, the Garden of Eden, complete with an apple tree and a serpent. But it showed more than just the first family of the Bible. Around the perimeter of the garden human figures were depicted, standing, sitting, and generally carrying on with daily life—the normal existence of ordinary people, oblivious to the beauty that surrounded them.

"It's blasphemous," was all Father Thom could say.

The Cardinal's hearty laugh echoed through the great hall. "Blasphemous! It is only a painting, Father Thom! The wild imagination of an artist, meant to be enjoyed, not reviled."

"But still. It suggests a story contrary to what we teach."

"That's the beauty of art. Each man takes from a painting exactly what they want, or need. There is a lot more to the Church you serve than you will ever be aware of. And from what it appears you have stumbled onto suggests it is a Church in trouble. But, let's have a quiet evening before we get down to business."

They entered the dining hall from the anteroom through a door that blended so well into the wallpaper that Father Thom did not notice it until the Cardinal touched a button on the wall and it swung open. The opulence of the stately villa stood in stark contrast to the dilapidated wooden structure he called home. Thom suspected that a single piece of art or sculpture exceeded his annual budget many times over. Like a multinational corporation, the Church accumulated its wealth for the privileged few.

There were two place settings at one end of the twenty-seat dining table; the large candelabra in the center of the table provided only a small circle of light. The first course was a sumptuous feast of broiled quail in wine sauce. It was soon followed with pesto-infused angel hair pasta, tomato salad, cheese, and finally a rich helping of tiramisu. Thom's wine glass was kept full throughout the meal with a decade-old vintage of Chianti. Locally made, the Cardinal assured him.

During the meal he consumed three glasses of wine to each one of the Cardinal's. By the time the dessert dishes were removed, a cloudy pleasantness filled his head. Thom clumsily followed Agostino as he stood up and left the dining table, traversed the entrance hall and into an oak-walled den. The rich wood-paneling and thick area rugs were exactly what he would have expected of such a room, except for the bank of computers and monitors sitting atop a massive cherry wood desk along one wall. No one was at the computers, but it was clear they were staffed regularly, as evidenced by the coffee mugs and notepads strewn about.

"We will work here tomorrow. As of the rest of the night, my valet will show you to your room to sleep off the effects of the wine. Have a good sleep." With that the Cardinal retreated from the room.

This was no ordinary room, Thom surmised as followed the valet down the hallway. There was more research going on here than the Cardinal let on. He wondered what interest the Church had in such clandestine operations.

15

The sun barely peaked over the Tuscan horizon as Agostino sat down in front of one of the monitors, reciting a few commands into a small microphone set up on a tripod on the desk. He invited a bleary-eyed Father Thom to pull up a chair then turned back to the monitor as soon as the welcome screen appeared. The bright screen in the dark room displayed a crest of a winged horse carrying a sword-wielding knight. Thom was curious about the crest but said nothing. He wondered what branch of the church the Cardinal of Siena represented. He also wanted to know who had so quickly heeded his research.

The crest dissolved as Agostino voiced a few more commands. Thom faced a blank screen for a moment before a spreadsheet appeared.

"Here it is." The Cardinal opened the spreadsheet. "I may be old school, but technology will not defeat me."

Thom recognized the spreadsheet as the one he had sent. However, more information had been added—his research was being duplicated by others.

If that were the case, then why did they need him?

"My spreadsheet," he said out loud.

"Interesting research. What made you start to track the demise of organized religion?" Agostino came right to the point. He needed only one answer before he was done with the frontier priest.

"Mathematics always held a fascination for me, so when my parish began to experience a mass exodus of its congregation, I got curious."

"No pun intended, I'm sure," the Cardinal interjected.

Father Thom smirked at his choice of words. He turned back to the computer screen before continuing. One column of numbers in particular caught his attention. He pointed, his arm extending past the Cardinal's chest, "What are you trying to imply by that—"

Agostino cut him off. "What is of importance to me—*why I brought you here*—has to do with *your* research."

Father Thom was proud of the work he had compiled. It was why he sent it to a minor clerical priest who worked at the Vatican, a man he met only once at a synod a few years earlier. And now he was in Siena presenting his findings.

What he had discovered could help bring people back into the pews. It was just a matter of applying the same methods that drew the congregation away in the first place. He sat back, put his hands behind his head and stretched out. He came all this way to sell the hierarchy on his concerns. It was no time to questions their motives.

"I used a parallel co-efficient of numerous communities and parishes, first in North America, then Europe, and finally the rest of the world. I compared congregation lists, which have been recorded since the late eighteen hundreds. I then applied the formula to the other major religions: Judaism, Islam, even Buddhism."

"What did you find out?"

"The trend was alarming, but no more so in the latter half of the twentieth century than into the first decade of this one. A century ago our world revolved around the church. Just take a look at every city and how the center of town is dominated by a church tower. You should be even more aware of the history of the church than most. It is very evident as we were approaching the airport in Rome. Each small village that I saw from the air was dominated by a spire, or dome, or both."

"Most of them survive on tourist dollars. We've become an organization of tour guides, not deliverers of faith." Cardinal Agostino spat out the words. Not that the Church was his only concern. To reclaim the past glory of the organization, it was necessary to understand the forces at play that were laying waste to the true Church. What he needed was the information that Thom possessed.

Father Thom continued.

"I then plotted the movements away from the Church during times of significant cultural and historical shifts: world wars, social upheaval, technological advancement, medical breakthroughs, and so on. The world has changed so fast since Eiffel built his tower to regale Parisians in 1890, but the Church has not kept pace."

Thom pointed to the graph on screen, placing his finger on the bottom of each peak showing the falling attendance of the church. "Crisis brings them in; technology drives them away."

"Fascinating."

"Not fascinating, devastating. The last peak you see on the chart represents the Internet. See the spike. The Internet dominates the consciousness of the world. Its penetration rate is exponential. The spike represents a rise in power; the trough represents religion."

"So that's what you concluded." The Cardinal was relieved. Maybe the naive priest really did not see the correlation he was expecting to hear.

"No. That was just the beginning. I thought maybe it was the Internet, until I started to compare the Church growth in the undeveloped countries, where Internet growth is just as strong. And religion thrives there. So it could not be the Internet itself. It had to be something else. Look at the green line on his graph," Thom pointed the computer screen, "It shows the real cause of the downward blip in attendance."

Cardinal Agostino stared past the figures on the computer screen. The label below the green line was what threatened him. He paused before speaking. This young priest discovered a trend that was supposedly a closely guarded secret of the Order, a secret that could not be revealed at any cost. Too much was at stake. For the Order. For the world. For him.

"Seventy-three million by my count," Thom concluded as he sat back in his chair.

"That is beyond understanding."

"Look at the calculation. It takes into consideration every conceivable possibility." Father Thom was emphatic. He spent the better part of the morning in the opulent surroundings of the Cardinal of Siena's estate, pouring over his research like a small child might explain a trip to the circus.

Cardinal Agostino neared the end of his questioning. He had exhausted the explanations of the Canadian priest, because it was important that he find out everything the young man knew. He needed to corroborate it with his own findings. It was clear from the information the Father Thom presented—it was clear that the Church was almost ready. The Order needed that. He needed that.

Then it would be important to make sure there were no loose ends.

Agostino excused himself. He hurried to a private office at the other end of his home and locked the ancient olive wood double doors behind him. He placed a set of headphones over his ears, adjusted the mike against his right cheek and dialed a number. He then settled into his familiar leather chair. A moment later his call was answered. Agostino spoke, delivering the salient features of Father Thom's research to the listener at the other end of the line. Then, with finality, he issued some detailed instructions. Once he finished relaying his demands, he rose abruptly with an air of anticipation.

Twenty minutes later Father Thom found himself back in the black sedan, heading back to Rome. Cardinal Agostino bid him a hasty adieu then quickly retreated as the driver ushered Thom out of the chateau and into the waiting car.

A brilliant blue Tuscan sky had replaced the gray clouds that greeted him the day before. The sun was reaching its zenith as the sedan made the on-ramp to the E35 south to Rome. Thom dozed off as the car sped back to the cradle of Christianity.

By four o'clock he was deposited outside the steps of his two-star hotel. The driver handed Thom an airline ticket for a flight the next day. Then, without a word, he sped off, into the throng of the mounting rush hour.

That was not at all what Thom had expected! He expected them to welcome him with open arms, to give him access to the Holy of Holies, to drink in the history of Christendom. He had come all this way and he was not about to leave without spending a few days exploring the Vatican. He hurried to his room to make a reservation for a tour that he wanted to take the following day, then he called the airline and cancelled his flight, unaware of the chain of events he had initiated by his short visit.

Agostino sat staring at the numbers on the computer screen for a long time after his visitor's departure. Father Thom's spreadsheet showed the figures, the effects, even the entire collapse of the Roman Catholic Church. But something else disturbed him more than the mass exodus from organized Faith. Something else was happening. The world was not unfolding as Agostino had expected. While he was busy making preparations for his star to rise, something had gone horribly wrong. The timing was perfect, and yet nothing seemed right. He hoped that it was not too late to realize the true purpose of Thought Mechanix.

16

Jason had been thinking about their trip to New Jersey, to the studio to film the third segment of Hans's new series. He was contemplating the conversation about the origin of Thought Mechanix and was anxious to carry on with that conversation.

So he waited for Hans to return.

As he thought about the taping session, Jason could not determine the great revelation that Hans had promised. He must have missed something, because the message was no different than what he had heard before, except that Hans spent a considerable amount of time stressing the need to focus the thought energy in the right direction. Focus was the key, likening the sensation to the effect of a laser pointer. By the end of the session, he promised to explain the need for the intensity in the next session.

First focus, then reveal. That was how he left the taping.

An hour passed. Jason had surveyed every inch of the office he had been in a hundred times before. He took the time to peruse the sixty pages of the Talon offer, answer his emails, and make a few phone calls to the office to change the rest of his afternoon appointments. Once everything was done, time crawled at a snail's pace. While he waited, Jason made the rounds of the massive corner office, re-admiring the artwork and sculptures, the numerous pieces filled the room like a cluttered English library. There were a few additions to the room, a new mask on the wall behind the ornate desk, a signed photograph of President Miriam Hansford, the current resident of 1600 Pennsylvania.

He was getting impatient. Waiting was not something he did well. The antique grandfather clock struck another hour when Hans burst into his office just as Jason was considering leaving him a note. He was going to suggest that Hans call when it was convenient.

Hans sat down at his desk and began the meeting, offering no explanation for the delay. There was no mention of the upcoming taping session, despite Hans's promise to explain the entire RoP II philosophy.

"The changes that are coming will be profound, a message that I was supposed to reveal at the Stern. After the bombing, it is necessary to use a different approach. I have come too far to stop now. By the time the new series of RoP II is released, the world will be enlightened and nothing will be able to stop the avalanche of awareness from enveloping the global consciousness—"

"What are you talking about?" Jason thought Hans was babbling. He seemed distracted, less focused than normally.

"I promised that it would be done, that what *they* started would be unleashed. I have continued to pursue their plans even after my mentor disappeared. Now with the arrival of this notebook…" Hans lifted a thin, leather bound burgundy notebook for Jason to see, "I'll need to show you where it all began. But first let's dispense with the Talon deal," he stated.

Before Hans called Jason, he had studied the slim notebook in detail, shocked by the level of knowledge they had about his activities. He thought that he'd hid his private intentions rather well, but apparently that was not the case. Everything he had done in the last few months was meticulously documented in the notebook. It also laid out a detailed account of the events that led to Jason's departure from his firm, the reasons for which knocked Hans off balance—Jason was to be used to carry out the elaborate plans outlined in the notebook.

Although the plan presented in the notebook was expected, given the original objectives, Jason's involvement was not. Most surprising was that, clearly, he had played directly into their hands, like a puppet on a string. It drove him mad to think they exerted such control of his life. Despite his angst, Hans dove into the project with renewed vigor.

But there were forces at work that had nothing to do with the recent intrusion in his perfect world. Someone else was trying to derail his plans, and they were not afraid to eliminate people in the process. The expectation that he use Jason meant his exposure was going to be complete. It would put the accountant at risk, inextricably connecting him to the final plan. But Hans knew that what he needed to do was the right thing to do. Jason would prove the perfect conduit.

Before they could get into the proposal, the phone rang. Jason sat and waited again. Hans stood next to his glass-covered cabinet, listening, not speaking. Jason set up his laptop on the round cherrywood meeting desk. A few times the self-help guru tried to edge in a comment, only to be stopped in mid-sentence. He glanced over at Jason and shrugged as if nothing of importance was discussed, but Jason sensed that the call was unexpected, maybe even unwanted.

Hans hung up abruptly.

"Who was that?" Jason inquired.

"It was nothing," Hans responded without conviction. Jason detected a brooding look of concern behind the charismatic smile. "Now, let's look at the Talon deal."

"Talon is offering a lot of money for you to use their global network to distribute RoP II." Jason had read the offer an hour earlier as he sat waiting. It was a ridiculous offer of fifteen billion dollars. Thought Mechanix was profitable, but not nearly profitable enough to warrant such an exorbitant price. The age of technology seemed to dispense with the usual rules of prudent business practices. And yet there were countless examples of Internet-based enterprises raking in mega-dollars for their unproven concepts.

"It's a bogus deal," Hans replied to Jason's comment. "Talon has no desire to bring this concept global. At least not the way you may think. Can you tell them for me it is no deal?"

"Are you sure? Fifteen bill—"

"Listen, Jason, the money is irrelevant, as you will soon understand. I need you to bring a message forward. In a way that you have already been doing, only more significantly."

Jason swallowed hard. He sat in silence while his mind fired a billion synapses as he thought about the implications of the comment. The room around him went fuzzy.

"Great, but Wakefield and Associates is dead. The partnership has asked that I leave."

"Yes, I know."

"You do?"

"Rumors travel fast in New York. I probably knew before you did." Hans smiled, "But it doesn't matter, does it?" Hans made eye contact and held it.

"No," Jason answered somewhat perplexed at the intensity of the gaze. He felt drawn into his gaze like a moth to a flame.

"I am ready to concentrate entirely on Thought Mechanix, to build a network of offices to bring the philosophies of your company to the international business community. The projections suggest that within three years there would be Wakefield Greer Consulting offices around the globe. Take your infomercial and bring it into the mainstream of the economy. So, have you thought about my proposal?"

Hans Pedersen smiled at the choice of words. Hans didn't think recruiting Jason would be quite so easy. Everything that Siena told him, revealed in the notebook, was coming together. As instructed, the energy had been focused, not only on Jason's dissenting partners, but also on the young accountant. But to meet his objective it would be necessary to educate his protégé. It was time to reveal the truth.

"The real energy of what we do is in London. It has been there for some time. So I'd like you to set up in our offices. Integrate into TMI."

"London and a merger? Not quite what I expected." Jason's head reeled with the implications.

"You will achieve much more by joining forces, believe me. When you get back to your office you can start planning. I've put together a dossier of entities I need you to visit. The first meeting will be the most important. I've taken the liberty to set up accounts for you to draw from, for working capital and other capital needs. I'd like to you to get started right away."

Jason stared at his client before speaking, not sure what to say. It was as if Hans had anticipated this. Hans never ceased to amaze Jason in the way he could hypothesize the future. *Never mind,* he thought.

"It's important that you focus on *every* step when you present the process. These entities must implement the process exactly to get the desired results. But of course you already know that. Do not hesitate to recruit people from each organization to help implement the strategy. If your business is to succeed, it is important that your approach reach critical mass as quickly as possible. Your involvement is crucial to me. To TMI."

"You seem to have anticipated my position."

"At least it came soon enough."

"Soon enough for what?" Jason was dumbfounded as he stared across the room at his mentor.

"The explosion at the Stern has convinced me that the message of Thought Mechanix has hit a chord with certain people who wish to preserve a state of ignorance in the world. I was hoping to change that. You are going to help me succeed. But before you start, it's time I tell you about the origins of Thought Mechanix." Hans delivered the speech as he had been instructed.

"What are you talking about?" Jason asked. "I know everything about your rise to fame and fortune."

"I know you are aware of the tablets." Hans pointed to the glass encased display across the room. "But what you don't know is where they came from originally. Although the theories of thought energy are not new, nothing has ever been revealed to you about the genus of the concept."

Hans paused to sip from his drink of choice, a glass of oxygenated sparkling water. He hesitated a moment before continuing, his face strained, as if he were wrestling with the direction to take.

"Eight thousand years ago the people who populated the earth suddenly evolved from virtual cave dwellers to creative thinkers. No one knows how or why that happened. Historians and theologians differ in their opinions as to the source of this new wisdom. Keep in mind that organized religion started at about the same time. Men created the theology to ensure a truth stay buried, considered by the sages of the day to be reserved for the select few—for those in a position to exert the right amount of controlled benevolence. These people became known as god-kings. They held court, designed a theocracy, created language, initiated politics.

"Known as the cradle of civilization, this advanced society continued for over a thousand years, then, just as mysteriously as their rise to prominence, they disappeared from the annals of history. Brushed over and forgotten. Yet every thought that was generated by that advanced group of people was documented. Written down for others to learn and follow."

Jason had been listening intently, part of him thinking that the rotund business man-cum-motivational speaker had slipped into insanity. "Who are you referring to?" he asked.

Hans ignored the query and continued. "The earlier generations were thought to be the forefathers to the Sumerians. What historians do not know is the origin of the original god-kings. They appeared, exerted their knowledge upon an unsuspecting group of semi-advanced humanoids and then dissolved into the ether. The names of the god-kings were unlike any uttered before. If you delve deeply into the Christian bible it hints at the fact that these men came from another place. Many scholars have attempted to equate them—"

The telephone rang, interrupting his history lesson. Hans cradled the phone between his ear and the rolling layers of skin circling his neck.

Jason waited. He looked about the office, waiting for Hans to finish his conversation. Hans listened for three minutes before he hung up the phone. Jason sensed that the mind guru was no longer into the theological conversation he had begun a few minutes earlier. The silence that followed enveloped the room like a sticky fog. Jason stared at Hans and then at the case containing the tablets, then back to Hans. He started twice to respond, only to find that no words came. Struggling to absorb the information that Hans thrust his way, to understand what Hans was trying to tell him, he could not think of anything to say.

Finally Hans broke the silence, carrying on as if there had been no interruption.

"According to the Catholics, there is no way to prove or disprove the Old Testament. They continue to stress the literal stories of the Bible despite scientific evidence to the contrary. Most intelligent men and women take the Bible to be a figurative story, meant to inspire faith in God. The Church, however, continued to espouse the literal interpretation of the Word despite the countless contradictions present in the Gospels. What the Order of Sumer taught me, and what I believe is the ultimate proof, is the truth of creation."

Jason felt a litany of arguments forming in his brain. Just as he was about to rebuke Hans's claims, he was bombarded with more information to take in.

"You don't need to struggle with your belief system, as your mind is doing now. I went through all the same arguments when I was in Siena fifteen years ago. It became clear to me. The origins of ROP are not what you think. The originals of the plaster-cast tablets in that case..." Hans jerked his left thumb at the glass case adjacent to his desk, "provide irrefutable proof as to our origin. I know they do because I have had the opportunity to study the originals, which are safely stored, to be made available only when the time is right. They are too valuable to entrust with just anyone. Yet the burden of their existence has taken its toll. That was what we...I wanted..." Hans corrected himself, but not without an upturned eyebrow from Jason, "...needed...to reveal at the seminar the other night. Organized religion has deceived their followers for over four thousand years. It's time to let the world know the truth."

"What truth is that?" Jason asked as he stood up at walked over to the case that held the tablets.

"That the fundamental laws of nature have been hidden from all of us since the beginning of human consciousness. The Rules of Possibility were an attempt to regain the foothold to our destiny that organized religion stole from its subjects."

"I think you've lost me, Hans." Jason struggled to absorb the information presented, his skeptical mind challenging the conversation. He believed in the power created by the Thought Mechanix Rules of Possibility. But this explanation was beyond his grasp of comprehension.

Hans was about to continue when the phone rang again. A brief discussion ensued. Concentration enveloped his round face. He turned white as he hung up the phone.

Hans started again, slowly this time.

"Jason, you have to believe me when I tell you that there is much more to what is going on than you could possibly imagine. I need to know that I can trust you."

"Of course..."

"You will help me?"

"Just name it."

At that moment Amy opened the door. She stood just inside the room, the rectangular frame creating a portrait of exquisite beauty. Jason cast his gaze from Hans to Amy, caught by the seriousness of her facial expression.

"We have to go…NOW." That was all Amy said as she turned and left, not acknowledging Jason's presence.

It was all that the Thought Mechanix founder could do to bid a hasty good-bye to Jason as he rushed towards the door of his office. He turned once as if to speak, catching Jason's eyes then fled behind Amy.

17

The grandfather clock chimed four symphonic bells as Jason stood aside to let Hans bolt from his office. He sat quietly for a few moments in order to absorb what he had been told. It seemed ludicrous that the world could have had the wool pulled over its eyes from the dawn of civilization. He was more bewildered than he was before the day began.

With no answers forthcoming, Jason packed up his laptop, abandoning the Talon offer on the otherwise uncluttered desk of the Thought Mechanix founder and left the office.

Amy emerged from a side door a few paces behind Jason. She grabbed his shoulder as he reached the reception area.

"Sorry, Jason," she began casually, as if there was nothing untoward about her intrusion into Han's office or the motivational speaker's abrupt departure.

"Hans had an urgent meeting he could not miss." Amy looked around before leaning into Jason, her voice lowered, "Did Hans tell you anything during your meeting?"

"What do you mean?" Jason cocked his eyes at her, hesitant to delve into the strange conversation. "We just spent an hour together going over the Talon deal. You knew that."

In fact, Jason was surprised that Amy was not at the meeting. His mind was reeling at that fact as he watched Amy's pale face reveal her distress.

"He didn't give you anything?" she pressed him again, more urgently.

"What's the matter?" Jason was looking into the eyes of a frightened child.

She was sent to him to deliver a message that was not needed. Somehow she seemed unsure of what to do, being caught in her lie. A moment later the calm demeanor she learned on the streets returned. Amy corrected herself. It was what anyone would expect from Hans

Pedersen's right hand. Amy tossed back some strands of hair with a casual brush of her hand, as if the last minute never took place. She smiled. Her radiance was disarming.

"It's nothing," she laughed. "He told me he was going to give you another deal to review. He'll call you later. Come on, I'll walk you through the gambit of security." She grabbed Jason's hand and headed for the exit. She said good-bye, kissed him on the cheek then turned back into the building.

Jason watched her disappear into the elevator.

Amy's mind was reeling. Something was amiss. Why wasn't she told that Hans kept his meeting to discuss Talon? Amy worked too hard to get close to the founder of Thought Mechanix to be shut out now. Was it possible Hans was having suspicions about her motives?

Jason stood on the sidewalk outside of the Plaza looking up at the top floor. He had been whisked away so quickly by Amy that he barely had time to digest what had just happened. As he reviewed the scene in his mind, it was clear to him that Amy was scared, if only for a moment, and then it had passed. He had always known her to be impetuous… but never scared. He dismissed the notion, deciding to wait for Hans to call later in the week.

Without giving it a second thought, Jason turned to follow the cacophony of noise from midday Manhattan to his office. Taxis honked as he made the tail end of a walk signal, content that the traffic would ease around him. Several angry honks met his dash, despite sidewalk signs instructing drivers to avoid the use of their horns. Street vendors outside the entrance to his office were noisily exchanging prices with eager tourists, loudly enough to drown out the executives barking orders into their bluetooth devices.

Jason pushed through the revolving door into his building, grabbed an open elevator and made his way to his corner office. He threw his briefcase onto one of the leather client chairs, tossed his suit jacket onto the other and walked over to the window.

"So, what happened?" The suspense was killing Timothy.

Jason turned to his friend and shot him a sour grimace. A moment later, Timothy's face registered disappointed. Then Jason let his pent-up grin replace the feigned rejection.

"We've got it?" Timothy squealed.

"Not only do we have it, Hans wants us to go global."

18

Snow filtered through the dense clouds of the midsummer alpine sky. The mountains were being assaulted by an unexpected cold front as the wind picked up speed, bending the tops of the mountain pine trees to the breaking point. Perched atop a bluff overlooking the valley near Salzburg, a solitary building was being buffeted by the tempest raging outside. Inside, away from the storm, a group of men sat in rapt attention at a round, ornate table inlaid with finely carved cherry and olive wood swirls. The table had been used for the meetings of the Order of Sumer for the past forty years. Prior to that, its owner was another man who harbored visions of world domination.

An eighth man entered the room. He looked around the table, resting his gaze for a moment on each of the faces, a smile no longer evident on his otherwise good-humored visage. The situation had reached a crisis point. It was not their intention to release the knowledge in its current state. They were faced with a responsibility to guide the course of history; but despite keeping the plump man under wraps, watching his every move, cautiously spoon-feeding his ego, they had lost control. The man who had been unknowingly cast upon an unsuspecting world had outgrown the teacher. They had narrowly avoided exposure from his latest endeavor—now this.

"How did he unravel the truth?" one of the men inquired.

Another man spoke, his English thick with Slavic undertones, "How could he have even found out about the Books?"

"Who told him?" The eighth man boomed out the question above the din raised by the others.

There was only silence from the seven men who comprised the council of the Order of Sumer. The eighth man was bound by ancient rules, commissioned with a responsibility older than written history. He was on the brink of destiny, only to have it taken from his grasp; a duty bestowed upon him by prior generations of kindred spirits, a responsibility that was handed down for eight millennia was about to be broken because of one man.

The others in the room shared his concerns, but for different reasons, reasons that the man used to his advantage. They had been recruited by the Grand Master to ensure the fulfillment of his responsibility.

Another joined them at the table. His face was hidden behind a black hood that covered up any possibility of identification should the men around the table raise suspicions as to their motives.

The room went silent.

The visitor spoke. "From what I have gathered, Hans Pedersen was more aware of his circumstance than we originally thought. Early on, he recruited help to understand the source of his success. He was coached, even from the beginning, in Siena. He also has an Italian contact that has led him to the object we have been seeking."

"Does he know what it means? After all, he is not really one of us."

"What do you mean?" The youngest of the group spoke up, still unfamiliar with the protocol of the group. "He is *him*," said the young one.

"Silence," the leader screamed across the table. "Do not speak until it is your turn." Each one would speak in turn without questioning the views of the others. Then they would reach a consensus, for the good of their objective, the leader, for his view of mankind. "Enough of my tradition has been jeopardized by what was revealed in Siena," he went on. "We need not risk any further compromise. We have dealt with that situation...I also know the person responsible for the breach of trust. We must deal with the product of his indiscretion."

The novice member of the council bowed his head in deference, knowing well enough now not to offer an apology.

The leader continued. "He is not him. There is no *him*. Surely all of you believe that to be true. We are one, there is no him. It has always been that way, since the beginning. It is the secret we hold, the truth we protect. Man requires nurturing to survive. They cannot survive if they know the truth. For all of us to be enlightened means the end of humankind. It has been that way from the beginning, content with the knowledge that they must answer to a higher being." He paused. "I'll tell you how the sacred idols were taken... our purpose has been compromised from within by someone with a much different agenda."

"So what does it matter? Let's terminate the project to prevent any further abuses," an Indian man said with a soft, musical voice. "We can go back to where we were."

The Master spoke. "I wish that were true. The evolution of the human brain has reached a point of divergence with its past. Wheels set in motion a decade and a half ago may be too late to just ignore. We have to do what we can to reverse the effects. We cannot let the evolution of the process continue on its current path. If ever there was a time to honor our forbearers it is now. If we do not, then I fear the end that was foretold will surely be wrought upon an unsuspecting world. It's time to take back control."

The leader, the Grand Master of the Order of Sumer, had voiced what everyone else was thinking.

It was time for the Guardians.

19

It did not take long for the two mavericks of the newly formed global advisory firm of Wakefield and Greer to uproot from the downtown Manhattan to make their mark on London, England days after an astonished group of former partners licked their chops at the ease of the partnership divorce. Jason had smiled inwardly as each of the partners signed the agreement, only a slight pang of regret that he had not fought harder to keep his firm. He knew his new direction would be much more rewarding. In the end, they had agreed on just a cash settlement for their capital accounts at the value of the business left behind. Jason and Timothy also agreed to indemnify the firm for any future exposure to the Thought Mechanix advisory practice.

As he watched his former partners, he could see the dollar signs of future earnings in their eyes. In return, the former Wakefield partners agreed to a non-compete, in particular, to Blair Stanford's insistence that TMI advisory services not be offered to any of the existing clients of the firm. And Jason insisted that the firm change its name.

"The signs are already ordered," Blair Stanford had quipped.

Jason unloaded his Manhattan apartment for a sum just shy of four million and had the money transferred to the London Merchants Bank, adding to the three million after-tax he took for the practice. London Merchants wasn't Jason's first choice, but Hans Pedersen provided the referral. The bank had been around since before the Pilgrims departed the Mayflower, was as solid as a rock, and eager to do business with a confidant of the great TMI founder.

At the age of thirty-eight Jason Wakefield had more money than he ever expected, and now he was in London to launch his second firm. He surveyed the London cityscape from the cab he had taken from Heathrow while his mind wandered back to his life growing up in Wyoming. From the age of five until he left for college to pursue a life beyond the rigors of prairie farming, Jason was taught that money was something that others possessed. He grew up hearing the constant preaching that money did not buy happiness; that the love of money was the root of all evil; that nobody who was rich earned their money honestly; that all rich people were lazy; and a litany of other platitudes.

He smiled at his dim reflection in the cab window. He was not unhappy, evil, or dishonest, and he certainly was not lazy. And the interesting thing of it was that the money was irrelevant. He suspected that others in his position felt the same way—life just threw you a basket full of opportunities to enjoy. Money was only the scorecard. Those who saw the green stuff as a tool for survival missed the point.

It was too bad that his parents were not around to enjoy his good fortune. As the cab arrived in front of the Savoy, he felt a momentary twinge of melancholy as he remembered the devastating day of their death. James and Sherry Wakefield were avid hikers. The two were on a trek through the Coyote Bluffs, near the Utah border, when a freak rainstorm washed their party of six from a thin path high up the cliffs of Cardiac Canyon. Beaten and barely recognizable, the bodies washed up a mile from where they had fallen. Death came quickly, the coroner stated. Hardly a consolation to losing your entire family.

Jason settled into his room then ventured out to meet his partner. Timothy had arrived in London a week earlier to set up the office with the help of local employees of Thought Mechanix. Hans Pedersen had ensured them the full support of his London team, together with several thousand square meters of office space. The offer came with a few strings that the two accountants were happy to pull. They had met with Hans a month earlier, getting a final set of instructions as to what was expected once they hit London.

"Europe is the birthplace of Thought Mechanix. The concepts are inherently better accepted over there. I based my production operations in New York because I like it here, but London is where all of the action really happens." It had sounded like Hans missed the place.

Jason was surprised and stated as much. Although he had been doing Hans's tax and accounting work for a while, he had never seen any activity indicating a London based operation.

"I thought that the business activities in the U.S. were the extent of your operations."

Hans laughed, causing his body to shake like a bowl of jellied salad. "The extent of Thought Mechanix goes far and beyond the production of my Rules of Possibility DVDs and the infomercials that drive the American psyche. My organization in New York represents only a small part of the extent of the Order."

Jason threw the round man a sideways glance then looked over at Timothy and mouthed the word *Order.*

"You heard me correctly. There is a larger picture than just what you see. I have benefactors who demand my attention. I was in the process of separating myself from their influence when the Isaac Stern explosion took place. Now the plans have changed somewhat, which is why I need you there."

"Who are these others?" Jason started to wonder if the affiliation with TMI was such a good idea.

"Thought Mechanix Foundation is based in London, which is why I want you there. The two of you have been able to take the basic tenets of what Thought Mechanix is all about and deliver it with resounding success. So much so that we want you to design a template to allow the Rules foster within any organization—corporate or otherwise. I'll have you start with several organizations that are primed to go. If we don't do this now, I'm afraid it will be too late. In fact, it may already be too late. You will know soon enough."

"Too late for what?" Jason probed.

Again the rolling laugh. "Let's hope that I am just being paranoid." Hans dismissed Jason's question. "I know you think that Thought Mechanix is something that I started. Several times in the last year I tried to tell you about the bigger picture, but the time just never seemed right. There is a bigger picture. Trust me when I tell you that because once you get to London what you have done for me so far will seem trivial."

"The place is amazing," Timothy spouted, placing a pint of Guinness in front of Jason. "In fact, this whole town is amazing."

"London *is* the bastion of civilization." Jason held up his beer and clinked glasses with his friend. "A toast."

They were sitting in a corner, next to a table of loud insurance men from Lloyds. At least, that was what they surmised from the stack of files piled amid the empty pints on the table next to them. The Golden Boar was a self-service bar, that is, unless you were prepared to wait for the fleshy cherub with the ample bosom to make her way to your table before the lunch hour was over. Few waited. They did, however, all enjoy the girl as she shoved her way through the crowded room, cleaning up after the liquid lunch crowd.

Jason chuckled with the rest of the mob as, inevitably, a newbie tried a pickup line, only to be shot down with a once-over look and a roll of the eyes from the cheerful maiden.

"So what's so amazing about Thought Mechanix London?" Jason raised his voice to be heard over the din.

Timothy pulled back and took a drink of the frothy beer.

"Nothing like a Guinness." He took a large mouth full of beer before explaining. "TMI London occupies over half of the Gherkin." Timothy pointed to the cone-shaped St. Mary's Axe across the street from where they sat, and kitty-corner to the world's insurer, Lloyds of London. The conical shaped building stood forty stories high in the center of the financial district, amongst a plethora of centuries-old architectural beauties.

"The what?"

"The Gherkin, as in pickle. It's the nickname they gave the building when it was first proposed to the City's development board, for obvious reasons. Although, in the last week, I have heard it referred to as the Towering Innuendo, the Crystal Phallus, and the Glass Dildo."

Jason stared past the Lloyd's table at the round spire that crested into a spherical point. It rose so much higher than the buildings around it that it dominated even the farthest corners of Central London.

"Anyway," Timothy continued, "when I first arrived I was met at the airport. My name was on a placard and everything—the royal treatment. After setting me up at the Savoy, they brought me down to the Axe to get acquainted with *our space*, as they put it.

"At first I thought maybe Hans was playing a trick on us, like I, we, were being punked. But the infrastructure was too established. They set us up on the thirtieth floor. When I walked into the place I almost shit myself. Our name was on the wall across from the elevator, in bold letters—Wakefield and Greer—and below that, Management Consultants. The receptionist spoke to me in a cute British accent: 'Welcome to London, Mr. Greer,' she said, before handing me a coffee with, yes, you got it, two sugars and a cream. Hans made sure they knew how I liked my coffee. That was surprising enough. Before I could ask, the girl, Sandra, how she knew, she said that it would be no problem for me to go to the gym at lunch and handed me a membership card to a fitness facility in the building. It was as if she could read my mind.

After I settled in the office, another secretary came by and asked if everything was satisfactory. She must have sensed my discomfort as I stammered a response. She told me that their instructions were to make us feel at home. Well, it's like they took my office straight out of its New York skyscraper, right down to the same dictation equipment I used in Manhattan."

Timothy caught his breath as he sat back and breathed in the atmosphere.

"So what do you think?"

"I've always known Hans to provide only the best. But I've never known him to go overboard for anyone other than himself. He must really want us to deliver."

20

Jason stood at the window of his office in the Gherkin watching the London fog devour the city below the twentieth floor. He closed his cell phone, ending his conversation with Hans. The man sounded more anxious than ever, insisting that Jason meet with Lord Barton as soon as possible. Today was preferable. *He has the information that you will need to continue* were Hans's parting words.

"The strange thing is," Jason pointed out to Timothy as they prepared for the meeting, "that Bristol Canneries does not exactly fit the profile that Thought Mechanix is looking for."

"I don't think that Hans cares. Bristol, and its founder Lord Barton, are first on his list of contacts. The instructions he provided you were very clear. Contact each person on the list in order, as soon as we were set up in London."

"Time is of the essence were his parting words," Jason recalled.

He went back to his office and made the call. Lord Barton seemed expectant, even urgent, that the two of them meet to discuss "developments" as he put it. Jason wondered what that meant.

"Today, at the Club." Lord Barton instructed he would send his driver immediately. Lord Barton insisted, as it seems only the British can do, that Jason would meet with him at precisely two p.m. He promised to provide Jason with the required contacts he would need to be successful.

Lord Barton proffered Jason Wakefield his utmost attention. He was led into the opulent surroundings of the Discover's Club after a comfortable ride in Lord Barton's Rolls Royce. An hour earlier, when he settled into the back of the Rolls, he was handed three fingers of Glenlivet in a baccarat crystal glass, no ice—just the way he liked it. Jason spent the drive to the appointed meeting contemplating who these people were on the list provided by Hans. But when escorted into a private den off the main entrance, Jason knew he was in the presence of true wealth and power. The den smelled of old money, as if it had been infused into the oak paneling and high-back leather chairs. The bookshelves were filled with what looked like leather bound first editions. Adam Smith's *The Invisible Hand* was propped up on a stand just to the left of the entrance.

"We like to remember the reasons for our success." A soft yet authoritative voice roused Jason from his state of awe. The door locked behind the man who entered.

At six-foot three inches, Lord Barton was taller than Jason expected. With his silver-grey hair and his ultra-thin body, he carried off the Savile Row suit like the true aristocrat that he was.

"Mr. Wakefield. Hans has spoken very highly of you. Said you were the one to get us out of our current crisis."

"Crisis?" *Hans never said anything about a crisis!*

Jason took the man's hand, grasping it lightly as if afraid to break any bones. Barton looked like he was in his late eighties; he was bent slightly forward, as if he had spent a lifetime tacking into the wind.

Lord Barton gestured Jason to sit in one of the high-back leather chairs, which looked as if it had comforted a battalion of dealmakers during its service to the Club. He called for drinks and made small talk until the servant left. Taking a sip that would have made only a hummingbird seem ravenous, he set his crystal tumbler on the oak side table and shifted slightly in his seat towards Jason.

"Hans has spoken to you about his situation?"

"Situation? Crisis? What's going on?" Jason looked at the octogenarian. "Hans has recruited my firm to establish a series of training seminars to—"

"Stop," Lord Barton's voice echoed in the small chamber. "You do not need to be coy with me, son. We are on the same team. Now, let's talk about the release of the knowledge that Hans has bestowed upon you. He promised me you were ready."

Jason was more than just a little confused. *Had this geezer gone off his rocker?* He decided to play along to find out what Hans had obviously omitted from his briefing on their assignment. He had no way of knowing whether Lord Barton was just a demented old man or if he truly was as important as Hans seemed to indicate.

"The time has come to release the origin of the Rules of Probability to a needy world." Then Jason stared intently at Lord Barton, trying to evoke a reaction that would indicate if the man was all there or not.

"Exac—"

Lord Barton's enthusiastic response was interrupted by loud yelling from outside the door.

Within seconds, several elderly men had entered the room. One of them was grasping a remote in his bony hand. He pointed it at the painting above the fireplace. The oil canvas, which depicted a polo player on his pony, was ascending into the ceiling, revealing a large plasma screen television, already tuned to CNN.

The second gentleman cranked up the volume of the television rather than his hearing aid. Instantly the room was filled with the shrieks of a hysterical woman who was standing in the front of what was clearly the Plaza in New York. The scream had pierced the steady rain of noisy Manhattan.

Jason saw his office building in the background.

"Hey, that's—"

This time Jason was cut off by the old man wielding the remote, who held up his hand to silence the room.

The amateur cameraman was following the woman, who had come from the opposite side of Park Avenue where his office was situated. The footage was grainy and unsteady, as if being taken by a cell phone video camera.

Jason stared at the screen. The screaming woman looked vaguely familiar. But the camera continued to pan the crowd and the anguished woman lifted her hands to the sides of her head, effectively covering her face.

Her wails had drawn the attention of some pedestrians, who were now weaving their way between the stopped cars, seeking out the source of the shrieks.

The cameraman continued to follow the crowd as it converged on the entrance to Hans's building. On the Plaza side of Fifth Avenue a scene of unbridled chaos erupted as the crowd of people rushed to the east side of the Thought Mechanix building.

The audio of the cell phone picked up a man's voice off camera, gleefully announcing that it was a jumper.

"Splat" — Jason heard another voice say.

The cameraman quickened his pace, covering the large mall in front of the Plaza in seconds, making Jason slightly ill as he watched the undulating sea of people through the unsteady movement of the camera.

The young woman, her hand now to her mouth, tears streaming from her eyes, stopped in front of the camera, a look of disbelief staring straight at Jason and the other men six thousand miles away.

"He's dead. I can't believe he's dead."

Amy. She was the screaming woman. His heart skipped a beat. Her blond hair was soaked by the continuous rain. Her clothes were drenched and her makeup was smeared. Mascara trickled down her cheeks like black tears.

"Who's dead?" a voice asked. The cameraman was the most likely source of the question.

Amy stared at the camera. Her eyes were hollow sockets, as if her soul had been ripped from within. It was as if she was looking directly at Jason.

"*Him*. The man who said all was possible. He changed my life. I saw him fall, from up there." Amy turned and pointed upward but to no particular spot.

Warm bile enveloped Jason's tongue as the situation registered in his brain.

"He just jumped," she repeated

"Why?" the voice asked.

"He told me it was never going to be possible—"

Just then another woman came up to Amy, wrapped a wool blanket around her shoulders and led her away. The cameraman tried to follow, but he was held back by several men in dark slickers.

A man's face appeared on the screen as the cameraman continued to film. In the background a local news team was setting up their equipment.

"Who jumped?" the cameraman persisted.

A businessman stood a foot away from his inquisitor and looked at the camera as if it had two heads.

"Hans Pedersen, of course. Is there anyone else who mattered?" he snapped, skirting his interviewer and disappearing into the crowd.

The room went quiet as the audio was muted. Jason had not noticed the people entering the room as he watched the broadcast. Now he looked around to see that about two dozen old men had gathered around the plasma screen. The men stared at Lord Barton, waiting for a reaction. The seconds ticked, but there was no response.

Then before Lord Barton could speak, voices were heard outside the door, getting louder, sounding more aggressive. A moment later screams echoed through the room, just like the ones on the screen moments earlier.

The screams were drowned out by the sound of gunfire.

Jason looked around at the faces of the octogenarians, who seemed strangely calm, almost as if they were expecting the interruption. Not one of them moved.

Jason on the other hand reacted swiftly. Although glued to the TV screen seconds earlier, he dove toward the windows. Instincts of a delta-force fighter, not of an accountant, told him that staying in the library with these oddly placid old men was not a good idea.

No more than ten seemingly-endless seconds passed from the first sound of commotion outside to the inevitable intrusion. As Jason fumbled for a latch that would provide an escape, a burst of gunfire splintered the wood around the heavy lock that sealed the door.

Then the old men began to topple one by one, as blood spurted from the shots to the head.

Jason found the lever and yanked the large window toward him. Poised to jump out, he glanced back and noted that the lone gunman was selecting each target with calm detachment. But the composure of the old men struck Jason as truly odd. They didn't flinch or flee. Each one took the hit like an expectant child waiting for approval. Jason watched, paralyzed, as Lord Barton took the next hit. The bullet entered just above the left eye, leaving a dark cavernous hole.

Then, out of the corner of his eye, he spotted the remote-toting octogenarian reach out and press a series of numbers into a keypad just as the gunman squeezed the trigger to end his life.

A loud horn began to wail throughout the building.

The gunman turned to Jason.

Their eyes locked and time froze. Breaking the stare, after what seemed like an eternity, Jason turned from the carnage, grasped the edges of the window frame and lifted himself over the sill.

It was only a few feet down to the gardens. He hit the lush lawn and rolled once, trying to recall the survival training he learned during a corporate boot camp he took his employees to in the Pacific Northwest.

A few yards from the window a large oak tree provided cover. Jason scurried behind the tree as several bullets planted themselves where he had landed a moment earlier. Then he bolted for the gated entrance to the Discoverer's Club. He stood for a moment in clear view of the window he had just exited, half expecting a bullet to stop his progress. None came. Instead, a chilling, bone-shattering explosion sent a shockwave across the ground, knocking Jason sideways into the Rolls Royce that had brought him to see Lord Barton. He landed on the pavement beside another body. Like the others, there was a bloody hole in the man's head. The chauffeur.

Behind Jason, the entire front of the three-hundred-year-old Discoverer's Club had disappeared in an instant. Bricks and chunks of dark wood paneling fell around him. He covered his head as he dove under the Rolls for protection. The spot where he had jumped out of the window was now just a hole in the ground—the same spot where the shooter had stood moments earlier. Whatever had leveled the building was powerful enough to do some serious damage.

What the hell was going on? Jason's analytical mind reviewed the past several minutes. He wasn't sure if the gunman had survived the blast. And if the gunman had not survived, then who set the explosion? His mind raced through the events that had placed him under the Roll Royce.

A moment later his question was answered as a black-clad figure emerged from the trees half a block past what was the Discoverer's

Club. Again their eyes locked. Jason started to look for an exit strategy, when the gunman turned away and ran up the street away from where Jason lay.

Could the dead Discoverer who had punched the numbers into the keypad have deliberately set the explosion to destroy the building, and its contents? But why? What knowledge did they possess that was so important that the death of Hans Pedersen and the corresponding invasion from the gunman invoked a need to self-destruct the building?

The sound of sirens began to infiltrate his numb brain as fire engines and police descended upon the venerable old club. Jason shook off the debris and sprinted across the street to the safety of Hyde Park. He was not going to subject himself to the scrutiny of Scotland Yard. Besides, he had no answers.

Only questions.

21

Rain fell in sheets across the mushy lawns of Hyde Park, pooling in areas where fall leaves clogged the drainage system. Jason barely felt the cold pellets as he traversed the grounds towards the tube stop at Marble Arch. He vaguely heard the latest orator spout off against the loss of privacy in the modern world. The unshaven, shoddily-dressed speaker tried to get Jason's attention by throwing verbal barbs his way as he passed within spitting distance of the man. He did not notice the splendid Arch as he passed beneath, lost in the confusion of the events that drove him forward, away from the carnage. For a fleeting moment his mind recalled the London Walks tour guide explaining that in the early eighteen hundreds John Nash designed the arch based on the Arch of Constantine in Rome. The Arch had been originally erected on The Mall as a gateway to the then new Buckingham Palace. It was moved to its present location during the building of the east front of the palace. According to urban legend, the arch was moved because it was too narrow for the Queen's state coach, although unlikely, as the gold state coach passed under it during Elizabeth II's coronation in 1953.

At Speaker's Corner he headed for the Tube to board the Central Line back to the Gherkin. The rain pounded as Jason crossed Cumberland to enter the subway. He was feeling light-headed. A woman stopped him in the concourse on the way to the trains to point out that he was bleeding profusely from his leg. Jason looked down to see a trail of blood behind him. While the oozing was evident, it was not constant. The blood was dripping from a large splinter of oak sticking out of his calf. At that precise moment, as he acknowledged his injury, he felt the pain. A moment later the color drained from his face as he collapsed onto a nearby seat. He watched the woman alerting the tube officials for assistance.

Jason did not remember the wood entering his leg, but it did not surprise him given the amount of debris from the Discoverer's Club that rained down on him after the explosion. A half hour later, with his leg professionally bandaged but without even a query as to how he had contracted the errant splinter, he was traveling down the Central Line to his office. Questions surpassed answers by a staggering margin, but he was too numb to think. He only hoped that Amy was alright.

It was twilight when he emerged from the Circle Line. A glimmer of sun on the western horizon tried to beat its way past the dark clouds for one last moment of daylight. A taxicab almost clipped him as he crossed Beavis Marks and headed down St. Mary's Axe. The polite driver of the cab waved an apologetic hand as Jason passed Eat, a smoothie bar where he had become a regular. It was great having the eatery so close to where they worked. Healthy food was not that easy to find in London. Jason took pride in staying in shape, despite the ridiculous hours he worked. He credited that to a regimented exercise program and a constant vigil on his food intake. It seemed to work.

Twilight melted into darkness by the time Jason made his way along Undershaft. The streets were deserted, relatively speaking, as the main rush of foot traffic had already found their way to the Tube or to a pub at the end of the workday. He was lost in thought about the Discoverer's Club attack as he rounded the corner to his office. In his distracted state he almost walked into a barricade blocking access to the street leading to his building, oblivious to the chaos that surrounded the Gherkin. Ambulances and fire trucks were blocking the main entrance to the streets around the building and police were directing people to other arteries, away from 30 St. Mary's Axe. The foot traffic was being re-directed across the street to the futuristic façade of the Lloyds of London tower.

Jason blinked at the scene before him, a sinking feeling in the pit of his stomach. Frantic thoughts raced through his mind as he glanced up to the thirtieth floor, already prepared for what he saw. Gaping holes replaced the windows where Jason had stood speaking with Timothy a few hours earlier.

Making his way to the entrance of the building, Jason pushed past firemen and panic-stricken business men and women trying to vacate. Struggling his way through the torrent of people and into the lobby, he walked towards the bank of elevators that would take him to the thirtieth floor. A constable stood guard at the entrance of the corridor, barring his way to the elevator.

"Sorry, sir, no one is allowed up these elevators." The constable held up a hand blocking Jason's approach to the elevator, the cockney accent sounding slightly comical. Another policeman looked over and spoke into his two-way radio.

"What happened?" Jason queried, despite a sickly feeling that he already knew the answer.

"Explosion." The policeman said without elaboration.

"I have an office on the thirtieth floor..."

A thin expression of angst crossed the bobby's face as he replied, "Not anymore ya don't. That floor's gone, as well as all the floor above."

Jason felt a prescient fear that this incident and the explosion at the Discoverer's Cub were somehow connected. He wondered if the apparent suicide of Hans Pedersen was also related. Then his mind raced back to the present.

What about Timothy?

"Were there any casualties?"

The policeman looked at Jason as if he had two heads, with one of them on fire. "Don't believe the floors were occupied. Apparently the fire alarm vacated the floors before the explosion. There were a few people who did not heed the warning, however. I was up there—"

The cockney policeman was interrupted by a taller man in a dark and rumpled suit who had emerged from the elevator. He spoke to the policeman before turning to Jason, giving the policemen a slight nod. The officer immediately retreated toward the chaos in the lobby.

"Mr. Wakefield?" The detective spoke in an upper-crust nasal voice that indicated an Eton education. He sounded more like a tennis pro than a policeman.

"Yes," Jason responded tentatively, as he accepted the outstretched hand of the well-dressed man.

"I'm detective Barry Bryan. I was told by the building receptionist that you were out of the office at the time of the incident. Do you have any idea why your firm would be a target?"

"What are you talking about? Why would someone attack a private consultancy firm?" Gunter Tang's face flashed across his mind, but he quickly dismissed the thought. The man was a criminal, but he did not harbor a grudge. Business was just business.

Or, maybe not.

"That's what we were hoping you could tell us. But I also need to ask you a few questions." He took out his notebook and flipped it open. "Could you let me know where you were this afternoon? Why you left the office?"

Jason paused for a moment. He didn't just fall off the turnip truck. He needed to know what it was they thought he knew, what they were thinking. *Did they know about the Discoverer's Club incident already?*

"I was at a meeting…"

Detective Bryan pointed to Jason's torn pants and blood-soaked bandage.

"What kind of meeting? You look a little banged up. Were you attacked?"

"Could you let me know what it is you know? What happened here?" Jason turned the line of questioning around by asking one of his own. He learned early in his career that the best way to gather data during a negotiation was to be the one asking the questions rather than the other way around.

"You have no idea what happened? This attack was incredibly sophisticated, planned and coordinated. It wasn't a like a suicide bomber running into a crowded market. In fact, I would say that the place looked like it was designed to self-destruct."

Jason could feel the blood drain from his face. His knees buckled as he leaned onto a nearby pillar for support.

Self-destruct.

He could see the old man at the Discoverer's Club pressing a code into the panel on the wall moments before the building exploded into a fiery grave. He was certain the Discoverer's Club was destroyed intentionally. Now, his offices in London had also been destroyed by what the detective thought was an intentional demolition.

Did both of the incidents happen at the same time?

"Are you okay?" Bryan called over at one of the policeman milling about, "Bring us some water."

A few minutes later Jason sat with his back to the pillar, sipping on a bottle of water.

"Why do you think it was premeditated?" Jason looked up at Detective Bryan.

Detective Barry Bryan let out a soft chuckle that seemed to get stuck in his cheeks, as if releasing the humorous thought was considered undignified.

"Follow me and I'll show you."

Jason lifted himself off the floor and followed Detective Bryan to the elevators. The doors opened onto the thirtieth floor, now a hollowed-out shell. A gust of wind swirled around the floor. Nothing remained of the offices that Jason had left just a few hours before. Only the blackened skeleton of the perimeter walls of St. Mary's Axe remained, with a few charred corners of desks and what looked like computer monitors littering the darkened floor. Most of the offices had been leveled, except those on the far side of the bank of elevators. In several spots, ghostly white sheets covered forms that Jason realized were bodies. He could feel bile rising to his throat.

"What the hell happened?" Jason looked around him searching for anything that he could recognize as being part of his new firm. "The officer told me that there were no survivors…"

"There were five people on the floor when it exploded. Janitorial staff mainly. The people on the other floors survived. The damage was not as extensive, but as far as salvaging anything, highly unlikely. Fortunately it happened at the end of the day."

"Timothy? Do you know if my partner Timothy Greer was…" Jason was not one to panic but could not maintain his calm with the realization that his best friend may have been killed.

"I believe your partner was one of the people taken to the hospital. He was severely burned but alive when they took them away."

"Could you find out if he is going to be okay?" Jason implored.

"I will have one of the officers contact the hospital for an update." He spoke into the small microphone that was attached to a thin wire draped around his neck and connected to an earpiece.

"I have never seen an incendiary device as sophisticated as that used here, even in the decade I spent in Ireland dealing with attacks by the IRA. This was different. I am certain that the devices were planted in the walls."

"What do you mean?"

Detective Bryan led Jason to one of the pillars in the center of the floor. It was more charred than the others. He knelt down and pointed to a spot on the pillar that looked like a bracket of some sort.

"The fire guys think this is one of the hot-spots. There are about a dozen of them scattered throughout the floor. The explosions seem to have emanated from each of these spots. We don't know what accelerant they used, but early indications are that it is military grade. Like napalm, only much stronger, more accurate in its destructive path. We've sent samples to the British War Office to see if they can identify the substance."

"So what about that leg then?" Detective Bryan was not about to let it go.

Jason made a quick decision. This man would help him. Sitting on the charred edge of one of the desks he explained why his leg was cut. The Detective's casual expression knotted with concern as Jason described the executions at the Discoverer's Club, the recessed keypad and the explosion. He started to explain the suicide of Hans but thought better of it.

The detective prodded Jason to give him more information. He had none really, but he continued to answer enough questions to fill the detective's notebook. Although Jason was eventually given permission to go home, Detective Bryan instructed him to stay close by.

But Jason had other plans. He left the building feeling light-headed. From the Discoverer's Club devastation to the Axe bombing, he was suddenly confronted with the harsh reality that his new firm was under attack.

From what he could gather, based on the activity in the building when he arrived, whatever happened must have been done simultaneously with the attack on the club from which he had barely escaped. There was nothing that could explain who would attack him or his firm. He had been in London only a few weeks and, despite his best efforts, he'd not had a lot of time to make many contacts let alone enemies. Nor could he forget that Hans Pedersen had apparently committed suicide by jumping from the top of his office at the Plaza in New York. Jason did not believe in coincidences. Something was happening that he could not explain. He needed to get back to New York to make sense of what was going on in his "new" world.

First, he had to make sure that Timothy was okay. Jason felt responsible for putting Timothy in harm's way. Not that he could have predicted the wild events that happened in the past day. Once he was certain that Timothy was in good hands, he would go to New York and connect with the only person who may have answers—Amy Glass. From what he could see on the television, she was distraught beyond comprehension. Of course she would be devastated; Hans had rescued her from a life on the streets in abject poverty. He had treated her like a daughter. As far as Jason knew, she did not have any family, or even close friends, outside of Thought Mechanix.

She would probably welcome a familiar face.

22

The wheels of the Boeing 767-300 landed hard on the tarmac of JFK airport in New York. The pilot had fought through turbulence during the last half hour of the flight from London, so most of the passengers actually welcomed the hard landing. Jason had slept through the rough ride, but it had been a fitful sleep. Before boarding his last-minute flight back to the States, he'd spent a few hours visiting Timothy at the Chelsea and Westminster Hospital Burn Unit. He wanted to understand the extent of his partner's injuries in order to help Timothy in any way possible. He felt responsible for his best friend and partner.

Over a quarter of Timothy's body was burned, so it was necessary to ensure fluid replacement as the primary objective in treating the burn. The burn damages the skin cells, the doctor explained, and burns make the cells porous, so that where normal cells will stick together, the damaged cells release huge amounts of fluid out of the tissue. If not controlled, the excessive leakage could lead to hypovolemic shock, and possibly death if not properly treated.

Timothy had entered the burn unit in shock and had only been stabilized a few minutes before Jason arrived. The doctor explained that Timothy was lucky, as he was facing away from the incendiary device at the time of the explosion, so his face did not sustain any significant damage. Jason smiled at the sedated body of Tim, knowing he would be pleased to have preserved his boyish good looks. It would be a long road, but Timothy would be alright.

Several others who were brought over from the St. Mary's Axe explosion were not so lucky. The distraught, grieving families of the victims consoled each other. Talk of a terrorist attack was the easy way to explain any unforeseen calamity. Fear was evident in the eyes of the families, the staff, as well as the doctors. The memory of the Tube bombing a few years earlier was all too fresh.

But Jason knew this was no random terrorist attack. The men who blew up the offices of Thought Mechanix and the Discoverer's Club knew exactly what they were doing. Thinking back on the person who had punched the keypad at the Club, and the Scotland Yard detective's explanation of the planted explosions, the only conclusion that seemed logical was that both "attacks" were self-inflicted. Two buildings, both connected to Thought Mechanix, were destroyed at the same time.

More importantly, Jason thought, as the plane taxied to the jet bridge, the decision to do so must have been prompted by the news that Hans Pedersen had apparently committed suicide by jumping from his penthouse office. Looking around the plane, he could only surmise that his fellow passengers were either oblivious of the recent events that had rocked his world, or totally desensitized to the random violence that seemed to be a common occurrence in a media-saturated world. They were only excited about going to the Big Apple.

Without luggage, Jason made his way curbside within minutes of deplaning. By the time the baggage conveyor started to roll, he was comfortably in the back of a Lincoln Town Car headed for Manhattan, still groggy from the six-hour flight. He dozed off until the driver gently woke him as they entered the Holland Tunnel.

"The traffic is going to be a brute. Some guy 86'd himself downtown, yesterday, where ya wanna go. Do ya want I drop ya off someplace else? He was some big shot PR guru, Ya know the guy, Hans Pedersen. He created the Rules of Possibility. Got 'em right here," the driver pointed to his CD player. "Media circus hasn't stopped. The clowns of Network America love a jumper, 'specially the famous ones. I wonder what could depress a man so much as to do that. And a person who's entire life was dedicated to helping others succeed?"

Jason could only mumble his instructions to the driver, to take him to his original destination.

The driver shook his head at the callousness of his passenger who seemed indifferent to the tragedy.

It had been less than a day, Jason realized, since he had been standing in the private den of the Discoverer's Club watching the footage moments after Hans fell to his death. But Jason couldn't believe that Hans was dead, and apparently of his own volition. The man had established himself as an international icon, like Madonna or Warren Buffett. He had ridden his success train aggressively. Only two weeks earlier Hans had been on set, taping his latest program, the Rules of Possibility II. The man seemed on top of the world. Unstoppable.

Yet there was the strange disappearance at the office before they discussed Jason's move to London. And the urgency of the request that he get on with his program. Hans insisted that Jason make contact with Lord Barton as soon as he established himself in London.

Something did not add up. For an accountant, the facts always had to add up. The balance sheet had to be equal on both sides. It was a matter of logic. But the man's urgency to get Jason set up in London, his zealous attention to the design of their new office, even before Jason and Timothy arrived, and his subsequent conversations with Jason the week leading up to Jason's move were not logical for someone who just committed suicide.

He needed to find Amy to figure out what was going on. He needed to find Amy to make sure she was alright. He knew that they would never be together—they were too different—but he knew that, right then, he really needed Amy.

The Lincoln Town Car pulled up in front of the Plaza amidst a cacophony of car horns, blathering news reporters and mobs of devoted TMI followers coming to pay homage to the man they saw as their savior. Church leaders were gathered in the fray, seemingly recruiting at a time that the lost souls looked desperately for a place to turn.

Jason paid the driver and exited the vehicle, making his way through the mass of people to reach the entrance of the building. As he approached it, he was surprised to see the doors guarded by a cadre of private security, a contingent of New York's finest, and what looked like a SWAT team. They were interspersed among the throngs of people trying to get into the building, trying to get closer to anything that connected them to their icon, Jason supposed.

He pushed his way to the front of the throng, where he was stopped at the door, like everyone else, by a thick-necked man in blue.

The officer guarding the door held up a hand in Jason's face. "Sorry, sir. This is a restricted area. No one is allowed in the building."

"I need to get inside. Hans was a close friend. I work with him in his London office—"

"Sorry, sir, no one's allowed in." The officer moved his imposing body in front of Jason as if to form a second barrier in addition to the revolving door.

"Could I speak to your commanding officer? It really is important that I speak to someone from Mr. Pedersen's organization." He mentioned Amy Glass. Jason had been trying to contact her since leaving the hospital in London, but for some reason, he kept getting a "no longer in service" message. Jason figured the only way he was going to contact Amy was to track her down at the Thought Mechanix New York office.

Jason provided his name and other details at the officer's request. The officer spoke into the microphone pinned to the shoulder of his uniform.

Eventually he turned to Jason. "Seems like someone up there knows who you are. My commander will be down shortly to speak to you personally. You must be important." The man in blue shrugged his shoulders and directed Jason to stand out of the way and wait.

In the short time it took the elevator to travel the forty stories to the lobby, the commander was approaching Jason. The man was dressed in a full SWAT outfit—complete with bulletproof vest, helmet and jack boots. Commander Jackson Thorne was every bit the military man. His rugged face was etched with deep creases, each one a reminder of the many battle zones he had survived. The dark intensity of his eyes unnerved his colleagues as much as the terrorist targets he pursued and captured.

"Mr. Wakefield. I was told you were looking for Ms. Glass." Thorne's penetrating voice was strong and direct.

"I was looking for Amy Glass to find out what happened. Her cell phone seems to be disconnected. I'm a business associate of Hans Pedersen. And a friend. Amy was one person I was hoping could help make sense of what happened. I was in London when I heard the news—" Jason did not have a chance to finish.

"Do you have any idea what *exactly* happened here, Mr. Wakefield? Why *I* am here?" Thorne stressed this last question as if any fool would be able to surmise that a calamity of unspeakable proportions was the only thing that would rouse him from his command post.

Thinking about the carnage he just left, Jason was afraid he knew exactly what to expect, but he kept silent. Something that he was sure he would regret later.

"Perhaps if you just came from London you can help explain to us what happened here?" Thorne continued, "Follow me."

Five minutes later they were standing in the middle of the same type of devastation that Jason had left in London twelve hours earlier. The entire area that had housed the sophisticated security equipment was reduced to a blackened pile of rubble. As in London, the interior walls were gone, only a few resilient pieces of computer hardware and structural components of the building remained. Jason noticed several brackets on a nearby pillar that were like the ones in the St. Mary's Axe office. This building was also set to self-destruct.

Thorne noticed the recognition in Jason's eyes. *This man had seen similar devastation before.* Sensing that Jason was in a quandary, Thorne provided an explanation, "From what our bomb experts have been able to determine, highly sophisticated incendiary packets were built into the leaseholds. These were put here by the owners, or by someone that wanted to destroy the premises at their will. Why would anyone do that?"

Thorne left the question hanging, staring at Jason as if willing the answer to be extracted from his mind.

"I don't know." Jason spoke slowly, not sure if he should reveal the similarity to the destruction in London. He was afraid that he might be implicated. Two similar bombings, in two cities a continent away, and he seemed to be the only one still standing. What if they suspected him to be behind the destruction? What if they also connected him to the Discoverer's Club bloodbath? All of a sudden he felt a need to get out.

"Are you alright?" Thorne's voice softened. He might be wrong about the young man, although he doubted it. He survived three decades as a terrorist specialist because he was able to judge the reactions of people. Jason Wakefield knew something but was not sure how to express his knowledge. Eventually it would surface. For now, Thorne chose to interpret Jason's anxiety for mild shock over the devastation he had just witnessed.

"Did anyone survive?"

"From what we can gather, the building was empty, maybe a few night janitors. There were deaths, but we have yet to identify any of the human remains," Thorne replied without emotion. The thought of one death or one hundred deaths had no effect on him after two tours in Vietnam as a gunner on a whirly-bird.

"Come on. I'm sure you've had a long flight and you're tired." Thorne led him down the elevator away from the destruction. Once they were back in the lobby, Thorne took Jason's contact information. "Just in case we need to ask you anything further."

"When did this happen?" Jason asked as he was led out the door.

"Around four this morning." Thorne handed Jason a business card. "Don't go anywhere. I'd like to know how I can reach you if there are any more questions."

Jason took the card. "What do you mean? Do you consider me a person of interest regarding this? I wasn't even in the country."

Thorne looked hard at Jason like a schoolmaster admonishing one of his students. "I'd like you to stick around in case there are more questions. I don't expect you to leave the country."

"I have to go back. My partner is currently in a London hospital with multiple burns over most of his body. He needs me."

"No traveling without my permission. You have my card," Thorne said brusquely as he left Jason at the door.

Jason quickly calculated the time since he had left the Discoverer's Club. Twelve hours. A sense of dread flooded his mind as he realized that the Plaza explosion occurred at exactly the same time as the two London bombings. Someone wanted all things tied to Hans destroyed.

Moreover, they had planned for the eventuality that it would need to happen.

Who would orchestrate such an elaborate system to ensure the destruction of everything connected to Hans? And why?

23

It was a few minutes before two, Thursday afternoon in New York, a time when the city hung in limbo between a hectic business zoo and a street fest of white-sheet vendors and high-strung tourists looking to energize the town that never sleeps. Jason stared out the window onto Fifth Avenue from his perch inside Starbucks. He sipped on a chocolate banana Vivanno laced with a double shot of espresso to give him the needed energy to do what he had to do next. The cool drink soothed his battered throat, rough from a day of breathing in fumes from smoke-filled buildings.

Jason mulled over the events of the last twenty-four hours. His world had imploded. Everything he'd worked towards had disappeared in a burst of flames, literally. As was his nature, he turned to practical requirements. He needed to talk to the human resources people of his old firm to tie up some loose ends for Timothy. Make sure his insurance coverage they had negotiated on their exit was still intact. Fill out some forms to get money to him in London.

Jason looked around as he entered the lobby. Wakefield and Associates had transformed in the brief time that he had been away. Gone were the bright colors and the trendy artwork. The stainless-steel sign showing the name of the firm had been replaced with large wooden letters announcing the new regime: Stanford and Dixon. Blair had finally achieved his wish—a firm under his thumb. Yet he wasn't powerful enough to prevent Miriam Dixon from garnering a place on the letterhead. Jason smiled at the thought.

The modern art pieces that had adorned the walls of his firm, all borrowed from prominent New York artists, were replaced with gilded frames of landscapes and portraits. It looked like a golf course clubhouse from the seventies. His receptionist was also gone. Collateral damage, he surmised. In her place, a fifty-something lady, dressed as if for a funeral, was manning the phones.

He strode to the reception desk. He decided to ask to see Miriam, figuring she was the safest one to seek out. Maybe she could enlighten him as to what was happening at Thought Mechanix since his move to London.

"Mr. Wakefield, it's nice to see you in one piece," the receptionist smiled up at Jason as he approached the desk. "You must have had quite the ordeal in London. Mr. Stanford and Ms. Dixon said we might expect a visit."

"How…Wha…? Jason stammered at the unexpected greeting.

"I'm Joan Wetherill. Spent thirty years at Morgan Stanley before Blair enticed me over. I make it my business to know what's going on in my firm, Mr. Wakefield. Your ordeal in London has been all over CNN for the last twelve hours. They even have footage of you walking from the Discoverer's Club explosion…" She left the comment hanging, as if there were more to the story. "You must be here to pick up the package."

Without waiting for an answer, Ms. Wetherill stood up and walked into the anteroom next to reception where the couriers and other outgoing client records were sorted and stored for later delivery. She reappeared a moment later with a package the size of a milk carton. On top was an envelope, bound to the package by an elastic band. She handed the package to Jason then promptly sat back down at her station to take an incoming call. She mouthed an acknowledgement to him that she would buzz Miriam.

Well, maybe not so bad a change, he conceded, as he sat down in one of the new leather armchairs adorning the waiting area. He did not have to wait long. Miriam Dixon rounded the corner into the reception area less than a minute after Jason sat down.

Miriam was a forty-eight-year-old Big4 product who had joined Wakefield on the heels of Blair Stanford. Rumor had it that the two of them were involved, but Jason only saw them engage in a hard-fisted professional relationship. Not that she wasn't worth the trip. Miriam was a stunning redhead with a fiery body to match. She and her husband were weekend warriors on the Ironman circuit and her physical presence left many of her colleagues, both male and female, only guessing what she'd be like in bed.

Miriam wrapped her shapely arms around Jason in a fashion that landed somewhere between a warming relief from an elderly aunt and a clutching embrace from a long-lost lover. Jason returned the squeeze, feeling the intensity and heat of the embrace. Miriam released herself and led Jason back to her office.

"I am so relieved that you're okay. We've only heard snippets from the news. Even our contacts at the Times were tight-lipped about what they read on the wire. Is it true that the two floors of St. Mary's Axe were virtually destroyed by the explosion? CNN only showed footage from outside the building. Apparently, the entire building was locked down by the police. Your name was mentioned…"

Another fishing expedition, Jason noted. Just like the receptionist. Since he didn't really know what was going on, he figured he'd better find out what they knew. But first things first.

"Timothy was injured. Quite badly burned. "

"Oh my God. Is he alright?" Miriam's shock revealed itself as the blood drained from her face.

"He's in the burn unit at Chelsea and Westminster Hospital in Central London. It's the reason I came here."

Miriam's eyes shifted to the package on the chair next to him as he explained the purpose of his visit. Jason wondered if they thought he knew the package was there waiting for him.

"I'd like to ask if the firm could make sure his medical coverage stays intact as well as arrange to get him back to the States. It would mean a lot. It's fortunate for Timothy that I negotiated a two-year post-departure extension to our participation in the benefit plan."

"Of course, Jason. Anything to help. It's a real shock. CNN did not mention any casualties." Miriam smiled with true sincerity. It was why Jason spoke to her and not to Blair.

"I haven't had time to watch the news. I've been traveling for the past twelve hours. Can you enlighten me?"

Miriam stood up and walked over to a bar fridge, retrieving two small bottles of San Pellegrino, handing one to Jason.

"No one really knows anything it seems. And since the suicide and explosion next door, they have been running interviews with all sorts of crackpots who have an opinion about Thought Mechanix—

conspiracy theorists, religious zealots, TMI converts, Republicans—the usual crowd. The news people are trying to create a connection between Hans and a radical religious faction, that there was a falling-out between Hans and these people, and that *they* were the cause of the explosions. There is no thread of proof, but it's the story people want to hear. Everyone needs to have a reason for the unexpected, the black swans in life that blindside our sensibilities."

"And me, you mentioned that I was part of that story."

"CNN especially seems to want to connect you to their theory. You were present, or almost present, at every explosion. You were deeply involved in TMI, even leaving the country to pursue a closer connection to Hans—"

"Wait a minute," Jason blurted out. "How do they know where I have been in the last two days?"

Miriam held up her hand to hold back his tirade, "Someone must have tipped them off. A reporter was here an hour after the explosion next door, looking for you, specifically. They don't know enough to connect the dots. That's why Blair and I were...*are* happy that you came by. We know you. We know how passionate you are about what Hans was doing."

"But—"

"But...before we go and defend you against the media, we wanted to hear your side of the story."

Jason could feel his blood start to percolate. He had a hot temper when his well-controlled ego was threatened. This was unbelievable... they actually thought he might be a terrorist.

His voice rose as he spoke, thankful that he was behind closed doors. "What the hell are you saying? That you think Timothy and I are involved in some sort of plot?"

"Of course not, Jason. At least, I don't. I know you too well. You are all business, no political ideology as far as I've ever seen. But we want to sound credible when we go to the press."

"Miriam, believe me when I tell you, I know nothing about what Hans might or might not have been involved in. He had asked me to do some unusual assignments in London, but they involved more PR than anything. He seemed anxious to get his latest round of the Rules of Possibility activated, like he was on a tight schedule to deliver. I was helping him set up the channels. My life has been in a state of chaos since yesterday…"

Jason stopped himself. He had no idea what was going on or why Miriam, and especially Blair Stanford for that matter, would give a rat's ass about what he was up to. They fought too hard to get him ousted from his own firm to care what happened to him now.

And then it dawned on him.

"You're concerned about the reputation of the firm. That's all there is to this!" Jason sat back and laughed as he noticed a deep shade of red spread across Miriam's cheeks.

"Of course we care about that, Jason." Blair Stanford's booming voice growled from the doorway. The grey-maned business man entered the room. "But this is different."

Jason turned and started to get up, bile rising in his throat.

"Blair," he managed to spit out, with a slight nod of this head.

Stanford ignored the greeting and continued. "Despite our professional differences we care about you and Timothy. It seems that you may have pissed off some very powerful people who have a very high level of influence with the press."

"What do you mean?"

Miriam spoke up. "Blair spoke to his contacts at *The Times, The Journal* and NBC after we saw the footage from London and heard about the connection CNN tried to make between Hans, you, and some clandestine group called the Guardians. They have all been fed a storyline that amount to the same thing. It was well orchestrated. We discussed it." Miriam looked over at Blair. "You were a very convenient person in whatever complex game is being played. You were meant to be where you were when you were."

Blair picked up the thread. "So, I'd like you to tell me your side so that I can have the FBI back off any investigation concerning you and Timothy. You win and we avoid a scandal."

Jason wanted to leave. He had no desire to repeat the story he just gave to Miriam. But he needed to be sure his old firm, and his former partners, would be there if he needed them, for whatever reason.

Despite his resentment, he repeated his story, right from when he arrived in London to start his new company.

Fifteen minutes later, he had the distinct impression that Blair wasn't really interested; there was nothing in Jason's tale that would help or hurt his new firm. Jason stopped midstream and changed the topic.

He picked up the package. "So do you know where this package came from?"

"Amy Glass dropped it off. She made sure it was delivered directly to me." Miriam stood up and retrieved three bottles of water and handed them around.

"Amy…when was she here?" Jason's mind whirled when Miriam mentioned the Guardians. It was the same organization that Amy spoke of on the phone. *Who was she really, and who were the Guardians?*

"Yesterday." She thought for a moment. "I was heading out for the day. She seemed anxious to get rid of it. Amy told me that I was only to give it to you when you showed up, not to mail it to London under any circumstances. She was adamant about that."

"Did she say why did she delivered it here? She knew I was no longer part of the firm. She knew where I was in London; in fact, she was there a few days after I arrived for meetings."

Jason looked between Blair and Miriam for any sign of why Amy may have acted so unusually.

"She said that she wanted me to make sure the package was safe, and that you would be back here when the time was right. As she was leaving, Amy grabbed my arm, as if to reassure herself that the package was in safe hands. I assured her that the letter and package would be safe and secure."

"What did she mean by that?" Jason was perplexed.

"She said that when you read the letter you would understand."

24

Jason's mind was frantically trying to sort out the events of the past few days. He sat in a food court drinking a Coke, recalling the events. People bustled around him, grabbing their late-afternoon snacks before returning to their offices to finish off the day. Mothers with strollers, tourists, and teens with time on their hands lingered in the plastic seats around him, making noise, laughing at their own jokes. Jason blocked out the noise. He began to piece together the events that led him back to New York. The open package given to him by Miriam Dixon, his former partner, sat on the table next to his drink, its contents lying in his lap. He focused on the letter. There was a key taped to the letter. Putting the key in his pocket, he read the letter for the third time:

Jason,

If you are reading this, then it has already begun. You are my only hope because you understand the power of the Rules. A power that has caused a catastrophic shift in consciousness that Hans had no knowledge of when he began. This shift in human consciousness was intentional, and Hans was manipulated into being its creator. When he found out what was happening, he tried to stop the momentum. His seminar at the Stern was the start of his revelation. At first I thought he was crazy about the effects that the Rules of Possibility were having, but I have since learned the truth.

What you do not know about me is that I was placed at Thought Mechanix by the organization who was manipulating Hans. I was recruited to report back to them on everything that happened at Thought Mechanix. All of Hans's actions were relayed to my superiors. That was up to a few months ago, when I realized what was happening. Since then, I have been trying to help Hans reverse what he had been manipulated into doing.

Hans became obsessed with his desire to release us from the bonds of religious-created beliefs, a manipulation that he had become a party to in an experiment gone horribly wrong. The concepts had dangers right from the beginning, dangers not known to my superiors. They had manipulated Hans to start a chain reaction with the introduction of the Rules of Possibility. As the movement grew, it took on a life of its own. People began to change. The world began to shift away from religion, something unexpected was happening and it scared him. He naively believed in the inherent goodness of man, but it became clear the Rules took hold of the popular consciousness in ways that even my superiors did not expect. They saw it as a path to success. What they did not foresee was the cost to the millions of unfortunate people who were…are being manipulated by negative forces.

These negative forces have been created by the teachings of Thought Mechanix just as all of the positive influences. Whatever my superiors were hoping to achieve has long since vanished. There is a pervasive negative energy that has taken hold in the world. A force so powerful it has the potential of choking the positive healthy energy that Hans thought he was activating in people. Han was convinced that thought energy could connect in some visceral way to free the world from the limiting bonds of man-made religion. To him, the real power of TMI was the freedom from the constraints that have been controlling the human mind for thousands of years. He was sure he had figured it out.

It was during a trip to Italy that Hans discovered something that opened his eyes to what was going on. He was doing research on the origins of the power of the Rules when he learned the truth. It suggested the original Rules were creating unexpected consequences, which were frightening to him. He was devastated by the news and confided in me after his return. After learning the truth, I came clean to Hans about my involvement with his handlers. The men who did this to him were not aware that I had told Hans.

Feeding false information to my superiors allowed Hans to begin the ROP II series in secret. The new series of thought energy mechanics was an attempt to try and reverse the effects of the initial series. But the people for whom I worked learned of his clandestine work. They confronted him, convincing him that he caused the negative shift in human consciousness and that he alone was responsible for the effects that ROP had on the world. Hans became obsessed with fixing what he had done but quickly lost faith in his abilities. He became despondent, convinced that he had gone too far and could not reverse things.

That is why, by the time you read this letter, he will be dead; destroyed by an organization that put the safeguards in place so that what he had built could be destroyed by one simple push of a button. The button was pushed minutes after Hans plunged to his death. What you need to know is that ROP II was his attempt to try *and reverse the effects the first series. The original Rules were derived from ancient teachings, written on a cuneiform tablet known as the Third Book of Eden. It was referred to as the Book of Thought. What Hans and I did not know was that by creating and distributing the Rules, an unspeakable power was unleashed. Please read the papers or watch the news on television to see what I mean.*

You are also a victim—another link that needed to be eliminated. But I refused to do it. I'm sorry that I got you involved, but I need you. I am not able to finish what Hans has started. They will know. I also cannot carry out the task they have asked of me. You need to help me. Hans believed in you. He told me several times that you were the person with the conviction to bring his ideas to the world. You believed in the good of Thought Mechanix, using it as Hans had intended. I know that the pundits believed it was about ridding the world of organized religion and replacing it with the one and only Truth. But it was much more than that.

You recall the four tablets in Hans's office? Three are replicas of the first three Books of Eden. The fourth was a re-creation of what was rumored to be the fourth and final tablet. He told me that he discovered a link to the existence of this fourth book. Its existence is as much legend as fact. He referred to this book as the Book of the Journey to the Source. He swore me to secrecy. I was torn between my loyalty to the Guardians and my faith in Hans. I felt that I should have told my superiors but feared my life would be worth nothing. I feared for Hans.

I am a true disciple of Hans's vision of the world. The deceit that he suffered at the hands of the organization that set him up in the first place led to his death. Now that he is dead, any chance of reversing the destruction caused by his misguided teachings diminishes. He was right, but he was convinced he was wrong. Now I know the Book of Thought was not the elixir it was said to be.

Perhaps the fourth tablet will provide clues as to what went wrong. In the package enclosed, there are three DVDs, the first cut of the initial segments of the ROP II infomercial. Hans said that if anything happened I was to give them to you. I entrusted this letter and the DVDs to Miriam Dixon. You always spoke highly of her integrity. I couldn't think of anyone else whom I could trust. Hans drafted his commentary on the DVDs to provide the instructions needed to understand the Book of Thought, to understand what is needed to effect any change in the current pattern of negative consciousness.

Hans said he had knowledge as to the existence of the Fourth Book of Eden. That it was not a myth. He never told me how he discovered its existence, but from his telephone records I had pretty much figured it out. He spoke numerous times to a woman in Italy whose name is Carmen. I kept a journal of my discussions with Hans just in case I needed to defend my actions to the Guardians. I dare not reveal what I wrote in the notebook, as I do not know what will become of this letter once I leave it with Miriam. The notebook is hidden in my apartment. You'll find it inside my most favorite thing in the world.

I fear that if we meet in person you will be a target. So I will stay away from you to protect you from my deceptions. You will know what to do once you read the journal. The contact information for Carmen is in the notebook. Make sure Hans did not die in vain.

Love, Amy

P.S. The Guardians are dangerous.

Jason stared at the letter in disbelief. How could Amy have let Hans die? She knew what was going to happen. So what if these people were powerful, without regard to any borders? She was a part of them, yet she cared about Hans. Just not enough to save his life. It was not the Amy that he had grown so close to in the past few years. Somehow, though, she must not be the monster that appears to have allowed the man she loved be killed if she had the foresight to try and make sure that his work was carried on after his death. Jason had to believe that Amy must have been incapable of stopping what transpired.

One thing was clear to Jason—Hans Pedersen did not commit suicide. He was murdered. Probably by the same people who coolly blew up three buildings on two continents with the precision of an atomic clock. The three buildings were connected to Hans Pedersen and Thought Mechanix. Destroyed simultaneously. More perplexing was the method used. All of the facilities were hardwired for self-destruction right from the beginning. They were built to be eliminated, presumably in the event of circumstances that threatened the organization. Hans's suicide seemed to be the triggering event.

Jason contemplated briefly his predicament. The FBI was asking questions about his involvement; possible links to terrorists were being touted by the media. Clearly somebody beyond Hans was in control. It was that realization that stumped Jason. He had known Hans for a long time, a period of time in which the little ball of energy never alluded to being connected to anything bigger than his own greatness. As far as Jason was concerned, when it came to Thought Mechanix and the Rules of Possibility, everything began and ended with Hans Pedersen.

That thinking was clearly wrong. It was evident that the person or people responsible for destroying the Thought Mechanix network were ruthless. He had no idea how many people died in the three explosions, and others, like Timothy, who were lucky enough just to be alive. Jason had no idea why he was still alive. *Was that by accident or design?*

After finishing his drink, Jason threw the plastic cup in the waste bin beside the door. He turned to exit the food court when the picture on the late edition of the paper caught his eye. Amy's tear-stained face stared back at him from the page. Her picture was below a headline that read "The Face of Mourning." He picked up the section of the paper and settled back into a chair to read.

Amy was quoted as saying that Hans Pedersen seemed out of sorts since the Stern Auditorium explosion. She identified herself as head of Public Relations at Thought Mechanix. Jason though that was unusual, but dismissed it as a misunderstanding as he read on...

"No one is really sure what was going on in Mr. Pedersen's head. One minute he was the gregarious person that everyone identifies with in his infomercials, and the next he would tear a strip off of you for no reason."

Amy Glass, executive assistant to Mr. Pedersen, was distraught as she fought back tears to answer this reporter's questions. Thought Mechanix creator Hans Pedersen seemed to be a very unlikely candidate for suicide. His popular CD instruction series, Rules of Possibility, espoused the belief that we all had control over our thoughts. The program reputedly saved hundreds of people from committing the very act that ended the life of one of the great men of our century, indeed of any century.

And yet we need not be reminded of the recent spate of turmoil that had gripped his world. Opponents of Thought Mechanix, including this journalist, have cautioned readers about the negative power of the application. Each time I personally tried to discuss these issues with Mr. Pedersen I was rebuffed. Perhaps, now, a glimpse into his greatness shows all of us that it is never as perfect as we would like to believe.

Amy Glass left me with a sobering thought as she too mourns the death of her boss and mentor.

"Hans Pedersen was only an inch away from ending his own life when he came up with the concepts that evolved into the Rules of Possibility. He used this as a way to avoid moving that last inch. He was as vulnerable as the rest of us. There is no cure for our shortcomings, no matter what one may think. Even the great Hans Pedersen was haunted by his own demons."

Jason stared, eyes frozen on the white and black newsprint. He could not believe what he'd just read. The words were quoted as Amy's, but it was ludicrous to think they were hers. Especially after reading her letter. She adored Hans, worshipped the very ground he walked on, and never stopped believing in the power for good that was possible when applying the Rules of Possibility—potential under any circumstance. Her comments made no sense. Jason could only think that maybe whoever destroyed the Thought Mechanix offices in London and New York had regained control over Amy and were forcing her to disparage Hans to the world.

A light drizzle fell on the sidewalk as Jason walked up to the hotel he had booked before boarding the flight from London. His stomach growled. He looked at his watch and was surprised to see that it was already past nine. He tried calling Amy at her home number, but there was no answer. After leaving his old office, he bought some clothes and toiletries, having left London without any luggage. He decided to check in and drop the bags off at his hotel before heading out to find a late dinner.

An hour later he was sitting in Mark's at a corner table, enjoying a medium-rare steak with onion rings and a glass of dark red Oregon merlot. Jason was not a wine snob, but he had spent considerable time trying to understand the grape varietals, especially the supple art of matching a wine to different foods. He let the velvet liquid swirl in his mouth for a few seconds before swallowing, the thirteen percent alcohol content having the desired effect.

"Haven't see ya around here much, Mr. Wakefield."

Jason looked up and smiled as Bruno G, his favorite waiter, took the bottle of wine and filled his glass. Jason used to eat at Mark's at least once a week when he first started his own firm, often by himself when he just wanted a good meal with no social interaction. It was a place where the waiters respected the privacy of the restaurant patrons, often forming long-term bonds with customers. Bruno served Jason his first steak in New York when he was a young accounting student. Besides being an exceptional judge of character, Bruno had an ear for his customer's emotions.

"No. Not much. I've been working in London."

"Yeah, I heard about the coup d'état at your office."

"More like a lynching," Jason laughed with Bruno at his own expense.

"I'm sorry to hear about Hans. He was one of the great ones." Jason and Hans spent many late night dinners at Mark's under the watchful eye of the burly, bald-headed waiter. "That why you're back?"

"Yeah, that and I needed to finalize a few things with the old firm." Jason lied, and he knew Bruno knew he lied. A brief glance from Bruno as he backed away from the table said it all: *Let me know if you need any help.*

Jason motioned him back. "Bruno, have you read the article about Hans in the paper? The quote from Amy?"

"Strange. She was here the night before the article came out."

This time Bruno took a seat next to Jason, glancing up briefly towards the maître de for approval. It was granted with a slight nod. Mark's was one of those places in New York that the regulars and the waiters were on a first name basis. *Casual elegance* was how Mark Jackson, the owner, once described his restaurant to a critic from Zagat's. The remark received a stiff rebuke from the preeminent rating Czar. The notoriety only fuelled the restaurant's success.

"You've seen Amy?"

"Like I said, she was in here two days ago. She sat in the lounge. There were five of them talking in hushed tones. They all listened intently to a fourth man who clearly directed the conversation. When Amy saw me she averted her gaze. When they left it looked like Amy was being led out of the restaurant."

"Against her will?"

"Didn't think much of it at the time, but…with that article, I wonder."

"Did you recognize any of the people?"

"No. They looked foreign. The suits looked like a European cut. If I were to guess, I'd say Italian."

"Bruno, you have a good eye for clothes but not that good. I've seen you in your street clothes."

The two of them laughed at this. Bruno, despite the black pants and white dress shirt he wore at Mark's usually donned sweats and a tee-shirt.

"They were Italian for sure."

"And you know this because…"

Bruno smiled like the cat who ate the canary, ready to expose a dark secret. Leaning forward, he lowered his voice to a whisper.

"To begin with, the talkative one was a Cardinal, red robes and all, like he was usually wandering the halls of the Vatican."

25

Jason thought back to the last time he met with Hans at his office—the quick departure and phone call from Italy that required his immediate attention. Amy dismissed him that day by suggesting the call was routine. Obviously she knew what was going on. The Guardians kept her in the loop. Amy was now reunited with these men, who appeared to be connected to the Church. He wondered if Amy was in trouble. Now he really needed to find her, doubting she was still alive. The thought that she too might be dead sent a cold chill through his body. Despite his fear, he knew what he needed to do next.

It was eleven by the time he stepped out of the taxi outside of Amy's apartment. The streets were emptied of the busy daytime pedestrian traffic. The apartment was in a trendy, restored brownstone building a block from Central Park in a revitalized Harlem a few minutes from the famed Apollo Theatre. Year's earlier it would have been a death sentence to wander the streets past dark in this section of New York. Now most of the area was more or less safe, although the back alleys, where drug deals still went down regularly, were best to avoid.

Sidestepping a young couple exiting the building hand-in-hand, Jason took the steps to the front door three at a time to catch the door before it shut. The young couple did not bother to look back as Jason slipped through the door and headed up the stairs to Amy's third floor apartment. He had only been to her apartment once after a TMI release. He woke up on her couch the next morning after having a few too many glasses of single malt scotch the night before. Amy nursed his hangover with a strong coffee and a greasy breakfast before sending him on his way. Since that day, Jason had developed a special attachment to Amy, although, for some reason, he never pursued the possibility of a relationship. Amy was too connected to Hans Pedersen to take notice of him.

The apartment was one of two converted attic lofts that were accessed by a half set of stairs at opposite ends of the third floor. Jason turned to the right as he reached the third floor landing and made his way along the narrow hallway to the attic staircase. He was halfway to the stairs when he slowed his pace, realizing that something was wrong. A dull light from the top of the attic stairs illuminated the entrance to Amy's apartment.

"Amy? Amy, are you in there?" Jason called out as he ascended the stairs.

"Amy, why is your…door open…"

He finished the sentence silently as he walked into the midst of an apartment that had been torn apart. The disarray before him was cyclonic in magnitude. Furniture had been ripped apart and toppled over, all of the pictures taken forcibly off the walls, each one systematically ripped apart and left where they had been dismantled. In the small kitchen, all the drawers had been emptied of their contents, the bottom drawer of the stove tossed aside. The fridge and freezer were also empty, save for a tub of Ben and Jerry's Rocky Road ice cream, leaking from its plastic container.

"What the—"

Jason jumped at the lyrical voice behind him, swerving around in a defensive stance that defied any martial arts training; but he tripped on a box of granola, which sent him flying backwards against an open cupboard door. A second later he watched as the person who had uttered the question faded into a dull grey. Then the unfamiliar face disappeared altogether.

"Are you alright?"

Jason had just opened his eyes. He was looking up into the dark eyes of the woman who had startled him and sent him flying into the cupboard door.

"Are you alright?" the lyrical voice asked again. "That was quite the fall."

The woman was sitting next to him on the floor, holding a cold cloth to the back of his head. She was wearing a yellow sari accented with an equally vibrant yellow pashmina that hung loosely over her shoulders. Her eyes were framed by a thick, flowing mane of dark hair, brushed to a beautiful sheen. Her voice was rhythmic, lilting and sweet. Only an East Indian accent could do that to the English language.

"Yeah, yeah, I'm fine. I think." Jason reached back to feel the bump on the back of his head. He sat upright beside his kneeling angel of mercy.

"What are you doing in Amy's apartment?" Her tone did not evince suspicion or concern as to whether the intruder was either guilty or dangerous. It was like a mother querying a child about a broken cookie jar.

She handed him the wet cloth for his head. Unlike many other cultures, the female members of the Hindu population grew up with an unerring knowledge that they were powerful, intelligent beings whose contribution to their society was important, at least as important as their male counterparts. As a result, they were confident when dealing with unusual situations, like the one Jasmine found herself in. She, too, had noticed the dull light coming from Amy's apartment when she arrived. When she went to investigate, she startled Jason in the kitchen. From his comical attempt at self-defense, Jasmine quickly surmised that he was not dangerous.

Still, she wanted to know if this man had something to do with the trashing of the apartment. "So, why are you destroying Amy's apartment?" Jasmine asked, intuitively knowing that he was not responsible.

She had worked as a foreign correspondent for a major newspaper, that is, until recently when the latest market meltdown decimated the economy and her newspaper. She had been with that newspaper since graduating from the London School of Journalism six years earlier. As a child who had grown up amid the strife in Kashmir, in northern India, she was a natural investigative reporter, unafraid of any situation. The region was in a constant state of flux, as both Pakistan and India claimed the resource-rich region as their own. Jasmine knew as a small child that she wanted to be a reporter, to be able to tell the world that her homeland was better than the political bickering that made it a hell on earth. After required service and two university degrees, she landed in New York.

"I…it was this way when I arrived…hey, wait! I'm a friend of Amy's. I should ask you the same question. Why are you here?"

"Amy and I go to Pilates together. When I saw the door open I came to investigate. That's when I was attacked by you." She tittered softly.

"Yeah, well, you did sneak up on me." Jason laughed with her. "I'm Jason Wakefield, by the way." Jason held out his hand.

"Jasmine Shah," she replied with a slightly deepened voice, taking his hand and pumping it twice in mock formality. "So you're Jason. Amy spoke of you a few times. The bright accountant, she called you. You may be bright but not very careful." Jasmine laughed again as she took the cloth from his head and went to re-soak it in the sink.

"Expect danger when you least expect it. I must have slept through that lesson in accounting school." Jason smiled then grimaced, as the expression had caused him pain. He looked up at Jasmine as she stood at the sink, the stream of water cascading over her soft hands. Her profile was exquisite: high cheekbones framing soft, oval eyes, made up ever so slightly with a warm shade of earth-toned eye-shadow. Her dark hair fell down over her shoulders, lightly touching her breasts, which drew Jason's attention for a moment. They were perfectly suited to her slender body, a prominent feature, like palms trees on a beach, accentuating the beauty of the landscape. Her nipples were hard, probably from the cold water, but Jason paused for a moment to enjoy the way they strained to break through the silky fabric.

"When was the last time you saw Amy?" she asked, turning. She caught Jason's stare, then smiled as she pressed air into her lungs to improve the view.

Jason noted her movement and the glint in her eyes. Then he flashed a guilty smile. "I haven't seen her in a few weeks, since I moved my offices to London. What do you think happened here?"

Jasmine bent down next to Jason to apply the cloth to the back of his head, holding there with a slight pressure. "The last time I saw Amy was at Pilates class on Saturday. Now that I think about it, she seemed distracted. When we came back here, she asked me if I had seen anyone come around in the last few days. When I told her I hadn't seen anyone, she seemed relieved."

"I was speaking with a waiter at Mark's Steak House who said Amy was with a group of strangers. One of them was a Catholic priest of some sort. He said she looked intensely preoccupied."

"I didn't see anyone around here that matches that description. Do you think they tore this place apart?" Jasmine looked around at the destroyed apartment.

"Maybe, but I doubt it. Bruno at Mark's said that Amy seemed to know the men at the restaurant. Someone rougher did this. They must have been told to search for something. This place is too torn up; the people who did this didn't know where to look."

Jason glanced over at the Indian beauty, trying to decide if he should confide in her the reason why he was in Amy's apartment. He felt a comfortable confidence in the woman that suggested she could be trusted. "I came here to find something that Amy told me she hid in her apartment," Jason commented finally, more of a statement than a question.

"From the looks of things, someone got here before you and probably found it," Jasmine replied. She started to stand up but then stopped. "I guess I shouldn't move anything. We should probably call the police. I suspect they will want to examine everything for evidence."

"No," he blurted out, sounding slightly guilty. Jason thought about the encounters he'd had with the police in London and a few hours earlier at the Plaza. If they found him near one more disturbance like this one, connected even loosely to the Thought Mechanix organization, he was pretty sure they'd take him into custody and throw away the key.

"So what did she hide in her apartment that is so important that someone would destroy the place?"

"A very important notebook. It contains information that may help to explain why Hans Pedersen supposedly killed himself."

"I saw that on the news. In fact, I saw Amy. She was interviewed."

"Yeah. She was saying some weird things about Hans, stuff that just wasn't in character. I know Amy well. She loved Hans Pedersen."

Jason found himself defending Amy to Jasmine, who was one of her friends.

"People say unexpected things in a time of grief." Jasmine moved closer to console Jason. "I would be surprised if she meant what she said."

"Where do you think she hid her notebook?"

Jason looked up at the brown beauty that had startled him a few minutes earlier. She stared back with a look of concern. He wondered, briefly, if maybe she trashed the place, and came back in when he arrived, hoping he could help her find what she was unable to locate.

"I…she…it…" he stalled.

As if she could read his mind, she replied with a small laugh and a little pressure on his head wound.

Jason grimaced in pain. "Ouch, why'd you do that?"

"Do you think that I would be nursing your head if all I wanted was the location of some notebook? If I had done this," she swept her free arm around the room, "you can be certain I would have you in a compromising position to find out exactly what you might know that I don't."

"Fair enough," Jason conceded. "In the instructions that Amy left me, she said that I would find it inside her most favorite thing in the world."

Jasmine smiled instantly, exposing two rows of perfect white teeth framed by a pair of beautiful lips.

"I know exactly where it is." She stood up from the floor and headed for the kitchen. She grabbed the tub of melted Ben and Jerry's Rocky Road ice cream and opened the lid.

"You did say inside."

"That's what she wrote."

Jasmine thrust a hand into the ice cream. A second later she pulled out a small notebook sealed inside a plastic bag.

"She always was one for the extreme. Here you go," she said triumphantly.

Jason was now standing beside Jasmine at the counter. She slid the notebook out of the plastic bag and handed it over.

"Let's open it and see what Amy wrote."

"Maybe we'd better leave. You never know if the people who did this will be back."

As if on cue, two uniformed men appeared at the entrance to the apartment, guns out and pointed to the ground in perfect assault style. The insignia on their jacket sleeves identified them as private security. Jason recognized the design, a globe with a lightning bolt piercing it from pole to pole, used by the international private security firm Secur-Tec. He had known a few mining and oil exploration clients to hire this private police force in countries where safety needed to be purchased. This time, however, unlike his previous encounters, the men standing in the doorway to Amy's apartment did not bother to identify themselves before raising their Walther close-action pistols and firing.

The first bullet ricocheted off the granite countertop of the kitchen island that Jason was standing beside. The second bullet pierced the wood, a foot from his head. Jason had spent many summers playing paint ball and he was not one to panic under pressure. But in the three years of weekends spent with seasoned paint-ballers, he had never seen anyone act with the guile and agility of Jasmine.

A millisecond after the first bullet hit the granite countertop, Jason watched as Jasmine spun around and reached for the knife block. He clumsily ducked behind the kitchen island as the shiny metal of a carving knife sailed above his head. A moment later he heard the grunt of expelled air and a thud, as one of the men collapsed in the doorway, assuring Jason that Jasmine's improvised defense had found its target.

The distinctive *pfft* of the silenced pistols stopped as the surviving attacker hesitated, the realization dawning on him that an easy assignment had somehow gone horribly awry.

The hesitation was all that Jasmine needed. She seemed to anticipate it. Spinning on her heels to avoid a direct shot, she turned to face the remaining attacker, bringing her left arm forward to release a second knife she had slid out of the wooden block a moment earlier. Before the man could react, the blade found its home on the right side of his neck, piercing the jugular.

The man grasped his neck in a futile attempt to stem the bleeding that he already knew would kill him. As the life drained out of his body, he could only stare in silent disbelief as the Angel of Death wrapped in yellow silk seemed to glide across the room. His last thought was the captain's deep voice inside his helmet, "Easy as pie, get in, kill the accountant, and get out. No noise."

26

"Who ARE you?" Jason asked as he watched Jasmine drag the two dead men deeper into the apartment and close the door.

Without answering, she pulled the Kevlar coated helmet from one of the dead men and placed it against her head to listen. With her free hand she put a finger to her lips, indicating that Jason should be quiet. Jasmine was practically wearing the helmet as she strained to listen.

"What the hell is going on, Penske? Isaac? Acknowledge your situation. This is Mackenzie. Is the target down? Shit! Something's wrong. Send in backup…"

Another more authoritative voice invaded the helmet: "Backup's on the way."

"Come on." Jasmine pulled Jason up off the ground and led him to the bedroom. She took three quick strides across the room, Jason in tow. Pulling back the curtains cautiously, she took a tentative look outside before opening the window onto the fire escape. "They must have thought it was going to be an easy in and out. No real backup to cover an escape. Follow me."

Jasmine climbed around the locked gate of the fire escape and made her way to the ground below. The fire escape opened onto the main street. She deftly landed on the pavement, crouched low like a cat and ducked into the alley next to the metal fire escape.

Jason followed like a trained puppy, still unaware of what was going on. A dull glare bounced off the wet pavement from the one street lamp that still worked. It helped to light their way. A siren blared in the distance. Jason wondered if it was headed their way, but the sound grew fainter as they reached the deadend street.

He leaned against the wall beside Jasmine to catch his breath. She stole a glance around the corner of the brick wall, stained with city grime. Harlem's outside veneer had changed, but the cracks and crevices of the alleyways still showed its true character of poverty and pain. Many New Yorkers felt that the beautification of Harlem, especially around Columbia University, was like putting lipstick on a pig. In many ways, the sentiment was not incorrect. Jason felt grit in his palm as he leaned against the wall.

Jasmine sized up a black late model SUV parked a block away from the entrance to Amy's apartment on St Nicholas Avenue. She could see that that this was a coordinated attack. People were waiting for Jason to appear before they acted. The doors to the vehicle opened as men poured out, one of them remained by the vehicle, watching as two of his colleagues disappeared into the building.

Jasmine turned to head the opposite way down the alley into St Nicholas Park. Jason followed her blindly, still not sure he should trust this woman. He heard men yelling behind them. He glanced back to see if they were being followed, but the tall oak trees in the park blocked his view.

"They won't be following us." Jasmine had stopped a few hundred feet into the park and sat down on a bench near the basketball court. It was empty except for half a dozen teenagers mimicking plays on the darkened court, making out like they were NBA hopefuls. She straightened her clothes and watched the game, her breath a little quick.

Jason dropped on the bench next to her. His breath was also short, gasping, like he had just completed a ten-mile run. It had been two days since he ran from the explosion at the Discoverer's Club in London where his world was literally blown away. Nothing seemed plausible to him. He was sure in a moment he'd awaken from this nightmare, drenched in sweat and still in his London flat. But he was beginning to realize that nothing could to be taken at face value. He had witnessed three buildings destroyed by some sort of prearranged, orchestrated attack. Whoever was behind these explosions knew that the buildings might have to be destroyed and took measures to prep them far in advance. As the detective at the Plaza said, even when the leasehold improvements were initially done. Even Hans must have been aware of it.

But why?

He looked over at Jasmine, who watched as a crowd of youths whirled around the basket. Who the hell was she anyway, coolly dispatching two soldiers for hire like she was dicing vegetables for a salad? He wondered if she ended up in Amy's apartment by accident, or if she even lived there.

"You just killed two men back there."

"If I hadn't, they would have killed us. I don't know what sort of accountant you are, but you must have some powerful enemies if they are prepared to hire mercenaries to kill you. These men usually work in war-torn Africa, or Iraq. What are they doing here in New York on a hired hit? So, what's your story?"

Jasmine leaned in as if to listen to a confidential story, her soft, schoolteacher voice posing questions better asked by a seasoned veteran of foreign wars.

Jason stared into her eyes to see how deep her soul was buried in the dark pupils. She stared back, a small, friendly smile curling onto the edges of her mouth. She seemed to be an angel but, like Loki, he wondered if she was dispatched to bring death, not life.

"Don't change the subject. Who are you and how did you learn to protect yourself so adroitly. And don't tell me it was from your Pilates class."

Jasmine laughed, her head moving to the side as she leaned back, clasping her hands behind her neck.

"Very well, I'll tell you who I am first. I was born in Kashmir, near Kargil, a village that was constantly being overrun by soldiers; Pakistanis for a while, then our own Indian troops, and again Pakistanis. Many died in the streets of the village I lived in. My father taught me early to take care of myself, how to fire a gun, how to defend against an unprovoked attack. He was thinking maybe it would protect me from being raped. It didn't, but it did save my life. I cut off the man's penis as he satiated himself over me. The animal's wild screams brought a few other soldiers into our home to see what was going on. I shot each of them as they came through the door, then ran out the back and hid in the tall grasses. I watched them slaughter half the village, my parents included. But now I'm a journalist, or at least I was until the paper went bankrupt."

"Jesus Christ. I'm sorry."

"Don't be. Life is karma. We each live out our time on earth as the Universe has chosen. If I didn't have those experiences, I'd have to endure others, maybe worse. Because of them, I was able to save you tonight." Jasmine reached over and touched Jason on the arm, moving closer to him on the bench. "So, what's your story?" she repeated.

Jason mimicked her move and clasped his hands behind his head, slouching down on the bench. He relayed his experiences since moving from New York to London, ending with the reason why he had gone to Amy's apartment.

They had been sitting on the park bench for over an hour, the late-night basketball players long gone. An eerie silence enveloped them as Jason finished his story, the only sound coming from the buzz of the subway vent near the park entrance.

"So why do you think somebody wants to kill you?" Jasmine went right to the meat of the matter. Destruction was not only following Jason, it was trying to catch him.

"Hans told me that last night before I left New York that certain people, the people I went to meet at the Discoverer's Club, would explain the real reason he wanted me to join Thought Mechanix. He said that they understood better than anyone what he was trying to do at the Stern Auditorium before his presentation was prematurely stopped by a firebomb." Jason described in detail the firebombing of Hans's show that night.

"I heard about that at my paper. Grant Holmes covered the story. He and I had done a few overseas jobs together. He wrote a good piece, but the editor pushed it onto page four. Bigger news that day, I guess. So, what do you think is in the notebook?" Jasmine asked as casually as possible, not wanting to appear anxious.

27

Amy sat alone in the small, dark room. They had brought her here a short while after she was accosted, after her meeting at the restaurant. Hans warned her that the world was going to unravel, that he could not continue to defy their wishes without a reprimand. Amy still was not sure what to believe anymore, despite the assurances she provided Jason in the letter. God, she hoped he got the letter. She hoped he was alright. But these people were not whom she'd expected. They were not part of the Order. She had no idea who they were, but she was determined to stay resolute.

As she took the punches from the Asian, she did not see any strength of character. She saw only the face of greed. She looked into his eyes as he delivered each blow and saw nothing, said nothing. Her mind began to play tricks in the darkness. Images appeared before her, like a montage of her life on fast forward, pausing on the key events that brought her to this dark room. She rewound the images that seemed relevant, stopped on the critical points to analyze them from every angle.

And still she did not know what to believe. What was right? Wrong? False? True? Nothing made any sense. Hans was dead. Dead. By his own hand? And yet he was convinced that he could fix everything. There seemed to be no reason for him to die.

She was in this dark room because she believed him. Believed that what he was about to do was the right thing to do. Now she wasn't sure what was true. All along she believed that the people who took her out of the rain were all the same. They were not the same. She did not know who these people were, but she was determined not to succumb. Her fate meant nothing, except to find out the truth.

Amy ran her dirty hands though the clumps of blood-soaked blond hair. Broken blood vessels circled the bright emerald iris of her left eye. She gingerly touched the swollen cheek that threatened to block out her vision. She was used to pain. It was a daily occurrence in her past life at home with a drunken father. She could take it. She could dish it out, too, if she had to. Life was about survival. At least, that was what it had become for her until she met Hans. Since then it had been about hope, a vision of the world that didn't require thirteen-year-old girls to live in Central Park to be safe. Hans believed that he was creating such a world.

She knew better. She saw the signs happening around her. The news was not getting any brighter. People were not getting any more generous, sympathetic, or compassionate. Murders happened, rapes happened, theft was endemic. The human character was not improving from the teachings of the Thought Mechanix Rules of Possibility. It seemed to be the opposite. Hans finally saw it as well after his discovery in Italy. He had been merely a pawn.

But he was determined to reverse the momentum that he helped to start. It was supposed to have begun at the Isaac Stern Auditorium, with the new ROP II seminar. A complete transformation from the effects of his first program, a rebirth of character, a tough kindness was going to take over from the callousness of the existing human spirit—a purposeful intention of hope.

That had all changed with the plunge that sent Hans to his death. An event that set off a prearranged chain of destruction, ending any hope of fixing the manipulation of the human spirit that he had inadvertently began.

But if she had changed, so could the world. All her life she knew that being tough showed strength of character. She knew that this strength was all she had left. She also knew that it would not be up to her.

As she sat in the darkness of the small room she hoped that Jason would find the strength as well.

28

The werewolf-moon peeked through the velvet curtain from its perch above the early morning skyline of Manhattan. Jason moved from the living area of the deluxe one-bedroom suite he rented at the Four Seasons on Fifty-Seventh. It was only a few blocks from his old office, and the now destroyed offices of Thought Mechanix at the Plaza. The sky was clear, showing a promise of a beautiful fall day in the city. The street below was nearly vacant, except for a few cart-vendors setting up shop for the day and the ubiquitous taxis enjoying a period of light Manhattan traffic. Jason had moved from his other hotel to the Four Seasons after they returned from Amy's apartment. He insisted that they stay together, as there was no question about Jasmine returning to her apartment after what happened.

It was a few minutes after two by the time they settled into the suite. Jasmine headed off to the shower as Jason sat down to read Amy's notebook. The writing in the book was a jumble of scribbling nonsense and journal-like comments. It seemed to be a chronology of events since she first met Hans. The little anecdotes described events as they unfolded at Thought Mechanix. As Jason read, he formed the impression that Amy was building a case against Hans. He gathered from what she said in the letter that this was part of her responsibility to the Guardians. The reference was on a page dealing with comments regarding their first meeting.

Jason heard the shower stop. He closed up the notebook, placing it, the letter and the small package containing the DVDs in one of the desk drawers.

Jasmine came out of the bedroom wrapped in a bath towel, her damp hair falling over her shoulders to rest on the exposed skin of her upper chest. She walked over to where Jason sat, slowly loosening the towel and letting it drop to her feet, standing there silently as she let Jason take in her naked energy.

He slowly took in all aspects of the sensual brown body that stood in front of him, from her inviting womanhood to her firm yet curvaceous stomach surrounding a small belly-button, leading up to her firm navel-orange sized breasts. She was pleasantly affected by the cool air pushing out of the ventilation. Her naked body had the desired effect on Jason, his body reacting as he reached out to her.

Jasmine led him into the bedroom, helping him undress and leading him to the bathroom where she helped him shower before they lay on the bed together. She straddled him, knowing that the position held certain obligations. He touched her wet skin, feeling her body tingle from the touch of his rough fingers. They moved slowly at first, enjoying the feel of their bodies. After a while they moved more urgently, the moisture on their bodies glistened in the light bouncing in from the moon. In time, she felt her body tense, stifling a scream until Jason released into her.

Then they slept, exhausted from the night's activities, awakening only after the sun found its way into the opening in the curtains. The sun piercing the room through a crack in the curtains hit Jason square in the face. He rose quietly, leaving the bedroom to order breakfast, waking Jasmine once the food arrived.

They ate ravenously, neither of them sure if the hunger came from their lovemaking or from the events of the past evening. A short, awkward silence was broken by Jasmine.

"I'm sorry," she said demurely.

"For what part? Trying to kill me or trying to kill me?" Jason looked down into his lap and smiled devilishly, knowing full well she was talking about her seduction. It was answered with a mini-bagel to his chest.

"Hey, no more target practice. I think you proved last night how capable you are at throwing things." Jason picked up the bagel and took a bite.

Jasmine feigned being insulted before becoming serious.

"So what are we going to do now? I suspect we should go down to the police station and let them know what happened in Amy's apartment last night," Jason commented.

"I don't think that would be wise. Whoever sent Secur-Tec to that apartment will be looking to finish the job. The fewer people we tell the better."

"What about the dead bodies?"

"From what I know about private armies, they do not leave evidence behind. I know of two companies who have used Secur-Tec in the past to protect their people in hostile countries. The men and women who sign up with these sorts of companies are usually on the fringe of the law. Unsavory and very skilled, these men and women are often trained by the same terrorist groups around the world that they combat every day. The bodies will be taken away, their remains disposed of, and their families will receive a letter and a sizable financial settlement for the bravery and valor in which their loved ones died."

Jason looked at her in disbelief. "Are you serious? Hired murderers receiving a hero's funeral?"

"No funeral. Just the niceties of battle for the mourning families. From what I've seen, they don't expect to survive. But they don't like to lose. Chances are they are scouring the city to figure out where we went. So what do we do then? If what you say is true, I can't go home, and I'm currently unemployed," Jasmine stated.

Jason looked over at the woman who, in one night, tried to kill him, saved his life, and gave him the greatest sex he'd ever had. He was not sure exactly who she was, but after reading Amy's letter he was not sure who anyone was anymore.

"We should stay together until we figure out who sent these men. They clearly knew my whereabouts. I just wonder if they knew why I went to Amy's apartment."

Jasmine was silent for a moment as her roving journalist's mind scanned the events since she first encountered Jason. She needed to make sure he was the right person to help her accomplish her objective, the reason why she was at Amy's apartment the night before. She needed to find the people Amy was working for.

"You were not the first person to trash the place. Somebody was there before us."

"What do you think they were looking for? The same thing we were?" Jason thought about the letter. Amy had left revealing clues about the nature of the package she was leaving for him, as well as every other detail surrounding her defection from the Guardians.

"The only item in the letter that Amy was obtuse about was the whereabouts of the notebook. She said it was *inside of her favorite thing in the world*. Not very many people would know that, except her close friends. Whoever came here before us must have seen the letter but did not know what Amy meant by her favorite thing."

Jason sat back. Having just consumed a scrumptious breakfast, he was ready for more coffee. He picked up the coffee carafe to refill their cups.

"What are you thinking?" Jasmine could tell that Jason's mind worked like her own. He formulated thoughts like fireflies, letting them dance about in his mind until they shone bright enough to form a connection.

"Whoever ransacked the place must have seen Amy's letter. It is the only logical explanation. If it were the ecumenical folks Amy was seen with, they would not have had to tear the place apart, as they had a direct relationship with the occupant. If it were the people who sent the hired soldiers, then why did they bother to shoot before asking why we were there? The question is who did Miriam Dixon share the information with?"

Jasmine finished his thought: "And why?"

From his wicker-backed chair, Jason stared over at Jasmine. He knew that there was only one way to survive the nightmare he had been tossed into and that was to discover what Hans intended on revealing to the world. Amy had left him with a quest to fulfill in honor of Hans. He was committed to completing her wishes and realized he could use all the help he could get.

"You want to help me? I could use your company, and more importantly, your protection."

She smiled at that.

"I thought you'd never ask. I happen to be looking for a position."

Jasmine smiled lasciviously, jumping out of her chair to hug Jason. *Perfect,* she thought.

"Let's get started."

29

Gunter Tang was not accustomed to failure. He particularly deplored people who could not deliver on a promise, especially if he had already been paid in advance. It was not the usual way he did business. After years of working to shed his criminal pedigree—at least on the surface—Gunter stood adjacent to the titans of international business. Most businesses that supplied his vast array of commercial enterprises did so eagerly, anxiously and, in most cases, expectantly. He ruled with the CEOs of the Fortune 500 and would be listed among them if he disclosed his true net worth.

Clear to those who negotiated with Tang Enterprises Incorporated and its egocentric CEO, you did not try to take too much off the table in a deal. Bad things happened to companies who pushed too hard. Bad things happened to their management. Bad things happened to their families. Gunter Tang was able to build an international business of magnificent proportions, but he was not able to do it without some competitive casualties. He had used a multitude of methods and resources over the years to achieve the results he desired.

Recently, he employed one of his shadow subsidiaries, the private army and for-hire security firm Secur-Tec, to secure details from one of Hans Pedersen's associates. They were only partially successful. Forming the private for-hire army firm was the brainchild of Anthony Lee, a former lieutenant of his father's criminal network. Lee went to work reluctantly for the son of his boss after the elder Tang was killed. For a few years he acted in the background, contacting Gunter surreptitiously whenever a problem needed to be solved. So a competitor's business would become the victim of a fire. Suppliers that needed to be reminded of a pricing agreement would lose a few trucks. Boating accidents. The tactics were reminiscent of Chicago in the twenties and thirties, except that Gunter stayed far away from the proceedings. Often he would wait months after a misfortune to resume stalled negotiations.

Lee soon grew tired of the charade. He approached Gunter on going legit with the security firm idea. Within a few months recruits from criminal organizations all over the globe signed on to work with the new subsidiary of Tang Enterprises. Secur-Tec soon became one of Gunter's most profitable divisions. The crowning achievement was the signing of a multi-billion dollar contract to protect American interests in war-torn regions around the world. The beauty was that the company was making so much money protecting American interests abroad that they did not need any criminal entanglements. Not that their tactics were always ethical. Gunter let his special-ops teams loose for extraordinary situations, like the one that he was about to discuss with Lee.

They agreed to meet at a diner just off 122nd Street, a few blocks from Amy's apartment. Gunter arrived first, having sped there after getting the phone call regarding the botched job. He ordered a coffee and waited for the arrival of Lee and the project coordinator. The diner was old, the coffee tasted like it was the first pot ever brewed in the place, and the large black waitress looked like she may have poured the first cup. A blanket of smoke eighteen inches thick clung to the ceiling, fed by a half a dozen men scattered throughout the cramped space, smoking despite the posted ordinances to the contrary.

Lee arrived just as the waitress was freshening Gunter's stained and cracked coffee cup for a second time. He was followed into the booth by Sean Mackenzie, the Secur-Tec project coordinator.

Mackenzie was an inordinately tall man dressed in a black undershirt and black battle pants. Beads of sweat trickled down the man's neck as Lee's boss stared down at the security leader. He only knew Gunter by reputation and would have been happy to have kept it that way. After the fuck-up at the apartment, he cleaned up the mess, had his men search the vicinity for their target, and only then called Lee to give him the news. While he waited, he rehearsed in his mind the series of events that sabotaged the simple operation.

It was only when he entered the apartment, observing firsthand how his two team members were killed, that he realized that the accountant was not alone in the apartment. It was clear from the bio they had on Jason Wakefield that he was not capable of killing his men in such an efficient manner, if at all. As the dead men were removed from the apartment, he reviewed the security recordings they set up to cover the building during the incursion. Jason arrived alone. The only other person to enter the building during the time they were recording the entrance was an East Indian woman dressed as if she were coming from a ceremony of some sort.

He sent a picture of her face to their database, linked by special arrangement to the Homeland Security databanks in Virginia. The link was a favor to Secur-Tec by the previous head of the nascent organization and was never taken away after he resigned in controversy over a recent terrorist attack. The link remained in place without the knowledge of the existing leadership at HSA.

It turned out the woman was a foreign reporter with a keen interest in Thought Mechanix. Sean suspected that her arrival was not a coincidence.

"What happened?" Gunter spoke with cool efficiency.

Mackenzie responded in kind, "We were given the details of the apartment, tore the place apart just like Mr. Lee requested. There was nothing our men could identify as remarkable or special. We were not able to identify anything that might be construed as being 'favored' by the occupant. So we waited for your guy to show up. It took two days. We waited for him to come out. He never did. So I sent in two of my men. When they didn't check in, we went in with the team. You know the rest."

"Do you know if they found the notebook?" Gunter queried.

"Not for certain, but probably. On the kitchen counter there was an open tub of ice cream, scoops of the stuff melting in the sink. They may have found it in there."

Gunter could sense that the man was right. It was logical. He was upset. Ever since he saw the power of Thought Mechanix he needed to possess the secrets of the system Hans developed. He wanted to be in sole control of its potential.

"We need to find the accountant and this woman. I want to know what they know."

30

Hans Pedersen appeared primed and ready as the camera zoomed in on his face. In the background a large plasma screen streamed the latest enhancements to the Rules of Possibility. It was soon lost from view as the camera was adjusted to pan into the rotund head of the Thought Mechanix founder, his smiling face drawing the viewers to his message. Poised on the edge of his seat, the camera in position, Hans began to speak…

Jason stared at the state-of-the-art plasma screen, waiting for the first segment to begin. After he and Jasmine had finished breakfast, he had pulled the DVD from its protective case and inserted it into the player tastefully hidden in the armoire.

According to Amy's notes, there were supposed to be instructions regarding how to locate the Fourth Book of Eden that Hans had discovered. Jason was still not sure what the fourth tablet might reveal, but he was certain they would unlock the mystery surrounding Hans's success, and death. He also felt that they were critically important to certain people, given recent events affecting anything associated with Thought Mechanix, including his recent brush with death.

"So what do you think we should do first?" Jasmine called out from the bathroom as she towel-dried her hair.

Jason put the DVD on pause. "What do you mean?"

"From what I gather, the taped segment of Hans's new program is supposed to reveal the location of the fourth tablet, book, or whatever it is. But the information in Amy's notebook suggests that Hans's source may have the answers that are in the DVDs. Which do you think is easier—to try and decipher the cryptic messages in a bunch of DVDs or go to Italy and seek out the one person that helped Hans construct his theories?"

Entering the room, her hair hanging damp and loose around her shoulders, Jasmine walked over to the bar and poured them fresh cups of coffee from the ceramic carafe left by room service.

"A bird in the hand. I would suggest that we try to figure out what Hans tried to communicate to us in the DVDs. Hans hid the message within the DVDs for a reason. Maybe because it is something that this Carmen does not know, or maybe he is afraid to implicate her in whatever is happening. If we can find out that reason, then maybe searching out Carmen will be next."

As they waited for the DVD to run through its opening credits, Jason gave her the Cole's Notes version of the Rules of Possibility. He spoke highly of Thought Mechanix and about how it had affected his life.

Jasmine listened with rapt attention, laughing at his animated descriptions of the Rules. But her true interest in the man behind the phenomenon was very personal. Showing up at Amy's apartment was not a coincidence. She had a specific agenda. Her task was thwarted by the presence of Jason and the subsequent attack from the Secur-Tec soldiers. As a foreign reporter, she had to think on her feet. Her momentary surprise at finding the tall stranger in the apartment made her react. She quickly concocted her story, which left Jason with the impression she was just a concerned neighbor. After years of foreign assignments in unfriendly places, Jasmine knew better than to disclose too much information too soon. Now, sitting on the couch after a night of survival and lovemaking, she felt guilty. Looking over at the naïve accountant she wanted to blurt out the truth. But something held her back. She decided to wait until the time was right.

They spent the next three hours listening patiently to Hans as he laid out his new Rules. They were not the same as the original Rules, but they weren't different, either. Each one seemed to reveal a little more about how it worked, and not just how to achieve the desired result. If there was any subtext about the message he was trying to communicate, it was lost on them both. The Books of Eden were not mentioned once in any of the seminars they had spent three hours watching.

"Maybe we should start by finding Carmen and see what she knows about the fourth Book."

"We could try that, but I get the impression from Amy's letter that the existence of the fourth Book may be a myth."

"What do you mean?"

Jason picked up Amy's letter. We don't even know what these clay tablets are all about? Amy refers to them as the Books of Eden."

"What do you think she is talking about? Do you think she is talking about the Garden of Eden?"

"All that I know is that Hans somehow used the knowledge he obtained from them to construct the Rules. The entire structure of Thought Mechanix, and its success, stems from whatever is revealed in these Books."

"What do you know about the Garden of Eden?" Jasmine asked.

Jason took a sip of the hot coffee before responding. He had gone to Sunday school as a kid, never really paying much attention to the nun as she recited the same stories each week. His religion was weak, which perhaps explained why he was attracted to the Rules of Possibility.

"Only that it was where Adam and Eve lived after they were created by God. Of course, there was that whole serpent and apple thing."

"When my friend wrote that exposé about Hans Pedersen, he spent a lot of time researching websites that tried to uncover the falsehoods of what he taught," Jasmine answered, her knowledge gleaned more recently in her search to understand the truth behind Thought Mechanix and its enigmatic founder Hans Pedersen. Jasmine was the author of the article but she chose to weave a story about a friend writing the exposé to hide her true involvement.

"Because of my unbiased non-Christian religious background, my friend found it enlightening to share his discoveries with me. According to one conspiracy-theory website, the Garden of Eden plays a key role in the creation of the Rules of Possibility. It stated that Hans had found the lost Books of Eden. The Books were hidden because they revealed too much about the true nature of our relationship with God. The knowledge would have destroyed the very existence of the religions founded on the myth of creation by revealing the true events that took place in the Garden of Eden."

"So the serpent thing isn't true," Jason stated in mock disbelief.

"A quick, two-minute search on Google will tell you that. The fairy story that you were told as a child was written for readers in seventeenth-century England, when the King James version of the Bible was completed. The authors of that ill-fated attempt at translation felt that the populace of the time could relate to serpents and apples rather than to a more esoteric evaluation of the events. For one thing, the original text refers more specifically to a fig tree, not an apple tree. But in reality, many scholars think that the tree— there are in fact two mentioned—refers to *texts*, not trees. One of them was called the Book of Life and the other the Book of Knowledge of Good and Evil. It was when Adam—at the behest of Eve—*ate* from the Tree of Knowledge that they were struck by the reality of their own consciousness of their world. For that, they were banished from the Garden to join others who had not reached the same elevated state of enlightenment."

"Because…" Jason asked.

"According to the Jewish tradition, not Christian doctrine, man and by extension woman, achieved free choice once they ate from the tree, or in other words, *read from the book*. Since they now had free will, they lost their connection to immortality, their direct link to the gods, and thus, had to go out to the world and survive on their own. Some say that the myth can be translated as man's ascent from being hunter-gatherers to becoming farmers."

"So explain one thing to me."

"What?"

"Why does Amy refer to the four Books of Eden when there appear to be only two according to anything I can search on Bing?"

"I have no idea." Jasmine stared at Jason as a thought formed in her mind. "But I think we would be better off tracking down this lady who seems to know the location of the fourth Book of Eden. Where did Amy say that Carmen lives?"

Jason picked up the notebook, "Her full name is Carmen Salvatore. She lives in Florence and works at the university."

31

Piazza del Campo baked in the late summer heat as the black Mercedes sedan rolled through the crowded streets. The car inched its way down the steep Via d. Porrione in the center of Siena, narrowly missing a group of German tourists blocking the path to their destination. One of the occupants of the vehicle sat in quiet contemplation of the fate that would be decided in the next few hours. August Piccolomini, a Brother of the Order of Sumer, was wedged between two less than holy members of the monastery. He had been wrested from his bed in the Austrian mountain retreat that had been his home for the past three years.

Piccolomini was not alone in his convictions as to what they had built with Hans Pedersen. He spent the last fifteen years converting many to his truth. He did not feel that an error was made. It was time to enlighten the world, just as he predicted so many years earlier when he and the seniors of the Order of Sumer sent Hans out to create his destiny. Piccolomini had watched the news three days earlier, as Hans was pronounced dead in front of a disbelieving crowd of onlookers outside of his office building in New York. A victim of his own ego. Now, everything that they built seemed lost. He suspected that soon he would be told why the man took his own life just when everything they had worked for was so close.

A scorching sun beat down on the balding head of August as he was taken from the car and hustled into the privacy of the walled area of the Siena enclave. They walked up a set of stairs to the chapter house where the monks would meet daily to discuss the business of the monastery.

The Siena Monastery functioned as a full-fledged member of the Benedictines. They recruited young members into their fold and carried out the duties of a normal functioning group of monks. The Order of Sumer used this façade to gather the very best candidates to their own, more crucial calling. They rarely made errors in their selection process.

As a brother, Piccolomini rose through the ranks of the Order to eventually obtain the key title of Master of Recruiting. A young monk who quickly saw the importance of the Order, he learned all there was to know and gained the trust of the Elders to become the youngest ever to hold the post. Too young and too eager—that was how the Grand Master described his main weakness. So Piccolomini was forced to fight for his very survival. Piccolomini took his role to an extreme, recruiting people of like mind from all denominations. They formed their own council, meeting in secret in the Austrian alpine retreat to shape the future of the world.

The chapter house was guarded by two men who, like his escorts from the mountain retreat, looked more like they belonged in a café in Sicily than a modest Holy Order. Piccolomini followed his retinue inside. He sat down, clasping his hands gently into his lap, realizing full well the magnitude of the meeting. What he didn't know was how much his nemesis knew about what was unfolding around his carefully laid plans.

"Hello, August," Cardinal Franco Agostino began, trying to sound more confident than he felt. A terrible death occurred and it was crucial he discover what Piccolomini knew. Agostino was blindly content with the knowledge that Hans Pedersen was not aware of the strife he caused. The man was driven too much by his ego to see the bigger picture of what was happening. That was why he had taken the time to enlighten him about the truth behind Thought Mechanix.

Unfortunately, he could not have predicted that Hans would now be dead.

"You have no doubt heard of the unfortunate death of Hans Pedersen. What you may not be aware of is that his death has prevented a catastrophe. Had he succeeded in carrying out the plans, what we were empowered to protect over the multitude of millennium would have been destroyed."

Piccolomini stared up at the man and smiled. He grew up knowing Franco Agostino as a family friend who he had seen as an uncle. It was Franco who had recruited him into the Order at such a young age.

He spoke to him now as if they were strangers. A thin smile crossed Piccolomini's lips as he scanned the face of the man who had become his confessor.

Piccolomini spoke slowly.

"The world is changing faster than we can keep up. Your actions in London and New York to contain Hans's work will not stop the momentum that has been building for the last decade and a half. Surely you realize the progress made in the study of quantum physics and in understanding the connection that all energy has to the universe. Since the advent of supercomputers, scientists have been able to duplicate, in a small way, what Hans Pedersen has been doing—to harness the intention of thought. The time is right to expose our spiritual origins to the world. Hans thought he was improving the lot of humankind. He did not recognize that he was giving them a glimpse into their souls. A view that most people are not prepared to see.

"Let us not forget that the Order of Sumer's sole purpose is to protect the discovery of the information contained in the clay tablets referred to as the Books of Eden. We have strayed from that path."

The two of them stared at each other in silence for a few moments, lost in their conspiracy to ensure the translation of the third tablet known as the Book of Thought and to propel Hans Pedersen to greatness. Each of them knew that they had different motivations. Motivations that clashed as the results of the dissemination of the Rules of Possibility began to take effect. Once it got out of hand, the two men realized that their destinies were on separate paths. One was trying to stop Hans, the other to take advantage of the scenario that was created. But the control of the outcome had shifted. It was clear that whether or not the world was ready for its transformation no longer mattered, as neither man could ignore the inevitable flow of fate that brought them to where they now stood.

Neither of the men really knew what the other was protecting. Agostino knew the truth that he shared with Hans in secret. So did Piccolomini. But neither of them knew what Hans had discovered— the Fourth Book. The very existence of the Fourth Book was a myth to most. Now they knew the truth: there was an additional clay tablet.

Piccolomini had heard rumors over the years. All unsubstantiated. Hans Pedersen used his considerable wealth and influence to carry out a worldwide search. Obviously with success. Piccolomini knew he needed to possess the power of that fourth Book. It was what he and the others had planned since discovering the deception of Agostino. As the Cardinal of Siena, Agostino was a religious zealot who wanted greatness for his Church.

"Why did you direct Hans to continue his search, given the risks? A risk you took a solemn vow to protect," Piccolomini challenged the Cardinal.

"You cannot believe that I had anything to do with this. Pedersen acted independently. We lost control of our prodigy. But even you can agree with me that he accomplished everything you, and I, dreamed." Agostino turned to avoid Piccolomini's gaze. There was no way this man could know his true intentions.

Finally Piccolomini spoke. "We all have to make choices."

"A choice you made." Agostino's voice echoed across the chamber.

Piccolomini played the tortured soul, knowing full well the deception of Agostino and the wasted line of questioning he had to endure to determine if the man knew anything about the location of the fourth book.

"It was not my intention to compromise the Order. I did help Hans, despite your insistence that he be ignored. What we all failed to realize was that Hans Pedersen understood as well as anyone the power of the secret protected by the Order. He used that knowledge to make the human condition more tolerable, until—"

"Do you really believe that the human race would survive with the knowledge that we possess? Look at the proof of what Hans Pedersen created. Criminals have used *his* techniques to convince the world that they should be robbed, or raped, or worse."

Agostino's voice rose an octave. His entire world was collapsing around him and he needed to lash out at someone.

"Furthermore, the teachings allowed a multitude of people to use the legitimate financial system to rake in millions from unsuspecting investors. Hardworking morons poured their pennies and dollars into worthless paper. The techniques that Hans espoused allowed those in power to convince hapless investors that it was the right thing to do."

"We had a plan. What you did helped to unleash a potential that has put man more at risk than he has ever been. No, they are not ready to learn about their origin. They can barely cope with the technology they have created already," Agostino whined.

"Do not forget that it was you who let Hans develop the Rules in the first place. What did I do that was so different?" Piccolomini retorted to remind the Cardinal of their joint deception.

"What you did was give him the power of transference. I only wanted him to think he could use our teachings on an unsuspecting world. Let him believe that he was doing some good. By convincing him to search for, and then to find, the very knowledge that we have sworn to protect, you opened a window to the universal truth. And he was about to push that window wide open."

Agostino trembled slightly as he thought about the implications. Everything he had worked for since Hans Pedersen landed on his doorstep fifteen years earlier was on the verge of being lost forever. He had no choice but to act as he contemplated the future. He watched his subordinate, looking for recognition, anything that could tell him whether his grand scheme had been compromised. Agostino needed everyone to believe that the project was over. He wanted the realization of its death to sink like a sharp knife against Piccolomini's soul.

Piccolomini mulled over his own vision. A vision that would terrify the pathetically shortsighted old man that sat as his accuser. He sensed that the power struggle between him and his mentor had reached an apex. He stood up, facing his accuser, to give him what he wanted to hear. It was important that it looked like his ideological world was destroyed. To emphasize his supposed loss, tears began to form at the corner of his eyes as he fought against the rising tide of reality. He played the part, burying his head in his hands and wept.

Agostino watched as his subordinate crumbled. What he thought was to be a defiant battle with a man obsessed with destroying his plans had become a mission of mercy. He held his haughty smile in check. Piccolomini and his Guardians were still needed to complete their search so that he could fulfill his destiny. The revelation of the true purpose of the Books of Eden was at hand. The Church—his church—would become the only way. It was time to bring Piccolomini back to his camp.

"I thought that today was to be your last. But I can see that you are repentant. It is with relief that I absolve you of your sins against the Order. I will need your help to ensure that the damage is contained. We have received word from New York that Hans Pedersen has left behind details about the location of the fourth book. It appears that Hans's protégé has disrupted our attempts to contain this problem. Although we have lost sight of the accountant, it appears he has an accomplice. Her name is Jasmine Shah. We think that Jason Wakefield might be with her."

Piccolomini nodded to Agostino, concealing a triumphant smile behind his calm demeanor. He was still in control. He had his people in the right place. His Guardians would continue to enforce his will. More importantly, Agostino was unaware of the significance of Jason Wakefield. The Thought Mechanix organization that Hans Pedersen created was now history, but the energy of its existence was still active. With luck, nothing would prevent Piccolomini from realizing his vision of the world.

32

Sandra Larksmum was no ordinary killer.

She grew up as Sandra McKay in a mid-American nuclear family. She enrolled in the State college after high school—she excelled— dated the quarterback, and obeyed the rules laid down by her fiercely protective father. By all accounts Sandra should have ended up on a small hobby farm with three kids, a dog and a husband who pulled in six figures selling life insurance. But life is funny. At eighteen and home from college for reading week, she had an encounter with an uncle who pursued her like a drunken tobacco salesman at a smokers' convention.

On his third attempt to mount his niece, Sandra had had enough. After a family barbeque, when her uncle drunkenly fell on top of her, planting slobbering kisses and groping her ass, she reached over her head and grabbed the first thing she could find. It turned out to be a fireplace poker. With the deftness of a picador, she rammed it between her uncle's shoulder blades. As the inebriated slob fell back in surprise, Sandra retracted the implement and proceeded to shuck the man's balls as if they were oysters. He died en route to the county hospital, speechless about the cruelty to which he was subjected.

There was an arraignment, which Sandra skipped out on. As a fugitive, she stowed away on a college cruise to Italy under the name Sandra Larksmum and never looked back. Occasionally, she missed her mom and wondered if her dad ever recovered from the loss of the family honor. Despite the gruesome murder, the eighteen year old was by all accounts an outstanding human being—except for one thing. Sandra Larksmum realized that she enjoyed killing people.

Once in Italy she found herself without financial resources or contacts. Within a few days, she was shacked up with a low-life who fancied himself a player in the Florence underworld. He was a two-bit hustler named Rollo Biancci who knew just enough keep his prick whetted and his wallet full. He was Sandra's second victim—a case of jugular-interruptus with the help of a pen-knife.

The Italian prosecutor took a liking to the vivacious blond, looking the other way at the evidence and eventually setting her up in an apartment to take care of basic primal needs, a situation that eventually and sadly ended a promising law-enforcement career.

Sandra attracted the attention of a fringe group of people who spent their lives protecting the arcane interests of a small group of men known as the Order of Sumer. She never got the politics but understood a good thing when she saw it; they needed the raw and emotionless killing potential of the renegade Yank, and she needed the protection of their private organization. They called themselves the Guardians. What they were guarding she never really cared, but they emotionlessly dispatched anyone who got close to the Order's secret, or left them in such a state of fear that their silence could be assured.

Now in her late forties, Larksmum was the matriarch of the Guardians, sending her troops around the world at the bidding of the Order. Her charges called her Lady Larksmum. Stories of her exploits with the Guardians were legendary. Death and mayhem were her way of life, as she carried out the carefully orchestrated plans of her benefactors. As of late, she was rarely involved in black work, having satisfied her lust for blood years earlier. But the current situation was different. She was summoned and given instructions directly by the head of the Order.

As she entered the complex, she sensed an energy that startled her. Several of the brothers diverted their eyes as she walked by, not because she was a woman, but because they knew who she was. She offered a warm smile nonetheless as she left the courtyard and entered the conference hall.

She took a seat across from the man who directed her actions.

"This is delicate." The man spoke in a soft hush brought on by years of speaking in the hallowed halls of the monastery.

Larksmum leaned forward to catch all of the words.

"Sandra, you have been valuable to us over the years. I would personally not want to ask you to do this for me. But the matter is of grave urgency. It requires your immediate attention. It is crucial that you succeed."

"Have I ever failed you before?" Larksmum queried.

"You have been a devoted servant to our cause, never questioning, never remorseful over the burdens we place on you. You never question our purpose. I can only tell you that for everything you have done for us there is a purpose greater than the victims who have been dispensed by your hand. They only stood in the way of our purpose, a purpose that is greater than all of us, even me. Please accept my thanks for your dedication."

The leader of the Order of Sumer looked at the others sitting around the table, his expression bore a frightened responsibility that puzzled Larksmum. The other men sat solemnly in their places, each one intent on the words of the speaker. An air of desperation hovered in the room. It felt like the panicked energy that surrounded her when she took someone's life. The energy—good or bad—affected how Larksmum approached her assignments. She could feel fear, or in some cases exaltation, as her victims realized why she entered their lives. Most of them knew it was coming, for whatever sin they committed against her employers. She never knew, never asked.

"I am happy to oblige. I serve at your discretion. You took me in when I was lost, without judgment or criticism. You forgave me my sins, taught me that human life is not sacred if it is not purposeful. It is with my hand that many were able to be freed of their demons. Human life does not affect me."

Larksmum cared little for the people she killed at the behest of these men who sat around the table. They saved her from her own death, taught her that life was only precious if it were lived with the intent on giving back to the greater consciousness. Those who threatened the universal good needed to be eliminated. It had been her mantra for over thirty years. After all, she was a Guardian of the Books of Eden.

"Our time runs short. There are energies that threaten the sacred task that we, and others before us, swore to protect." The man began to ramble. "Four millennia ago our predecessors embarked on a journey to salvage mankind from extinction. Now, despite our efforts, that may no longer be possible."

A few of the others nodded in agreement.

"All that we represent will be challenged by this task. But I need you to do this for us. If we were to have asked another, I would be afraid of the consequences."

A hollow silence filled the vast hall as Larksmum opened the envelope containing her latest job. Larksmum stared at the name on the page, trying to hide her shock. With great difficulty she tried to control her emotions. Her voice faltered for a moment before speaking.

"I will do your bidding," she said weakly.

Larksmum stood up, accepting the task without another word. With a polite nod she left the room. The men did not stand as she exited. They expected her to oblige their command, thankful for the small fortune they paid her to perform her services with brutal efficiency. She never questioned their motives, and they never questioned her methods.

As she left the monastery, however, she was convinced the Order must have made a mistake this time. She had done her best to conceal her reaction in front of the council. She doubted whether she succeeded. It was the first time they ever saw her weak side.

Three hours later Larksmum was in her apartment, staring out over the Arno and trying to figure out what to do next. She removed her Dior dress in front of the full-length mirror in her bedroom, examining her body as she stood only in bra and panties. Her shoulder length hair was now snow white, in stark contrast to the rest of her youthful, athletic frame. The work she did was demanding. The result was a body of a thirty year old, firm and curvaceous. Her hand caressed a small scar on her right side, just below her breast, a reminder of the danger of her chosen profession. She changed into comfortable track pants and a tee-shirt, opened a bottle of wine, and sat down to plan her assignment. The name on the bottom of the letter given to her by the Order of Sumer stared up at her.

Carmen Salvatore was a thirty-six year-old associate professor at the University of Florence specializing in the Etruscans, an ancient civilization that had settled the hills of Tuscany four millennia earlier. The woman had more than a passing interest in the history of the ancient civilization of which many Tuscans shared a bloodline. There was also much more to Carmen than just her dull and arcane field of study, which touched on the subjects near and dear to the Order. There was a personal attachment.

Carmen Salvatore was Larksmum's lover.

33

The shrill metallic ring programmed to sound like a fifties-era landline was enough to distract one of the men weaving his way through the crowd at JFK. He cursed his men in Manhattan who had missed the targets at the Four Seasons by minutes, despite the lead from a well-paid doorman. Another large gratuity gave Sean the destination of the white male and the East Indian woman, bringing his team to the airport to scour the crowds. Glaring at his subordinate to shut his phone off, Mackenzie turned away for a moment, missing the young couple as they entered the concourse and headed for the Air Italia check-in.

Unaware that the two had again slipped past his dragnet, he made his way outside to the taxi stand to follow up with the taxi-dispatcher who had made a lucrative decision to watch for a particular cab. A moment later he crashed his way back into the terminal, signaling his man to follow him to the check-in counters.

JKF was crowded with tourists taking advantage of a weak British Pound and a rebounding domestic economy. British Airways, as well as most of the transatlantic airlines, were offering deep discounts to London and beyond. Frantic travelers were struggling to make their way through check-in and security on their way to the departure gates. A computer glitch that had delayed several dozen flights that morning only added to the mayhem.

Jason, led by Jasmine, joined the hordes of people making their way through security. With no checked luggage, it took only a few minutes to get their boarding passes from the self-serve kiosk. Each of them dragged a small carry-on suitcase full of essentials they had purchased at Macy's that morning. Still unsure of who was trying to kill Jason, they opted to leave without retrieving any personal affects.

Jasmine was thankful that Jason did not suggest they return to her apartment. She refrained from telling Jason more about her real reason for showing up at Amy's. Now she wasn't sure how to broach the subject. Her instincts told her that the time was not right. It was necessary to continue to build trust between them if they were both going to succeed, especially after they found out about Amy. Jasmine was still not sure the news had sunk in.

They had been watching television after arranging their flights to Italy when the news broke. Amy's body had been discovered by a jogger in Central Park early the previous night. According to the report, she was apparently a victim of a random attack.

Jasmine contacted her old publisher to get more details. It took him less than an hour. Her grizzled boss, an inch from retirement, knew when the police were covering something up. After some pressure and a few favors, he was given the details on the promise not to go public until the police were ready. Amy's body was riddled with intricate wounds that suggested torture. As the publisher described the condition of the body, Jasmine recalled another time when she had seen similar techniques used—techniques used during interrogations. It was clear she had been dumped in the Park after she was killed.

Jasmine shared the details with Jason, who stared blankly back at her for a few moments as the news registered. His jaw tightened in a way that told Jasmine he was gearing up for revenge. He would wait to mourn her death.

Jason was lost in thought as the TSA security agent asked him for his boarding card. Jasmine took it out of his hand and gave it to the agent. He snapped out of his reverie long enough to walk through the metal detector, collect his suitcase, and retrieve his shoes. Jasmine was held back, her body sounding the alarm. It took the TSA female scanner a full two minutes to wave the wand up and down her body to detect that the various snaps, pins and buckles of her dress were not dangerous weapons. But she had to give up a tube of expensive face cream she had just bought, since it exceeded the allowable size by a few milliliters. She offered to empty half of it out, but to no avail.

"We have to get to the bottom of this conspiracy," Jason intoned as they sat down to wait for the Air Italia flight to board.

"Why would you call it that?" Jasmine reached for his hand and placed it in her own.

"I am an accountant, trained to see logical connections, trace information back to source, and accumulate details so that shareholders can get a snapshot of what is happening in their business. Transactions tell individual stories about what is going on in a company. Each one reveals a little something about the aspirations of an organization. From the time I met with Hans to discuss my company joining his organization there have been little events that seemed like they were telling separate stories. Each event seemingly independent of the others. Until now. There is something much larger going on, larger than anything even Hans was aware of. He may have been a part of a group that rigged his buildings for destruction, but he was not in control. Amy's death is a clear signal that something has gone off the rails—"

"Because she was tortured?" Jasmine asked.

"Not just because she was tortured, but because her body was found so quickly. I think whoever did this is sending a message."

"Do you think Hans could have prevented his death…and Amy's?" Jasmine added tenderly. She had to phrase her questions carefully. She did not want Jason to discover the extent of her knowledge of the Thought Mechanix organization.

"I'd like to think so, but I doubt it. He once told me that the Rules of Possibility were tied somehow to the origins of human thought. When his production at the Isaac Stern Auditorium was sabotaged, he alluded to the fact that others might be trying to prevent his revealing the truth. Hans was on a mission that was decidedly different than the people who had him, and Amy, killed."

"Do you think the priest that Amy was arguing with was involved in her death?" Jasmine looked past Jason at the crowd, searching the faces for anyone registering recognition. She had been in enough situations to know that the people they had encountered in Amy's apartment were not going to go away. With luck, they would be able to stay one step ahead of whomever was financing their pursuit.

"That is why the threads connecting all of the events of the past week are taking us to Italy," Jason answered without conviction.

He was no longer concerned about fulfilling some crazy quest for Hans Pedersen. It was now personal. He stared past Jasmine at the Airbus 320 waiting to be boarded, the gate agent readying herself to call for the invalids, infants, and gold-elite. A strange anger overtook Jason's trademark calm demeanor. Now his only purpose was to find out who killed Amy and make them pay. He never thought of himself as a vengeful person, at least not in his business dealings. Most of the time he gave up too easily. Nothing really mattered enough for a fight. But with his best friend sitting in a hospital bed in London, his mentor splattered all over a New York sidewalk, and now Amy tortured to death by some very sick people, he could feel an emotion welling up inside that he had only experienced once before.

His mind flashed back to the tenth grade: he saw the senior football star, drunk with too much cheap bourbon, taking advantage of a girl from his grade. Repeated attempts to disentangle her body from the large brute were met with jeers from the other partiers. Jason snapped, grabbing the large athlete from behind and yanking him off the girl, who scurried away, clinging to her tattered clothes. The price he paid was a broken nose and suspension from school, consequences that had shaped his reaction to adversity from that moment on.

A sad smile crossed his lips as he let the memory slip back into the forgotten recesses of his brain. *Shit happens to everyone,* he thought. That's why the degenerates and the bullies of the world prevail, because people believe that misery is meant to exist. There is always one more victim, one more unfortunate, one more weakling who thinks that abuse is the human condition.

Hans Pedersen had tried to change that notion. He stood as a beacon of hope for millions looking for a new answer, an answer that would expose the hypocrisy of some dogma convincing them of the frailness of the human spirit. Whatever was revealed to him about the formula of true existence worked itself into the hearts and minds of anyone ready to listen. It was a new connection to the universe's energy, and he was about to share with the world its secret. By Hans's actions, powerful forces were unleashed.

Yet there were those who were either unwilling or unable to part with their hold over the knowledge they possessed. Jason wondered if they were frightened of what it might do to a species not ready to embrace the truth. *Or were they scared of losing their carefully designed basis of power?*

Either way, Amy was forced to suffer some unspeakable death because of it, and that unleashed in him the uncontrollable anger that had long ago impelled him to defend an innocent girl at a high school party.

A surge of focused energy enveloped Jason as they boarded the aircraft. He held Jasmine's hand with a comfortable ease throughout the flight, dozing off for a few hours over the Atlantic, waking once to eat, then sleeping again until the plane touched down on the darkened runway of Rome's Fiumicino airport.

Bleary-eyed, the pair steered their small, wheeled suitcases through the thinning late-evening crowds to the car rental kiosks.

They were too tired to notice the men watching from across the nearly empty concourse as they exited onto the sidewalk.

34

Dusk was settling on Florence, the red-brown sky casting a dark shadow down the street as Larksmum made her way into the apartment. She stood ramrod straight in the small garden outside the four-story apartment building where Carmen Salvatore lived. The building was on the Via dell'Oriuolo, a short scooter ride to the university. The dome of the Cattedrale di Santa Maria del Fiore dominated the skyline from the balcony of the apartment. Larksmum enjoyed the view from the rooftop balcony where she and Carmen occasionally made love. Tonight would possibly be the last time she would enjoy the view.

Carmen answered the door breathlessly, having run down the two flights of stairs as soon as the buzzer sounded. She was radiant in a light-blue summer frock held up by invisible straps. Her braless excitement pushed though the thin, see-through fabric. She liked wearing the revealing dresses. This made it difficult for students of both genders to concentrate during her lectures. If they really cared about the subject, she surmised, they would get past the visual distraction.

Her colleagues were another matter. That was deliberate torture. What she gave out in the halls of the university, she gladly accepted back in the privacy of her own home. Carmen lived up to her name when it came to her sexual appetite. She liked it interesting, whether she was in control or not was determined by her partner. Her tastes were not gender biased, as she enjoyed the company of adventurers whoever they were.

Six months earlier Carmen had literally bumped into Larksmum while leaving a nightclub near her apartment. The woman was bleeding from a cut in her arm, a large stain already forming on the front of her blouse as she staggered down the street. Delirious from a lack of blood, Larksmum was taken back to Carmen's apartment and patched up. They became friends, then lovers, with Larksmum taking the dominant role, Carmen accepting her subservient position with vigor.

She never asked about the cause of the knife wound. Larksmum never volunteered an explanation.

Entering the apartment and quickly closing the door behind her, Larksmum took in the beauty of the five-foot-four Carmen. She looked deep into her hazel eyes, stroked the silky black hair that hung long over her shoulders, then with her right hand grasped her ample breast through the thin fabric of the dress. They kissed for a long time before reluctantly detaching their bodies. The intensity of the passion surprised Carmen, who was used to Larksmum starting their evenings more casually. Regardless of the reason, she liked the urgency.

Carmen's apartment was a collection of artifacts and artwork of the civilization to which she dedicated her career. Delicate stone pots, clay tablets with glyphs pronouncing the events of the day, and a plethora of textbooks cluttered the shelves along three of the walls in the tiny apartment. In contrast to the radiant beauty of Florence, the walls and tile floors of the apartment were drab and grey. Yet the colorless walls only served to heighten Carmen's own vibrant beauty. Besides the sheer dress Carmen wore, the only other color in the room was a glass vase full of gladiolas, sunflowers and roses.

Carmen went into the kitchen as soon as they were upstairs, speaking with excited animation as she poured Chianti from a carafe into two ancient Etruscan wine goblets. The goblets were a gift from her PhD thesis professor, after a weekend he would never forget. Unlike the other stodgy professors who graded the theses of aspiring PhD hopefuls, he came to all of her Etruscan civilization lectures as she worked to earn a spot on the faculty. He watched intently as her eyes shone with an electric intensity, capturing her students as she traversed the lecture hall, looking for minds to challenge her theories. He had been eager to please too, and he was married to a beautiful woman who had no sexual boundaries. Carmen proved it to herself by personally bedding the woman. She was like an animal in a primal state, seemingly deprived of affection, eager to explore all aspects of Carmen's insatiable desire.

Yet Carmen was born to teach, and even without the mind-altering sexual experiences, her other gifts were a guarantee to a tenured position at the university. But she was always astounded by the depths for which human lust could manifest success.

Tonight she and Larksmum made love on the rooftop patio under a dark autumn sky that was caressed by a light breeze making its way across the Arno. It was a passionate entanglement that lasted longer than both of them expected, neither willing to give in to the surge of ecstasy building from deep within. Afterwards, they sat wrapped in each other's arms, watching the lights bounce off the Cathedral dome. Larksmum leaned back into the younger woman, allowing her hand to softly rub the taut muscles of her upper thigh. She knew that such an intimate moment was not how she wanted to remember Carmen.

A moment later she reluctantly pushed herself away. Getting up from the foam mattress, Larksmum went to the bathroom.

She splashed a handful of cool water onto her face as if to wash away the conflict that weighed her down. It was unsettling to be planning the death of her lover. She was always able to detach herself from the victims of the Guardians. This was personal. She could not shake the connection that she had a responsibility to Carmen. The arguing in her head was moot as Larksmum was sworn to carry out all requests of the Guardians, her death assured if she failed them even once. As she contemplated the death of her lover she understood why they chose her. It would have been impossible for her if they had sent someone else who would not be as kind.

Larksmum would miss the vivacious professor's company, particularly the sweet scent of her body. The lovemaking was more enjoyable than most of the men she bedded. Although just a distraction in her life, the companionship was the closest she felt to having "family" since she ran away from home at eighteen.

Although Larksmum was mulling over the methods she would have to employ, she was having reservations. The Order of Sumer was like an onion, each layer more secretive than the next. Although they did not share their motives with the outside world, nor with the people whom they employed to enforce their will, Larksmum had been around long enough to deduce that the group possessed some powerful knowledge. She knew of the relationship between one of the significant members of the Order and Hans Pedersen, the founder of Thought

Mechanix, because she had been dispatched to bring back intelligence about one of their own who went rogue.

Most of the Guardians never learned why they were summoned. It was enough to be needed for their unique talents. But Larksmum had a curiosity that bordered on OCD. She was relentless in her attempts to understand her employers. So it was not routine for her to accept the sanction on Carmen Salvatore without some enquiry. This was the not first time Larksmum questioned the motives of the Order. But this time she wondered what it was that Carmen could possibly know that had prompted them to authorize such quick action.

Larksmum decided she would find out before proceeding with her assignment. She needed to know why she had to make such a sacrifice. Clearly, she was not going to be able to fulfill the demands handed to her by her employers. Her brain was a mixture of blind emotion and intense conflict as she tried to come up with a solution. She needed all of the knowledge Carmen possessed regarding her arrangement with Hans Pedersen, information that had her benefactors trembling in abject terror. Once she was able to extract that information, she could deal with eliminating Carmen from the scene. Her employers would not have to know that the professor was not dead, as long as she disappeared.

"You seem preoccupied tonight." Carmen tossed a pillow towards Larksmum as she exited the bathroom. Catching it mid-flight, Larksmum realized that she now held the potential murder weapon in her hands.

"I was just wondering about you," Larksmum smiled down at the Tuscan beauty. "You are so vibrant in your lovemaking, but you are involved in studies of such mundane topics. How do you cope?"

"I just imagine what life must have been like when the Lydians first arrived from the Middle East almost three thousand years ago to live amongst the Etruscans. To come from such a barren land to the beauty of Tuscany must have sent them into rapture. I imagine the men and women finding their private places amongst the dense brush that covered the area, copulating to the sounds of the birds and the smell of the lavender in the air. They created a civilization that served as the basis for all great cultures that followed. The Greeks and the Romans owe a significant portion of their historical influences and innovations to the Etruscans. The artistic explosion of the Renaissance stems from the originality and creativity of the Etruscans. They were the first civilization that truly understood how to harness the enormous power of the human mind."

Carmen was animated as she described the culture, art and innovations of the Etruscans. She sat half naked on the edge of her bed looking up at Larksmum, who, by this time, had settled comfortably on the settee for the discussion, hoping that whatever it was that possessed the power of the Order of Sumer to sanction this execution would be forthcoming in her casual inquires. She was incapable of torturing this exquisite woman in order to understand their motives. If they demanded such a sacrifice of her, they had better be ready to deliver an equal reward in exchange. She would make sure that it happened.

"You are passionate about this. I haven't even heard of these people. Does the rest of the world know their history?" Larksmum was intrigued.

"Many Westerners are ignorant about the Etruscans, whose existence is rarely spoken of outside of central Italy. History remembers the Greeks, it remembers the Romans, but speaks little of this small tribe from Asia Minor, the first to conquer the European continent.

"They were a small tribe indigenous to the hills of Tuscany and Umbria before such places were known by those names. Something happened around the year 700 B.C. that changed all of that. Once a nomadic group of disjointed families, the Etruscan civilization was consolidated by a smaller group of people who emerged around that time from Asia Minor. No one knows exactly where they came from but similarities in early writing and other artifacts closely linked them to the Lydians. Biblical and historical accounts speak of the Lydians dealing with a great famine that forced the leader of the Lydians to send half of the tribe away. They were sent west in search of more fertile lands. Historians believe they eventually settled in the hills of Tuscany after decades of migration.

"The Lydians had no means of protection from the more aggressive Etruscans and soon found themselves immersed within a warrior-like group of local hill men. Grossly outnumbered, lacking in sufficient war-like tendencies and unable to hold back the more aggressive locals, you would think that the Lydians would have been slaughtered. But the funny thing is they weren't killed. Not even close. Within a few short years the migrants were ruling the local hill people, intermarrying with their offspring and prospering. The interesting point is that the Lydian assimilation was more than just an acceptance of one tribe over another. It was more like slow, methodical conquest. Etruscan rites and culture quickly converted to the customs of the implanted Lydians. The men and women from Asia Minor soon forgot their roots, so that within one generation they had become Etruscans. It was as if their past was a stain to be removed and forgotten."

Carmen rolled over on the bed to rest on her stomach, her hands under her chin and her legs bent at the knees like a sorrority girl gossiping on a Saturday night slumber party, her appearance completely at odds with the IQ she possessed and most likely due to the wine she had consumed.

Larksmum wanted her to continue. The history lesson was riveting. She sensed it was leading her to a story she wanted to hear.

"Is it that unusual that one tribe assimilates with another rather than killing them off? After all, wasn't that what made the Romans so successful?"

Carmen continued after taking a mouthful from her third glass of wine, feeling tipsy but alive with the passion of her life.

"Precisely. In fact, despite massive evidence supporting the theory, it is generally a very little advertised fact that much of the Roman elite, including possibly Julius Caesar, was of Etruscan descent. More importantly, the lineage goes further than that. Many of the leaders of Western civilization and culture were descended from the original Lydian families who comingled with the early Etruscans."

Carmen punctuated the comment with another gulp of wine.

"Why are you so intent on proving the lineage from the Lydians?" Larksmum asked, now anxious to hear the response. "What makes them so special?"

"The Etruscan civilization is part of my heritage. I grew up in Tuscany with a knowledge that my family comes from ancient bloodlines. I studied with my peers, closely observing to see what the expectations were of me. I wanted to know more about the happy Tusci farmhand who settled in near my uncle and aunt, collecting artifacts from the surrounding hills. The more I studied, the more I realized this was no ordinary union of two distinct cultures. What I discovered was far more revealing than I could have ever imagined. There is a reason why the Lydians were able to subdue the indigenous hill tribe from Tusci, why their influence could be felt from the time they appeared on the horizon of the Italian peninsula seven hundred years before the birth to Christ, and why the legacy they left behind in Tuscany and elsewhere is so important to grasp."

Carmen was tipsy. She spoke with a slight slur as the alcohol took hold. Sworn to secrecy by her superiors not to discuss the latest discovery until the time was right, she held back. Dean Franco Simonyi was adamant. They were well funded by their benefactor from the U.S., to the tune of over ten million Euros a year, to continue their research of the Etruscan's connection to the Lydians. Details were fed through an intricately disguised pipeline to the man with the checkbook.

Now, that benefactor's death could have a significant impact on her research. It could mean the end of her department. She knew that her latest discoveries were what nudged the millions their way. Her epiphany had to be kept secret until a solution could be found. Carmen considered Dean Simonyi erudite in his scholarly pursuits of the Etruscans but naïve about the world of funding research. She knew the cash would stop soon. If she was to continue her research, there would have to be a new strategy, and looking over at Larksmum from her prone position on the bed an idea started to percolate. She had no idea what her lover did, but it was clear by the Ferragamo shoes and Dior dresses that she was wealthy.

"So what was it you discovered?" Larksmum asked quietly, hiding the anticipation with a nonchalant sigh. Larksmum knew it was just a matter of coaxing Carmen to reveal it. *What was it that made her so dangerous to the Order?*

The night had become cool, as a northern wind chilled by the Dolomites descended upon the city. Carmen moved from the bed to close the windows, the breeze pushing the silk robe away to reveal her nude body.

Larksmum cooed her approval of the sight, momentarily forgetting their conversation. In return, she received a seductive smile. Carmen looked over her shoulder as she latched the window, blew a kiss, then returned to sit across from Larksmum in a leather recliner. Curling her legs up on the chair gave Larksmum a pleasant view of the delights she would enjoy later in the evening.

"I shouldn't really be saying anything. Our department is under tremendous pressure to deliver on our research from the people who provide the funding. One of our benefactors died recently, and that could mean the end of my department, even the end of my career at the university. Right before I was about to deliver my greatest discovery surrounding the Etruscans."

"Who died?" Larksmum asked, knowing perfectly well she was referring to Hans Pedersen.

"It's not important. Listen, let's forget about all this and enjoy the evening." Carmen stood up and removed her robe, walking over to Larksmum, who lay back on the settee.

The discussion, and Carmen's fate, would have to wait.

35

"I think we're being followed."

Jason stole a glance out of the back of the white Fiat taxi they had hired at the Florence airport after a few minutes of haggling. The car was not an official airport taxi, just a local cabbie trying to make a buck without paying for the official airport tag he needed to pick up curbside at the terminal. This suited Jason fine, as the tagged cabbies in Florence were reputed to rip off unsuspecting Americans.

Gino, the driver, spoke passable English and agreed to take them to their destination. In the first few minutes of the journey Jason secured the man's services for the day, just in case they needed to move around the city quickly.

"Which car do you think it is?" he asked Jasmine as he scoured the crowded lanes of traffic from the small rear window.

Jasmine was watching the same scene from the passenger side mirror. "Three cars back, outside lane, a silver Mercedes sedan. I recognize the men from the airport in Rome. They got into the car just as we were pulling away from the curb at the airport. The driver pointed our way, which I noticed but thought nothing of it at the time."

"You have keen eyes or were you just expecting us to be followed?" Jason rubbed the back of her shoulder from behind as he let out a small laugh.

"Journalist…duh." Jasmine mocked a Homer Simpson reply. "From everything that has happened since I met you, I wouldn't be surprised about anything. But my journalistic sense tells me that we had better be observant."

"Rrrright," Jason replied in his best Dr. Evil voice.

They had travelled halfway from the airport to the University of Florence, hoping to meet Carmen Salvatore as soon as possible. Thoughts of a hotel room and a shower were dismissed.

"You guys ina trouble." Gino's English accent was thick. He glanced over his shoulder at Jason in the back seat. "You wanna me lose this car?"

"Would you mind…they think I'm some sort of Bollywood movie star…" Jasmine batted her eyes at Gino, who grinned knowingly.

"Hang on, eh," Gino yelled as he cranked the wheel, waving his fist at the driver of a semi-truck that veered to miss the near collision. *"Basta,"* he yelled through the windshield at the truck as it evaded the taxi.

Jason was tossed to the other side of the cramped backseat as Gino veered off the Viale Alessandro Guidoni into a construction site. The Mercedes followed by cutting off two lanes of nonchalant traffic seemingly immune to such antics, following the battered Fiat into the worksite.

After narrowly avoiding a dump truck as it lumbered out of a foundation pit, Gino was back on the street at Via Sandro Pertini. Fifty feet further, Jason was tossed back to the passenger side again as Gino made a two-wheeled turn into another construction site, this time of an apartment complex. Ignoring the one-way sign at the entrance, Gino gunned the engine and flew out of the narrow unpaved parking lot, barely missing a front-end loader that was turning into the site. A wave of his fist as he sailed past was met with a quick flick of the worker's hand under his chin.

Jasmine looked back at Jason, who was trying to keep planted in his seat, and then past him to the street they had just left. The silver Mercedes had turned into the parking lot just as Gino turned onto another side street.

Jasmine hooted as she could see that the front-end loader blocked the path of the pursuing Mercedes. Two men jumped from the car and were yelling at the driver to move, who sat dispassionately waving his arms for them to get out of his construction site.

Gino kept the pedal down as he maneuvered his illegal taxi through a number of side streets, parking lots and alleys.

"To lose the paparazzi for good," he yelled over the whine of the twelve-hundred cc engine.

A few quick turns later, Gino was traversing down a worn footpath beside a greenbelt, smiling sheepishly as he deftly avoided several couples on a late afternoon stroll. Cranking the wheel one more time to exit the path, the Fiat careened around an approaching delivery truck. After spinning the steering wheel half a revolution onto Via di Novoli, they drove the few remaining kilometers to the University of Florence.

The Mercedes was nowhere to be seen.

Gino continued to be wary of the pursuers, continually looking over his shoulder, flashing a smile at his two passengers with each small triumph. He weaved in and out of traffic, took small side streets, and even pulled into an alley to stop and watch the traffic for a few minutes in order to make absolutely certain he had succeeded in losing his tail. Despite his ability to lose the Mercedes, he did not let up on the accelerator, driving as if all of Florence was watching his magnificent feat.

"*Non male, eh*! Not bad, huh?" Gino smiled as they pulled in front of the University of Florence main campus building.

"Not bad at all," Jasmine smiled as he opened the door of the taxi.

"Let's hope that we can find Carmen," Jason said as he exited, handing Gino the driver a one-hundred Euro note. "You certainly earned it," he said as they departed with Gino's cell phone and a promise he would be nearby when needed.

They entered the university from the entrance on Via Antonio Magliabechi, after sidestepping a group of students who had stopped in front of the exit. They were focused on one member of their little group, a young man whose excited and animated demeanor seemed to hold them enthralled. Neither Jason nor Jasmine could understand his rapid dialogue or high-pitched Italian, but they heard the student mention the name *Salvatore*. A few of the students reacted with comments that Jason could only interpret as disbelief, as several of the girls covered their mouths with their hands.

"*Antonio, sei sicuro? Come è potuto accadere?*" One of the female students queried, her voice cracking with emotion.

Jason and Jasmine let the door close and turned back to the group of students who were now edging closer to their fellow classmate to learn more details.

Jasmine moved into the center of the group, cornering the student with the news. "Do you speak English?" she asked. "What was it you were saying about Ms. Salvatore?"

The small crowd made an opening in their circle for Jasmine.

"Yes, a little," Antonio replied hesitantly.

Jasmine continued, "Were you speaking of Ms. Carmen Salvatore, the Professor of Etruscan Studies?"

"She was my professor." Antonio looked past Jasmine at the girl who had now broken down in tears. *"Scusami…*excuse me," he held his index finger up for Jasmine to wait and went over to bend down to speak to the girl, who had dropped onto the curb.

"È 'alright, Bianca. Non preoccupatevi di Salvatore. Lei è una donna dura. Si arriva al fondo della cottura. Sono sicuro che è stato un malinteso. Te lo prometto." He wiped the tear from her cheek and gave her a hug. *"Aspetta un minuto, sarò subito."*

He stood up and came back to where Jason and Jasmine were waiting.

"I am Antonio."

Jasmine held out her hand.

"My name is Jasmine Shah. And this is Jason Wakefield. We are friends of Carmen's from America. We've come to visit her—"

"I'm afraid she is no longer here," Antonio gestured to the building behind them. "I was telling Bianca that everything will be fine. We went to class today and were told that is was cancelled. That Ms. Salvatore had been, how do you say…*licenziato*…fired."

"You mean she was let go by the University? Do you know why?" Jason moved closer.

"We don't know. No one would give us any answers. The administrator just told us not to come back to this class until further notice."

"Do you know where Carmen, ah, Ms. Salvatore, is now?"

"No idea. At her home, I guess."

Jasmine realized she told Antonio that they were friends, so he would expect them to know where Carmen lived. She'd have to be shrewd to find out the answer.

"We've never been to her house. The last time we were in town she visited us at our hotel. Do you know where she lives?"

Antonio shook his head no, but then turned to look at his friend. *"Bianca, dove Carmen si vive?"* He turned to back to Jasmine, "Bianca knows. She told me that she had been there once for coffee."

Bianca stood up and walked back to where they were standing. She wiped her cheeks with the edge of her sweater. "She lives on via dell'Oriuolo by the Cattedrale…the Cathedral… di Santa Maria del Fiore. It is about kilometer. Just walk straight up this street." Bianca pointed opposite of the way Gino had brought them to the University. "The street turns into via Dai Pepi. When you reach via Pietrapaina, turn left. Her apartment is number 29."

"Grazie." Jasmine gave Bianca a hug and a thank-you. "Don't worry, Carmen will be just fine."

She had no idea but thought at least she would make the poor girl feel a little better. Jason extended his thanks as they left.

The students started to talk all together in excited Italian pointing towards where Jason and Jasmine were going.

Ten minutes after leaving the group they were standing at 29 via dell'Oriuolo. They instinctively looked up and down the street, half expecting to see the Mercedes. Jasmine had no illusion that they would stay underground for long. The men chasing them were like dozens of other teams she had encountered in her life, brilliantly skillful at tracking the movements of people. She had hired similar, albeit less deadly teams many times to secure information, or safe passage, or both. By now she figured they would have located Gino, their illegal cab driver, by tapping into the Italian motor bureau and with a little persuasion, financial or otherwise, determined to know where he had taken them.

Jason should not have told Gino that they were coming to the University, nor should she have mentioned Carmen by name. It was gratuitous information that provided a direct link to their destination. But he wouldn't have known to do otherwise. Americans like to share information; it was what made them so vulnerable. She did not know how long they had but suspected there was not much time.

36

Gunter Tang paced behind his desk as he spoke into the Bluetooth earpiece. His goal was becoming a bigger challenge than he expected, even after convincing Jason Wakefield that the Thought Mechanix meddling in his business was tantamount to corporate sabotage. Despite his successful efforts to convince Jason's lackluster audit partners to arrange a coup, acquire Talon, and by default Finnstart— for twice its market value—to access Hans Pedersen indirectly he was still no further ahead than he was when he started his recent campaign. Even gleaning as much information out of Amy Glass as her strong-willed personality would permit was not conclusive. The only thing he learned from her was the double life she lived, and the name of her second employer.

He was no fool. His empire, despite some of his unsavory tactics, was considered by Forbes as one of the best-run companies in the country. It was a behemoth that fed on growth, synergies, and the massive talents of its CEO. Gunter often joked that running Tang Enterprises was no different than operating his father's Triad, except that he could sell products and services openly rather than trying to outrun the vice squads around the world. But with the power of thought energy he could reach a new plateau.

Gunter also knew a good thing when he saw it, and he saw the potential of what Hans Pedersen was doing from a million miles away. Control through manipulation was all that the motivational guru did to his disciples. The Rules of Possibility did to its devotees what years in a prisoner-of-war camp could never do—it released whatever thoughts the user fed to the listener into their subconscious. Hans, whether he knew it or not, had created the most powerful brainwashing technique ever devised. To be able to harness that thought energy would guarantee untold success—commercial success, physical success, psychological success, whatever Gunter wanted it to do. And Gunter Tang wanted to do it all.

Even though it was speculation, Gunter knew that if he could control Thought Mechanix he would be able to control how Hans Pedersen approached the development of his product. That was why he purchased Talon Enterprises. It gave him access to Finnstart, which gave him access to TMI—and Hans Pedersen. At least that was the idea. That was until the motivational guru splattered himself all over the pavement outside of the Plaza. It was no wonder the idiot did not accept the billions he offered to gain access and control over the Thought Mechanix premier product and the power it could unleash. The man had problems.

As did Gunter. The events since the unexpected death of Hans had him worried. Everything connected to Thought Mechanix was being systematically destroyed. There were very powerful people behind the TMI corporate façade, people who were as ruthless as his organization. He had no idea who they were, but it was clear that they wielded an unfathomable depth of talent, and power. They were unraveling the billions of dollars he had committed to gain control of whatever secrets Hans Pedersen held. It was clear that the people who killed Hans wanted to ensure that no one else could do what he had done.

Less than a week after the New York icon hit the pavement there was a well-oiled publicity machine spinning stories to discredit Hans's Rules of Possibility. Newsmen across the globe interviewed countless experts who testified to the watching millions that Thought Mechanix was nothing more than pabulum for the disheartened and disenfranchised. It worked much like voodoo worked—because the users wanted to believe it was true they convinced themselves that projecting thoughts, creating positive images, and avoiding defeatist notions would cure them. To many, just changing how they viewed the world changed their world; they still lived pathetic lives, but somehow they were now content. Hans Pedersen did not do anything but deliver regurgitated advice handed down to pathetic losers since Norman Vincent Peale suggested that thinking positive was the panacea. The general population bought the tripe, while only a few truly gifted people benefited from the exercise. It would not take long before Hans Pedersen and the Rules of Possibility were yesterday's news.

Gunter wasn't buying any of it. He saw what Jason Wakefield did to his employees at the Tang Enterprises subsidiary. The change was remarkable in two ways. Not only did the efforts of Jason and Thought Mechanix increase productivity by over thirty percent, there was a wholesale change in the attitudes of the employees. They worked twice as hard as ever before, and they voted to disband a union that Gunter wanted to get rid of for years. Most significantly, they were adding improvements to the production line and the products without being asked or prompted. He had never experienced a mass of people giving back as unselfishly as his workers after they completed Wakefield's course.

He needed the power that the process promised. To control that raw mental power, he needed to find out who was destroying the Thought Mechanix organization that Hans built. He needed to gain access to their secrets. Either that or he needed to find Jason Wakefield and convince him to divulge what he knew. Gunter was not having any success with either plan and his patience was wearing thin. He paced the carpet behind his desk as the cell phone connected through his Bluetooth.

Anthony Lee answered with a sharp hello.

"There is no way this can be happening. I gave you carte blanche to use whatever resources it took to find Jason and Jasmine. Eliminate her if you have to, but not until you can determine what she knows. I need them and I have to find out who is systematically destroying Hans Pedersen's empire before the man is even in his grave."

"They seem to have a sixth sense. Whenever we get close, they bolt," Lee explained.

Lee had his best men on the task. It was infuriating to him that Jason Wakefield was able to elude his men. Even his friend at Thought Mechanix succumbed in a matter of hours, despite the fact that she appeared to be surrounded with round-the-clock protection. Once they had her, he was certain of his ability to deliver everything his boss requested. But the bitch turned out to be tougher than he expected. She died without even providing a thread of useful information. So the trail returned to Jason Wakefield. And his newfound friend, Jasmine Shah.

"You lost them again in Florence?" The anger was rising up in Gunter's throat like unwanted bile.

"Temporarily. They picked up the tail and by some miracle chose a taxi driver who drove like he was in the Dakar Rally."

"What did you find out about Jasmine Shah?"

"Ms. Shah is quite a handful. A decorated war hero in the Indian elite forces, she was, until recently, working as a foreign correspondent for a now defunct British newspaper."

"Indian special forces? Who exactly are we up against?"

"She spent three years of mandatory military service with the Indian Army. The records were hard to get, but we have enough friends there that we now have a complete dossier. She is one talented soldier."

"So get rid of Shah. Once she's out of the picture, Jason will be easy to control. I presume he will lead us directly to the source of Hans Pedersen's power."

Gunter was no fool. There was something to the Rules of Possibility. He was even more convinced of that after the wholesale destruction of the Thought Mechanix organization and the spin campaign orchestrated to discredit it. He needed to find out how and where Hans Pedersen acquired his knowledge. It could not have been personal skill or some nascent talent. The round tub of a man was a great orator, a showman of immense skill. But the vodka- swilling motivational speaker did not act alone, even if he believed he controlled his own actions. No, Hans Pedersen was a pawn of a much larger organization, and Gunter was determined to steal their secrets. Anyone who stood in his way would be dead, or wish they were.

37

Jason squinted at the small print on the intercom at the entrance to the apartment building at 29 via dell'Oriuolo, finding a C. Salvatore on the top floor. He pressed the intercom. A moment later a woman's voice cracked through the ancient speaker.

"*Chi è?*"

Jasmine moved towards the intercom to speak. "Carmen Salvatore?"

"*Sì.* Who is this?" Carmen responded, her voice tight, like she had been crying.

"Carmen. My name is Jasmine Shah, and I am with Jason Wakefield. We were friends of Hans Pedersen—"

There was an immediate buzz from the intercom and a click of the door in response.

"Apartment 4c," Carmen said from the intercom as they entered the building.

The apartment was a tastefully restored house built at the turn of the century during a building boom in central Florence. Marble stairs wound up through the center of the building, framed by an ornate wrought-iron banister. An elevator was squeezed into the small space created by the circular stairs. Looking at the fifty-year-old contraption, Jason surmised that the climb up would be quicker and so headed up the stairs with Jasmine right behind.

The walls and ceilings of the hallway were decorated with flower-shaped molds, thick sconces holding electric candles, and bold ceiling medallions in the center of each landing. Each floor opened onto a small hallway with four sturdy-looking wood doors. As they reached the top floor, they saw Carmen. She was waiting for them in the only doorway at the end of a small landing. Her face looked like it had endured a month of tears, her eyes bloodshot and her hair disheveled.

After introductions, she escorted them in, offered drinks and led them to the living room. Jason sat on a small ottoman while Jasmine sat beside the professor on the blue leather couch. A warm breeze came in from the open window bringing with it a fresh smell of rosemary and sage from a small herb garden on the balcony.

"Hans Pedersen sent you," she said tentatively. It was more of a statement than a question. Carmen edged out the words as she held back another burst of tears. Her world was being twisted out of her grasp and the fear made her long to have Larksmum by her side. She no longer felt the confidence that she radiated around the campus of the University of Florence. She was once again the shy schoolgirl who walked home alone, ashamed of her thoughts, the stronger girls tugging at her adolescent insecurities for their own gain. She needed her new lover to make certain she would be okay. She was thankful that Larksmum planned to drop by later.

"You were fired today," Jasmine began. "Do you know why?"

"It was sudden. Unexpected. There is nothing I did that would warrant such an action. The Dean said he was not comfortable with the recent events, especially the suicide of Hans, that he felt it best that I take an extended leave of absence." Carmen spoke as if she were reciting a speech, her Italian accent ending each word with a quiet, fading vowel.

"Why would your Dean be concerned with the death of a motivational speaker halfway around the world?" Jason and Jasmine exchanged a glance.

"Let's back up a minute." Carmen focus intensified, looking at one then the other of her unexpected guests. "You came here looking for me. How did you know to seek me out? As I asked before, did Hans Pedersen send you to see me?"

"In a manner of speaking. Amy Glass was a woman who worked closely with Hans Pedersen. After Hans jumped from his building in New York I tried to contact Amy from London. I never connected with her, but she left me instructions on how to locate a notebook she kept in her apartment. That notebook left enough clues that led me to you. Before that I was unaware of any connection between you and Hans. I'm only now beginning to realize the extent of your involvement.

After Amy betrayed this knowledge to us, she was murdered," Jason explained, a strain of sadness in his voice.

"Oh my God. This can't be happening. I told Hans that my search was tentative. I was confident in what I have discovered, but it may not be the relic he has been looking for all these years. He warned me to be careful, that certain factions were as anxious as he to validate the finding. And now look at what is happening! Are you sure she was murdered?" Carmen burst into another round of tears.

"Convinced she was murdered, yes. Certain it was connected to the insane series of events that have occurred in the past week, no. But I racked my brain. I can only speculate that her complacency with Hans was somehow responsible for her death."

"Hans Pedersen was an exceptional man. He changed the lives of millions," Carmen mumbled.

"Not always for the better," Jasmine quietly noted.

Jason looked at her for a moment, her comments gave him pause. He caught her eye and thought he detected a hint of anger.

"Not always for the better, that is true. In many cases, his lessons have caused the less desirable elements of society to be more successful thieves, or blackmailers, even murderers. Perhaps it was one of them who has wrought destruction on Hans and the organization that he secretly fronted."

"What are you talking about?" Carmen asked.

"You don't know?"

Jason and Jasmine locked eyes for another moment.

"Know what?"

Jason explained what had been going on, both before and after Hans's death, his own move to London, the bombings in London and New York, the trails that led him to Amy's apartment, his meeting Jasmine, as well as their discovery of Amy's meeting with the Cardinal, and finally her death. By the time he finished, he felt that the story seemed more like the plot of a Ludlum novel than real life. Even he didn't think it seemed real.

The emotional tension in the room was palpable. Only Jasmine maintained a calm demeanor as she listened to the exchange. She had lived with death her entire life. A lifetime of neighbors killed and innocent bystanders blown to bits had the effect of dulling the sensation to the loss of life. That Hans Pedersen was dead, that Amy Glass was dead, that Timothy Greer was in a hospital bed with a body covered in burns were just tragic chapters in the human destruction she had witnessed her whole life. But now she knew she was right. Hans Pedersen had discovered something significant in the history of the Etruscans that catapulted him to stardom.

Something that was not meant to be discovered.

She had been tracking Hans and his Thought Mechanix organization for a long time, trying to discover the secret that caused her own brother's self-destruction. Now she was close to finding out who was responsible for his death, close to finding out the factions alluded to by Carmen. With luck, she would be able to put that chapter in her life behind her.

Carmen offered them a seat and a glass of water, then spoke quietly as she sat down. "Sometimes I feel I should never have begun my quest so many years ago, when Hans first came to me to explain the Books to him."

The door chime broke the momentary silence that had enveloped the room. A few minutes after leaving the living room to answer the door, Carmen returned with a forty-something woman, her snow-white hair striking against her black leather suit. Carmen was beaming as the woman moved into the room and introduced herself.

"Hi, I'm Sarah Larksmum."

Larksmum could not believe her good fortune. Sitting across from her in Carmen's apartment were the two people she was instructed to find. After her last failed attempt with Carmen, she had been summoned to locate two others who had emerged on the trail left by Hans. She was to find these two, an American accountant and a British journalist, at all costs. This link to Hans Pedersen needed to be contained if they were to succeed. She was to take the utmost care to insure their safety, particularly that of Jason Wakefield. She was also tasked to uncover what information Hans had shared about his latest research, which he was about to reveal to the world before his death.

The cancer that the Order of Sumer had wrought upon itself, the malignant stain on their legacy was released by one of their own in a plebeian attempt to speed the evolution of mankind. Piccolomini spent time with Larksmum, bringing her into his confidence in a last ditch effort to gain control. He told her all about Hans Pedersen and gave her as much of the history of the Etruscans as he could so that she would understand the consequences of her failure.

Armed with that knowledge, Larksmum now knew why it was crucial she act. But she needed to bide her time. The Order of Sumer needed to consolidate the knowledge that had resulted in the success of Hans Pedersen and the Rules of Possibility. More importantly, it needed Jason Wakefield. What a fortuitous coincidence that he was now sitting in Carmen's living room. She knew what had to be done. It was time to extract the necessary information sought by her benefactors. And bring them Jason Wakefield.

She spared Carmen's life the last time they were together, a mistake she was certain would cause the Grand Master of the Order of Sumer heart palpitations. She was wrong. They were relieved. It turned out that she still had information crucial to their plans. Now she could accomplish all she wanted in one night with the unexpected appearance of Jason Wakefield. All of the loose ends had coincidentally come together. By the end of the night she would be finished her last assignment, able to fade out of active status with the Guardians after three decades of carrying out their wishes. She was ready to stop the killing, her lack of remorse equal only to the nagging angst over its absence.

The presence of the other woman was problematic. She would be a threat, a threat that should be eliminated. Larksmum surveyed the room. This woman would be difficult to dispatch. She had an air of quiet confidence that alarmed Larksmum. With the need to take Jason in alive, she would have to act swiftly. She was quickly formulating a solution, when, just as quickly, she stopped short to take in the late afternoon sun as it streamed through the open window, creating a halo affect behind Carmen.

Outside the apartment, the shadows of the roofline cast a dark stain on the white wall across the street. In the distance, the dome of the Cattedrale di Santa Maria del Fiore looked like a boldly lit beacon in a sea of haze. Daylight was fading to dusk as the night air lay heavy in waiting along the river Arno. It would be impossible for her to destroy this angel of love. Larksmum smiled warmly as she set her new course of action and settled into the evening.

38

After introductions, poured wine and plates of cheese and fruit, Carmen sat down across from her three guests. They stared back at her with the anticipation of school children, their curious faces barely able to contain their anxiety. Carmen reached out and took the hand of Larksmum into her own, thankful she'd arrived. During their last encounter, she had almost revealed to her the secrets the University bound her to keep. But it didn't matter now. She had been unceremoniously canned, fired by a frightened Dean who saw only ruin in the discovery she had made. The death of Hans Pedersen proved to her that she had been right all along. There was credence to the theories she had been studying her entire life. Carmen knew it was time to share her story.

"When I was twelve years old, I went on a school field trip to an Etruscan burial site north of Siena. The curator of the site, a Brother from a nearby Monastery, told a story that day that changed my life. His name was Brother Agostino. He spoke of the wonders of the Etruscan civilization, how they influenced the Greeks, shaped the very fabric of the Roman culture, even laid the foundation for many of the rituals adopted by the early Christian religion. He spoke that day of an ancestry that extended to the root of civilization itself, and told tales of how a small group of people integrated themselves into the local tribes, changing them forever.

"That day was just another memorable field trip for a curious child. But those stories stuck with me, despite their being nothing more than romantic fantasies of princes from faraway lands, epic battles of bravery and cunning, great intellectual pursuits of scholars and artists. Yet it was so much more. What I remembered the most about that day was that a small tribe of people, the Lydians, ingratiated their way into the lives of the people from Tuscany, the original Etruscans, to eventually create one of the most enigmatic civilizations the world had ever seen.

"At night in my bed as I drifted to sleep I wondered who these people were. What was so great about them that they could alter entirely the future of the simple people who lived here and then, after a few centuries, fade away into the fabric of those other kingdoms they helped to create? I have spent my life trying to understand Etruscan history.

"While I was a student here in Florence, I was approached by a little man who asked me to help him with some research. It was Hans Pedersen. He told me a story of some lost cuneiform tablets that the Lydians possessed. He shared with me a tale of intrigue and mystery concerning secrets that the Lydians brought with them to Tuscany. I was hooked. I have spent many years since searching for these lost tablets, funded surreptitiously by Hans and his organization. About six months ago I made a discovery that will challenge the status of all we know. All we believe in. It is what I have waited my whole career to prove. It is something I could not have done without Hans Pedersen. He started it all."

"What did he start?" Jasmine almost whispered.

Not one of Carmen's audience of three moved a muscle, but she stood up to get another bottle of wine in order to refill the now empty glasses. In the half hour she had been talking, the sun had settled quietly behind the horizon, the night sky lit only by the thin slice of a crescent moon. A steady stream of scooters and taxis provided a quiet drone beyond the open window.

Jason excused himself to go to the bathroom, returning to find the three women discussing the latest Italian fashions. He interrupted.

"You were saying that Hans Pedersen was the reason you started your research. But I thought it all began from the childhood memories of a twelve-year-old schoolgirl."

"Hans Pedersen came to see me to ask questions about the Etruscans. I was just a grad student at the time, writing my doctoral thesis on the migration of the Lydians. He started to question me about certain artifacts, clay tablets that the Lydians may have brought with them. He seemed particularly interested in pre-Lydian culture. Interested in how the Lydians might have acquired some of their knowledge."

"Are you referring to the Books of Eden, in particular a fourth tablet?" Jasmine blurted out.

"How do you know about them?" Carmen stared across at the woman whom she had only just met, shock clearly evident on her face. "No one knows about it. I only told Hans about my discovery of the fourth tablet a month ago."

"Hans had an assistant who gave us the background before she disappeared."

"The four Books of Eden? What are they?" Larksmum perked up. "Just a minute." Larksmum stood up and went to the kitchen to retrieve another bottle of wine, intending to keep the conversation as loose as possible.

Carmen took the opportunity to head to the bedroom to retrieve her correspondence from Hans. She had saved all of the communication between them. They served as a chronological history of her research from the time she started receiving Hans's grant money. They contained the real story behind the search for the fourth book of Eden and the power it possessed.

With the wine served, Larksmum settled in next to Carmen on the floor, across from Jason and Jasmine, who were sitting close together on the leather couch.

Jasmine glanced over at Jason, his eyes locking for a moment in quiet acknowledgement. Time was of the essence. A few hours earlier they had barely outrun and lost an aggressive tail that had been following them since New York. At least, that is what they suspected. Whoever was following them had something to do with the death of Amy Glass. They wanted what Amy had hidden in her freezer. They wanted what the two of them now possessed—Carmen Salvatore. She was the key to whatever started the destruction of Thought Mechanix and the death of Hans Pedersen.

Jason was aware that whatever he learned from the fourth tablet, the fourth Book of Eden that he was about to reveal to an anxious world, made some people very nervous. Nervous enough for him to be killed and his organization destroyed. The secret would have died with him, except for the file folder that Carmen Salvatore just retrieved from her bedroom. Jason knew that the men who pursued them in Florence wanted what they wanted. By coming to Carmen's apartment, they had put her in danger. Luckily, the men were momentarily lost.

But for how long?

They would figure it out soon enough; it would only take a little persuasion of one cabbie.

"So, what is this fourth book of Eden?" Larksmum asked again as she curled up beside Carmen, a warm smile disguising her impatience.

Carmen smiled down at Larksmum and then at her two other guests. "Before I can tell you about the fourth book, you will need to understand the entire story."

39

"You all know about the Garden of Eden, right? God created man in his image, etc., etc. Eve led Adam to the tree in the middle of the Garden, where they ate from the tree and were banished from the Garden."

All three nodded in bewilderment.

"That tree, called the Tree of Knowledge of Good and Evil, is in fact the second tree in the Garden of Eden, not the first, despite the fact that it is referred to first in Genesis."

"The first is the Tree of Life," Jasmine interjected.

"Right," Carmen answered, as if she was addressing a student in one of her lectures.

"But these trees were not made of bark and wood. The Trees are just an allegory. True Bible scholars know that the Trees refer to sets of clay tablets. Cuneiform tablets, or early forms of books. And eating from the tree refers to accepting the knowledge of the 'book' as truth. Once the truth of the Knowledge of Good and Evil was accepted, then Adam and Eve could never return to their old existence—to that blissful state of ignorance they previously lived on earth, as the Bible states in Genesis 3."

Carmen then quoted from memory:

See, the man has become like one of us, knowing good and evil; and now, he might reach out his hand and take also from the tree of life, and eat, and live forever'—therefore the Lord God sent him forth from the garden of Eden, to till the ground from which he was taken. He drove out the man; and at the east of the garden of Eden he placed the cherubim, and a sword flaming and turning to guard the way to the tree of life.

Jasmine again interrupted: "So Adam and Eve now possessed the knowledge of the gods, or God, and were banished from Eden and had to act accordingly. They became like real men. So we all learned this in Sunday school. Nothing new."

Carmen reached over and opened the folder she had of her communications with Hans. "The story is not that simple. How well do you know your Bible?"

"I'm Hindu," Jasmine laughed. "I only know a little from my comparative religions classes at NYU." She looked over at Jason, who was drinking in the story. He was probably raised a Christian, but like most Americans only knew the short sound bites they were fed at Sunday school, a fantasyland of truncated parables and misinterpreted ideology. But the message worked as comfort food to the masses, so the sound bites remained blissfully sweet and simple. Jasmine had to be careful. Already she had revealed more than she dared. It had been a long road of research and late-night journalism to discover what she had learned so far. And Carmen was clearly the key to whatever new paradigm Hans Pedersen had been creating. She was too close to discovering the real cause of her brother's death to be careless now.

Larksmum shrugged her shoulders.

Carmen continued, "Well. If you read earlier on in the first chapter of Genesis...

Then God said, 'Let us make humankind in our image, according to our likeness; and let them have dominion over the fish of the sea, and over the birds of the air, and over the cattle, and over all the wild animals of the earth, and over every creeping thing that creeps upon the earth.'

So God created humankind in his image,
  in the image of God he created them;
  male and female he created them.
God blessed them, and God said to them, 'Be fruitful and multiply.'

"We all know that God created Adam and Eve on the sixth day," Jason commented.

"Ah. But that is where most people go wrong. It is a natural mistake. Your Sunday school teacher never read for you the subtleties of the Bible. For instance, on the sixth day God created man and woman. But are you not also taught that God created Eve from the rib of Adam? That he has the two of them sequestered in the Garden of Eden? There is no mention of children in the Garden of Eden. At least not until they are banned from the place."

"Yes, but—"

"Let me explain. It is relevant to why the two of you are here. Genesis continues:

In the day that the Lord God made the earth and the heavens, when no plant of the field was yet in the earth and no herb of the field had yet sprung up—for the Lord God had not caused it to rain upon the earth, and there was no one to till the ground; but a stream would rise from the earth, and water the whole face of the ground— then the Lord God formed man from the dust of the ground, and breathed into his nostrils the breath of life; and the man became a living soul. And the Lord God planted a garden in Eden, in the east; and there he put the man whom he had formed. Out of the ground the Lord God made to grow every tree that is pleasant to the sight and good for food, the tree of life also in the midst of the garden, and the tree of the knowledge of good and evil.

"Now this is where it becomes tricky. Man and woman were already created on the sixth day. But according to this next passage, God forms man, Adam, from dust, breathed life into him and man became a living soul. There are many theories about whether Adam, and of course Eve, are somehow different than the man and woman God created on the sixth day. That they are somehow closer connected to God because of the reference to the soul.

"When Hans Pedersen first came to me about my understanding of the Tree of Life and the Tree of the Knowledge of Good and Evil as defined in the Bible, he asked if they were really clay tablets connecting Adam and Eve to the common existence of man and woman. He did that because he brought me undeniable proof of the existence of a third tablet."

"A third? I thought we were talking about a fourth book, not a third," Larksmum asked.

"We are, or we will. But before we talk about the fourth book, I have to give you a little background. The third clay tablet is known as the Book of Thought. It is the power behind the evolution of man, so to speak. Hans Pedersen brought me a rendering of the clay tablet he had taken from the Siena Monastery. He wanted me to translate it. He had thought that because it was an Etruscan relic, I would be able to read it. But it wasn't Etruscan. In fact, it wasn't any language I had ever seen. So I took a few passages and distributed it to the linguistic community to find out if anyone could help interpret the language. Hans came to see me every week for months. Finally, I received a reply from National Linguistic Centre in Iraq. The rendering was written in an early cuneiform style, identified as Sumerian.

"What do you mean by cuneiform?" Jason asked.

"The first known cuneiform writing came from the Sumerians. But the term is deceptive, as most people think that it's some type of writing system. It isn't. Cuneiform can mean not one but several kinds of writing systems, including logo syllabic, syllabic, and alphabetic scripts. The word comes from Latin *cuneus*, which means 'wedge.' In other words, any script can be called cuneiform as long as individual signs are composed of wedges.

"The important point here is that the clay tablet rendering that Hans gave me was Sumerian. Once I figured that out, Hans asked me to have it translated. But he was very careful. At my suggestion, we sent different sections to different linguists, only piecing the entire transcript together once the interpretations were returned. The final product was not any clearer to me than if we had been trying to read the original Sumerian cuneiform text. But it was a revelation to Hans. I remember at the time how his eyes shone, like he had all of a sudden discovered a cure for cancer. He thanked me for my help and told me he would never forget. It wasn't until later that he told me the truth."

"What truth?" Jasmine sat on the edge of her seat.

Larksmum, who had moved to a more comfortable ottoman sat up. The revelation was getting close.

"The Book of Thought, known as the Third Book of Eden. That was what he brought to me all those years ago. It formed the premise of his entire metamorphosis from a lowly doctoral student at a second-rate university to a global icon. The Book of Thought is what Hans used to create the Rules of Possibility. It gave him the power to transform the secrets of the Book of Thought into Thought Mechanix, eventually becoming the single most successful converter of minds since Constantinople catapulted Christianity into the largest religion in the world."

"Why do you refer to it as the Third Book of Eden?"

"I'll explain that later," Carmen promised.

"Do you think that the monks at the monastery in Siena knew what they had?" Larksmum just had a revelation of her own. The small monastery in Siena that Carmen referred to was the same one from which the secret cabal known as the Order of Sumer originated. Of course they knew what power lay within the clay tablet they guarded. It was the sole reason for their existence. For her existence. She needed to know whether or not Carmen knew this.

"Hans once told me that he had never meant to deceive the men of the monastery. With the help of one of the Brothers, he was set up in New York and given direction, seed capital and media resources. They set him up to succeed. Whatever the Brother's motivation, he understood the enormous power that he had unleashed. What Hans told me was that once the power of the Book of Thought was released through his Rules of Possibility concept it could not be stopped. His benefactor only wanted to bring religious peace to the world. Hans carried out his end of the bargain, becoming enormously rich and successful in the process.

"He sure as hell did that," Jason commented.

"About three years ago, Hans showed up on my doorstep. I had not seen him in over a decade. He had with him the same rendering that we had translated a dozen years earlier. He told me that in his opinion there was more to it. There was a look of desperation in his eyes. He was not the same man who frolicked like a beachball when we were together in Siena. He had the look of a cornered animal. He was ranting that there had to be more, a message in the writing, something that proved there was more to the truths revealed in the Book of Thought."

"Why do you think he believed that?" Jasmine asked.

"Hans said that the Order of Sumer, where he first learned of the Books of Eden, existed to protect the secret of the Book of Thought. He told me that this organization was created over three thousand years ago. Hans said that the Brother could no longer shelter the truth now that he, Hans, had released the energy contemplated by the Book of Thought. The Brother felt certain that the path hidden in the third tree needed to be found. That there was rumored to be a fourth tree that would help them better understand the Book of Thought. Something about the time being right."

"So what was it?" Jason was on the edge of his seat. He had experienced the incredible power of the Rules of Possibility. And to think that there might be an even greater tool made him giddy with the possibilities. His mercurial mind for business was already inventing the franchise.

"Hans didn't know. That was why he came to me. So I've spent the last three years trying to find out to what the monk might have been referring."

"Why didn't Hans just ask the Brother directly?" Jasmine queried.

"He tried but was stonewalled. He was told to leave well enough alone. That it did not concern him."

Larksmum tensed. She realized that Carmen was referring to Cardinal Agostino, the man that compromised the Order of Sumer.

"Which brings us to why you are all here, the millions that Hans spent had finally come to fruition. I wasn't sure what I had when it first arrived, not until I went back and compared the discovery to the rendering of the clay tablet Hans had provided years earlier."

"What was it that you found?" Jasmine asked.

"A few months ago an artifact came onto the underground market. In was of Sumerian origin, similar in age to the clay tablet that Hans told me the monastery possessed. What I have referred to as the Third Book of Eden. The clay tablet supposedly came from the ransacked treasure of the National Museum of Iraq during the second American invasion. The clay tablet interested me because of its carbon-dated age being so close to the other clay tablet, which produced the rendering from Hans. We figured it may hold a clue that would allow me to answer the question that Hans left for me to discover. The tantalizing clue promised by the monk who disappeared that sent Hans searching the globe for an answer."

"So? Did it?" Jason asked.

"Hans arranged for me to purchase the tablet. He wanted it for himself. I was not comfortable buying the clay tablet on the black market, so I made discreet introductions. Hans must have arranged its purchase because a few weeks later he called to let me know he was emailing the rendering of the clay tablet to have it translated. I was so excited I couldn't wait to get started. It took me a while to understand the text, even though the tablet was written in much simpler cuneiform than the Book of Thought tablet. It was like it was written by a child, not an educated man."

"Remind me again why you think this clay tablet is tied to the others, the ones that are supposedly referred to in the Genesis story of the Garden of Eden?" Larksmum asked.

"The carbon dating is important, but not as important as the message it contained. The clay tablet from the National Museum of Iraq and the clay tablet from the Siena monastery were definitely connected. It fact, even though the text differs in sophistication, they were written by the same scribe."

"How do you know that?"

"No different than modern-day handwriting analysis. Each cuneiform tablet has a certain style to it, no different than the glyphs in Egypt or the cave drawings in the Pyrenees. The author has a certain style that can be identified."

"So why do you think there was a difference in the complexity of the message if both tablets were written by the same scribe?" Jasmine asked.

"It could be that the scribe was transcribing information from two different people. But my theory is that the Iraqi tablet was written by the scribe himself, after he realized the importance of the other messages he was creating."

"What does the Iraqi tablet say?" Jason looked over at Jasmine as he asked the question.

Jasmine looked down at her watch. They had been there for over two hours. Time was running out. It was inevitable that the tail they shook at the airport would eventually figure out their destination. She only hoped it wasn't before they had enough information to proceed with their search. Looking over at Jason, she wondered if it might be wise to alert him that they had been followed from the airport.

A moment later it was too late.

40

Finally, a break.

Sean Mackenzie of Secur-Tec was poised with his team outside the apartment. He could least afford another debacle like New York, yet despite his best efforts by his best men it appeared to be happening anyway. Losing his targets in the Florence traffic was unacceptable. How was it possible that they found the one taxi driver in the entire city who was capable of driving like he was in the Le Mans twenty-four hour rally? It was important that Jason Wakefield be found. The fact that they lost him within spitting distance of the airport really pissed him off. More importantly, he needed to understand how Jason was able to connect with a military-trained expert like Jasmine Shah.

The information he is privy to must be very important if his security is as well trained as she appears.

But his men would not make the same mistake they made trying to corral Jason Wakefield in New York, which had made a bad situation worse. The botched interrogation of Amy Glass had forced him to call in a few favors with New York's finest to get one of his men released to his custody. His men became overexuberant. Amy was a feisty captive, who proved too strong-willed for his black-ops interrogators. One unnecessary step was all it took to send the woman to her death—a painful but fruitless death that yielded no intelligence. That slipup alone placed Secur-Tec in a difficult position. He'd have to deal with it later, before anyone could connect the dots to his employer.

Sean's cell phone began to vibrate in his breast pocket. He pushed the button on his earpiece.

"Mackenzie."

"What's the status in Florence?" Anthony Lee spoke without emotion despite his growing anxiety. Gunter Tang rewarded success and punished failure. Right now, Anthony Lee could see only an excruciating personal punishment if they did not quickly find out everything that Hans Pedersen knew before he died. Jason Wakefield was now the only link they had to get inside the workings of Thought Mechanix, to learn the secrets of the TMI organization so that Tang Enterprises could reap the benefits.

"It took a few hours, but we were able to locate the cabbie that picked up Jason Wakefield and Jasmine Shah from the airport." Sean reported.

"And?"

"They were dropped off outside the main entrance to the University of Florence. We thought we'd hit a dead end. Thankfully, we were able to get the cabbie to remember most of his little escapade. It'll be the last ride he'll take for a while. Anyway, the cabbie heard Jason mention the name Carmen as he exited the taxi. We had our computer people do a quick search of the students and faculty at the University. Three names came up. The first two were quickly ruled out. One of them was an elderly cook in the cafeteria, the other a first-year foreign student from Madrid. The third, a Ms. Salvatore, turned out to be the right Carmen. She's a professor of Etruscan studies, specializing in ancient languages. After a brief reconnaissance of the woman's apartment, we're certain our targets are inside."

Anthony Lee could feel his blood pressure drop. Maybe something was finally going his way. "Maybe they just found us our real target. From the little we were able to glean from Amy Glass before the end, Hans Pedersen had a source in Italy."

"So what would you like us to do?"

"Extract Jason Wakefield. Get this Carmen woman. Dispose of Jasmine Shah in any way you see fit."

Sean smiled as he signaled for his men to take up positions.

41

Dark clouds slid past the falling sun, obliterating the long shadows that minutes earlier decorated the busy tourist-filled streets of Florence. With the fast-moving clouds dusk came earlier than expected, hiding the movements outside on the street as two men dressed in black started to enter the ground floor of 29 via dell'Oriuolo, with another pair making their way around the back of the block-long apartment complex. A third team entered the adjacent apartment building fifteen minutes earlier to strategically set up on the roof above the target property, waiting for the signal.

A light rain together with increased wind threatened the quiet street. This pleased Sean Mackenzie. It would mean white noise to drown out the inevitable sounds his teams would make as they carried out their attack. After deactivating the alarm, Sean directed his men. One team, led by a mean-spirited Algerian, made its way through the front door. Anton, the Algerian, had his Glock pistol at the ready. A second man followed him inside, his compact Uzi held at his side.

On Sean's jacket sleeve, and on the sleeve of every member of the elite team that he'd recruited from Secur-Tec's Belgium office, there was a clear plastic sheath containing the pictures of Jason Wakefield and Jasmine Shah. His men were not provided with visual ID of the intended victim, so they would have to rely on the process of identification by elimination. The third person in the room would be the new target—Carmen Salvatore.

Sean listened carefully to the voices in the apartment above. As with every surprise operation he counted to fifteen as he rehearsed the pending assault in his mind. When he finished counting he nodded to the Algerian beside him on the landing, who was already slipping through the front door as his boss spoke to the others.

"Go," was all the other five needed to hear to swing into action.

Carmen's apartment was on three levels, a small entranceway led to a set of semi-circular stairs that curled up to the second-floor bedrooms before continuing up a floor to the main living area. Unlike many of the apartments in the building, hers had been substantially renovated by previous owners. The original configuration called for only one bathroom on the second floor. The renovations undertaken created a second powder room on the main floor, attached to a private den, where Carmen did most of her research. Above it all was the rooftop garden, the site of so many enjoyable evenings for Carmen and her lover.

Carmen smiled as she watched her guests discuss the revelations she had just divulged over a few bottles of wine. It had been like a pleasant evening with friends. Jason and Jasmine sat on the couch, quietly talking. Larksmum rose to walk down the small hallway to the upstairs bathroom. And Carmen was in the kitchen, measuring out espresso beans to make lattes. She looked over her shoulder to say something when she saw the man in the window.

She screamed.

Jasmine heard the sound of footsteps on the stairs right before Carmen's scream pierced the air. A second later, breaking glass scattered across the apartment as men entered the room from both sides. Jasmine quickly counted four as she spun off the couch towards the coffee table. Her instincts kicked into action: four men, small-arms weapons, two machine guns, clear-plastic ID sheaths on the insides of their jackets. In the four seconds it took for the men to gain entry to the room and survey their landscape, Jasmine was able to determine what each man was assigned to do. All of the men had their index fingers on the triggers of the weaponry they were carrying, the barrel of the guns pointed at only a twenty-degree angle towards the ground. From her own incursion experiences she knew that such an angle close to horizontal meant they were to shoot to kill. A quick glance at her first target confirmed that the gun safeties were off.

Stealing a glance at Jason, she grinned to herself as her mind processed everyone's actions in slow motion. Jason had pulled his arms over his head to avoid the flying glass and was propelling his body towards the floor. Without her level of experience he was going into a classic defensive mode. That was what most people would do. Insurgents knew that the shock of an attack was what allowed them to establish control. It ensured a quick death.

Jasmine had no intention of giving them the upper hand.

"Get down, get down," the first man up the stairs was screaming at Carmen as he entered the small kitchen area, his gun held at a twenty degree angle.

That's a good sign, Jasmine thought as she focused on the man coming up the stairs behind the apparent leader. *He's not here to kill indiscriminately.*

It was clear to her that the second man up the stairs was assigned to her as she watched his eyes lock on hers for a moment, then go back to the clear plastic casing on his arm to ensure identification.

It was the second Jasmine needed.

She rolled her body over the coffee table, grabbing a small knife from the appetizer tray. Pinching the blade between her thumb and index finger, she flicked it towards the assailant.

As the man looked up from his ID label on his arm, his eyes widened slightly when he saw the blade spin across the room. It entered his neck on the right-hand side, a few inches from center, directly into the jugular vein.

As if in slow motion, Jasmine watched as he screamed out in pain. His submachine gun clattered to the ground as he reached for his neck. A moment later, his blood-depleted brain stopped sending signals to his body and he collapsed next to his gun, both hands still clutching at the wound.

The world sped up. She could hear shouting. As she made her way towards the dying man she turned to see who was entering from the window.

Two men were bearing down on the room, their guns now raised horizontally. The first one to crash through the window was a square stub of a man, no more than five feet tall without any visible neck. His eyes bulged from their sockets as he saw his slain colleague. He froze.

Jasmine seized the opportunity. Twisting her body to the left of his line of sight, she rolled onto the floor, her right shoulder curling under as she half-somersaulted towards the dying man's discarded weapon. A second later she grabbed the butt of the gun, spun it around as her finger found the trigger to squeeze. A short, powerful burst sent her backwards towards the stairs, the bullets ricocheting harmlessly into the ceiling as her body spun out of control down the stairs to the second floor landing.

A moment later, as she tried to shake off the fall, her body contorted miserably in the small space, she looked up to see the gunman take aim, a wry smile of satisfaction forming on his pudgy face. Jasmine scrambled to locate the short-barreled Uzi that had sent her cascading down the stairs. Her eyes spotted the weapon lying on the bottom of the stairs by the entranceway. As she struggled to right herself, she looked back up to the top level into the eyes of her executioner, her only thought being whether Jason was still alive.

Jasmine heard the gunshot before she saw the flare from the nozzle of the gun, as she instinctively shielded her face with her arms. Waiting for the pain of the bullet that never came, she lowered her hands to see the square-bodied assassin falling head first towards her. She squeezed her body against the doorway to the bedroom as the now very dead man careened down the stairs. Jasmine noticed an entrance wound in the middle of the man's temple as he sailed past her.

Jasmine looked up, expecting, for some strange, illogical reason, to see Jason staring down at her with his goofy told-you-I-could grin plastered on his face. Instead, she was staring into the knowing eyes of someone accustomed to killing.

Larksmum stared down at Jasmine as the Belgian mercenary fell to his death. The bullet in his brain had come from the pistol she held in her left hand.

The two women locked eyes, each of them registering the knowledge that the other was more than they appeared.

Larksmum kept her gun leveled on the East Indian beauty as she contemplated her next move. It was clear that Jasmine, together with the accountant Jason, were on the same trail of information that she was pursuing, the same secret information that she was to extract from Carmen on behalf of the Order. She didn't know what their true purpose was, at least not yet, but she knew that they were a threat. Despite the countless men, and women, whom she'd dispatched during her career, she was never one to kill indiscriminately, at least not someone who was as beautiful and as enchanting as Jasmine.

As they held each other's gaze, it took only a moment for each of them to relay their intentions towards the other.

Larksmum aimed the pistol at Jasmine, took two shots then spun away from the stairs towards the kitchen. There was an eerie silence in the stairwell.

Jasmine had watched in horror as Carmen's friend calmly pulled the trigger, aiming the gun slightly over her head. She looked back at her would-be killer sprawled on the floor by the front door to see if he had been the intended target, quickly concluding that the angle of the shots were completely off. She wondered why Larksmum had shot and intentionally missed.

Only a few minutes had elapsed since the intruders first entered the house. It was clear to Jasmine that things had not gone according to plan. Two of the men were dead, with the other two still upstairs. She was familiar with operations like this one. Five minutes was a lifetime. In all likelihood they were outside the time limit they allowed themselves to get in and out before invoking a Plan B. It would not be long before a backup team came upstairs to investigate.

Carefully moving her body into a crouching position, she took a mental survey of her aches and pains. Her body was sore, but there did not appear to be any broken bones. Standing cautiously, Jasmine took two steps up towards the main floor, stopped, then quickly doubled back down to the ground level to retrieve the Uzi. The gun was underneath the dead intruder, so she pushed the body onto its side. The vacant open eyes stared back at her as she picked up the machine gun. She checked the clip as she headed back upstairs.

The yelling from the main floor registered as she reached the last half-dozen steps. She stopped before the top. Rather than burst into the room, Jasmine shrunk down onto her haunches, lifting her head just above the top step to see what was happening. She listened to the exchange going on, trying to determine the best course of action.

"Stop and drop your gun!"

It was voice of the black man who had gone directly into the kitchen when he arrived.

Algerian, thought Jasmine. There was a hint of panic in his voice.

Jasmine glanced over the top step to survey the room. She sucked in her breath as she caught sight of Jason, who was staring wide-eyed into the barrel of a gun, held steady at his head by the fourth intruder.

Larksmum was aiming her pistol at the black man as she stopped inching herself closer, a look of concern curled her brow. The black man, who had targeted Carmen as soon as they burst into the apartment, now held the terrified professor, his left arm wrapped tightly around her chest, his Glock pointing at her temple. Carmen was sobbing uncontrollably, her tears dripping onto the massive bicep that held her tight.

"If you shoot him, your boss will die," Larksmum directed her words to the man holding the gun on Jason.

The man glanced over at the Algerian.

"You know our orders," was all the man said, as he tightened his grip on their intended target, now clearly an unexpected pawn. He had gotten himself into an unscripted scenario. There were only supposed to be three people at the apartment. Whoever this fourth person was, she was not someone that would be easily dispatched. This was someone to be reckoned with. The white-haired woman had shot the hapless Belgian with cold precision, only to then shoot the Indian woman who had fallen down the stairs. Now she had turned her sights on him. She was calm. Proficient. The man quickly realized that the tide of events was not going his way. He needed to disarm the situation quickly. He grabbed for his mike switch to provide a warning to the second team.

For a moment no one spoke. Jasmine looked on, unnoticed, at the three gun-wielding participants in the Mexican standoff. Her mind processed the various scenarios open to her. It was clear that these men were not to harm either Carmen or Jason. At first she thought that maybe it was only Carmen who was not to be killed but for the last comment from the Algerian. Whoever sent them wanted Jason alive as well; otherwise the fourth man would have already pulled the trigger.

She took aim just as the front door two stories below burst open.

42

Sean Mackenzie waited three minutes longer than he wanted. He listened through his earpiece as the events unfolded. The snatch-and-grab was routine and his team were experts. But somehow he felt uneasy. Since this operation began, nothing had gone right. Sean did not feel comfortable in Italy. He had dealt with Italian mercenaries in the past, never with good results. That was why he brought in a team from Belgium, old-timers reminiscent of the African wars. But somehow he knew that this was not going to be an easy five-minute drill—get in, kill the East Indian woman, grab the accountant and the Italian professor, and get out.

His uneasiness increased as he listened to the unexpected gunfire. He waited. It wasn't until he heard the thud against the front door that he realized something had gone wrong. He yelled into his microphone at the backup team before heading into the apartment and up the stairs.

A minute later, he tried to burst through the door, only to see it was blocked by the body of one of his men lying prone in the entranceway. Pushing inward, he was able to force open the door enough to enter the landing. He glanced as his watch. They'd hit the five-minute mark. The second team would be swinging into action. They were to follow the path of the first team, enter the adjacent building and access the apartment from the roof. Two sets of teams to infiltrate the building, in waves. Since the first group failed, the second wave was activated to complete the mission. The second team had better not fail. As his second team activated on his command, the mike squawked out a warning from the apartment above.

Too late.

When the front door opened, Jasmine turned to look just as a large man, someone she recognized from New York, entered the apartment. She remembered his face. He was one of the men outside Amy's apartment. He was with Secur-Tec. She wondered what they had to do with this.

Jasmine swung her gun around just as the first volley from his semi-automatic sliced into the stairs below her. Taking careful aim as the man stumbled over his fat, dead partner, she pulled the trigger. A short burst from the air-cooled nozzle hit its target in the thigh, the elbow and the shoulder knocking the gun from his hand as he fell backwards against the half-opened door.

Jasmine wondered when the neighbors would start reacting to the gunfire as she started up the stairs to assess the Mexican standoff. Cresting the stairs, she reached the main floor just as the second roof team entered the room with their guns firing. It was a mistake that cost them their lives.

Blinded for a moment by the bright lights of the apartment, the two men had no idea of the scenario they were entering, assuming that their presence as the backup team required immediate firepower. Jasmine watched as the first volley cut down their partner who a moment earlier had his gun aimed at Jason.

A stray bullet found its way across the room into the kitchen.

Jasmine ignored the gunshots and screams coming from Larksmum as she calmly splayed the window cavity, hitting both men with a deadly burst of gunfire. The men collapsed onto the apartment floor, landing on either side of a petrified Jason. He looked up and gave Jasmine a feeble smile.

In the short gun battle, however, a stray bullet had found Carmen, hitting her beneath the eye and causing her eyeball to explode out of her head.

Larksmum watched in horror as Carmen's body sagged forward, held up only by the Algerian's strong grip. Enraged, Larksmum emptied her pistol into his chest and face, spewing flesh and bone fragments across the kitchen cabinets. The Algerian and Carmen fell in a silent heap onto the floor.

But the Algerian had returned fire even as he was falling. Two of the bullets had hit their intended target, one in the arm and one in the upper chest.

"Are you alright?" Jasmine directed her question at Jason.

Standing in the center of the room, she quickly cast her eyes around the apartment, watching for movement. She glanced down the stairs, taking note that the New Yorker was gone. She did a quick tally: six dead, seven if you counted Carmen. Jasmine saw Larksmum in the kitchen, cradling Carmen's dead body in her arms. Blood seeped onto her clothes where the bullets had ripped into her, but she showed no evidence of pain.

Jasmine waited for a moment before she reacted. Picking up the Uzi, she held it at an angle of twenty degrees. She walked into the kitchen and pointed it at Larksmum.

The two women stared at each other. Neither of them said a word. The guns that they held were not raised in a position to fire, but each of them held their fingers on the trigger. They were adversaries and both of them knew it.

Jasmine's instinct told her that to let the woman leave would be a mistake that she would pay for later. But she also knew that they had a common enemy, and she thought of the lesson from the Sun Tzu: *The enemy of my enemy is my friend.*

Larksmum looked one more time at Carmen's grotesquely deformed face before glancing back at Jasmine. She gently placed the dead professor onto the floor.

A moment later she was heading down the stairs and out the door.

"What the hell was that all about?" Jason asked as he picked himself up off the floor, "And who the hell *are* you?"

Before Jasmine could answer, sirens filled the emptiness of the Florence night. The distinctive two-toned pitch of the Polizia di Stato seemed to come from everywhere, as the streets were suddenly alive with activity.

"Come on, we'd better get out of here." Jasmine moved towards the broken windows.

"Where are you going?"

"We can't very well leave through the front door, now can we?" Jasmine smacked Jason lightly on the head as she walked by.

Jason followed her out onto the balcony.

"Wait." He headed back inside.

"Where are you going?" Jasmine hissed. She could see people starting to mill about down in the alley and looking up at her.

Jason appeared a few moments later, clutching a folder. "We're going to need this."

He tucked the folder that contained the notes about the translated clay tablet into his shirt and followed Jasmine onto the roof.

43

Cardinal Agostino of Siena worked his way up the power grid of the Vatican by taking advantage of his opportunities. He went out of his way to support the core group of Cardinals who felt that the church needed to remain true to its historical roots. Over time, he even voted for controversial decisions that restricted the growth of the church in order to preserve the integrity of Roman Catholic dogma. He had a vision for the Holy See that went beyond the small minds of the Cardinals who holed up inside the Vatican, thinking that they could convince themselves that the world was not changing.

But the world was changing faster than the speed of prayer. A steamroller of transformation was enveloping the consciousness of the six billion human residents of the earth, and if the Church did not do anything to embrace the momentum, they would be left far, far behind, a relic of outdated, irrelevant and disappointing traditions.

Agostino carried out his duties as a Cardinal of the Holy See with care and diligence. He was a model follower of Christ. But it was only a role he played until he could fulfill his destiny. If the Vatican knew of his true purpose, he would be more than likely excommunicated. It took persuasion, a few timely events, and several carefully planned campaigns to discredit his opposition, but he achieved the role necessary to carry out his long-term plans, plans that began fifteen years earlier when he convinced Hans Pedersen to embark on the development of a simple motivational program designed around the teachings of the small monastery that had nursed him back to health.

He used the secret the Order of Sumer was ordained to preserve to create his future. He had arranged for Hans to design the powerful system that he sold through infomercials and presentations. It was the culmination of years of preparation and waiting to find the right man to carry out his strategy. Once the Order of Sumer discovered the truth about what they were protecting, he knew what needed to be done.

It started at the beginning, from whence everything came. The early prophets did not realize the significance of the knowledge they possessed, or where it came from. When men took control of the direction of human religion, they designed their teachings to control the hearts and minds of men with fear and mysticism. Knowledge was power, and it was all about power. Even the Order of Sumer had no idea of the power behind the secret they were protecting. It was not for lack of trying. They just did not have the capacity, or the belief system, to allow the information to be revealed. Agostino, on the other hand, saw the writing for what it was—an instruction manual to the energy created by directed thought.

But Agostino picked the wrong horse to ride to his victory. Just as the power he had been seeking his entire life was within his grasp, the tide shifted. He had no idea how he lost control of everything he helped Hans build. It was important that he find out who was behind the destruction, as time was running short. The chain of events that abruptly ended the career of Hans Pedersen and his Thought Mechanix organization was skillfully put into motion. Although he did not relish driving the man to his death, it was necessary. His death would be the catalyst needed to implement the next phase of his plan, a plan that he was ready to implement without delay if it had not been for the meddlesome Hans Pedersen and his incessant search for the fourth Book of Eden.

And Hans had been surprisingly successful. Agostino could see his world unravel as Hans reversed roles, taking control of the message that was being delivered, trying to reverse the wave of criminality and despair that was gripping the world. A desperate man seeking a solution that only he, Agostino, the next leader of the Roman Catholic Church saw as his destiny.

That was until the death of Amy Glass. And now, with the unexpected attack on Carmen Salvatore, he saw no hope. He needed the Italian professor to explain what they had discovered. The information that Hans possessed had died with him. Now she was dead, at the hands of some unknown assassins. It was clear to Agostino that he had lost control. Someone else knew more than he did.

If he did not do something soon, his dreams would be thwarted, and if his guess was correct about what Hans Pedersen discovered, then more than his ambition was in jeopardy. The world was on the brink of a cataclysm that in all probability could not be reversed.

44

They drove all night, crammed inside a bus crowded with budget tourists and backpacking students heading north to Venice. At first they were going to rent a car, but paranoia trumped their judgment. These men, whoever they were, seemed able to find them wherever they went.

The tourist bus had left the Firenze Santa Maria Novella train station at ten o'clock that night just as the late summer sun was starting to set. There was only one hour-long stop in Bologna just before midnight. By two-thirty the bus rolled into Piazzale Roma in Venice, depositing Jason and Jasmine together with the thirty other late-night travelers onto the deserted plaza on the outskirts of the fabled canal city.

Jason did not take any chances. He wanted to disappear. Find a place where he could try and figure out what was going on. To get to know this woman who could kill with such cold dispatch, who had skills he thought only people in spy novels possessed, a woman who could make love as passionately as she could kill.

After they fled the apartment, Jasmine insisted that they return to track the people who attacked them and killed Carmen. She wanted to follow them to try and find out who was directing their actions. Jason insisted on getting as much distance between them and the assassins as possible.

"It's better to be close to your enemy," she insisted.

Jason's fear of being thrust into a world he did not understand prevailed.

They withdrew money from a half-dozen ATMs using their various debit and credit cards and horded as many Euros as the machines would spew out from their daily limits. Without thinking about a final destination, they boarded the first bus leaving Florence. By two in the morning, a light drizzle falling, they walked across the bridge into city of Venice.

45

Gunter Tang put down the report he was reading and leaned back in his Corinthian leather chair, his hands clasped behind his head. He stared up at the crystal chandelier over the dining room table, his eyes following the reflections of light as they pierced through each of the two-hundred or so Baccarat crystal beads.

He had purchased the chandelier at Sotheby's the year before and had it hung in his New York apartment. The lighting fixture had once graced the entrance to the Scottish palace of the Duke of Edinburgh, the route it took to the auction house a story of its own. Gunter bought the fixture, together with an entire lot of furniture from the Duke's newly restored and modernized home. He liked the chandelier in particular because it was made by an ancestor of the Hong Kong partner of his father. He liked to know about the things he owned.

The report rested on an equally exquisite late-eighteenth century cherrywood bombe end table crafted in Seville. The gentle curves of the wood gave the table the appearance of having overstuffed drawers. Gunter picked up the report again and thumbed through the pages. It was a hastily drafted summary of the state of research on quantum physics as it related to the energy created by the brain. Scientists appeared to be on the verge of proving what Hans Pedersen must have known—that thoughts are energy. And that all energy was somehow connected.

It all seemed to be a load of crap to him, until he observed firsthand the influence the TMI sessions had on his managers. Jason Wakefield had created a commercially viable program out of the Rules of Possibility that had a profound impact. When he first saw the productivity increases, he thought that the numbers must have been manipulated. Then the profits started to materialize, first in the level of sales, and then in the increased price of this stock. But then he noticed that his employees' morale had taken a positive upswing too.

However it worked, he wanted to control it. The report he just read indicated that the power of intention of masses of people could control the outcome of an event. Cheering crowds helped the home team have an advantage. Collective prayer helped heal the sick. Pessimistic investors could influence the direction of the stock market. What intrigued him the most was that the report suggested it was not the actions of these groups that created the results—it was their thoughts.

Gunter was convinced that Hans Pedersen had somehow managed to contain that thought energy in a way that enabled those properly indoctrinated to achieve whatever they desired, whether it was more money, more power, or increased contentment, whatever. From what the report implied, the effects of the energy could be directed to good thoughts or bad intentions. It didn't matter. The energy only created an absolute return; it did not distinguish between positive and negative. It was all energy.

Whoever, or whatever, affected Hans Pedersen to such a degree that he took his own life must also believe that Hans possessed a powerful weapon. Hans himself must have been distraught when he realized what he had released into the world. Whatever it was, Gunter Tang wanted it for himself.

He stood up and walked over to the floor-to-ceiling plateglass window. Staring out at the New York skyline, he imagined the immense sense of power he would feel with the ability to control and direct people to answer to his beck and call, even more than fear and intimidation had already accomplished. All previous successes would pale in comparison.

As he contemplated the possibilities, the quiet of his apartment was disturbed by the shrill ring of his private security phone. It was a call he was expecting. After sending Sean McKenzie to Italy, he had sent Anthony Lee to follow him and to report back. Gunter picked up the phone—maintaining his calm—expecting, but never prepared to accept, the worst.

"Tang here."

"I'm afraid to report that things did not go well in Florence." Anthony Lee stated somberly.

"What is the status?"

"All of the men are dead. The professor, Carmen Salvatore, is dead. We have nothing at this time. The carabinieri are swarming. After they left, I called a contact in the local department who told me there were nine dead. The police are trying to formulate a story to give to the media. As long as it's something that makes sense, the journalists will not dig. I told him that our company was tracking a potential terrorist threat on behalf of a client. I suggested the woman, Salvatore, was involved. The detective liked the angle, took some fabricated details and thanked me. That should be the end of any connection to us."

"Where are Wakefield and the woman?"

"No idea. Not among the dead. They could be hiding out in the building."

"Why didn't you check?" Tang could feel his neck burning red as the frustration built up in his body. He hired the best, trained the best, paid top dollar, and yet somehow Wakefield and the woman seemed to be outsmarting him at every turn. He held his tongue, waiting for an answer.

"There may be a more important break. Shortly after I lost communication with Mackenzie, I observed a woman, fiftyish, leave the apartment by the front door. From what I could see, she was injured. She was tucking a firearm into her purse as she left, careful to walk in the opposite direction of the advancing police. I decided that Wakefield could be tracked easily through passport or other financial searches, so I decided to follow the woman." Anthony Lee was certain his decision was the right one.

"And?"

"And I kept on her. She seemed to know I was following her, but didn't trying to elude my tail. She went to a late-night pharmacy, then wandered into a local Marriott, where she spent a few minutes in the ladies room, addressing her injuries I suspect. That was two hours ago. Right now I am in Siena, across the square from the entrance to a monastery."

"A monastery?"

"Yeah. The woman was expected. She was greeted at the door the minute the taxi pulled up. Two Brothers met her and escorted her inside."

"The Order of Siena," Gunter Tang said, almost to himself.

"The Order of what?"

"Never mind. You did well. I want you to stick with her. You can be certain she will lead you back to Wakefield and the woman."

Tang hung up the phone, a broad smile crossing his contented face. He just had his suspicions confirmed. The source of the information used by Hans Pedersen to create the Rules of Possibility would soon be within his reach.

46

As hotel rooms go, this one was suspect, pathetically small, adorned with two twin beds separated by a narrow side table, a television bolted to the equally secure chest of drawers, and a bar strung up next to the entrance with three empty hangers twisted from misuse. Paint hung in loose folds from the top of the walls, hardened by age, the plaster behind the paint begging to be restored. The establishment was strictly cash only; the unkempt proprietor did not ask and did not care who handed the Euros through the metal gate at the front desk.

They were in Venice. A city neither of them were familiar with, but it was the final destination of the bus they took when they hurriedly left Florence. The hotel was near the Rialto Bridge, off the main canal, in an alley not frequented by tourists. They selected it because it was close to an Internet café that would come in handy. After paying cash for the accommodation, they walked the two blocks to a late-night grocer to buy some food before returning to the room for the night. Venice was quiet in the early morning hours, the late-night revelers had sequestered themselves and the early morning delivery skiffs had not yet materialized on the canal. Only a few people stole furtive glances at the couple as they walked the near-deserted, rain-soaked streets.

Jason closed the door behind him and followed Jasmine up the circular stairs to their first story room above the ground-level nightclub. A techno-rock song was blasting through the floor beneath their feet. The proprietor promised the music would stop by midnight. It didn't matter. Jason was sure he would not be sleeping that night after the events at Carmen Salvatore's apartment.

He had only known Jasmine breifly and already he had been involved in two gun battles and she had saved his life both times. After the showdown at Amy's apartment he had tried to find out who she was, but he never received an answer. Now, after what he'd witnessed at Carmen's, it was clear to him that this woman did not just happen upon him at Amy's apartment. She had an agenda and it was connected to Hans Pedersen, which was now intertwined with his involvement.

"I'm going to take a shower," Jasmine announced. She began to take off her shirt and was looking around the tiny room for a clean place to put her clothes. Not that it mattered. They had been wearing the same clothes for three days. The hotel did not have a concierge, but its payment policy would ensure they could remain hidden while they contemplated their next move.

"Not so fast." Jason walked the two paces to the other side of the room, grabbed Jasmine around the waist and tossed her onto the bed. She bounced off the middle of the sagging mattress and rolled onto the floor. Jason followed her over the bed, straddling her twisted body and pinning her arms over her head.

"You've been telling me that you would explain your involvement with Amy Glass, and Hans Pedersen, and exactly where you acquired extreme skills to keep up both alive. I didn't just fall off a turnip truck. It's clear that you did not just *happen* to be at Amy's apartment at the same time I was there. So, time to confess."

Jasmine looked up at Jason, who clearly had no idea how vulnerable he was at that moment. Feigning a cramp so that he would release a little pressure, she swung her legs upwards until they locked onto Jason's shoulders. From that position, it was just a matter of applying a little pressure before both of their bodies changed position.

A second later, Jason was pinned to the ground, his head firmly jammed into the tight space between the floor and the bed frame. She bent down and kissed him firmly on the lips, lingering a while as she ground her body into his.

"Don't distract me," Jason groaned.

Letting go, she jumped up, stripping as she made her way to the bathroom. "Fine. All the details. But I *am* going to take that shower now."

Midday and the pair were hunkered in their room, eating the few morsels of food left over from their trip to the market. Noises from the street below drifted up into their hotel room: vendors selling their souvenirs, tourists squawking over the majesty of the canals, dogs barking, and horns of passing boats honking. It was white noise that reminded them that the world continued to function as if none of the events of the past few weeks ever happened, or mattered.

Jasmine sat on one bed, her legs crossed in the lotus pose. Jason lay prone on the bed across from her, listening intently as she detailed her life, the village, her training in the army, and the discovery of her exceptional skills for killing. Mostly she talked about her life as an investigative journalist. She avoided some of the more personal experiences, choosing to share those when the circumstances were better. After a while, she began to talk about her brother.

"Peter was five years younger than I was. The atrocities that he witnessed were too much for a boy his age. He was, maybe, seven when the wars began, when the two sides on the Kashmir conflict continually overtook our village, both of them were taking and killing as if we were the enemy. It took me a long time to get him to understand that it was not our fault that our parents were dead and that we were still alive.

"I thought he was alright, but he kept fading into depression, hanging with the wrong crowd, getting into trouble. He quit school a few times. He never held a steady job. He lived on handouts. I don't think that he resented my success, but he didn't applaud it either. About three years ago he enrolled in a Thought Mechanix seminar. He learned and adopted the Rules of Possibility. It changed him. He would call me all the time, talking about the virtues of Hans Pedersen, about the seminars, and the incredible power he felt. He would talk for hours about the concepts of thought energy, about connecting to the grid. He said he could feel the pain inside me, because of the thoughts emanating out of my head. I thought he had gone completely off his rocker.

"About a year ago his calls became less frequent. I was happy for him. It seemed that he had found some direction. For the first time that I could remember he seemed happy. Then several months ago he called me out of the blue and was ranting about the Rules of Possibility. He was demanding in his tone, telling me I had to listen to the CDs. I had to go to a Hans Pedersen presentation. That it had changed his life. That for the first time he had complete control over everything that was happening around him. He told me during one of our last conversations that knowledge was just energy, and that he had found a way to tap into the knowledge of anyone just by focusing in on their thoughts.

"By the end of the conversation, I was worried that he had converted to some sort of cult. So I flew to New York, where he had moved to pursue some big deal, to make sure he was okay. He was dead by the time I arrived. I had no idea that he had turned into a criminal mastermind of some sort. The police gave me a brief history—from petty thief to head of a massive crime syndicate in less than a year. How is that possible?"

Jasmine slumped down on the bed. Tears no longer came when she thought about her brother. His death was a tragedy. She just wanted to know why it had happened.

"I'm so sorry about your brother. I could tell you all the good things about Thought Mechanix…" Jason offered as he leaned over to touch Jasmine lightly on the arm. "People have accomplished some amazing stuff after following the Rules. Me, for example."

"Maybe. Maybe not. After I found out what he was involved in I started to investigate Thought Mechanix. I convinced my Editor that it was an important piece, so she let me run with it for a while. I settled briefly in New York, from London, to investigate. Then, out of nowhere, I was told to back off. When I didn't, I was fired."

"What was your brother involved in that was so bad?" Jason reached over to the small bedside table to grab the last piece of Gruyère cheese.

"According to the police, he was involved in a plot to kill several prominent people, people who had taken sides on the fight for Kashmir. Apparently, he assembled a group of ten or so accomplices. NYPD provided video surveillance, together with taped conversations obtained from an informant. In all of the tapes Peter is clearly the leader —directing, ordering, suggesting and plotting. In a few of the tapes you can tell he is agitated that others around him cannot see the big picture."

Jason piped up, "Your brother was a criminal. It's sad, but you said yourself he never recovered from the death of your parents."

"My brother was a petty thief. He had no ability to hold more than a few cohesive thoughts together at one time. I loved my brother, but he was no genius."

"So you think that the Rules of Possibility had something to do with it?"

"My instincts are pretty good from years of investigative journalism. He converted to the lessons provided by Hans Pedersen like a fish to water. Hans Pedersen turned my brother into an international terrorist who cared about his homeland. My only thought is that Peter was somehow brainwashed into believing things that never mattered to him before. So I made it my mission to find out."

"Amy Glass. How did you happen to end up in Amy's apartment the same time that I did?"

"Amy was actually a friend. We were introduced a few years back, at a media event I had attended about motivational speakers. At the time, I did not know my brother had gotten involved with the Rules. So to me, the organization was somewhat benign. After my brother died, I contacted Amy to discuss Thought Mechanix."

Jason looked quizzically at Jasmine.

"Amy never mentioned you."

"Did she talk about all of her friends and acquaintances?"

"We were close."

"Probably because she didn't think I was that big of a deal. She told me that what I had discovered was closer to the truth than I might have imagined. Amy said that the explosions at all of the Thought Mechanix locations were not accidents. That the transformation she noticed in my brother was happening everywhere, to hundreds of thousands of people. That Peter's use of his newfound knowledge was not unique.

"Anyway, the night that I—we—were at the apartment, Amy had contacted me. She told me that there was something at her apartment that could help me in my search for answers. She never told me where it was. But she told me to be careful."

"She told you to be careful?" Jason stared at her incredulously.

"You don't believe me?" Jasmine noted the look of disbelief on Jason's face.

"It does seem a little far-fetched."

"Be that as it may, it's the truth. I can't prove it, but I hope you believe me. We need each other now."

Jasmine moved over to the other bed and nestled herself into Jason. He wrapped his arm around her body, feeling her energy drain as she fell asleep, content that her pain was shared with someone who cared.

47

Jasmine luxuriated in the five-hundred thread count Egyptian cotton sheets as she sat up and sipped her coffee. She stared out the window at the potted plants and grasses that adorned the top of the canopy above the hotel entrance.

After the first night, Jason contacted his private banker in London, who arranged a sizable amount of Euro traveler's checks so they could pay for the room at the five-star hotel with the necessary discretion. A day later, a courier arrived with a Swiss bank-routed cash card. Untraceable. By midday, they were settled into Hotel Metropole, near Piazza San Marco. It was discrete, luxurious, and available.

Jasmine reached over and grabbed the last biscotti off the plate that Jason had left on the edge of the bed before heading into the shower. He leaned over and kissed Jasmine, stealing a piece of the biscotti. Jasmine pulled his towel from around his waist.

"Try to restrain yourself," he joked.

"Looks like you're the one that needs restraining. Make your shower a cold one. We have a lot of work to do," Jasmine retorted as she raised her eyes and smiled.

Jasmine lay back on the bed as Jason disappeared behind the bathroom door. She thought about her brother again. The discussion the night before brought back painful memories. Thoughts that made her even more determined to find out who was really behind Thought Mechanix, who had controlled Hans Pedersen. Clearly, given everything that happened, the people chasing Jason around the globe had significant resources.

Whoever they were, Jasmine concluded, they were not amateurs. And it was clear from the weaponry and the tactics that they were not amateurs. They were too organized and methodical in their approach. The attack was textbook, which explained why she was able to avoid getting herself and Jason killed. It was too bad about Carmen. Her death was a mistake. She saw that in the eyes of the shooter. As soon as the gun was fired, a look of incredulous disbelief swiftly followed by panic was apparent. Jasmine knew that look, for a number of reasons.

So if they were not amateurs, then they were desperate, which was why they failed. But they would return, and they would not make the same mistakes the next time. It also meant that they were backed by some influential people—people who would have access to information not available to the ordinary person. So if they charged something, called someone, flew anywhere, used their laptops or BlackBerrys, their digital fingerprints would be scattered across banks, airlines, internet service providers, and God knows what other organizations accumulating their data. They would be easily traced. Until they knew who they were up against, it was decided they would do their best to fly under the radar. They had spent the first night in the cash-only hellhole in the center of Venice to avoid detection. Untraceable cash and the Hotel Metropole were more appealing.

They decided to stay in Venice until there was a reason to travel. They had spent the day going over the folder Jason had taken from Carmen's apartment just as they escaped through the roof on the heels of the Florence police. Whatever Amy Glass wanted them to know would be in that folder.

Carmen Salvatore was thorough. She had kept fastidious notes on all of the conversations with Hans since she met him as a young grad student helping out a fellow Etruscan expert with a few areas of joint interest. The file was thick with notes recounting the meetings she shared with Hans as he tried to understand the secret so closely guarded by the Order.

It became clear as Jasmine and Jason poured over the notes that Hans had uncovered a significant link to the ancestors of the early Etruscans. An article dated a decade earlier tied into the myth that the Etruscans were somehow connected to the early Hebrew gods. No proof, just conjecture.

Having showered, Jason put on the new clothes he had purchased that morning with his new Swiss cash card and sat down at the desk. He flipped through the folder as Jasmine showered. Ten minutes later he lingered over a memo buried in the middle of the thick folder.

"Holy shit," he said to himself. Then louder, "Holy shit! Look at this!"

Jasmine had scrambled from the shower at Jason's first yell. She was now standing at his side, dripping onto the desk.

"Careful, don't get the files wet."

"Sorry," Jasmine covered her long hair in a towel, wrapping it around her head in a single movement.

"Listen to this memo: '... *proof of the existence of a fourth cuneiform tablet that outlined the history behind the eventual sophisticating of the somewhat simplistic human mind. The tablet is reputed to provide the first reference to the existence of more than two Books of Eden. From what I can gather, it was stolen from the National Museum in Baghdad and circulated among private collectors. The stencil of the tablet you sent to me...*' The memo was addressed to Hans, the wavy signature of Carmen on the bottom. Below the signature was a handwritten note suggesting Hans call her as soon as he could. The memo was dated six months before the Stern Auditorium explosion."

"Listen to this: '...*the scribe appears to chastise the writer of the tablet.*' "Jason pointed to the column of the memo at a hastily written note suggesting a crucial link between the third and fourth tablet. A single Xerox copy of a translation to a cuneiform tablet was attached.

They read the translation together, each holding an edge of the page.

... Kuhhake Civilization time is done. Our destiny comes to us not from what we have done but from what we have become. We protected our own for too long, became complacent, stopped growing, staying away from the natural evolution that is inevitable. Our ending was predicted, as are all endings, and all beginnings, which must be for there to be order in things. We succeeded in our desire to perpetuate the cycle of life, made use of the energy to improve the Source and to establish a new race for what has for us become stale, predictable, devoid of intensity. What was the fabric of our success became the fuel of our extinction. The source is from where we came and the source is where we return. It embraces us, sheds our outer shell so that once again we come unto our self. We no longer make the source stronger, without the required intensity of struggle, of conflict, of teaching, changing, and of learning. Not like we have done in the past. That time is behind us, unknown to us. Our history is as forgotten as footsteps in the sands of time. We will be remembered only from what is recorded in this text, written in solace without direction or command. Civilizations come and go, remembered in victory, forgotten when vanquished. These passing conflagrations of peoples do not assemble. They are necessary fuel for the Source. Our link is only a roadmap through a foggy landscape. Once the way was discovered, it was coveted as the greedy protect their desires. It caused us to challenge the Source until there was no other solution but to remove our essence. When your time comes for the chosen one to discover the secret written herein, to learn of the true symbiosis with the Source, then a new energy will be born. This roadmap was contemplated by our sages, who opened the door to our fate. The frail mass of you, evolved from single cells into a complexity of connections and processes, can give but faint hope to achieving what is proposed. To find the direction too soon is cataclysmic; to find it too late, despair. Like all things, the Source changes, evolves, grows and expands. We too came from the same primordial ooze. We developed quickly, nurtured by our understanding of everything that springs forth from this celestial body and a multitude of other similar ones, yet we were unprepared. Eli came to us and we nurtured him into our image, taught him to think beyond his understanding. We took a piece of him and created another. When the time was right, we enticed them to eat from our thoughts, to absorb our wisdom, and to delve into their soul so that they could envision their path to the Source. In Eli's mind we left two paradigms, calling the first the Book of Life and the second the Book of the Knowledge of Good and Evil. Then we sent him away. The first book gave Eli and his companion guidelines to ensure the growth of his understanding. In time, this will be a connection to all physical manifestations. Gone from our presence, they will no longer exist as they have until now; like animals, their primary thought processes focused on survival. The second paradigm provided them with the ability to think consciously, to be aware of thoughts, feel emotions, and sense how the two fuse together to dictate action. Seeing both sides of the Source ensured that Eli would rise above the rest of the creatures, using emotion to respect the nature of all living things, be able use the other species as necessary, and to continually improve connection to the Source. The other books are deliberately hidden, making only shadowy appearances outside the subconscious. To grow with the experiences of the conscious mind, to improve consciousness beyond the Source means to understand what they cannot yet understand. To do so would have destroyed Eli and his line. His mind would not comprehend esoteric thought or the freedom from the connectivity of our thoughts to ensure his own survival. There is a truth that will reveal itself, a truth that survives evolution. It is recorded in the Book of Thought, teaching that essence of energy unharnessed by the mind, channeled beyond the physical. It is the hidden sense. To learn to use this sense is to have the first glimpse at the Source. Once released, the collective thought will control the mind. It cannot distinguish positive from negative. My deception is only a gift if discovered at the correct time. Otherwise, it will lead to the destruction of man. The key is to unlock the journey to the Source, which has been written in a fourth book. This journey to the Source is hidden beyond the Book of Thought. The key to control thought is hidden in the understanding of good and evil. The key to finding the path of the journey is hidden in thought. Written by the hand of Anuk, scribe to Eliitiah.

"Do you realize what this is?" Jasmine stood mesmerized as she stared at the page, the edge still held tightly in her hand.

"It must be a hoax. Someone trying to cash in on some Biblical connection perpetrated into a hoax achieved?"

Jasmine looked skeptical. "Even if this is a fraud, and let's assume for a moment that it is, why are people getting killed to gain access to the information it holds?"

"This memo is only halfway..."

Jasmine stared at the page as Jason spoke, barely hearing the words. She stared at the passage near the end "*...once released the collective thought will control the mind. It cannot distinguish positive from negative.*"

Jasmine looked over at Jason, who continued looking through the folder, back to front. She formed words in her brain but could not speak. A moment later Jason looked up to see Jasmine staring off into space, her mind elsewhere.

"Jasmine?"

Jasmine stood still for a moment longer, then looked down at Jason, who had reclaimed the couch, his feet crossed over one another in a relaxed pose.

"Jasmine, are you alright?" Jason began to worry.

"Don't you see? Don't you see, Jason? The Book of Thought is what the Rules of Possibility are all about. Only Hans and his benefactors did not know that he could not control the direction of the collective energy his millions of followers unleashed as they trained their minds."

48

"You told me the other day that Hans created the RoP II as a change of direction."

"That's right. He told me that it was crucial the truth come out, once and for all." Jasmine perked up, the third espresso having its effect as the caffeine started to speed up her mind. She walked over to the bedside table to grab her bottle of water. The water was warm but still quenched her thirst. She didn't like the re-circulated air in hotel rooms. It always made it difficult for her to breathe if she stayed indoors for too long.

"So do you think that Hans felt he needed to explain this to Carmen? Or do you think that she discovered something that he did not expect?" Jasmine felt a sensation she knew to be intuition. A tingling in the back of her brain as all the pieces of the puzzle came together. One more piece and the entire picture would burst forth into her consciousness.

"Hans continued on with his research because he knew that there was something that needed to be found. One time, when I first met him, he told me that the methodology he had studied to create the Rules of Possibility was just one piece of a bigger picture, that he continued to search for answers that had eluded him, the existence of which even those in the Order of Sumer have refuted. Carmen discovered the link to that past with this translation from the obscure tablet that was stolen from the museum in Baghdad."

"Do you think Hans realized that he needed to find this link?" Jasmine asked as she readied herself for the inevitable truth.

"What? So you mean, do you think he was anxious to find a link?"

Jasmine stood up and started to pace. Her mind began to line up the puzzle pieces, collectively forming a picture as she spoke.

"I think I know exactly what happened. Hans spent a decade, maybe more, building his motivational seminars. He helped millions of people to realize their true potential. If what that translation implies is true…Hans realized that the true potential lay not in the bettering of minds like he had thought, but in the strengthening of the universal consciousness."

"What appears to have happened is that the disciples of TMI energized themselves, the power of thought energy becoming a self-fulfilling prophecy." Jason looked over at Jasmine, her face was contorted, like she was afraid of the next thought to emerge from her brain.

"Exactly. Except he didn't realize one important factor: human beings are designed for survival, to take the shortest route, to build the strongest fortification, to make decisions that better one's own position."

"What about empathy, altruism, contribution? Man's ability to help each other is enormous."

Jasmine smiled, a wry look curled her lips and crinkled the skin around her eyes. "Most people I know who give back have their own personal motivations in doing so. There are very few truly Mother Theresas in the world. Mankind's direction is not one of goodness. It is one of greed, gluttony and glory. It is a path of least resistance to achievement. Hans must have also observed what I saw happening to my brother. The Rules of Possibility, despite their good intentions, began to eat away at the most human needs and wants. Quest for power, wealth and manipulation began to take shape over a period of time.

"The people who entered the program began with only the best of intentions, and that would be what motivated most people. Once they began to see the effectiveness of the Rules, they began to realize that they had an upper hand over people who had not adopted the Rules. Things began to go their way: careers were enhanced, relationships improved, goals achieved. Those who succeeded started getting more daring. They raised the bar of what they wanted, started to achieve in areas that they never would have without the Rules. The power was intoxicating. Then there were the people with a natural predilection for breaking society's laws who completed the program, adopted the Rules of Possibility, and sought out the power it provided. These criminal elements began to exercise the influence afforded to those who achieved perfection with the Rules. Just like a worldwide catastrophe will cause grief to permeate the global consciousness, crime began to increase, as it represented the shortest path to wealth. Even those who thought they were being good helped to fuel the flames as they began to accept their omnipotence over other— "

Jasmine stopped speaking as the reality set in.

Jason stared at her as she stood motionless, unraveling the links in her mind one at a time. They looked at each other across the silence of the darkening hotel room. Then it dawned on Jason what Jasmine was thinking. As they looked at each other the reality of the situation hit them both squarely between the eyes.

"Hans Pedersen had unleashed a fury upon the world. The realization of what had happened terrified him as his life began to implode. The fifteen years of his lifeblood was sucked out of him by the passions for success he'd fostered."

Jasmine was breathing hard, the implications of her theory raising her adrenaline.

"So that was why Hans spent a fortune trying to prove the existence of the Fourth Book of Eden. He was determined to find the antidote for the sickness he had released upon an unsuspecting world." Jason grew excited, as they began to unravel what they believed to be the truth.

"So then why did he kill himself?"

"I do know that he received a few stressful phone calls during our meetings prior to my departure to London. Amy said it was nothing, but given her compromised position as a plant for the organization that was apparently manipulating him, I wonder just whom she was protecting. From what Amy said in her letter, if we chose to believe it, Hans was manipulated one last time into thinking that he would never be able to stop the juggernaut that he'd created. Perhaps it was too much for him."

Jason paused, getting up to refill his coffee from the silver carafe on the room-service trolley. After pouring coffees for both of them, he settled into the leather executive desk chair and leaned back.

"I still find it hard to fathom that everything that Hans accomplished was based on some larger agenda. Everything that the man did personified a greatness that seemed unstoppable. Do you think it is possible that the Rules can be used as deliberately as you are speculating?"

"Look at what you were able to do. You listened to Hans late one night, got hooked, went to a plethora of seminars that cost a fortune, then proceeded to build a firm of accountants that was the darling of New York. Talent flocked to your doors. You continued to expand. It was all because you adopted the Rules of Possibility. Do you think you could have accomplished the same thing without the tricks offered by the Rules? Without the ability to manipulate those unsuspecting people around you who thought you had some innate talent? You are a product of the Thought Mechanix machine whether you like it or not. You may think that what you did was for good, but it was really about you building a bigger and better firm than anyone else. Altruism was not at the core of what you did and it is not at the core of what my brother did. The Rules of Possibility just fine-tuned whatever particular vice drove you the most."

Jasmine's voice became stern as she released her pent-up emotions about Thought Mechanix and its founder. She spent a long time after the death of her brother trying to piece together who or what drove him to such extremes. Now that she knew what she believed to be the truth, it was time to exact some revenge.

Jason started to feel a sense of anger percolate from deep within. He had not felt that way in a long time. Those thoughts were suppressed as his success grew. Even when Blair Stanford stole the firm right from underneath his nose, he did not feel the outrage—Blair was buying something that he did not want anymore. He wanted greatness. Jasmine was right about that, although not so right that he was willing to admit. Jason knew that his path to immortality lay on the same highway that Hans Pedersen built, a highway that was destroyed by an unknown hand who had designed the route right from the start.

"Wait a minute!" Jason's voice rose a few octaves higher than normal. "My success has nothing to do with Hans Pedersen. I built a great firm because I developed a practice that helped its clients.

Everything I did was to help my clients. It was the core of my success. It's simply not fair to say that I had ulterior, empire-building motives."

Jasmine had hit a nerve, but she could not bring herself to stop.

"Jason, I've not known you for very long, but you do not appear to be the sort of person who faces a challenge head-on. You ponder, you avoid potentially dangerous conflict, you wait to see what I am going to do—"

"I'm not an assassin for hire. I'm an accountant. The events of the last few days were not exactly my area of expertise, unlike you—"

"Our interest in the origins and destruction of Thought Mechanix are different, Jason. I don't pretend to care about what Hans Pedersen did or did not do according to Amy Glass or Carmen Salvatore. I care about what he did to my brother. Peter was a good brother. He was not a bad guy, maybe just a little misdirected. But he was not a criminal mastermind or mass murderer. He was not a terrorist. What he did came from somewhere else. It came from the brainwashing he received at the hands of Thought Mechanix as he consumed the Rules of Possibility and allowed them to extract untoward crazy ideas that were not his own.

"What? Are you saying that everything I did, the entire development of the Thought Mechanix inspired management tools that I created and implemented were the product of Hans Pedersen through some sort of mind control?" Jason's voice was rising, as he could not help but feel that his unofficial protector had crossed a line. He tensed, rose from the chair and began to pace.

The proverbial cat was out of the bag. *Was it possible that she would withdraw the insinuation?*

"I don't believe that millions of people from all walks of life could embrace—religiously, socially, economically, politically—the tenets set out by the Rules of Possibility on their own. It is impossible for me to fathom that a collective *rightness* to the decisions currently being made in the world is possible as millions of people abandon their historical religious and other beliefs systems. It's like everyone who participated in Hans Pedersen's program developed the same sense of personal entitlement in whatever they considered possible to achieve. By his own admission, Hans had breached the secrecy expected of his mentors.

He determined what was possible for his own success, then went out and achieved it beyond expectations."

"You seem determined to prove that Thought Mechanix was a hoax perpetrated on an unsuspecting world," Jason said with a hint of indignation in his voice.

"I want to figure out who was responsible for the death of my brother and to exact revenge. Nothing more, nothing less. I don't care if Hans Pedersen was the greatest con man of all time or the most enlightened prophet."

"A prophet who held a mind-warp of some sort over *all* of his converts?"

"What I do know is that there was an organization that spurred him on, lost touch or contact, or whatever, tried to take charge of his development, but somehow fell out of favor. They manipulated Hans to his death and they're now trying to regain some semblance of control. What did Carmen call the organization? *The Order of Sumer?* I intend on confronting the people who set this nightmare in motion, who killed my brother."

"So you don't think your brother was responsible for his own actions," Jason commented.

"Jason, look at you. You are a great guy, good-looking, smart and focused. But from what I have seen in the last week, you are not a leader. You do not face a crisis head-on, like all great leaders. You do not take charge to ensure the desired outcome. Like great leaders do. Three times we have been in compromising situations and you have not acted. It didn't matter that your life was at stake. On the contrary. I have *seen* great leaders—they act when threatened. Always."

"I don't think I like what you are insinuating. I created a very successful advisory firm. From the ground up. I did that."

"Thought Mechanix did that. The Rules of Possibility did that. Jason Wakefield was just a convenient vessel."

"I resent that." Jason could not take the edge off his voice.

"My brother was a small-time punk kid who was not bad at heart. He had seen his share of indiscriminate death, but he was not jaded. He would not have done what he did without some significant change to his personality. The sort of influence he had from Thought Mechanix."

242 - |Derek Schreurs

"So you only care about revenge. What about stopping whatever this Order of Sumer is trying to do? They seem to have an agenda that Hans discovered and wanted to stop. He asked me to help him. I am going to do that."

"I have seen too much death and destruction in the world to care what the Order of Sumer has planned. Whatever it is, it has to be better than the current world situation."

"How can you believe that? Please don't tell me that you really believe what you just said."

"Religion has killed more people than any criminal organization. At least criminals are not intent on changing how you think. They only care about physical possessions. They leave your mind alone."

"Alone and living in fear? Is that fair?"

"Being afraid is a state of mind. I lived the first eighteen years of my life not knowing whether I'd be alive the next day, not knowing if the next patrol of power-drunk soldiers would decide to rape me, or worse. Every day was a day I could have lived in dread. But instead I acquired skills to protect my brother.

"Fear is relative, Jason. Humans adapt. The problem is that the security in which most affluent Westerners live has muted their ability to self-adapt, expecting that someone will protect them. It is a conceited idea that has existed for only a small part of human history. Whatever happens, people will adapt."

Jasmine marched over to the closet to retrieve the backpack and the few clothes she had purchased that day. She started packing without a word.

Jason fumed as he thought about what Jasmine had said. Is it possible he could never have created Wakefield and Associates without Hans? Is it possible that he had been manipulated right from the start? There was no way! He was fully aware of every decision, every success, every new client he brought in. Hans wasn't even a client those first few years he was in business. *He* had sought out the motivational guru.

Or had he?

Maybe Hans Pedersen met him first. Jason started to speak a few times as Jasmine packed, but could not find an appropriate retort to her accusations.

"I'm leaving, Jason. You can go and try to save the world. Personally, I am not sure it's worth saving. I have a date with a monastery."

With that Jasmine Shah was gone.

49

Agostino moved with the speed of a man much younger than his years, the recent discoveries increasing his energy level beyond his control. Decisions were made, events planned, contingencies considered. Sitting in the near-dark comfort of his Siena mansion, the log fire heating the majestic stone walls surrounding him, he contemplated the multitude of seemingly disconnected occurrences that brought him to this particular point in history.

In the span of less than two weeks, fifteen years of carefully laid plans had dissipated into the ether, like so many of the souls sent to the next world. And like those souls, he had no idea where they congregated, when their next destiny was to be ordained, nor could he envision any other path to be taken. Even after being forced to confront Piccolomini, it was apparent that no amount of preplanning could have predicted the events of the previous two weeks.

Hans Pedersen was a force that Agostino had not reckoned with when he set the stage for the young man's rise to international stardom. Pedersen was good, too, much more than Agostino had ever hoped. What he did not count on was the man's ability to protect his territory. Perhaps he should have revealed the grand scheme to Hans. Perhaps he should have shown why it was necessary to use the power of the Book of Thought at this time in history.

It was now up to him to see the program through. To do that he needed to discover how close Hans Pedersen came to truly understanding the power of the Rules of Possibility, which were carefully crafted from the ancient instructions as laid out in the Book of Thought. It was necessary to find out what information Hans left behind, and why, if he was to have any hope of succeeding in his own carefully set-out plans.

Agostino realized that the Holy See was in such a state of denial that nothing could save it from ruin. As Cardinal of Siena, he did not consider himself any less pious than the current sitting Pope.

He, in fact, revered the current Papal leader. Pope Clement XV was everything the church thought it needed. He was technologically savvy, aware of the yearnings of the youth of the Church, and cognizant of the changing moral tide.

The current pope was born Richard Wilhelm Scott, a Boston Catholic who wrestled his way to the top of the Roman Catholic Church by purifying the ranks of the broken, disgraced American Catholic oligarchy. In less than a decade he excommunicated no less than one-third of the priests for their transgressions, helped the authorities prosecute the worst of the offenders, and told the remainder of his flock to act with the dignity expected of their role. In areas where there were no priests left to service the dwindling congregations, he connected his flock to the most popular priests through live webcasts at the behest of Agostino.

After attaining the papacy, he chose the name *Clement,* after an eighteenth-century predecessor facing equal if not dissimilar threats to Roman Catholic dominance. His namesake's first Encyclical mandate clearly defined his policy, which was to keep the peace with Catholic priests so as to secure their support in the war against irreligion.

But Clement XV had one major failing: he did not grasp the extent to which his or any other religion was threatened by outside influences. This was particularly disheartening to Agostino. Ironically, it was due to Clement XV's misunderstanding of the power of the Internet. The current Pope neither understood nor grasped the enormity of the shift in consciousness away from his religion—away from all religion. Clement was no different than his counterparts in the other major faiths.

A global consciousness was arising, spurred on almost four decades earlier during the advent of the Age of Aquarius, fueled out of control by the connected globalization of the Internet. Agostino saw it early. He used his position as the protector of the Books of Eden to ensure that when the tide of consciousness shifted for good, he would be ready. Hans Pedersen did not know it, but he was Agostino's insurance policy. An insurance policy that, as it turned out, did not pay out when it was needed. By the time Agostino realized that something had gone terribly wrong, it was too late. The momentous shift happened in a way that he had not predicted. By the time he contacted Hans to tell him the truth behind Thought Mechanix, it was too late to stop.

There was only one thing left to do. He needed the strength to reverse what he started—to gain control of his destiny for the glory of the Church. What he once wanted was now impossible, even if the current Pope was ready to capitulate.

Father Thom, the wayward mathematical sheep, was correct: millions of Christ's followers were formally abandoning the Eucharist. Agostino knew that it was just a matter of time before Clement XV resigned the Papacy. The man seemed to be drained of energy, unable to comprehend how his followers could be leaving after his efforts to fix their Church. He was despondent beyond hope. The Holy See was functioning only by the grace of God and the strength of Clement XV's closest advisors.

Fifteen years earlier it was Agostino's intention that the Cardinals come to him for salvation, especially after he brought the population of the world back to Catholicism. All of that had now vanished. In view of recent events, it was crucial that he discover where his carefully laid plans went so wrong.

Or maybe he was responsible for the destruction, not the salvation, of the religion he had devoted his life to protect?

50

Jason tossed under the covers, unable to catch sleep. He opened his eyes into the blackness of midnight. It was humid in the room, the damp air sticking to him like plaster. Outside, there were sounds of late-night partygoers returning from the bars. It had been only a few hours since Jasmine and he parted ways, the words she left behind still stinging in his ears. Was it possible that she was right? He wrestled with her accusations. It was true that before the Rules of Possibility he was wallowing in a nowhere career, barely able to keep his head in the game. Did he really pull up his bootstraps and turn his life around, or was it some outside force that guided his success?

Sleep came in fitful waves as he wrestled with his conscience. Was that why Hans Pedersen became such a close ally? Because Jason was just another vessel of his motivational manipulation?

A particularly loud banging outside his window woke Jason up for good. He grabbed his watch from the bedside table: 3:15 a.m. Rebuffing the demons in his head, he threw off the covers and headed to the shower. An hour later, with a half a pot of thick dark Italian roast coursing through his veins, he sat at the ornate wood desk, staring at the computer screen.

Hans Pedersen stared back.

Jason was watching the first session of RoP II for what seemed like the tenth time, listening for the instructions that Amy Glass had alluded to in her letter. It was no use. Whatever Hans was trying to convey about how to unravel the secrets of the Book of Thought was lost on him. He was about to turn off the DVD when Hans said something that twigged a memory. He was reciting one of the twenty-one Rules of the first series, laying the foundation for the new Rules.

"...the next Rule is crucial in its implementation. Separate the inner and outer mind. Only by doing so will you be able to discover the truth. You must release the bonds to the physical world to find the path to controlling your thoughts. In the

beginning you had a thought, a small kernel of an idea about who you were. Focus on who you are for a moment; keep that in your conscious mind. Now let that thought drift backwards to your subconscious…"

Jason reversed the DVD, listening to the segment for a second, then a third time.

Then it hit him.

"…drift backwards to your subconscious."

It was something Hans had said to him in the limousine on the way back from the taping of the third segment of ROP II. Hans was explaining the new series. Jason remembered him clearly speaking about the third installment that he watched being taped.

The third segment dealt with how the process of replacing our memories with thought energy actually works!

Excited, he removed the first DVD, inserted the third and scrolled through the chapters until he found the spot he was looking for. He pressed Play then waited for Hans to begin.

The program started with the usual symphony of music building to a crescendo as the sound of violins filled the room. A few moments later Hans's face appeared on the screen, his intense eyes boring into the viewer. Jason waited and listened for the right clues. It took fifteen minutes to reach the spot on the DVD.

Hans spoke as if were speaking directly to Jason.

"…forget all of your preconceived notions of what is going on in your brain. It takes clarity to achieve the closest connections to the thought matrix. For example, take of a glass full of water. Put it up to your eyes and concentrate on an image in front of you on the wall in front of you—a picture, or another object. As you stare through the glass you can see to the other side, but the image is distorted by the water. Sometimes you see two, or three, of the same image, depending on how the light reflects off the water in the glass.

"Now empty the glass and look though it again. As you look through the sides of the empty glass the image is clearer without the fullness of the glass, but it is still fuzzy from the light reflecting off the glass itself. Look at the image directly without the glass in front of your eyes. It is seemingly crystal clear compared to the other two views.

"Finally, close your eyes and think about the image. It's no longer physically visible. You can imagine the glass as a crystal-clear reflection, as if the glass was not even obstructing your view, or you can see it as if it were distorted by a full glass of water. How you see the image in your mind depends on what you choose to see.

"So is it with thought. The mind is distorted by the multitude of ideas that circulate in the brain at any point in time, just like the water distorts the painting. What you concentrate on is entirely dependent on you, except that those thoughts are distorted by the fullness of your mind. Thoughts that stay in your consciousness are influenced by the myriad of sensory inputs just like the glass of water influences your ability to see the picture hanging on the wall. To really see your thoughts, you need to shed the barriers that make them necessary to exist in the first place. If you empty your mind of all thought, you will be able to direct your attention to precise individual thoughts…"

Jason continued to listen as the guru spoke, unraveling the techniques that he had established in the first series of the Rules.

By the end of the DVD, Jason had still learned nothing. The computer screen went blank. What was Amy talking about? There was nothing that indicated how the Rules really worked. If Amy wanted him to help fix whatever it was that the Rules broke, then she was out of luck. He had watched the three DVDs a dozen times, without success. Maybe Jasmine was right. Perhaps there was nothing they could do to help. Maybe it didn't matter anyway.

Jason took the DVD out of the computer and reached for its case. As he was putting it away, the light from the halogen lamp reflected off the disc. He noticed writing on the inner edge. Bending the disc into the light he read the two word inscription: *other side*. Jason threw the DVD into the computer, this time upside down. He leaned back and waited for the computer to recognize the disc. A minute later Hans's voice erupted from the computer speakers

"Jason."

Jason jumped as he heard his name coming out of his computer speakers. The motivational guru's face appeared on the screen against a dark background.

"I want to apologize. I had never intended for you to get so involved. But you were selected. You presented an opportunity too perfect to pass up. A dozen times I wanted to tell you what was happening but was afraid of what it would do to

you. I used you, Jason. I'm not proud of it, but I did what I thought was right. You possessed the energy and intelligence to attain the level of distribution needed to achieve my objectives. But it's too late for subterfuge; the truth is the only way to reverse the colossal mistake that I helped to create. I need you to trust me one more time, so let me begin.

Thought is energy. It is not restricted to physical space. When we tap the grid of thought energy we are not just focusing intentions to achieve success. We are supplanting our ideas in the minds of others. People do what we tell them to do because the Rules, properly applied, let you decided what thoughts they would think. Like brainwashing in real time. I know this because of the research I've done. It behooves me to admit that since acquiring that knowledge I have not been entirely noble in its application. I am ashamed to admit that the recent decisions you made with Wakefield and Associates are examples of my transgressions. None of the participants of Thought Mechanix seminars who have mastered the Rules of Possibility have any idea how it works; they just know that it achieves a level of success that they want, so they continue to apply the Rules on their personal growth journeys. From what you may have noticed in the media recently, Thought Mechanix has received quite a bad rap. Certain individuals who have attended my seminars have achieved some notoriety. This includes people who have used the Rules to further their criminal aspirations. Indeed, a wave of immoral, unethical and illegal activity seems to have enveloped the world, centered in New York, where most of my seminars have been conducted.

I thought that I had things well in hand, but it is clear that not knowing the true purpose of the Book of Thought has wrought these unintended consequences that have stemmed from the Rules. I have spent millions trying to discover a way to stop what I have started. I've focused on locating the fabled fourth book, known to exist for centuries by the guardians of the Books. They are known as the Order of Sumer. The fourth book is known as the Book of the Journey to the Source. It is now clear to me that the third and fourth books work in concert, similarly to the first two books, which religious references refer to as the Tree of Life and the Tree of the Knowledge of Good and Evil. I postulated my own theory that the third and fourth books were written as a guide to give man access to their origins, but that they would reveal themselves only when it was deemed appropriate. The ancient protectors of the third book, the Book of Thought, were entrusted to keep the secrets, knowing that releasing the power of the Book of Thought without knowing the contents of the fourth book would be cataclysmic.

In my search for the Book of the Journey to the Source, I discovered something that shook the foundation of my beliefs. I am a fraud. Everything connected to Thought Mechanix is a fabrication. My entire involvement, from my initial accident in Siena to my indoctrination into the secrets of the Order of Sumer, from the rise of Thought Mechanix to the creation of the Rules of Possibility—everything up to the recent work I have been doing was controlled by the leaders of the Order of Sumer. A high-ranking brother, convinced of his illusion for a better church, put me in place, manipulated my innate skills, and controlled my own thought energy in order to achieve his own ends.

In the past few months leading up to making recording this session, I have been distracted by this knowledge. Certain individuals for whom I shared a common vision have helped me to cope, but it is no use. I will not be allowed to continue.

You need to finish what I have started. The fourth book must exist. Find it and use it to stop the juggernaut of destruction. You have to believe that the effect of millions of people applying the Rules in the way that was not intended can be reversed. I believe it can be stopped. It was my intention to reveal to the world the true nature of the deception propagated by the man who has manipulated me for the past fifteen years.

As you will recall, that seminar at the Isaac Stern Auditorium was sabotaged. Even without the information contained in the fourth book, RoPII was going to be my attempt to reverse the effects of my decade and a half of preaching thought energy. I had no idea whether it would have been successful, but I had to try.

Because of my actions, it is clear to me that my position at the head of Thought Mechanix is about to come to a swift and ignominious end. Cardinal Franco Agostino, the man who manipulated me, knew full well the power of the Book of Thought. I can only surmise that he was convinced that he had the ability to control its effects once they were released on the world.

Whatever the true intentions, it is clear that something has spiraled out of control. I believe that the discovery and interpretation of the fourth book is essential to stop the madness infecting the world. It needs to be stopped—"

The DVD abruptly stopped. Jason sat staring at the screen, unable to move, as the words jumbled around his mind: conspiracy, manipulation, fraud, mind control. It all seemed too far-fetched. And yet he knew to his core that everything Hans spoke of was the truth. Since Jasmine confronted him about his ability to create his company, his own doubts were surfacing. From an early age it was clear that he was never destined for leadership. He was the second string athlete who aspired to break the inevitable bench-sitting cycle but was never willing to put in the extra effort. He excelled at school only because he took a course load that afforded him the time to achieve the necessary marks. He was a grunt in the big accounting firm and would have stayed there except that, as was apparent now, Hans Pedersen picked him out of a crowd. Once he was identified, they read his thoughts and supplanted them with their own. Jasmine was able to see the truth. She was able to gauge his true abilities after knowing him for just a few weeks.

Oh my God, he thought, she was heading straight into the eye of this hurricane without even knowing its fury. The man who was really behind Thought Mechanix was powerful, motivated, and would not hesitate to eliminate someone like Jasmine who threatened to topple his carefully laid plans. Jason needed to warn her of the truth behind the manipulation of Hans Pedersen. He looked at his watch. 7:30 a.m. She had half a day's head start. He hoped he would be able to catch her in time to warn her of the true purpose of Thought Mechanix.

51

The HeliMax XT-109 set down on the edge of a sunflower field within sight of the Ampugnano Airport in Siena after a harrowing hour-long flight. The helicopter pilot grinned over as Jason, his passenger, disembarked, looking a little green around the gills.

"I get you here fast, no?" The pilot, a retired captain of the Italian Air Force, helped his passenger to the ground. He was over sixty, with thousands of hours in the air in a myriad of combat and civilian situations. When the young American approached him, he jumped at the chance to fly below radar to Siena. He speculated the return trip would be short enough that the tour guide would only just be arriving with the day's tourists by the time he returned to Venice. Besides, the price was too good to turn down.

"It was great," Jason commented shakily, unsure if he wanted to compliment the pilot on the trip.

But he had been lucky to find the pilot. After arriving at the Marco Polo Airport, he was not able to find a connection that would get him to Siena any faster than renting a car and driving. As he made his way to the car rental counters, he noticed the pilot attending to his helicopter behind the security gates near the rental cars. He walked over to the fence and called the man over. After determining that he knew a little English, Jason explained his situation, hinting at a "lover's quarrel" rather than revealing that Jasmine was in danger. The pilot agreed to fly him to Siena. Without a flight plan, the older pilot kept the helicopter low, skirting the trees and buildings as they flew. Jason's worry was assuaged by the huge grin on the pilot's face as he banked over the low-lying hills of the Italian countryside.

Entering the terminal after a short walk across the farmer's field, Jason rented a diesel Mercedes at the Sixt rental counter. Using the map offered by the rental agent, he headed into the center of Siena, towards the monastery. Inputting the address into the GPS from the notes in Carmen's folder, he let the pleasant, soft-accented English female voice guide him into the city. He parked the car on a side street a few blocks from his destination and walked the steep slope to the unobtrusive front door of the ancient monastery. It was almost noon. With the quick stomach-churning flight from Venice, he figured that Jasmine couldn't be too far ahead of him.

A short, balding monk who couldn't be younger than seventy answered the door, eying the guest quizzically as Jason explained that he was looking for his girlfriend, a tall Indian woman. He explained in halting Italian from his airport-purchased phrase book that they were supposed to meet here but had been separated after a quarrel.

The man gestured for Jason to enter and take a seat on the wooden bench in the portico. Then he turned and left. Fifteen anxiety-filled minutes went by before the man returned, followed by a much younger monk.

"You are also looking for Cardinal Agostino?" The monk spoke in English with just a hint of an accent.

"My friend...girlfriend...is she here? We quarreled," Jason repeated to the younger monk, "She was coming to meet the Cardinal—"

"What is your business with the Cardinal?"

Jason hesitated for a moment. If Jasmine had come here, he had no idea what sort of story that she may have concocted. He also had no idea if the monks in front of him were aware of what Cardinal Agostino and their monastery were protecting. From the information he took when they left Carmen's apartment, he gathered that only certain factions within the monastery were given the task of securing the Books of Eden. It was better to play his cards close to his chest.

"It was a matter between my friend and the Cardinal. I left her in anger but was hoping to find her and make amends. It was a ridiculous argument." Jason stopped explaining his situation and got to the point. "Is she here?" he asked again.

"She was here early this morning, arriving shortly before nine. I spent a few minutes with her. I am sure that the Cardinal will be able to help her in her quest. I suggested that she meet with him directly at his private retreat. Perhaps she is still there." The Brother was sympathetic to Jason's plight.

After thanking the Brother for his help, Jason left. He hurried now, eager to catch up with Jasmine and hoping to avert the danger her desire for revenge was leading her into.

As he raced down the slope to his rental, he had no idea of the flurry of activity occurring behind the heavy entrance doors of the monastery of the Order of Sumer. For the second time that morning, the young Brother who had graciously directed the unexpected visitors to the summer retreat of the Cardinal of Siena was speaking on the cell phone he kept hidden in the folds of his robe for these precise moments. The man was a junior recruit in the cadre of men sworn to protect the secrets of the Order. His immediate task was simple: since the death of the motivational guru, ensure that all people seeking council with Cardinal Agostino get exactly what they request. The young Brother was not a violent man, so he was thankful to have been given the task of simply directing the strangers into the hands of the Cardinal, who would deal with them in his own way.

52

Jasmine approached the Cardinal's house with caution. Having left the taxi at the bottom of the hill, she made her way up the long, winding driveway as it curved between rows of majestic Cypress trees swaying to a warm, late-morning breeze. The large villa was perched at the top, surrounded by scores of boxwoods, bay and yew trees. A small grove of olives stood off to the side, waiting for the summer warmth to begin their gestation. The front entrance was splashed with planters full of a thousand lavenders and roses, the air strong with the smell of rosemary and thyme as well as the scent of fruit trees blossoming in the early summer morning. The house itself was larger than most Tuscan villas, looking more like a castle than a farmhouse, constructed mainly of stones extracted from local quarries.

Finding the monastery of the Order of Sumer was easier than she expected. She had stated that she was writing a history of the Etruscans. She was precise in her description of the relationship between the Tyrolean tribes and the interlopers from Lydia, the information that Carmen had provided when she explained how the Books of Eden ended up in Siena. Jasmine just wanted to create a plausible enough story that would ensure her an audience with the Cardinal. Carmen's notes indicated that Hans and the Cardinal worked together to interpret the Book of Thought. With Hans dead, the Cardinal was the only link to the answer she sought—why her brother became a sadistic animal. And why he was now dead.

She told the young Brother at the monastery that she was given the name of the Cardinal from a colleague in New York who said that he was the preeminent expert in the Church on the subject of the Etruscans. Pleased that she had convinced the young Brother to introduce her to the Cardinal, she waited in the portico of the monastery as he extracted a cell phone from the folds of his robe and made a call. A few minutes later she was in a taxi heading to the Italian countryside towards the Cardinal's private retreat.

Jasmine used the large iron knocker on the door to announce her arrival. She could hear the tone of the iron ball against the metal plate reverberate inside the house. A moment later the door was opened by an older man in a flowing white cassock, tied at the waist with a red sash. He smiled graciously at his guest as he opened the door wide.

"Jasmine Shah of New York. You have travelled a long way to meet with me. Come in." Cardinal Agostino grasped her hands between his own with the affection of a grandfather.

Before Jasmine could reply to the unexpected familiarity, the Cardinal continued, "Forgive my directness, but I am afraid we do not have much time. I am truly sorry for your recent loss of a sibling."

Jasmine pulled her hands away, feeling unsettled. She expected a confrontation with the Cardinal. From what she gathered after listening to Carmen Salvatore and from reviewing her notes, Agostino was the direct link between the monastery and Hans Pedersen. It was Agostino that pushed Hans into creating Thought Mechanix for his own gain. Jasmine expected to show the man no mercy now that she had found the person responsible for the creation of the Rules that killed her brother. Not at all expecting the Cardinal's acute awareness of her personal mission, she hesitated, the planned speech in her head dissolving in the current revelation.

"How do you know so much about me?" she managed to ask, her anger spitting out the words.

"By accident, really. We have—had —a mutual friend. Amy Glass."

"Amy. She worked for you, I suspect. Is she also just a victim of your contorted vision?"

"What do you know of my vision?" Agostino threw the question back at her. "You know nothing of what was—is happening. It is tragic about her death. For that I will never forgive myself. I told her that she needed to stay away. I went to her to tell her that things had gotten out of control. She didn't believe me. She held me responsible for the death of Hans Pedersen. But I have no idea who killed him? Or her."

"How do you know of me?" Jasmine asked again.

"I know of you and your brother because that is what I paid Amy to tell me. She kept me apprised of issues that affected the functioning of Thought Mechanix. She first told me of your queries into Thought Mechanix long before the recent…incidents. I have been waiting for you. I have much to explain."

He led a reluctant Jasmine into the main living room towards a pair of Victorian side chairs facing the gardens. He gestured for Jasmine to join him.

A servant brought a tray with coffee and breakfast biscuits before retiring.

"What was your involvement in the death of Amy? Or the destruction of the Thought Mechanix properties? What about Hans? My brother! What about him? People are dead, Cardinal Agostino. And more are going to die." Jasmine felt her face heat up as she queried the aging Cardinal, her anger no longer contained.

"I know every detail about the death of Amy, of Hans Pedersen, of the death a few days ago of a vibrant young professor of Etruscan studies at the University of Florence. I know more than I care to know. It pains me greatly."

Agostino commented, his voice holding back a flood of emotion. They were but another few deaths in the fight for his religion, a fight that he saw as part of his struggle for power. Even a few days earlier he was able to hang on to the belief that everything he was doing was worth the cost. That was until he learned of the death of Carmen Salvatore. Her slaying made him realize that his long-laid plans were collapsing, even as he neared the end of his grand scheme.

Agostino held out his hands in a gesture of compassion, his face divulging a small emotional strain that he kept well hidden. The weight of his sins could not be revealed, nor accepted by anyone. He was sitting face-to-face with one of the victims of his failed drive for power. He thought of solving her pain as his absolution.

"I know you are angry, Jasmine, as am I. Please try to harness your anger for the appropriate time. That time will come soon, I assure you. If you will indulge an aging man of God, I promise that you will see that we are on the same side.

"Let me tell you a story." He looked over at Jasmine with a sympathetic eye.

"I discovered the enormous extent to which my project had failed a few months ago." Agostino spoke with a heavy voice. His body slumped forward in his chair as he tried to hold his coffee steady.

"Your project—"

Jasmine's query was interrupted by a crash in the foyer as the front door knocked over a bronze statute. The pair jumped from their seats and headed to the entranceway.

53

They came upon a scene that caused the Cardinal to gasp and Jasmine to break into fits of laughter. Jason, standing on the driveway, was brandishing a tree branch high over his head, looking like a wild animal. Two of the villa's servants lay on the ground behind him, clutching their heads, staggering to get up. He had a look of crazed fury in his eyes as he rushed into the villa. He swiftly closed and locked the door behind him to stave off his attackers. He turned and looked at the stunned faces of Jasmine and Cardinal Agostino.

"Jasmine! Are you alright?" Jason was clutching the branch, at the ready.

Only able to nod as she held back her laughter, Jasmine indicated that she was fine.

Agostino rushed past Jason, unlocked the door and attended to his two bruised servants, who were now standing and examining each other's wounds, speaking rapidly in Italian. Agostino spoke to them for a few minutes, nodding towards Jason and using a few hand gestures to calm his servants down.

Jasmine relieved Jason of the branch he was carrying then threw her arms around him, her lips finding their target.

"You came to rescue me." She smiled as she held him tight, looking into his eyes.

Jason nodded sheepishly, pointing at the branch on the floor, "Complete with an olive branch. Is everything alright? Are you alright?"

Jasmine looked past Jason at Cardinal Agostino, who was sending his servants around to the back entrance of the villa. She lowered her voice, "Not sure yet. The Cardinal was about to tell me his role in Thought Mechanix before your grand entrance."

"Pretty spectacular, huh?"

"Makes us even." Jasmine smiled as she kissed him on the mouth.

Agostino returned to the living room, introductions were made, apologies accepted. Jason devoured half of the biscuits on the plate, famished, as he had not eaten since the night before. Agostino called for lunch to be prepared. An hour later, sitting at the large wood dining table, the aromas of olive oil, sage and roasted duck heavy in the air, Agostino continued his declaration to the two unlikely confessors.

"Religion is dying. Catholicism is dying, a slow, painful fall from grace. Men of the cloth, once revered, are reviled by many as weak and sinful. I know it is just a small percentage of priests who have strayed, probably not many more proportionately than the general population, but their actions have left a general sense of unease in the hearts and minds of the shirttail followers of Christ.

"It's not just Catholics either. Muslims are being defined by the actions of a handful of political terrorists, hiding behind the Koran to carry out their atrocities. Fundamentalists are screaming bloody murder as they fornicate behind veils of righteousness. Jews continue to fight for a homeland at the expense of a displaced multitude of god-loving, caring people, turning them into demons for the sake of a few zealots. Politicians use religion as the banner to achieve their goals—like the Crusaders, like the missionaries. It has always been the same.

"Fifteen years ago I had a vision that a man would come to us, a man young and able, to change the direction the world was heading. It was to be a new beginning for Catholicism. When Hans Pedersen appeared at our doorstep I knew that my dream had come true, that there was a way to stop the decline in belief that was starting to permeate the popular conscious. So I nurtured Hans from the beginning. I showed him the ancient tablets that our Order was sworn to protect—*to protect until the time was right*. I convinced myself that the time was right, that Hans was the messenger. So I orchestrated his development of Thought Mechanix, assisted him in the creation of the Rules of Possibility, made him famous. I opened to him the power of the Book of Thought."

Agostino paused from his confession to look at his two guests, two people brought to him to help salvage his beloved Church. He meant well when he started. But he was too impetuous, too anxious for his own power to grow, too certain of his convictions. The Book of Thought was hidden from the world, protected by him and his predecessors for reasons that could not be explained. If there was to be any hope to reverse the damage already caused by his actions, he must try to explain.

"I released upon the world a force that is more powerful than the current human mind can comprehend. There are a few who have been able to harness the energy released by the covenant of the Book of Thought. These men and women were not the first to harness the power of the untapped mind. Many people throughout history have accessed the source of energy bespoke of by the Book without knowledge of its existence. In history books they are referred to as visionaries, luminaries, men and women of great creative genius, as well as men and women infamous for their deeds. Their ability to tap the knowledge of the universe helped humankind to develop in leaps, but at a pace that the human brain could tolerate. It also created men who sought only to destroy. Many of the great men of vision were killed as heretics or murdered for jealousy. Most of them were considered ahead of their time by future historians."

Jason was about to interrupt, to explain what they already knew.

Agostino raised his hand.

"Let me finish. The Book of Thought comes from the beginning of creation. Since you have already met the lovely Carmen Salvatore, God rest her soul, you know that the Book of Thought was the third in a series of four. The first two Books, as you are undoubtedly aware, are those two mentioned in the Bible: the Book of Life and the Book of the Knowledge of Good and Evil. These were handy instruction manuals for the men of eight thousand years ago, providing appropriate rules to live beyond the scope of mere survival. The evolution of man as a thinking animal began with those Books.

"Despite the teachings of grade-school religion, the Garden of Eden was not where man, the physical man, came into being. Man already existed, which provides no end of controversial debate amongst my colleagues. How else could Adam and his offspring have gone forth and multiplied? No one bothered to explain how and with whom. The Garden of Eden is not how man came into existence as a physical being. It is where *spiritual* man first evolved, with the help of God. His soul was created by God, giving him a link to the universe of energy and knowledge.

"Jason, you would refer to this as heaven. Jasmine, you know of it as the plane of existence *Swarga Loka*, or the place where the gods reside. Adam was spared the knowledge of how the connection worked, left with only the knowledge that he had dominion over the rest of the creatures of the world. Being of a human mind, the energy that connected him to the universe was overshadowed by other human emotional drivers. Over the millennia, that knowledge of the connection to the gods was diluted into the myriad of beliefs that we live with today—dozens of religions and thousands of sects, all of them screaming that they know the path to salvation.

"For the past eight thousand years the Order was given the task of hiding the existence of the other two books, the Book of Thought and the Book of the Journey to the Source. Almost three thousand years ago my ancestors split apart into two groups. Each group was entrusted with the protection of one of these ancient tablets. My forefathers settled in Tuscany, merging with the Etruscans. The other tribe headed south to the delta of the Euphrates, carrying with them the fourth tablet.

"In my vision it was clear to me that mankind had evolved far enough along to benefit from the secrets hidden within the Book of Thought. As to the fourth book, its existence, while known to the Order, was lost in its travels with the other half of the Lydian clan that settled at the mouth of the Euphrates. I had no real understanding of how the two books acted in concert, just as the Book of Life and the Book of the Knowledge of Good and Evil go hand in hand. My desire to save the Church that I so love clouded my judgment. All around me there are people ready to accept that their consciousness is connected to everyone else's. I was one of those people. Hans Pedersen was one of those people. Jason, you are one of those people."

Jasmine interrupted Agostino as the realization hit her, "My brother…"

"Your brother was one of those people, people who are able to harness the power of the *energy grid,* as the Rules of Possibility provide, giving them an ability to influence events beyond the control of a normal person, like the visionaries and luminaries who are provided with direct access to the tools of the gods. What I failed to realize was that not all people who were able to harness the power provided by the Book of Thought would use that ability for the betterment of mankind. Even I have to admit that the power it gave me filled my head with personal ambitions.

"The second thing I failed to realize was the extent to which the Internet would affect the dissemination of the techniques taught by Hans Pedersen in how to access the power of the Book of Thought through his Rules. It did not exist as it does today. Consequently, the number of people who gained access to the energy grid is multiplying exponentially. And now it is spiraling beyond control."

Agostino knew that he needed the help of the two young people seated across from him, so he told them everything he could to convince them of his sincerity.

"When I realized the extent of my folly, I contacted Hans to let him know what was happening, to try and find some way to reverse the effects of the Rules of Possibility. He told me that he also saw what was happening. He disclosed his own research regarding the fourth book. Together we searched the archives of ancient writings, studied texts describing the second tribe of Lydia to their final destination. Carmen Salvatore spent every waking hour studying their history to try and find a clue as to the location of the fourth Book of Eden. It was only by luck the Iraqi war brought about the kind of museum pilfering that would expose the ancient text that proved the existence of the book. Hans used his wealth and influence to obtain the tablet. It proved the existence of the fourth Book of Eden, but not its location. Over the last two years we assembled a massive research team, centered in London, to locate the fourth book."

"St. Mary's Axe."

"Precisely," Agostino confirmed. "In the meantime, Hans worked nonstop to develop his new series, RoP II, as a sort of antidote for the original series. It was an attempt to reverse the negative effects that the access to the energy grid was causing, the increase in violence, crime, abuse that was beginning to overtake the world. But Hans became disillusioned, convinced that it was his fault, not mine. Drunk with the power of his illusionary success, he decided that disclosure was the answer. He initiated a series of lectures, the first at the Stern Auditorium, to tell the world the truth. It was an act of faith that he believed would set the world right. He would not listen to me when I explained that nothing he did could change the direction taken with the release of the power of the Book of Thought. When Hans died, I acted. I destroyed the Axe and the Plaza so that they could no longer function. I was careful. I knew the risks if the information that I bestowed upon Hans fell in the wrong hands, if the Book of Thought went beyond my vision. So right from the beginning I planned with the proper contingencies."

"It was you who destroyed the Thought Mechanix buildings? Why?" Jason blurted out. "What were you hoping to achieve? People died."

"My planning was not perfect. I tried to make sure the buildings were vacant. Jason, I am sorry about your friend."

Agostino broke down, no longer able to continue. He had confessed his greatest sin and it had drained the energy from his body.

Jason and Jasmine sat with empty expressions as they watched Agostino agonize, scarcely able to bear the responsibility for the destruction he had caused to happen.

Jason stood up. "So did you kill Hans Pedersen?"

54

Agostino looked up at Jason with an expression of tired resignation, choking back his grief as he spoke.

"Of course I did not kill Hans. He was like a son to me. I believed that Hans committed suicide when he realized that his attempt at disclosing the truth to the world would not reverse the path he set. He spoke to me many times, through Amy, indicating how sorry he was for what had happened. Amy told me constantly how desperate Hans had become, that he was no longer himself. I just assumed from the news coverage…"

"Hans did not commit suicide. He was murdered. Just a few hours before he died, I received a call from him, making sure that I contacted the men at the Discoverer's Club. He told me they had information that would help me complete my mandate. He did not sound like a man about to jump to his death."

"Amy was adamant. Hans was beside himself with grief."

"Why would Amy tell you that? She knew as well as I that Hans was anything but grief-stricken. He was a man on a mission." Jason let the words hang in the air.

"Why would Amy lie to me? She was my *savant* when it came to Hans Pedersen and Thought Mechanix. She knew what we were trying to do right from the beginning. I told her everything, that our world was in a self-destruct mode, which had started with my desire to make it a holier place. She understood better than anyone that the only way to alter our destiny was by finding the fourth Book of Eden. She swore an oath to help find the access to the one truth that will bring our destructive forces in check, to bring our consciousness back from the brink of extinction."

"What about the Discoverer's Club? At almost the exact same time that Hans fell to his death someone attacked the Discoverer's Club. It was like they were waiting for the right moment before striking. Like they were waiting for me to arrive…" Jason paused. "Do you know anything about that?"

"They were a fringe group of lunatics who helped me finance Hans. They thought they controlled the activities of the company behind the scenes. A paranoid group of rich, useless old men convinced that the world needed to change to their liking. Although they were useful for a while, they had become problematic. They thought they held the secret to the origin of Thought Mechanix. I suspect that Hans confided in them. It was my belief that they were going to tell you where the fourth Book was located. When they were attacked, it seems their paranoia took matters into their own hands. Solved a problem for me."

"Who else would be trying to stop Hans? So who attacked them… me…at the Discoverer's Club?"

Agostino avoided the question, "I was only concerned that the secrets I had divulged to Hans Pedersen did not get into the wrong hands. So I acted, like it we always agreed it would be done."

"Who is *we?*" Jasmine spoke up for the first time.

"Amy and I. It was she who helped to orchestrate the building construction to the exacting specifications needed to destroy all evidence."

"That's ludicrous. Think of the number of people who could have been killed. There were people who were killed or injured. What right did you have to act like a terrorist?"

Cardinal Agostino looked defeated. His head hung low, eyes sunk like dark shadows into his face.

"The world was on the path of destruction. The church had no way of saving itself from imploding. People die every day. My vision was not ill-conceived. The outcome was unfortunate, but I would have done it all over again if need be."

"What about the Discoverer's Club. Did they panic? If it was not targeted by you, who would have attacked them…attacked me…and why did they initiate a self-destruct sequence?"

"There is only one other man within the Order who had the knowledge of Thought Mechanix. Brother Augu—"

"What's that?" Jason pointed to a red dot hovering on Cardinal Agostino's chest.

Jasmine saw the tiny dot just as the first bullet pierced the living room window and embedded itself on the left side of the aging Cardinal's chest, followed a moment later by a second bullet embedding itself in the middle of Agostino's forehead, an inch over his left eye.

He was dead before his body hit the floor.

"Get out of the way," Jason yelled as he leaped over to where Jasmine was sitting, pulling her out of her seat as the next bullet broke through the living room window.

The projectile tore through the flesh at the top of Jasmine's bicep as Jason pulled her to the floor. Another round followed the first, hitting the back of the plush upholstery of the Victorian chair, tearing at the fabric and shattering the wood, stopping only after it lodged itself into the hardwood floor.

As they backed away from the windows, a fusillade of gunfire rained down upon the room, smashing statues, breaking glass, and looking for a target. Jason pulled Jasmine backwards toward the kitchen as the gunfire continued unabated.

A more intense round of gunfire erupted from inside the house as the two men Jason had previously subdued entered the room, firing back at the assailants with powerful AR-15 submachine guns, firepower much more deadly than the precision rifles that killed the Cardinal. They ignored Jason and Jasmine as they burst through the living room towards the gardens. As they ran outside, they shot off a dozen bursts at the sunflower field beyond the gardens, where the assailants lay in hiding.

They did not get far. The field erupted with gunfire, piercing the bodies of the two men with scores of bullets and silencing their powerful submachine guns.

Turning from the carnage, Jason used his right hand to stem the blood flow from Jasmine's arm.

She screamed out instructions through the pain. "Tear off a piece of your shirt and tie it around my upper arm."

He ripped a thin strip from the bottom of his shirt and wrapped it around Jasmine's arm.

"Tighter."

"Are you sure?"

Without answering she grabbed one end of the makeshift tourniquet with her teeth, pulling the other end with all her might.

"Now—in a knot. There. Now, let's go before whoever shot the Cardinal realizes there is no more artillery defending the villa."

As if on cue, a small group emerged from the sunflower field and moved towards the house, led by a woman dressed in black, her silver-white hair forming a halo around a fiercely determined face.

"Oh my God," Jasmine gasped, "Larksmum."

55

A hard summer rain fell sideways against the windshield of the cab as it made its way along the motorway from Heathrow. The cabbie cursed at the miserable traffic moving at a snail's pace along the recently uprooted pavement. At ten o'clock, the city that was once the center of the universe was alive with a million people trying to get somewhere, anywhere, as the storm performed its paralytic affect. London was never good at traffic, whether it was a blocked waterway, the manure-drenched Victorian streets, or the modern carbon-blasting Opels and Fords that clogged the streets. No, the city was never very good at dealing with the human tides that flowed through the city. London was a place the rest of the world looked to for culture and cunning.

Somehow it seemed fitting to Jason that they would end up back in this city to unravel the nightmare quest that he had been thrust into by his one-time mentor.

Agostino had said that the fourth book had been located right under the noses of the men of the Discoverer's Club. So Jason and Jasmine surmised that it must be in London. Following Carmen's detailed notes, as well as her best guesses, they both deduced that the tablet stolen from the Museum of Baghdad during the first Iraqi war pointed to the British Museum as the location of the lost Book of Eden.

Not surprising. It was the only international institution that still regarded the accumulation of human history as a noble pursuit, a gesture to the greatness of the Empire. It was also one of the few museums with an endowment deep enough to afford the prices.

From the story that Carmen relayed to them before she was killed, it was clear that they would be looking for a small cuneiform tablet, no bigger than a table atlas. The existence of the fourth tablet was supposedly proven by another cuneiform tablet, written by a scribe who lived in the region of northern Turkey about eight thousand years before the birth of Christ—written by a scribe who had documented instructions that would allow man to connect with their god in a way that would reduce to ashes the religions of the world, some sort of direct link to humanity's posthumous existence, according to the translation they had read about the Kuhhake Civilization.

With knowledge of the existence of the fourth tablet, Hans had used his considerable resources at the Axe to track all artifacts that could be linked to the same era as the other tablets held by the Order of Sumer. He was back in London after following Carmen's conclusive notes that the fourth segment of the Book of Eden had been sequestered in the British Museum for the past decade.

It was ironic that what they sought was literally right under the noses of the hundreds of people who labored tirelessly at St. Mary's Axe to discover its location. More puzzling, though, was that Carmen clearly communicated to Hans where the fourth tablet— known as the Book of the Journey to the Source—was two weeks before his death, and yet he left it alone. Why?

Jason studied the research notes taken from Carmen's apartment during the flight from Rome. Jasmine had urged him to take a bus across Europe to avoid detection, but he thought she was being overly paranoid. Still not convinced that the bad men had stopped looking for them, she pushed her case, but in the end the urgency of the matter carried the day. Jason flew to Heathrow from the Leonardo da Vinci airport in Rome.

Jason thought of her and immediately wished she was with him. But she had insisted on staying in Siena to recuperate. When they spotted Carmen's friend emerging from the sunflower field, toting a rifle affixed with a scope, they both realized that Larksmum was clearly more than just a close friend of Carmen's. Without waiting to be reacquainted with the woman who had just murdered, execution style, a Cardinal of the Church of Rome, they raced to the back of the house, Jasmine stoically holding in her pain as they found the garage. Jason grabbed a set of keys from a rack next to the door and pressed the unlock button on the fob. Running to the flashing lights of the jet-black Mercedes, they exited the garage and sped down the long driveway.

Jason looked through the rearview mirror at the ramrod figure of Larksmum standing in the middle of the pebbled driveway, her rifle at her side, seemingly deliberating where the two witnesses to her cold-blooded murder would try to hide. That she did not raise the sniper rifle to shoot them suggested that they did not pose an immediate threat to her objective.

How wrong they were.

Jason lamented leaving Jasmine at the small hotel on the outskirts of Siena without protection or a reliable plan to reconnect with her when he was done in London. Jasmine assured him that they would meet up once she located the other connection to the development of the Thought Mechanix organization. Agostino had been about to explain who he was before he was shot. If he could be believed, Agostino did not kill Hans. It was clear to Jasmine that whoever employed Larksmum would be the one she must seek.

The cabbie veered left along the M4 as it entered the heart of the city near Earl's Court, dodging a double-decker bus making a wide turn onto the street. Jason sucked in his breath as he thought of Timothy recovering in the hospital only minutes away from where he sat anxiously waiting at a stop light. He dared not go see his friend until the ordeal was over, lest he put him at further risk. It was clear to him that the people chasing him would stop at nothing to achieve their ends. It was also clear that more than one group was tracking his movements. They would stop at nothing to extract from Jason whatever information they thought he might possess. What it was, he was entirely unsure.

A few minutes later the cab pulled up to the British Museum. Jason paid the fare and fought his way through the crowd to the entrance. After Jason's cab pulled away from the curb, a second one deposited a lone traveler onto the rain-soaked sidewalk. Glancing towards the entrance of the museum, he spotted his target climbing the stairs into the Great Court of the museum, unaware that he too was being closely watched.

Six cars behind the black cab, a similarly rain-drenched dark Bentley sedan followed from a discrete distance. The lone occupant in the back seat was relaxed, assured that the driver would remain undetected but in visual contact. When the right time came, the driver would know instinctively how to react. Whatever secret knowledge this young information-seeker possessed would be revealed before the night was over. He'd watched the transformation of his organization as his people employed the techniques bestowed upon them from his advisors. Now, whatever new power Jason Wakefield sought would soon be in his control. No one would be able to get in his way.

Trailing a minute behind the two cabs, the Bentley pulled into a private parking area to the east of the museum, after the two men entered. The driver listened for a few moments to the passenger in the back seat before heading through a side entrance of the museum, guided by a uniformed security guard.

56

Jason made his way into the main hall of the British Museum and was immediately struck by the grandness of the history stored within its walls. From the Help Desk he grabbed a layout map of the museum that displayed the location of each of the major exhibits. He carried the file folder he had taken from Carmen's apartment under his left arm. Most of the contents he had already memorized, as he had studied her carefully written notes on the trip from Italy. Carmen's final entries suggested that a cache stolen from the National Museum of Baghdad was eventually sold through several intermediaries to a British Museum curator. Carmen lost the trail of the artifact once it arrived in England. It was as if it had vanished into thin air, although her notes gave Jason the impression that it resided somewhere within the stone walls of this National British institution.

"May I help you?"

The question startled Jason. He turned to look behind him, towards the voice—a young woman dressed in a blue blazer over a white silk blouse, the top three buttons unclasped. Jason's eyes focused on the small brass nametag over her left breast identifying her as Angelina. She wore her hair short, the ends teasing the bottom of her earlobes. Her smile was infectious.

"I'm not sure. I have a friend who told me I just had to see the new display of artifacts that the museum acquired in a private sale from the Middle East. It is apparently quite the find."

Jason had no idea where the lie came from, or why, but it rolled off his tongue with ease.

"Do you know exactly which era? The museum is split into geographic regions. The early civilization displays are in the upper levels, rooms 54 to 59."

"Thanks. I'll check there." Jason turned to go.

"Wait." Angelina reached out and grabbed Jason's arm. "You said the display was new. How new?"

"I'm not sure. I thought it was in the last six months."

"Hmm. I've been here for five years and I don't recall any new displays being set up in that part of the museum. But the museum curators are constantly bringing in new finds from around the world. Would have thought that everything discovered or invented by man was already on display, but apparently there are constantly new finds coming into the dungeon. Are you sure it was early Levant or Lydian artifacts?"

"I'm pretty sure. The display was supposed to include a few samples of early cuneiform writing. I teach early civilization and communication back home. My students would be thrilled if I were able to bring back details of such a recent find. So far, I've not been able to find anything about it. I only have a few notes that my colleague from the University of Florence was able to provide. She was an expert in the Etruscans. According to her research, they were descendant from the Lydians."

"I'm sure if you want, you can go to the main information desk to inquire as to the possibility of a future display."

Jason let the fabrication continue. "I'm only in London for a few more days. It's too bad I won't be able to see these artifacts. You mentioned the dungeon. What's that?"

"It's in the lower two floors below the main museum. All new collections are brought there first to be sorted and categorized. Sometimes stuff stays down there for years and never gets displayed in the main rooms. It's a shame. There's some pretty interesting history stored away down there."

"Oh, well. Next time!"

Jason started to walk away with a look of defeat stamped on his face.

"Wait," Angelina said haltingly. "Maybe we can go to the dungeon and look around. I'm game for a little treasure hunt." She looked around as if the walls had ears and were waiting to tattle on someone ready to break the rules.

"Are you sure?"

"Sure, what the heck. It would be nice to help your students." Angelina smiled. She enjoyed the dungeon, taking every opportunity to go exploring through the stacks, always on her breaks when the curator was otherwise engaged. Besides, she told herself, she was there as a museum patron ambassador. It was her job.

They made their way to the end of the Great Hall before veering left when they passed the reading room. Using the white card hanging from a strap around her neck, she waved it against a security box next to the door. A moment later there was a click and a green light indicating the door was unlocked.

Jason followed Angelina down a flight of stairs to the first basement, where she waved the white security card over another box. From there, the stairs narrowed, as they led them further down below into the bowels of the building.

"This was used as a secret strategy room during the Second World War. At that time it was felt that even the Germans wouldn't destroy the museum. Churchill was aware of Hitler's love of art and figured if the lunatic ever succeeded in breaching the beaches of England, he would be more inclined to empty the coffers of our national treasures than blow them to bits. Now it's used as a storage and processing center for the museum. After the subway bombings a few years ago, we closed the museum to the public and moved the most valuable of the museum's treasures down here to the lower levels."

Jason listened attentively to her story as they wound their way further down. He was surprised that the building had such a subterranean structure, but then quickly realized how far down the escalators went at Piccadilly station when he took the Tube. He was about to ask how far down they were going to go when the stairs abruptly ended onto a large landing. On the other side of the landing were two massive doors to a freight elevator.

Jason glanced over at the unused elevators.

"Too many people milling about upstairs," Angelina said before Jason could ask why they didn't ride the elevator down.

Anthony Lee walked quickly from the car and followed the accountant into the museum. He made no attempt to stay in the crowd so as not to be seen, since Jason had no idea who he was or that he was even being shadowed. That surprised Lee, after the debacle in Florence created by his team of incompetent mercenaries. It didn't matter that they could not have predicted what they were up against. At the time it was clear they were going to have to deal with the deadly Indian woman; but the other woman who ended up killing Sean was what he liked to refer to as a *rogue element*. The fact that the Indian and the other woman managed to kill every one of his men was distasteful. The fact that the only one in the apartment to be killed was the person they were supposed to extract alive was inexplicable.

Lee still felt the sting of the rebuke delivered by a volatile Gunter Tang. Ever since the criminal entrepreneur realized the power delivered by Thought Mechanix, he was obsessed with possessing the knowledge of the dead motivational guru. Despite what his boss had told Jason Wakefield about the Rules of Possibility, Gunter Tang saw the effects on his workforce firsthand and he wanted the ability to control all of those to whom he came in contact. His former "colleagues" in the Hong Kong underworld assured him that their recruits performed more ruthlessly than ever after being indoctrinated with the Rules. The best part was that, occasionally, a shining star would be able to take the thought skills to a new level, providing an even more effective tool of wanton criminal gain.

Looking around the Great Court as he entered from the street, Lee almost walked right by Jason, who was speaking to one of the museum employees. He had been on the accountant's tail from Heathrow, following him right out of the customs hall. One of his informants for Secur-Tec had pointed him out on the departing flight out of Rome. After he lost contact with his team in Florence, Lee distributed the identification of Wakefield and Shah throughout his well-greased information network in Europe. It didn't take long to track their movements, despite their attempt to avoid detection. Lee was tracking all credit card transactions, passport swipes and known phone numbers. It helped to have a worldwide security organization to speed things along when information was required.

The Secur-Tec network came through admirably. As soon as he got the call came from Rome that Jason had purchased a British Airways flight to London, Lee was on the first flight out of New York, arriving less than an hour before Jason. He waited in one of the interview rooms

278 - |Derek Schreurs

at the customs hall until his contact retrieved him to identify their man. After that, the tail was a non-event, Jason completely clueless that anyone was tracking his movements.

Staying close enough to hear the conversation between Jason and the young museum ambassador, Lee quickly moved away when the young woman suggested that they search the dungeon of the museum for the artifact in question. He swiftly made his way to the east side of the building, to the location of the security offices.

Captain Miles Chesterton was responsible for the protection of the billions of pounds in wealth housed in the British Museum and all of its ancillary properties. Headquartered in a nondescript building near Scotland Yard, the National Antiquities Service employed a small team of dedicated officers who appreciated the need to safeguard the treasures pilfered from the rest of the world. They saw it as their duty to protect the history of the world—the way the British wrote it anyway.

Lee approached the ordinary grey door, knocked three times, then waited. A camera above his head whirred into motion. Lee smiled up at the dark cylinder and waved a friendly salute. A second later the door swung open. Captain Miles Chesterton held out a beefy, bloated hand to his friend and fellow fighter from the Congo wars.

"Anthony Lee, you crazy Chinaman. To what do I owe the pleasure?"

"Miles, I see you're still enjoying an occasional beer or two." Anthony rubbed his own taunt stomach, the abdominal muscles rippling under his tight white shirt.

Miles followed suit, rubbing his substantial gut, likening it more to a keg than a six-pack, his laugh tearing a gaping hole into the subdued atmosphere of the Great Court.

"Quick, come inside before the Curator himself shows up and chastises me for opening the security control to a complete stranger."

"Stranger my ass. I carried your sorry carcass six miles through the jungle to keep you alive. It's a good thing that your keg was just a mini at the time, otherwise I would have left you to the jackals."

They both laughed, remembering their pact. That heroic rescue was motivated more by Lee's need to corroborate a story than by any act of altruism.

"Those where good times." Miles slapped his old friend on the back.

"They were interesting times. We fought for a cause that no one understood. But that's what mercenaries do, I suppose."

"Well," Miles handed Lee a steaming cup of tea and sat down in the command chair, "I imagine you are not here to demand repayment of our old debt." Miles was referring to the extra portion they had stolen from the junta leader during their last tour in the jungle. He never expected to repay the money after the rescue and subsequent investigation. Miles kept Lee out of the Congo prison, and probably saved his live in the process. After that day, they had never spoken. Until now.

"I have some information that you might find interesting. At this very moment a young art thief out of America is intent on rummaging through the labyrinth of rooms below this building that holds the treasures that the National Curator wishes not to have on display, for various reasons."

Miles knew that Lee was referring to the contraband art, sculpture and other treasures of antiquity that did not have the proper pedigree to allow public viewing.

Few people outside of the museum upper management, the Queen, and Miles' security team were aware that such treasures even existed. The right to hold the contraband was included in the articles of the National Museum Charter: *To protect the history of mankind, in all forms, at all times, so as to protect the fabric of human development.* Some items that came into their possession were never meant to be found, as their disclosure to the rest of the world would disrupt the unsteady peace that kept mankind surviving and presumably prospering.

"When you say intent, what exactly do you mean?" Miles studied his old comrade-in-arms sideways, trying to figure out his angle. Anthony Lee always had an angle. "Who do you work for now?"

"A man named Gunter Tang. He is an entrepreneur originally from Hong Kong and now resides in New York."

"So, you have a wealthy employer who hopes to acquire a certain item from this museum, but he's been beaten to the punch by a young upstart. So he sends his best security man to call in an old favor and gather up the antiquity for his private collection. The person currently downstairs is a straw man, I presume, leaving your boss with the item he wishes to possess and the young thief dead. With no sign of the artifact in question. It's a neat trick."

"How is it you are able to so quickly interpret my motivations? Lee let out a small laugh, playing into the story Miles concocted from his own imagination.

"You were always an open book, Lee, even when you handed me double my share of the Congo loot. Nothing for nothing. You told me that once."

"So."

"So." A grin wider than his belly expanded across Miles' face. "Let's go hunting."

Larksmum did not have a difficult time tracking Jason after he left her in the driveway of Cardinal Agostino's villa. She was not surprised that they bolted after she revealed herself to them, after she and her team shot and killed the Cardinal. On instructions from the Order of Sumer, she would have killed Jasmine as well, but she told her men to be cautious. Jason was to be kept alive at all costs. Although Larksmum was not privy to the reason why the accountant was to be kept alive, the edge in Piccolomini's voice told her it was a command not to be taken lightly. *A mistake that would be beyond catastrophic,* he had emphasized.

Following the retreating couple was not difficult. She noted the cars tags, made a call to the Polizia di Stato and received hourly updates as to their movements. Larksmum took a private jet to Heathrow, arrived earlier than the commercial flight that was expected to disembark her quarry, and then followed him to the British Museum. She'd exited the Bentley as it pulled alongside the entrance to the British Museum, suspecting now that she only had to go to the museum, that her dearly departed lover provided Jason with enough clues to have deduced the location of the lost artifact.

What Jason had come to London for was not sufficient to stop the wave of violence and disregard for authority that had gripped the world. The fourth Book of Eden, if it really existed, was not about to reverse the chain reaction that Cardinal Agostino unwittingly released upon the world. It was going to take more than fiction and myth. It was going to take a miracle. Her assignment was to help Piccolomini secure that miracle.

As she entered the museum, she spotted the other tail that Jason had picked up since he left Italy. She recognized him but could not recall why.

Acting swiftly, she veered to the left of Jason and his unseen tag, took out her cell phone and snapped a picture of the Asian as he followed a security guard into a back room. A minute later, the picture was emailed to the Guardians' communications center with a request to identify the man from their vast network of intelligence databases. Whoever was tailing Jason would most likely be the same people who killed Carmen. Despite her thirst for revenge, it was the safety of Jason that concerned her more than anything.

57

Angelina led Jason into lowest level of the dungeon after bypassing three areas of security with her key card. It had been fifteen minutes since they left the Great Hall and made their way through a labyrinth of stairways and halls. Entering the final door was like opening a chasm into history. Racks upon racks ran down the long, cavernous room in rows, almost as far as Jason could focus.

"Each row is labeled, supermarket-like, with its era of history. The stacks run north to south, beginning with prehistoric times at the far north of the room and ending with modern- era artifacts at the south end. Let me see, you said the tablet you were looking for was Sumerian, so that's about 3000 BCE, putting it somewhere around the fifth row."

"You seem to know a lot about history, and these stacks," Jason quipped.

"I'm taking my Masters right now, in history. I love this place and spend as much time as possible down here, looking through the stacks, trying to guess the period and significance of a piece. I'm not really authorized to be down here, but the Curator turns a blind eye."

"Hmm, fun."

"Hey, I have a social life too, I'll let you know," Angelina said haughtily. "I even have a boyfriend," she added.

Jason had no doubt the sweet, curvaceous museum guide was entangled. She wore the standard museum blue uniform with a casual sensuality that was alluring. Any young man would be lucky to be entangled with her.

"I didn't suggest…" Jason put up his hands in surrender. They both laughed at his embarrassment.

Angelina walked over to a computer on a stand next to the elevator. She swung the screen around and typed in a password.

"So, what exactly was it you were looking for?"

This was the moment Jason feared. He needed to string Angelina along so that she still believed he was looking for a random sample of cuneiform writing and not the specific photo in the file folder in his hand.

"I have a picture of one of the pieces that, supposedly, was purchased by the museum. It was taken from an article in a history journal I subscribe to."

"Oh? Which one? I get a few of them delivered each month. It keeps me up to date on historical findings. I'm a bit of a keener."

"You probably don't know the publication. It's a small magazine from back home, *The Midwest Historical Gazette.*"

He could tell that his story was starting to sound weak but carried on the pretense. He handed Angelina the picture from Carmen's folder, not aware of the significance of the writing on the top edge of the print.

Angelina looked at him sideways, the way a mother might look at a child caught with his hand in the cookie jar. She recognized the writing straightaway, having dealt with the indexing of the museum for the last five years. Stepping back from the computer after signing off, she backed away from Jason a few paces.

"Who exactly are you?"

"I'm a history professor—"

Angelina put her hand up to stop Jason from speaking. "I wasn't born yesterday. Do you know what this is?" She held up the paper.

"It's a picture of a sample of cuneiform writing. I'm looking for its twin…" Jason replied weakly.

"What it is, precisely, is a picture of a piece of contraband cuneiform writing. This picture was taken by Interpol, the European police agency. Photos of stolen articles are circulated to all of the museums so that there is nothing purchased by us on the black market. If we happen to buy something hot, it is returned to its rightful owner. I saw this exact picture about four months ago. The curator asked me to search the stacks to ensure we had not inadvertently purchased this with the shipment that came in at that time."

Jason stared at her with an expression of defeat.

"So, exactly who are you?"

Deciding that it was no use continuing on with the charade, Jason handed Angelina the folder and explained why he had come to the museum. He walked her through the articles and notes made by Carmen as he tried to explain the significance of the find. He explained about the Rules of Possibility, the thought energy concepts and the meeting that he had with the Cardinal before the man was gunned down.

Twenty minutes had elapsed by the time he finished weaving his experiences into a coherent story. When he was finished, he stood silently looking past her at the endless stacks of civilization's treasures, letting her absorb the information for a few moments.

"To tell you the truth, I have no idea why I have decided to continue with this seemingly ridiculous quest, but Hans was a friend, and he never wanted to hurt anyone with his processes. I don't think he even knew that he was being manipulated. But it is clear that there are powerful forces who believe in what Hans delivered with the knowledge he possessed. And they seem to have no problem killing people to get what is apparently somewhere in this museum."

"Do you really believe that the Rules of Possibility caused an increase in crime and violence in the world?" Angelina read the daily headlines of violence erupting in the world but didn't really think it was any worse than in the past.

"Cardinal Agostino thought so. He never intended to abuse the power of the Book of Thought, but somehow it got away from him. From my experience, the Rules definitely improved the performance of some of my clients. At first I thought it was just a result of positive thinking, but now it appears that the process has some ability to harness thoughts, to direct energy to obtain a desired outcome."

"Positive or negative."

"It seems the universe doesn't distinguish. It only reacts to the energy released." Jason realized he just had an aha moment. *"It only reacts to the energy released,"* he repeated.

Angelina looked up at Jason from the computer. She had been searching the databases as Jason explained his theories about the Books of Thought and the mythical fourth book, the Book of the Journey to the Source.

Ping. The computer had found something.

"It looks like we do have an item similar to the one in the picture," she said in disbelief. "It's labeled as *'An artifact from early Mesopotamia'* and refers to an early example of cuneiform writing, referring to crops and pricing. It also says here that it is *'on loan from the National Museum of Baghdad.'* It was logged in four months ago by the curator himself."

She paused.

"You seem perplexed," Jason commented.

"It's unusual. The curator never logs in items. He is a political appointee and doesn't like to get his hands dirty."

"Why do you think he logged this item in personally?"

"More importantly, why did he have me search for it when he knew it was here all along? Come on," she said, as she tore the search results off the printer and headed for the stacks. "What you are looking for is in the fifth row."

58

It was a long walk to reach the halfway point down the fifth row of the stacks. Each row was the length of a football field, stretching into the weakly lit ceilings. It was like looking into the wrong end of a pair of binoculars. The sturdy metal shelving, where the thousands of items were stored, stretched right up to the small, naked light fixtures about thirty feet above. Jason wondered what was holding up the massive museum building that towered into life five stories above him with all this hollow space below.

As if she could read his mind, Angelina explained, "We are not directly under the museum. The stairways have taken us a little north of the main building, so the main courtyard is directly above. If you remember, there is a receiving bay on the far left-hand side of the museum. That is right above where the elevator sits."

Jason looked back towards the end of row five. They were about a hundred meters from the start.

"That puts us almost at the front gate."

"Exactly. The stacks end on the other side of Montague Street. See that ladder over there?" Angelina pointed past the stacks to the dark wall beyond. "It leads to an emergency escape shaft that opens inside of one of the row houses across the street. It was designed as a discreet way to extract the important artifacts in the case of an emergency."

Slowing her pace, Angelina turned to read the numbers on the sides of the cardboard boxes that housed the various pieces either not important enough, or too important, to be displayed in the galleries five floors above.

"Grab that ladder."

Angelina pointed to a ladder twenty paces further up the row. It was affixed to rails at the top of the stacks, allowing a person to stop along the row by simply sliding the wooden ladder along its track.

The young museum guide climbed up a dozen rungs of the ladder before she stopped. Jason looked up for a moment to follow her progress, then quickly looked down as the uniform she was wearing proved to revealing from his vantage.

She called down, "Slide the ladder over a few feet to the right. A little further...stop." She was quiet for a few minutes, then yelled down to Jason, "Got it!"

Angelina placed the box she pulled from the stacks onto a platform attached to the ladder. The platform was designed to be lowered or raised by turning a crank attached to the ladder. As the crank was turned, a set of gears moved the platform up and down. That way the larger and heavier artifacts could be put into place at the higher levels of the stacks.

"I'm coming down."

Inadvertently, Jason looked up at her as she descended. He caught her eye. She gave him a sly look, clearly aware of the show she had provided.

"Sorry about that. Guess I should have worn my slacks today."

Jason mumbled an apology.

"No biggie, she said, "I have older brothers."

"For protection, no doubt."

Angelina reached the bottom, grabbed the handle of the crank and began to lower the cardboard box she had placed on the platform. The box being lowered was twice as long as the file folder boxes he used to store records in his accounting office but about the same height.

"How long did you say this had been down here?" Jason asked as he ran his finger through the eighth of an inch of dust that had settled on the top of the box.

Angelina stopped turning the crank. She was about to answer Jason when they heard the elevator.

"Who could that be?" Angelina frowned. "There would be no reason for any of the research staff to come down here at this time of the day. They would be busy in the labs during operating hours."

Then, a voice emerged from the elevator, causing the pair to panic... "The security cameras showed movement on this level."

"They're here, I can sense it," another male voice said.

Angelina ducked into a small enclave that housed a desk and working area in the middle of the stacks. Jason followed her into the tight spot.

"It's the security chief, Miles Chesterton. He's with someone," Angelina whispered. "I don't recognize the other voice."

The voices moved in their direction.

"Hurry!" Angelina grabbed the box from the platform and led them through the stacks, stopping only when they reached the far end of the fifth row.

Because he was looking back over his shoulder, Jason didn't see the metal trolley at the end of the row. He crashed into it, sending it clanging loudly against the wall.

The voices at the other end of the stacks stopped and were quickly replaced by the sound of running feet on concrete.

Larksmum shifted her focus from pursuit to capture. After losing sight of the Asian who had been following Jason, she knew it would be necessary to gain access to restricted areas. The man she was following had inside friends, so that meant that Jason was in more trouble than he even knew. She looked around the concourse for someone who could help her achieve her objective.

The young guard was on the far side of the Great Hall, sitting against a wall and looking bored. She made her way to the other side of the room, occasionally glancing back to see if the Asian and his friend would emerge from the security room.

Just as she reached the bored guard, Larksmum turned to see her target and his inside accomplice emerge from behind the locked security doors. A moment later they disappeared through another exit, halfway from where she stood.

She needed to think quickly.

"Young man, I was wondering if you could help me."

"Of course, Madam."

As the guard rose, Larskmum lurched past him, falling just close enough to drag the young man down with her.

As if on cue, the guard latched onto her to break their fall. As they hit the ground, Larksmum reached out to keep the guard close. She grabbed him by the femoral artery on the left side of his neck and squeezed.

Within seconds the guard was lying unconscious on the ground next to her. Removing the security pass draped around his waist, she quickly stood up and called for help.

As a few others began to approach, Larksmum faded into the background, looking for the employees-only exit where the Asian had disappeared moments earlier.

After passing the security card through the reader, the door opened with a quiet click. Larksmum walked down the corridor as if she belonged there. She made her way down a long, narrow hallway, which branched off into several rooms and ended at a set of elevator doors.

A few people emerged from the offices and passed her in the hallway, neither looking at her in any particular way nor questioning her presence.

She glanced at each face as she passed but did not see either of the parties she was after. She relaxed as she reached the end of the corridor. No one was around. She exited through a set of double doors with her newly acquired security pass and made her way towards a freight elevator. Still, no one was around. She had no idea where the Asian and the security guard could have gone, but she had a hunch it was the same place she was going—to the subterranean labyrinth of storage beneath the museum.

59

Jason scurried to keep up, amazed at Angelina's strength as she toted the heavy box while running. They were now running along the far end of the stacks towards a set of double doors. He had no idea how many rows of shelving they had passed but figured they had been running for over a minute before the first shot whizzed by his head.

Angelina screamed as the men chasing them started to shoot. A second bullet implanted itself above their heads in a wooden beam that supported the roof. She could hear the head of security yelling at her from a hundred feet back, ordering her to stop.

She didn't.

She had no idea who this man was that she was helping, but his story had convinced her. The cuneiform tablet in the box she was holding was important. It was too important to give to someone who was willing to kill them and take possession of the artifact.

As she reached the end of the corridor, she jammed her electronic pass against the security lock to open the double doors leading out into the offices across Montague Street.

Nothing happened.

She dropped the box onto the ground as she quickly positioned her pass over the reader.

Still nothing.

A moment later it was too late.

"I shut down the security pass access to the exits, Angelina. Your card won't work. Move away from the doors."

Miles Chesterton heaved as he spoke, sweat poured down his face onto an already soaked shirt. The security chief of the British Museum had reached the doors that led from the underground storage facility to the nondescript row of apartments across the street used to move sensitive items in and out of the archives.

Angelina started to move away from the doors when she noted the emergency access button encased in glass on the wall on the right-hand side door. She put down the box and started to move towards the wall.

"Why are you shooting at us?" Angelina asked, her calm demeanor hiding the rapid beats of her trembling heart.

Miles Chesterton's accomplice stood silently beside the security chief, holding his recently discharged weapon loosely in his hand but pointed at Jason.

"Stop!" the Asian hissed. "It's clear that you are in the process of stealing artifacts from the museum. This man you are with is a wanted criminal. Whatever story he told you is a lie."

Miles let the fabrication stand.

"I don't believe you," Angelina retorted, haughtily moving away from the man as she spoke and inching toward the emergency button.

Anthony Lee did not answer. He had a mission to complete so was not looking to explain his purpose. He raised his gun and shot the young girl between the eyes.

The sound resonated throughout the large cavernous room.

A small red dot appeared on Angelina's forehead as the bullet entered her skull, splattering grey matter on the wall behind her body as it collapsed onto the hard floor.

The security chief was so stunned by what he saw his old friend do to the innocent girl that he didn't register when the bullet entered his own head an inch below his ear, passing upwards through his brain before its exit sent shards of skull into the air.

A few of the grisly pieces of bone hit Jason as the overweight security guard thudded to the floor, next to the girl.

Jason stared in horror at the dead girl near his feet.

"What the fu—"

"Shut up, Mr. Wakefield. Or you'll be next."

"Why did you do that? They were just innocent people helping out?"

"No one is innocent, Mr. Wakefield. You of all people should know that."

"You're the one who killed Amy Glass in New York, aren't you? And Carmen. What is it that you want?"

"I want what you want." Anthony looked down at the box that lay underneath Angelina's dead body. "I want that."

Jason was at a loss. Ever since he left New York he had been pursued by this killer, perhaps even before he arrived back in New York from London. Death and destruction were following him in his search for something he did not understand, something that had been of no interest to him a few weeks earlier. And it seemed that people were convinced that he knew what it was that he was looking for, that he knew the importance of the tablet lying underneath the dead girl.

"You can take it if you want. I have no need for it. Not really sure why it's so important really."

"You're not a very convincing liar. My employer has told me firsthand how potent your skills are with the Rules of Possibility. This thing," he gestured to the broken box, "will give you even greater strength, huh?" Anthony Lee smiled at his insight.

"Your employer? Your employer? Just who do you work for?" Gunter Tang's face entered Jason's mind even as he was asking the question. "You work for Gunter Tang. In fact, I know you. You're Anthony Lee. You attended one of the seminars I put on at Tang Enterprises."

"Well done, Mr. Wakefield. When Hans Pedersen refused to sell my boss Talon Industries, he decided that he had to learn the truth behind Thought Mechanix at any cost. After Pedersen killed himself, Gunter became convinced that you would be the source of any knowledge that he needed to control the minds of his people, the way you have so effectively demonstrated. So my team and I set out to follow you until you found what you were looking for after leaving Amy's apartment. When she was not forthcoming, my men and I turned up the heat in our little search."

"Well. Now you have what you came for. Take it." Jason moved out of the way to give Anthony full access to the box.

"Unfortunately, it's not that simple. I was also told to deliver you as well. Mr. Tang will need someone to interpret the tablet."

Without a moment's hesitation, Anthony Lee kicked the dead girl's body off the box with his boot. The cardboard box that housed the cuneiform tablet was beyond repair, so he tore it open with one hand as he kept the gun leveled at Jason.

The tablet was not heavy, weighing as much as a sack of flour. He signaled for Jason to pick it up. Leaving Angelina and the dead security chief behind, Anthony followed closely behind Jason as he directed him back towards the elevators.

"How do you propose to get this thing out of the museum?" Jason asked.

"Easily." Anthony smiled, holding up Miles Chesterton's security pass. "Now, come on. Time to go."

Jason moved along the narrow corridor with Lee following, his mind numb from the sight of watching Angelina falling helplessly to her death, a look of bewilderment frozen on her innocent face.

He blanched at the thought of it, her death seared his conscience. He was sick to his stomach with death. Sick of the thoughts of destruction—the explosions at the Discoverer's Club ripping human bodies to small, fleshy bits, destroyed buildings burning colleagues to a crisp, tortured friends, apparent suicides, execution-style assassinations, commando raids and now, a cold-hearted killer blowing the brains out of an innocent girl just doing her job.

He knew that the world was becoming a place where violence was passé, where everyone was numb to bullets and guns and blood. It was engrained in the heads of tweens, who were indoctrinated into the use of force to subdue enemies—gratuitous blood and gore the result of moving from one level to another in live-action video games. He had never been a fan of the genre. Now he knew why. Death is not entertainment. It is not the means to an end to attain a higher level. The rewards are not worth the price. He was sick of it and wanted it all to end.

His mind looped back, over and over the events that led him to the basement of the British Museum, carrying a rock that was older than history as some deranged killer held a gun to his back. He thought about Amy, who was dead. Timothy, burned and suffering. Hans, disillusioned and dead. Jasmine, struggling to find out why her brother invited the violence that killed him. And all of the others who had touched his life briefly for only a few moments.

All for this a two-foot by three-foot hunk of rock.

They had reached the elevator. Jason stopped, turned, and faced his adversary. He put the cuneiform tablet at his feet. He ignored the gun Anthony had leveled at his head. It didn't matter.

"I'm not going to do this anymore. If you want this tablet so badly, take it. I don't care what it signifies, or what power it may hold. I have had enough."

Jason turned away and pressed the button to call for the elevator.

"Pick up the tablet." Anthony's voice was slow, firm, deliberate. "Pick up the tablet or I will blow a hole in the back of your head."

"No you won't," Jason replied without looking back. "If I was expendable, you would have shot me already. I'd be lying dead beside Angelina and the fat guy at the end of the stack of dusty artifacts, just like the one you and your boss, Gunter Tang, is so anxious to have. So take it and leave me."

"I cannot do that, Mr. Wakefield. You know that as well as I. There are things we found out from your friend Amy Glass before she succumbed. Information that maybe you are not even privy to—"

Jason turned around to stare at the Asian. "What are you talking about?"

Anthony smiled. "You really don't understand, do you?"

Before Jason could answer, the elevator signaled its arrival with its distinctive bell. As he turned to face the opening doors, he was shocked when he saw who stood before him.

60

"What do you think he was talking about?" Jasmine whispered to Jason in the back of an S-Class Mercedes sedan that was heading up a steep road in the mountainous region northeast of Salzburg. The car's headlights skimmed the shoulders as it traversed the narrow road, receiving no illumination from the thin sliver of a new moon. The digital clock on the Mercedes dashboard showed the time to be 3:30am.

Twelve hours earlier Jason was led from the British Museum by Larksmum after a brief encounter that left a stunned Anthony Lee with a bullet between the eyes. As the elevator doors opened and Jason saw Larksmum standing inside, he did what seemed instinctive, from a B-rated crime drama—he pleaded pathetically for Anthony Lee not to kill him like he had killed the others. He blocked Lee's view of the elevator as he bent down to pick up the tablet he had put down only seconds before, watching the smug look of success on the Asian's face as Jason buckled under his intimidation. As he stooped to retrieve the cuneiform tablet, it was the only cue that Larksmum needed. Jason could feel the movement behind him as Larksmum exited the elevator and dispatched the Asian.

On the flight back to Italy Larksmum provided no explanations as to where and why she came to get Jason, and he really didn't care. She told him only that they had Jasmine, as insurance, to make sure he would return. He told her everything he knew of Gunter Tang and his involvement and knowledge of Thought Mechanix, leaving nothing out, as if she were his confessor. She listened intently but said nothing. Now they were driving towards some unknown destination on the outskirts of Salzburg.

"There was another member of the Order mentioned in notes that Carmen kept—"

"No need to speculate." Larksmum turned from her point position in the passenger seat of the sedan and looked back at the two Americans.

She smiled at them, feeling full of herself to have accomplished both of her objectives at once. The Cardinal had to be eliminated. He was soft and his motivations limited to his own desires. The Order had lain dormant long enough, protecting a truth that needed to be revealed. Only one person was prepared to lead the way to the new world.

"Who are you? And what was your involvement with Carmen Salvatore?"

"Who I am is of no consequence to you. Brother August Piccolomini is the one of whom the Cardinal spoke. You will be meeting him soon. All of your questions will be answered."

Larksmum turned in her seat as the Mercedes approached an ornate gate that swung open as the car approached. A young man in black clothes, wearing a ball cap and holding at his side a small semi-automatic machine gun, acknowledged the driver as he passed.

Jason looked up at the sheer cliffs as they made their way up the mountain. "I recognize this place. It's the Eagle's Nest, built for the leader of the Third Reich as a gift from his generals. I toured it during college. Why are we here?"

Larksmum turned back again to address Jason's comment. "The Austrian government kindly sold it to our cause after a school bus full of children plummeted to their death off one of the many switchbacks the road takes to the entrance shaft. They closed the site permanently after the tragedy. It has proven to be a most satisfactory location for the new Order of Sumer's headquarters. Piccolomini will explain everything. I am sure you will not be surprised as to your fate. Larksmum stared at Jasmine as she spoke."

"Fate?" Jasmine laughed. "I don't think this has anything to do with fate."

"On the contrary, Jasmine, this has everything to do with fate. It may even be your destiny. But for that you will have to wait. Piccolomini is sleeping. I will show you to your room, where you two can get some sleep. We will come and get you later in the morning. In the meantime, I'll keep this." Larksmum held up the backpack containing Carmen's folder, Jason's laptop, as well as the cuneiform tablet. "Sleep tight."

Six hours later, Jasmine was sitting up in bed sipping hot coffee and shifting awkwardly, trying to make the pillows comfortable against her neatly bandaged arm. The bullet had sliced cleanly through the soft tissue, missing the major arteries and bones. Jasmine took the injury in stride, as if it were an everyday occurrence. Her nonchalant attitude was unsettling for Jason, even though he joked about how she sought out danger like a mosquito seeks out an exposed vein.

"At least Larksmum made sure the wound wouldn't turn septic." Jason stroked Jasmine's hair as he helped make her comfortable.

"She seems awfully concerned for your welfare," Jasmine commented.

"What do you mean?"

"We're still alive. She killed Cardinal Agostino with impunity. When we were being attacked at Carmen's apartment, she killed with a ruthless calm. I've been in her shoes. She kills for a living; efficient, methodical, emotionless—all traits of a mercenary. Even though you could see her anguish when Carmen was gunned down, she kept focused. I thought she would have killed us at the time if I hadn't had the upper hand."

"So why not kill us when she had the chance, at the Cardinal's villa?"

"Exactly. Piccolomini must have given her instructions specifically not to kill us. But why?

'Their conversation was interrupted—their door was being unlocked.

"We're about to find out…"

61

An early morning sun broke over the snow-covered Alps surrounding the former refuge of one of history's most notorious butchers. The warm rays covered the rich wood interior of the residence with a comfortable glow. Outside the air was crisp. The forest gleamed with a layer of shimmering hoarfrost. A blazing flame burning in the fireplace warmed the interior of the room where Jason and Jasmine were being held.

At nine in the morning a pair of guards unlocked their apartment and led them to the entrance shaft that would take them to the elevator carved inside the mountain. Above the entrance to the tunnel was depicted a winged horse carrying a sword-wielding knight through a cloudlike stream that flowed into a golden urn. The hand without the sword was reaching down to the urn, holding onto the tail of one of the wispy clouds. Underneath was a Latin inscription that Jason did not understand.

Neither of the guards palmed their weapons but kept their distance behind the pair in order to react to any unexpected behavior. There was none. They walked for two minutes along the darkened tunnel leading to the middle of the mountain. At the elevator they were greeted by Larksmum and the Mercedes driver from the night before. They all waited a few minutes for the elevator to arrive.

The Eagle's Nest was built in the late thirties on the Kehlstein Mountain as a hilltop teahouse. It was built near a residence in an area known as the Obersalzberg. The residence was where Adolph Hitler lived off and on from 1928 as a tenant. He purchased the home in 1933. On the rock face above the residence Martin Bormann, his deputy chief of staff, envisioned building a retreat as a fiftieth birthday present to his Fuhrer. The project was a monumental achievement in efficiency and engineering. It was to be one of the great legacies of the notorious regime.

Leaving the elevator, the group made its way through a maze of hallways towards the grand hall. A man sat in a large wingback chair, staring at the flames of a robust fire burning in the thirty-foot-wide fireplace built from local rock.

August Piccolomini stared at the two people who caused him such a perplexing mixture of salvation and stress. He knew what he needed from Jason. He looked past him at his companion, not sure why he did not eliminate Jasmine. Her involvement was no longer essential, but he was not compelled to eliminate her. Perhaps it was because she kept Jason alive without knowing his true importance. Perhaps it was because she could be useful to him in the future.

He was thankful for the series of events after the death of Hans Pedersen. While the death of the motivational guru was not perfect, it did reveal Cardinal Agostino's intentions when he panicked, seeking out his former conspirator to help him achieve his weakminded goal to lead the Catholics into the next epoch. Piccolomini cringed at the man's naïve arrogance. The Cardinal had no vision of what could truly be achieved with the power granted to those who possessed the knowledge, those who understood the true significance of the Books of Eden. *He* understood what it meant to those whom he once swore to protect. He also understood what it meant to himself, to control those souls.

Now, he needed to convince these two of the humanity of his motives.

"It really is a beautiful setting, is it not?" Piccolomini turned from the large fireplace to the picture window overlooking the majestic Austrian Alps, addressing his guests but not expecting a reply. Nor did he begin with any pleasantries. There was not enough time.

"We don't typically resort to extraordinary measures, but these are extraordinary times. You have been brought here under duress because I feared you would not come on your own volition. Alliances have been created out of your quest to discover the truth behind the death of Hans Pedersen and of the destruction of his organization. You need to know the facts surrounding what you thought was an organization devoted to helping people find their potential.

"Thought Mechanix was a smokescreen created by the recently deceased Cardinal Agostino, a façade to bring a new set of beliefs to the world. He was a sadly disillusioned man who was consumed by a dream that was never to be his to realize. His vision is now dead. As deceased as he is. But there is a greater goal that is being pursued. A goal to which your own role in the events that are about to happen will be crucial."

"What are you talking about?" Jason asked.

Piccolomini continued, ignoring the question.

"Unfortunately, the Cardinal's blind ambition has released a catastrophe upon the world, a power unleashed for which the world is not ready. Undoubtedly, you have now discovered that Hans Pedersen received his inspiration from a manuscript known as the Book of Thought, one of a set of four cuneiform tablets that are believed to have been written at the dawn of creation."

Piccolomini paused as he sipped his espresso from an ivory-white and blue-crested demitasse, waiting to see if either the accountant or the journalist would comment. He was not disappointed.

"All of that we already know, as I suspect you are aware. You killed Hans, you killed the Cardinal, and Carmen Salvatore was on your list." Jason stole a glance at Larksmum, who stood quietly near the exit. "I suspect there have been untold others who have gotten in the way of your blind ambition. So cut to the chase—what do you need or want of me?"

Jason's delivery was hard-edged. He wanted to provoke a reaction. He learned from his experience in the battlefield of negotiations that you only get an advantage by placing the other party off balance.

"As Ms. Shah most likely is aware, I have everything I need, now. It was only a matter of timing."

Jason looked over at Jasmine. "What is he talking about?"

Jasmine directed her attention to Piccolomini rather than deal with Jason's query.

"Don't try and manipulate me, I have dealt with too many power-hungry megalomaniacs in my life to be fooled by your benevolence. You need us. Otherwise, we would not be here." Jasmine jerked a finger towards their female abductor. "She isn't here for the good of our health."

Jason turned and looked at Larksmum, who returned a sardonic smile. He turned back to Piccolomini and was about to say something when Jasmine grabbed his arm, her eyes imploring him not to speak.

Piccolomini continued.

"The knowledge of our cognitive connection to the past, present and future has been planted in the minds of millions by your friend Hans Pedersen with the application of his wondrous Rules of Possibility. That seed has now germinated and is growing. In the last few months the evidence of this connection has started to affect more than just the privileged few who were able to transcend the bounds of our locked minds. They have been influencing the collective masses."

"You still haven't answered my question," Jasmine retorted, now uncertain of the decisions she had made.

"Do not be impatient, my dear. There is much you will understand before long. Suffice it to say that once the entire story unfolds it will be clear why you are still among us, and particularly why Mr. Wakefield has been brought here to our little chalet in the clouds."

A young man had entered the room. He stood at attention near the door. He was dressed in an elaborately adorned military uniform, a scarlet double-breasted jacket with three gold buttons and golden epaulets on each of his broad shoulders. His pants were black with a twin golden stripe down each leg. On his head, a golden beret with the insignia of a winged horse carrying a sword-wielding knight.

Piccolomini acknowledged him with a slight nod of the head.

The young guard strode purposefully across the room until he was only inches from the Brother. He bent over and whispered in his ear. His message delivered, he took two precise, military steps back and stood, ramrod straight, waiting for a response.

"Tell them we will be just a few more minutes. I need to relate a short history lesson to our guests before we begin the session. Let the Imam know we will be along shortly."

Brother Piccolomini spoke clearly, looking directly at Jasmine and Jason in order to gauge what sort of reaction his mention of an imam would receive. But the pair seemed as bewildered as ever, watching the exchange without a glimmer of understanding. He was starting to think that maybe his theory about them was wrong.

The uniformed man left the room. Piccolomini gestured for Jason and Jasmine to join him at the breakfast table.

"You may want to something to eat. It could be a very long day." Piccolomini reached across the table and selected a croissant from a silver tray.

Still unsure what had befallen them and famished from three days of intense travel, they filled their plates from the cornucopia of delectable choices spread across the massive cherrywood dining table.

Jason ate like a man given his last meal. Jasmine fueled up because she knew she might need the energy to fight or flee, given the opportunity. It was a feast characteristic of their Austrian hosts—sweet pastries, croissants, cured meats, artisanal cheeses, freshly squeezed juices, and boiled eggs split open and stuffed with cream cheese and mushroom paté. A young waiter, dressed all in white, emerged from the shadows of the floor-to-ceiling post, bringing coffee in a sterling silver carafe.

They ate in silence, mystified. If the man sitting with them at breakfast felt no compunction to kill them, then there was something that he needed. Jason thought about the attack at the Cardinal's villa. Jasmine had been shot and yet he was not. In fact, as he thought about the exchange of gunfire, he was never in range of any of the shooting. He sat back for a moment and eyed their portly host, trying to determine what knowledge he was supposed to have that brought him here to the top of the Alps.

What had he learned in the past few weeks that could have caused him to become the object of this hunt?

Piccolomini continued to observe his guests from across the table. Their naïveté was beginning to unnerve him and he speculated that he may have blundered once again. Shaking off self-doubt, he stood up. It was time to find out whether his intuition was right. It was time to bring Jason forward to the Council.

"It is time to bring you into my confidence, Mr. Wakefield, and you too, Ms. Shah, as you have become intimately entwined in this adventure." He pointed to the bandage on her shoulder. "My instructions were explicit, but I am pleased that the circumstances prevented their execution…so to speak."

Piccolomini spoke with an arrogance that cut Jasmine to the quick—his smug stare was condescending, his thick torso reflecting a life of placid overindulgence. Like many men of the cloth who lorded over the ordinary people of the world, he was a man who viewed his worldly power as absolute.

She bit her tongue before speaking, but unable to remain silent, she spoke, choosing her words carefully.

"Life does not seem so precious to you, Brother Piccolomini. From what I gather, you are responsible for deadly attacks on innocent people, cold-blooded murder of your colleagues, and the destruction of three office buildings. I have no idea what your motives are, and despite the preaching of many world leaders, the ends never justify the means. My brother—"

Piccolomini stopped her, holding up his hands in innocent defeat. He needed to be careful, as it was clear that Jason would not be cooperative if they reacted to the adversarial nature of this Indian woman. And he needed Jason.

"Your brother is why you are here. I understand that. Your brother's life, and death, is, in a way, why I am here as well. It is why I had to do the distasteful things that you are accusing me of. His death illustrates precisely why Cardinal Agostino is now dead instead of pursuing his insipid dream of sitting in the seat of power within a dying religion.

"There is a lot that I need to tell you, so please indulge me. Be patient, and maybe you will change your mind as to whether the means might, in certain circumstances, justify the ends. It is now time to go to the main hall. Seven decades ago that room was used by the Madman of Europe to orchestrate untold atrocities, atrocities that will seem like a summer breeze compared to the storm that is developing in our world. Jasmine's brother was caught in the center of that storm, battling others caught in the maelstrom of shifting consciousness. Like the warm winds from Africa leading to storms of hurricane force a continent away, the indelible strength of Hans Pedersen's motivational oration has created a mental storm that is about to hit land."

Piccolomini fixed his stare on Jason, boring into his eyes as if trying to see his soul. A moment later he sat back, smiling, confident that this young man was exactly where he needed to be.

"Do you remember the first time you heard Hans Pedersen speak?" He continued without waiting for an answer. "I do. It was early on a Tuesday morning. You had come home from an audit wrap-up event, wired, unable to sleep, questioning your very existence. You were surfing the channels, settling eventually on the Rules of Possibility infomercial. It changed your life in an instant. You became one of the most successful converts to the RoP concepts. So successful, in fact, that you began to succeed in ways you never imagined. You started to apply the mental tools of Thought Mechanix to your life and to those whom you could influence. Everything you did brought positive thoughts into the grid. It was the start of a revolution, commercially speaking, for which you earned handsome fees."

Jason sat there with his mouth hanging open. "How do you know so much about me?"

Piccolomini laughed, "I'm not prescient if that's what you think. Hans kept me well informed of your progress. And I took a particular interest, for reasons that will soon become clear.

"To continue…think of all the positive energy that you were generating within Wakefield and Associates, within the business community you served —the people who came into contact with you every day. Profound, was it not? Even unexplainable—a truly universal shift in energy. Positive thoughts changing the world. The feeling of success was palpable.

"Unfortunately, elsewhere in the world, there were others who found the same infomercial program on late-night television. They were as affected by the message as you were. They bought the program from Thought Mechanix, just like you, and like millions of others who did the same thing they generated a significant amount of thought energy. But the people I speak of were not like you. They did not generate positive thoughts that served to create a growth of energy in the universe. Unlike you, the energy stream they generated was predominantly negative. In many instances, the thoughts were very negative, so much so that not only did they counteract the positive energy that you and your connections released, these negative influences overtook the power of your infectious positive thinking until a tipping point was reached."

It was true. The world was becoming increasingly uglier, from everyday interactions in the street to mass killings around the world. There was a marked increase in suicide bombers and drug wars. More neighborhoods were under siege and religious angst was intensifying around the world. Jason had stopped reading the papers because the news was so depressing. Lately, it seemed, anger permeated every interaction that he'd had with strangers. He simply chocked it up to a nagging suspicion that he had outgrown New York. Now it seemed like the world had embarked on a path divergent from his, without him even knowing that he was a part of it.

"What does this have to do with me?"

"Everything, Jason. Everything."

62

The place where the leader of the Third Reich came to relax and unwind had been transformed into a war room for new leaders of the Order of Sumer. Piccolomini had assembled the group of religious leaders fifteen years earlier, just as Hans Pedersen began his discovery of the power of the Book of Thought. He let Agostino believe that they were in agreement about the mandate of Thought Mechanix. While Agostino muddled forward with his dream of religious power, Piccolomini was creating a new world order. What he had not anticipated was the extent of damage done by the Cardinal of Siena's blind ambition. It almost destroyed everything he had worked so hard to achieve.

Piccolomini led his guests from the elevator. In the heart of the Eagle's Nest, below the majestic main entrance hall, was a fortified strategy room that had become a second home to the men sitting around the massive oak table. They had met countless times over the past fifteen years, waiting for the opportunity to capitalize on the efforts of the guru from New York. But they never anticipated that the rogue activities of the ambitious Cardinal Agostino would become the foundation of such a dangerous sequence of events.

The death of Hans Pedersen forced the group to meet with more frequency. However, they were careful to leave their respective congregations only long enough to avoid any suspicion. The devastation that was occurring in the world since the Cardinal had misappropriated the Third Book of Eden was increasing exponentially. They had to hope beyond hope in Jason if there was to be any chance of survival.

As they walked along the corridor to the strategy room, Jason noticed the pictures hanging on the walls. It was not a gallery he expected to see. Gruesome scenes of historical battles, depictions of religious persecutions, angry mobs and human suffering were the themes. Death and misery oozed out of every canvas. With the exception of one, over the entrance to the room at the end of the corridor. It was the rather hopeful picture of a young man and a woman, presumably his wife, sitting under a tree, protected by the leafy canopy as a storm raged just beyond the protective cover.

"It serves to remind us why we are here," Piccolomini commented as they entered the room.

The din of voices stopped as Jason entered. His eyes slowly adjusted to the dim room. Small halogen reading lamps illuminated the area in front of each of the men seated around a large circular table. Jason stared at their faces. He looked back at Jasmine, who was walking next to Piccolomini. He had insisted that she stay in the main entrance hall of the Eagle's Nest with Larksmum, but heaven and earth could not keep her from Jason's side.

Each one of the men sitting around the table was a de facto representative of the religion they represented. Their faces were solemn, as if the worry of the imminent collapse of their chosen faith was written in the lines that creased their anxious faces.

While Jason could not readily identify all of the formal robes the men wore, he did recognize the stern look of the Hasidic Jew and rightly assumed that the calm Indian man whose beard rested in folds upon his lap was a Hindu. He noted the saffron robes of the Buddhist monk and the worn woolen kufi on the head of an angry looking man in his early thirties. The casual attire of the middle-aged man, simple navy-blue slacks and light blue shirt, suggested a Christian minister, possibly Anglican. The others clearly represented numerous other religious denominations of the world unknown to him. Jason wryly noted the absence of any women at the table. Most of the major religions of the world revered women within their respective dogma but granted them no authority.

In the center of the room were four square display tables. Each of the granite tables held one of the four cuneiform tablets that made up the four Books of Eden.

Jason stared hard at them as they walked past. He wondered about everything that he had learned since he escaped death at the Discoverer's Club. *Were these tablets really the first instructions from the gods? Were they the earthly manifestation of the Tree of Life and the Tree of the Knowledge of Good and Evil as alluded to in the Book of Genesis? Was the fourth book of the Journey to the Source a map to God, a link to a stream of universal energy?*

The first three tablets were similar to the plaster casts that Hans Pedersen displayed behind the glass case in his office. The fourth one was the one that he and Larksmum smuggled out of the British Museum after setting off a series of fire alarms to distract the security staff. All four tablets were lit by individual halogen spotlights suspended overhead. Beside each one was a bowl of colored liquid.

As Piccolomini walked past each pedestal, he stopped, dipped his fingers in the bowl, and placed the moist tip to his forehead. Red, green, blue and yellow dyes soon mixed on his head to form a dark spot in the space between his eyes.

"I sum scientia , ego sum unus," Piccolomini chanted as he moved towards his appointed seat.

"I am knowledge, I am one."

The group repeated the chant.

A nervous energy filled the room as Jason was led further around the table to a seat opposite the door. Piccolomini gestured to the young assistant who had accompanied them to leave the room. As the hollow echo of the closing door faded, Piccolomini held his hands away from his body in a V formation and began to intone a well-rehearsed chant.

As each of the men chanted their responses, Jason watched their silhouettes flickering on the walls. Images of freemasonry and the occult flitted through his mind. His nervousness gave way to curiosity as the men settled back in their seats and waited, a sense of anticipation on their faces.

63

"Gentlemen, before we begin I wish to first introduce you to Jason Wakefield." Piccolomini looked over at Jason, nodding.

The rest of the men looked upon their guest as if he possessed a power that each of them coveted. Jason began to feel uneasy. He glanced over at Jasmine.

When asked, each man acknowledged Jason's presence with a slight nod of the head.

"For Jason's benefit I will summarize the circumstances that brought us to this particular point in history.

"Fifteen years ago this group accepted an obligation to deliver our world from its certain demise. Hans Pedersen was identified, trained, positioned and empowered with the skills to deliver our lessons to a world sorely in need of a new reality. We were on the verge of success when the ambitions of my once-revered mentor altered the path of our carefully laid plans. It is now clear to me that our desire to propagate the *new consciousness* has been irreparably damaged by the actions of Cardinal Agostino. His interference with the programming that we had so carefully nurtured in him has caused a surge of free will that is set to destroy the world as we know it.

"We had choices to make after we discovered the extent of the damage done by Cardinal Agostino. Hans was an unfortunate victim of this tampering; the men of the Discoverer's Club could no longer deliver on their ancient promises; dozens of other emissaries were sent back to their lives to wait for the opportune time to re-emerge, a time that we thought was lost.

"But I sit before you with a new hope, a ray of light not extinguished by the angry thoughts that are circling the globe. While we mulled over the exact way to deliver our new message of compliance with the truth, the truth disappeared. But we have redemption. Jason Wakefield is that ray of light, a cistern of energy which continues to abate the powerful forces stacked up against his own resources."

Jason was trying very hard to follow the oration. Clearly, he was a significant part of it, but, instead, he found his mind distracted by the thought of the trail of death and destruction that these men had left in his wake in pursuit of their own interests. He had no idea who these men were, what power they felt they wielded over him and the rest of the world, or what their true agenda was, and he wasn't sure he cared. What he gathered was that he had, somehow, attracted their attention at a time when their view of the universe was crumbling. Jason was still struggling to figure out what knowledge he possessed that made him so valuable.

As if on cue, Piccolomini seemed to address his unspoken questions. He turned to look directly at Jason, his deep grey eyes glistening with emotion.

"I believed that man was inherently good, that the evil that was done between men would stop eventually, if enough positive energy was created. It was my fervent belief that the power given by our Creator, passed down to us in the Books of Eden, was meant to ensure our survival. No, not just our survival, but our reconnection with the universe from which we came.

"As I studied the history of the Order of Sumer, I began to grasp the futility of its existence. For six millennia, our forebearers stood guard over the secret that connected us to the universe while, at the same time, they stood by and watched as men destroyed themselves in a kaleidoscope of religious dogma destined to pit one faction against another—brother against brother, neighbor against neighbor, tribe against tribe. A proliferation of sects, denominations, off-shoots, cults, factions, and religions scattered around the globe, each group believing that they alone possessed the answers to eternal existence. For those eight millennia we protected our secret as countless millions were killed in the name of one deity or another. We protected the truth from being revealed.

"So I decided to reveal the truth. As a young Brother to the Order I knew that my influence was weak. I approached Agostino, at that time the lead Brother, in an effort to gain support of the more powerful members of the Order. He listened, considered my suggestion, and then dismissed me, with no sign of support. I assumed my idea was ignored.

"Then, a few months later, I was asked to accompany him here to the Eagle's Nest. During the months that I had thought my idea to expose the truth of the Books of Eden had withered, Agostino had been busy assembling a group of like-minded men, disenfranchised by their respective religions. Gathering these men, who shared a common purpose to unite the religions of the world, we revealed the truth of the Books of Eden to them, and in particular the third book that the Order of Sumer so ardently guarded for so long.

"Seizing the moment those fifteen years ago, we identified Hans as the man to deliver our program to the world, to instill in people the knowledge that we felt they needed in order to live life the way it was meant to be lived, in the way *we* chose. But none of us suspected that Hans was being led in a different direction by Cardinal Agostino. In his desire to seek as many converts as possible for his Church, Agostino manipulated Hans and kept the focus of the rest of these men sitting before you today from enhancing their influence in the world."

The young Persian wearing the kufi cleared his throat as he interrupted Piccolomini, his rich Middle Eastern, English-educated voice filling the room: "Perhaps we should give Mr. Wakefield some time to absorb all this before you continue. I can see that he is already having difficulty staying focused."

It was true. Jason could feel his mind wandering. And yet he was still trying to understand how he fit into the picture.

"We have no time to waste. Jason must hear this."

The young Muslim nodded his acknowledgement.

Piccolomini continued.

"It turns out Agostino was controlling Hans from the very beginning in an effort to achieve his agenda. As the power of thought was being disseminated by way of the Thought Mechanix infomercials, Agostino was adding his own revelations, instilling them in the mind of our messenger. His hope was to create enough dissatisfaction with the status quo that eventually he could step in as the new Pontiff and bring order to the world, thereby showing that his Church was the one and only solution. Unfortunately, in his zeal to make the world in his image, he released a power of thought amongst the population that took on a life of its own, a very ugly, destructive existence that was granted by the energy of thought collectives, delivered by certain men and women who could control the energy—unbeknownst to anyone, even us."

64

Jason watched as the men around the table began to murmur their disapproval of the late Cardinal. The grumbling continued for a few minutes, but then the Indian yogi stood up. He lifted his hands as if in prayer, touching the tips of his fingers to his forehead and his thumbs to his lower lip. Silence descended upon the room as the rumbling dissipated. He kept his eyes closed for a moment longer before lowering his arms to his sides as he turned to face the young couple sitting across the table. He nodded imperceptibly at Jasmine who, with the slight tilt of her head exchanged the greeting.

"Namaste, my child. I am Yogi Ranunhandan. Is your pain gone?"

"I am well," Jasmine replied as she held her hands in front of her face and bowed to the Yogi.

Jason looked over at Jasmine, who just stared straight ahead. Did she know this man, he wondered? He then looked back at the Yogi, drawn into his intense gaze.

"Mr. Wakefield, Jason, I want to apologize for bringing you here under such mysterious circumstances. You have been through too much already, but soon you will understand. I can tell from your expression that you are angry and uncomfortable. Perhaps you have a right. That is not for me to judge. Do not believe your own thoughts. We are not evil people."

At this, Yogi Ranunhandan swept his hand around the table, acknowledging that he spoke for the group. Jason glanced over at Piccolomini, surprised to see that he had withdrawn, allowing the Yogi to take control of the proceedings.

These men were not all equals.

Yogi Ranunhandan smiled warmly at the two seated across from him. He was not as convinced as the others that they had found their messenger. Even Jasmine was not able to give him the assurances that Jason was the one. Despite the clarity of the actions of the accountant, he was still not convinced of the man's purity. The man needed to prove himself.

Jason remained silent as the last comment lingered in the stale air.

Everyone sat quietly.

But Jason could not hold back for long. "You people kill with impunity. You destroy what is not yours to destroy. You play like gods with your desire to protect man from God. Are you sure you are not evil men? Do you really think that whatever you hoped to accomplish was going to make the world a better place? Look at the world you have created. It's a mess, and the death and destruction you wreaked upon it are just a small indication of how warped your thinking was… is. I don't know what you want of me, but you must be delusional if you think that I want any part of your grand scheme."

Yogi Ranunhandan chuckled as Jason finished his rant.

"Perhaps you are right. But maybe we have done what we have done for precisely the reasons you say. Neither that nor the path taken to get you here is relevant. You are here now because we want you to be here. We are all here to be witnesses to who you are."

Silence enveloped the room as all eyes looked at Jason, waiting for him to acknowledge his place among them.

Jasmine sat quietly next to Jason, wondering if she had done the right thing—wanting to have done the right thing. It wouldn't bring her brother back, but it might stop the spiraling violence that gripped the world. She believed them when they told her to protect Jason, to make sure he was kept safe. Twice she left him alone since she was recruited to help. Twice she doubted what they said, seeing Jason only as the man he was: flawed, scared, and uncertain. She asked herself the question just as she knew Jason would ask it.

"What are you talking about? Who am I?" Jason heard himself asking as he watched the men around the table surge forward in anticipation.

Piccolomini spoke up from his location at the far end of the table. "You are the one who can fix what has happened to the world. To stem the tide of cascading violence. You had the ear of Hans Pedersen. He nurtured you. Those things you say about us you might as well say them about yourself."

Jason turned to face the man he saw as the face of madness. Their belief that he was somehow their messiah was ludicrous. He discovered the Rules of Possibility on his own while watching late-night television. No one approached him, cajoled him into joining the seminars, or remotely influenced his decisions to embrace the power developed by Hans or Thought Mechanix.

Before he could respond, however, the man continued.

"You still don't understand the power behind the program. The Rules of Possibility were only a delivery mechanism, a cleverly disguised set of prayers, if you will, to engage the mind to be activated by tools handed down to us through the Book of Thought. Naysayers would call it mind control. That does not do it justice. It is really more a channeling of unseen energy. You know it to be true. Think about what it was that Wakefield and Associates was able to accomplish for its clients—a complete transformation of corporate culture in twenty easy steps. You must have had some inkling that your abilities were somehow more powerful than others.

"In the beginning, when Hans was directed to us, we thought that we had found the person we had been looking for to introduce the Book of Thought to the world. It became clear soon after the founding of Thought Mechanix that Hans was not the right person. We used his abilities as a speaker to seek out the right person. Hans was told to look for certain characteristics in the many participants of his motivational seminars. The late-night advertising was specifically designed to flush out the person we were looking for—You."

Jason reeled.

Piccolomini stopped speaking and glanced over at Ranunhandan, who was now standing dispassionately to the side.

Jason locked eyes with Jasmine. She held his gaze for a moment before turning away. *He was not special,* he thought. What he did was a result of discipline and dedication. Not some innate connection to some concept of god.

"What are you trying to say, that I am some sort of prophet, a twenty-first century John the Baptist?"

"The first time you called in to order the program, that late-night infomercial plug that prompted you to phone in, was the first time we had hope. Most of the calls were monitored by people working in London, at St. Mary's Axe, intercepting any signs that someone, anyone, would call in who released an energy wave that would respond to the principles of the Book of Thought."

Piccolomini had risen. He moved to the end of the room, to stand next to Jason.

"Every once in a while a caller would exhibit unusually high energy levels, enough to cause us to send out a team to investigate. Then you called. The levels went off the charts. So much so, that after that day, all of our resources in London were redirected to follow your every move, to lead your career in such a way so as to continue to nurture the inherent gift you possessed. When we thought you were ready, we instructed Hans to create the opportunity for you in London. From there—"

"What do you mean *when you thought I was ready?*" Jason interrupted.

"The mind is an incredibly powerful tool and yet extremely fragile. Your ability to harness the thought energy around you is remarkable, even if you are not aware. But the mind, your mind, was also in jeopardy of resisting all thought energy, slowing you down like a governor does a golf cart. The brain is very good at self-preservation. So we helped to train and strengthen your mind. When we felt you were ready we moved you to London for the next phase. Unfortunately, in some ironic twist of fate the machinations of Agostino unraveled at the same time. The rest, as they say, is history."

Jason pointed to the fourth cuneiform tablet on display, "Let me guess. I have been prepared to help you somehow with the power in that rock. And you are all convinced that it is so profound that without me, it will be too great for any of you to survive the release of whatever secrets it holds."

At this point Ranunhandan laughed, as did a few of the others around the table.

A black priest halfway down the table chimed in, his thick accent revealing that he was from South Africa. "That seems like a good story, perfect for a thriller novel." He pointed to the tablet that Jason had taken from the British Museum. "We would all want to believe that Hans was somehow able to discover the existence of the Fourth Book of Eden, locate it with the help of his Italian professor, and have it hidden away in the archives of the British Museum until he was ready to unveil its awesome power to the world.

"The reality is much simpler. When Cardinal Agostino decided to use Hans Pedersen to cause the world to rebel so that he could come to its aid while at the same time save his church and catapult himself to its head, he had no knowledge of the tablet that you so kindly located. But what he did have was a fanatical desire to fulfill his ambitions. In doing so, he engineered the largest threat to man since Einstein proved the ability to split atoms. The negative thought energy that is currently enveloping the world is similar to the chain reaction of a nuclear explosion. It feeds on itself to create more energy."

"But even a nuclear explosion is finite," Jason commented.

Piccolomini spoke, his voice revealing that his patience was wearing thin. "Fair enough. The problem is we have no idea just how wide and deep this energy stream will go. Like any plague, it will eventually run its course as the virus has fewer and fewer hosts on which to attach and survive. Our fear is that it will not act like a fission bomb, but instead like its more robust cousin, a fusion bomb, which has no end until it has consumed every thought capable of being consumed."

"I still don't follow. What have I got to do with this?" Jason cast his eyes around the table, seeing if he could detect anything other than hope in the eyes of his hosts.

They all stared back at him with expressions of anticipation.

"We need you to take over from where Hans left off, to resurrect his organization, to become the next motivational guru, except with a different message: our story. To take what Hans has shown you and bring it to the world. Stop the unnecessary violence. Help create a peaceful world. A content world. A world *we* can guide into the next millennium."

"I am no Hans Pedersen, and I don't particularly like speaking in public."

"We can train you, give you the resources and the knowledge that Hans was given so many years ago. Only this time it will go further, now that we possess the final tablet. The source is now so close."

As he contemplated the thought, he caught Jasmine's gaze for the first time since they arrived. The expression in her eyes was a mix of disbelief…and fear. He had learned in the few weeks since they first met in Amy's apartment to trust her instincts. There was something that she knew but was too afraid to speak. Now her eyes spoke volumes. When they first entered the central chamber of the Eagle's Nest, it was clear that she had knowledge of some of these men, Ranunhandan is particular. Somehow she had to think that there was more going on, that he was the patsy.

So Jason did what he did best, he stalled.

"I'm not so sure I am interested. I will have to think about it. Everything is happening too fast. As an accountant, I am naturally cautious. I am sure you can understand. Give me some time. Despite your expression of confidence in my abilities, I am not sure you have the right person."

Jason stood up as if to leave.

The men around the table began to murmur, their agitation palpable. A few of them began to rise to their feet. Two men, whom Jason had not noticed earlier, now edged toward the exit, their hands moving inside their jackets. He suddenly realized that he was not here of his volition. Whatever they thought he was capable of providing, it was clear that refusing to participate was not an option. Their arguments thus far had carried a logical thread, a layering of the past to convince him that he was the chosen one.

Then, reality hit him like a ton of bricks: these men had no idea how Agostino and Hans Pedersen were able to harness the power of the Book of Thought. They'd been strung along, just like everyone else. It was clear from the look in Piccolomini's eyes. The man that Agostino had betrayed must think that Hans had bestowed some extraordinary knowledge upon him, giving him the keys to interpreting the fourth tablet so that they could, somehow, mold the collective minds of the world to create some sort of ideological utopia.

"You're wrong." Ranunhandan spoke softly, deliberately, to Jason as he moved in his direction. "You do not understand our purpose."

Jason knew that this man was not capable of interpreting his thoughts. He realized he was free to think what he wanted to think, to determine a way to escape.

"There is no way out of here…" Ranunhandan smiled benignly as he inched closer to Jason. "Do not jump to any conclusions until you give us a chance to show you the ability you have."

Jason could see that he would soon be wedged between two tables if he did not act quickly. He glanced over one last time at Jasmine to see if she was still committed. She stood transfixed like the rest of the people in the room as they watched the slow pirouette of the two men. Piccolomini had vanished. Jason could only guess that he had gone to summon Larksmum, his personal death machine. After a final survey of the room, Jason acted without thought.

65

The room moved in slow motion. Eyes averted to the fourth tablet, illuminated like a phoenix under the halogen lights, as Jason lifted it from its perch. Men started to move in chaotic unison as they reacted to what was happening. Two guards entered the room, looking towards their employer for some direction, but none was given, as the men stared in disbelief at the scene that was unfolding.

Jasmine looked at the same men too; then she reacted as expected, given her training.

Jason ran awkwardly, the heavy tablet tucked under his arm like a pig skin. As the hesitation behind him turned to reaction, he bolted through the unlocked doors of the main chamber. He ran through the exit and found himself at the bottom of a set of stairs. He took them two at a time.

Behind him, men started to shout orders. He heard boots pounding up a set of stairs to his right as he reached the main entrance, his mind forming an image of the female assassin who had brought him here with the promise of protection, and revelation.

As the world began to speed up to normal, the voice of Jasmine rose through the chaos. He wasn't sure if it was a warning or a threat as she shouted for him to stop his escape. He didn't look back as he ran outside and headlong into a torrential downpour. The rain tore across the sky as if pulling the rolling fog with it towards the cliffs. Within a few seconds the area where he stood was shrouded in a heavy white cloud, thicker than anything the sky over London could muster.

Jason stumbled up the mountain trail leading to the summit, still not sure what drew him higher up the slope rather than down it. The mist enveloped him, even as shouts and instructions sent people in pursuit. He ran as fast as he dared. Soon, the voices were lost in the clouds. They faded away on trails below him. He moved swiftly along the poorly marked path until he reached a refurbished wooden gazebo at the summit. It smelled of newly cut pine, the roof beams still without stain. The structure was twenty-feet round with a railing around the circumference. There was a three-foot opening at the far side of the structure. The only sound Jason could hear was the wind whispering like a ghost through the nearby pines, the voices chasing him completely gone.

As he placed the tablet on the wood table in the center of the gazebo, he cursed himself for being so stupid to run uphill. He sank to the bench and stared at the cuneiform tablet, trying to read the engraved symbols that had been chiseled into the stone six millennia ago. Somehow, he was supposed to be the spirit guide that would reveal the secrets of this tablet to the world.

"I doubt you'll understand anything written on that tablet."

Jason jumped as Jasmine's voice cut through the fog, her image materializing out of thin air as she stepped onto the gazebo.

Jason took a defensive step back.

"Who are you, Jasmine? Who are you really? These people, you work for them, they have some sort of hold on you. I saw the glance that Ranunhandan gave you when we entered the room. You know him."

"Let me explain." Jasmine took a step towards him, then another. In her left hand she held a small pistol, no bigger than her palm.

Without thinking, Jason grabbed the tablet and held it over his head. "Stop or I'll smash this thing into a million pieces."

"Do you know how ridiculous you sound? I don't really care if you throw the damn thing off the mountain."

"You came here to kill me." Jason pointed at the gun in her hand.

Jasmine laughed, her disarming smile causing Jason to follow suit. She looked down at the small gun, put the safety on, and stuck it into the pocket of her jacket.

"Is that what you think? I somehow connected with you in Amy's apartment in New York, traipsed halfway around the world, got shot at, saved your skin on more than one occasion, slept with you, made love to you, like newlyweds, just so I could wait for this moment to plug a bullet into you at the top of a mountain?"

"When you put it that way, it does sound rather ridiculous."

"Well some of what I said is true." Jasmine moved to the center of the gazebo and took the tablet from Jason. She placed it on the table.

"I am a pawn in this, just as you are. Ranunhandan recruited me to find and protect you. They were aware that Hans told you certain things of which they were not privy. They knew that Hans had located that tablet and they were convinced that he would use you to find it because he was being watched too closely. They wanted me to stay close to you and let them know once we had discovered its location."

"But they killed Hans. They admitted it."

"When he was ready to go public about the source of his knowledge about the mechanics of thought, he became too much of a liability. When the explosion at the Stern only strengthened his resolve to expose the secret that the Order had protected for the past eight millennia, they felt they had no choice but to remove him, and destroy his organization."

Jasmine sat down on the bench.

"Why did you help them?" Jason looked down at Jasmine as she searched for an answer. Tears were welling up in her eyes. She stared up at him, her pain complete. She would have done anything to save her brother from his fate.

"Piccolomini promised my brother salvation for his deeds. He was a good boy, ruined by the mind manipulations of evil men. When I first sought them out I was ready to kill them all— Piccolomini, Ranunhandan, Agostino—the whole lot of them. With their lives at my disposal, they talked me into avenging my quest by helping them instead. Until today, I did not realize that their power over me was yet another manipulation. When you left me to go to London, I ached inside, missing you, worrying about what was going to happen when you finally were brought back here to meet with these madmen. I realized that I loved you. It was all that mattered. I cannot do anything for my brother. So I did what I needed to make sure you…we…would be safe."

Jason looked into Jasmine's eyes. He lifted her up and held her in his arms. He kissed her, once on the neck, then for a longer time on the lips.

"I love you too. Thank you."

They stood together for a few moments, each quietly contemplating what to do next and watching as the clouds thinned out, revealing the winding path that Jason had blindly followed earlier.

"We need to leave now," said Jasmine, prompting them out of their silence. "We don't have much time."

"Time for what?" Jason asked.

Before Jasmine could answer, the clouds receded further, revealing the shape of another person, making her way up the path towards the gazebo.

66

Larksum watched her men deploy down the slopes from the top of the Eagle's Nest. She was ready for this, having sized up the young accountant on the trip back from London. Jason was not a hero but nor was he a patsy. From the first report that she delivered to her bosses after the fiasco in New York, she knew that he was a flight risk. What she didn't realize was that Piccolomini thought enough of her report to insinuate Jasmine into his life as insurance. Yet even that plan seemed to have gone wrong. It was clear to her that Jasmine cared a lot for Jason, enough to take a bullet to protect him in Siena.

She had caught a quick glimpse of Jasmine as she veered away from the throng of guards steaming down the hill to head towards the summit. Sensing that the Indian beauty went in the right direction, she turned up the mountain and followed, hidden in the shroud of mist that enveloped the rocky footpath. The fog cleared almost as fast as it had arrived as the cloud was pushed eastward. Larksmum could see Jasmine and Jason under the protection of the gazebo, holding tightly onto each other, revealing what Larksmum had long suspected.

"Not a very good exit strategy?" She raised the nose of her semi-automatic rifle as she approached.

Jason moved away from Jasmine, grabbing the heavy tablet and hoisted it over his head. "Stop or I'll smash this thing."

"Don't be so melodramatic. I couldn't care less if you broke it into a million pieces."

"Piccolomini does. Don't you work for him?"

"Indeed. I guess I should be more concerned. Nevertheless, I doubt you could destroy it to such a degree that it couldn't be restored soon enough. Now, let's just go back down the hill so that you can be properly indoctrinated into the Order of Sumer."

"I have no intention of helping Piccolomini and his group of zealots. They are power-hungry men with no desire to make the world a better place. They'll do anything and employ anyone to meet their ends."

"Like your friend." Larksmum pointed with her rifle towards Jasmine.

"She was a pawn in this just like me," Jason retorted.

"Tell him, Jasmine."

"Tell me what?" Jason turned to Jasmine

"I've told you everything that mattered."

"Have you told him about the explosions in London at the Discoverer's Club, at St. Mary's Axe?"

"It doesn't matter. I didn't know him then." She turned to Jason and looked into his eyes, pleading for him to understand.

"It was you? You did those things? You almost killed me. You critically wounded my best friend."

"I am so sorry, Jason. There was nothing I could do. I had to try and save my brother. I told you that. Believe me, I was not targeting you. I didn't even know you then."

"You are no better than they rest of these people. Men died. Many men died at the Discoverer's Club."

"I know. But you have to understand."

Jason was getting angry. He had fallen in love with Jasmine. She told him she loved him. Now he did not know what to believe. How could someone so heartless, so destructive, feel that way?

"Those men at the Discoverer's Club were not good people. Their only intention was to manipulate for their own gain. They killed themselves when their world was threatened. I did not push that button. I am sorry about Timothy. No one was supposed to be in the offices. I thought I'd made sure." Jasmine spoke softly, imploring Jason to believe her.

Larksmum had heard enough. It was time to finish this interlude and get back to what mattered, for the Order. As she stepped onto the gazebo toward Jason, she caught sight of Jasmine's hand moving towards her jacket pocket. Sweeping the rifle towards Jasmine, she took aim.

Jason stared in shock as Larksmum shifted her focus, lifting her rifle to shoot Jasmine. Reacting without thought, he followed her turn and hurled the thirty pound cuneiform tablet. The tablet hit barrel of the gun just as it went off, pushing the barrel towards the ground. The bullet missed its intended spot in the middle of Jasmine's chest but embedded itself in her leg.

As Jasmine fell to the ground, she freed her pistol from the pocket of her jacket and swung it around, firing the bullet sitting in the chamber. She watched as a red dot formed between Larksmum's eyes, whose expression went from victory to realization in the second before her body crashed to the slatted wood floor.

Jason turned to tend to Jasmine. The thumping sounds of spinning helicopter blades broke the silence as a pair of Black Hawks crested the side of the mountain, each one bearing the insignia of one of the smallest countries in the world.

EPILOGUE

"That's two bullets I've taken for you."

Jason sat in the grand hall of the Eagle's Nest beside Jasmine as a white-frocked physician carefully dressed the area where Larksmum's last bullet had entered and exited. He looked down at Jasmine's face resting in his lap and stroked her long raven hair. He watched as dozens of dark-suited men overtook the Eagle's Nest, taking photos and rounding up the last of the Guardians as they tried to protect their masters.

The four tablets were being carefully removed from their pedestals and placed in fortified containers. They were then loaded onto a small white helicopter, which eventually took off, veering south toward the Salzburg airport. There, the four tablets would be transferred to a Lear Jet waiting on the tarmac. And from there, the tablets would be ensconced in the archives of the Vatican, in a special section accessible only to the sitting Pope.

"You did all of this while I was in London?"

Jasmine grimaced as she shifted in her seat. It was the first time Jason had seen pain in her eyes. He wasn't sure if it was the bullet wound or the final realization that her brother was gone forever.

The grand hall of the Eagle's Nest was eerily quiet as the last of the Swiss Guards removed the evidence they would use to prosecute the men who had plotted against their religion. It would be a matter handled quietly—outside the normal channels of jurisprudence—the captain had implied, as the religious conspirators were led from the room. Piccolomini was led out separately. No doubt to be dealt with directly by his superiors.

Outside the sun shone brightly against a recently cleared alpine sky. Birds sang, as if rejoicing. The rain clouds that had hidden Jason as he ran for the summit were long gone but were still visible over a distant mountain.

Jasmine took a sip of vitamin water and squeezed Jason's hand, kissing him on the cheek before speaking.

"When you left for London I sat in the hotel room trying to decide what to do. Ranunhandan had used the temptation of the reincarnation of my brother's soul to keep me motivated to help them. When it was clear to the Order that I had shifted allegiance to you, Piccolomini used the threat of your life to force me to continue."

Jason smiled at her honesty and held her close.

"So I made a decision after the assassination of Cardinal Agostino. He was as delusional as Piccolomini and the other men we met today. He was just as power hungry, with his personal ambition clouding his judgment. And he was ruthless in his pursuit of his vision. But he did not deserve to die like he did. It was clear that I could no longer support or assist the Order of Sumer, despite the risks taken, even the risk to you. I decided to act.

"So I went to Rome, to the Vatican, with pictures I took with my phone of the dead Cardinal, hoping to use them as a bargaining chip to gain an audience with the Pope. It took a day and a half, but it worked. I spoke with him for two hours, laying out in detail everything I knew of the Order of Sumer. He knew an amazing amount already. About an hour into the conversation, he brought in a young priest from Canada to help piece together some of the facts that you and I had discovered about the rise of non-religion. The priest took me through the statistics he had collected to prove that the Internet-fed consciousness shift was real. Pope Clement XV was very attentive to my story. By the end of the meeting we had laid out a plan."

It was clear to Jasmine as she left the meeting that everything would depend on timing. Her rendezvous with Jason after Larksmum delivered him and the fourth Book of Eden to the Eagle's Nest was difficult; she knew her plan would be putting him at risk. She did not anticipate how Jason would behave on his own. It was a heroic move that probably helped the siege that she and Swiss Guard captain had quickly pieced together.

"I had no idea of how important you were to the Order of Sumer, that you possessed a special talent, similar to Hans, to control thoughts. I thought you just had some knowledge that Hans shared with you before you left for London."

"Believe me, Jasmine, I have no special knowledge. Quite the opposite. What I do know is that these so-called religious men are delusional. The tablets hold no power of their own, only what they believe them to hold. It's just hocus-pocus. The ability to influence others comes from a person's desire to believe, not what I, or Hans, or anyone does or says. The Order of Sumer believed that the Books of Eden were real, that what was written at the dawn of civilization was a blueprint for our existence, a guidebook to live like the 'gods' had lived. The Books of Eden were meant to inspire hope in mankind, to keep the people hoping and hopeful. That's why they protected them for the last eight thousand years."

Jason thought back to the last conversation he'd had with Hans. It had told the real story of the Books of Eden, a legend created to keep men hoping.

"You were right all along. Hans did share a secret with me." Jason smiled as he helped Jasmine to her feet.

"So…what was it?"

Jason looked out on the grandeur of the mountain scene that opened up before them as they stepped out towards the waiting helicopter.

"If I told you, it wouldn't be a secret, would it?"

THOUGHT MECHANIX
THE RULES OF POSSIBILITY

1. Thinking consciously
2. Think to be
3. Energizing memories
4. Thought reality
5. Tapping the grid
6. Channeling dreams
7. Training the sub-conscious
8. Listening intently
9. Think and connect
10. Ignore your open mind
11. Separate your inner thoughts
12. Training the brain
13. The script of intention
14. The myth of willpower
15. Escaping negative energy
16. Feed your mind, fuel your thoughts
17. Thought receptors
18. Precision thinking
19. The thought grid
20. Listening waves
21. Knowledge energy

ABOUT THE AUTHOR

Derek Schreurs lives in Kamloops, British Columbia, where he has practiced as a Chartered Accountant for over twenty years. This is his third novel after Debit Fund (2005) and The Augustine Pursuit (2007).

ACKNOWLEDGMENTS

Although this was a fun project, it happened to take a long time, and during the four or so years it took me to complete this novel, I was ready to quit many times. The continual encouragement from many of you who read my first two novels gave me the perseverance to carry on. I want to thank all of you for giving me the motivation to finish this book.

I want to thank my wife Lynn for always being there, for not reading the book until it was finished, and for keeping the bed warm during the late winter nights of writing.

Thanks to Nick and Judy for persevering through an early version of the book. There were many necessary corrections. Hopefully I caught them all.

Jim, thank you from the bottom of my heart. You have an amazing talent for spotting the smallest detail in my writing. The novel is better for it.

Finally, thanks to my editor, Victoria who provided me the comfort that my words could actually be tamed.